An Angel at the Highland Court

The Highland Ladies

CELESTE BARCLAY

OLIVER
HEBER
BOOKS

0 9 8 7 6 5 4 3 2 1

Published by Oliver Heber Books

 Created with Vellum

Sometimes the divine intervention we need to save us from ourselves sends the most unexpected people into our lives at just the right moment.

Happy reading, y'all,
Celeste

SUBSCRIBE TO CELESTE'S NEWSLETTER

Subscribe to Celeste's bimonthly newsletter to receive exclusive insider perks.

Have you read *Leif, Viking Glory Book One*? This **FREE** first in series is available to all new subscribers to Celeste's monthly newsletter. Subscribe on her website.
Subscribe Now

Have you chatted with Celeste's hunky heroes? Are you new to Celeste's books or want insider exclusives before anyone else? Subscribe for free to chat with the men of Celeste's *The Highland Ladies* series.
Chat Now

THE HIGHLAND LADIES

PREFACE

The Highland Ladies series is a spin-off to my first series, *The Clan Sinclair*, and follows the lives of ladies-in-waiting at King Robert the Bruce's court. If you are a fan of Highlander romances, then you've surely encountered the time period that spans the Wars of Scottish Independence, along with the rise and reign of Robert the Bruce.

While I was intentionally vague about the time period and royal couple in *The Clan Sinclair*, there is little way to avoid the history of Robert the Bruce when this series takes place predominantly at Stirling Castle after he was crowned king. I have taken creative license in a number of areas, but the events and clan dynamics are true to history.

In *An Angel at the Highland Court*, I rely heavily on the politics on the Isle of Skye and the MacLeods' of Skye legend of the Fairy Flag. To appreciate my story, I hope this little slice of history offers you context.

In *A Wallflower at the Highland Court*, we were introduced to the MacLeods of Lewis. The isle upon which they lived is really formed in two parts: Lewis and Harris. The MacLeods of Lewis, as told in the book, also held land on the mainland in Assynt. If you read *His Bonnie Highland Temptation*, this is alluded to with Siùsan's extended family. Additionally, they were also tied to clan members on the Isle of Raasay, which lies between Skye and the mainland. The MacLeods of Harris were part of the Skye branch through heredity and were not always on the best of terms with their neighbors, the MacLeods of Lewis.

The MacLeods of Lewis claim their branch was *Sìol Torcaill*, or "seed of Torcall", while the MacLeods of Skye (Dunvegan) claim their line comes from the *Sìol Tormoid*, or "seed of Tormod." The MacLeods of Skye is the older of the two branches, but they all descended from the same progenitor, aptly named: Leod.

The clans of the Hebrides were reluctant to join the politics of mainland Scotland for decades. Their shared lineage descended from both the Scottish and the Irish, which the clans felt set them apart from even the Highlands. John MacDonald of Islay, Lord of the Isles, has cameos in both *A Saint at the Highland Court* and *An Angel at the Highland Court*. The southern peninsula of the Isle of Skye is a region known as Sleat. John MacDonald's branch claimed Sleat as one of their clan seats. As I've referenced in both books, John of Islay was a notably ambitious man who "settled" for the title of Lord of the Isles when he wanted to be crowned King of the Isles. The lairds from Clan MacLeod of Lewis and Skye became vassals of the Lord of the Isles, and as members of the Council of the Isles, they were called the "greatest of the nobles, called Lords."

The MacKinnons of Strath, those who are part of this story, were a step lower than both MacLeod branches on the Council of the Isles. They were called "thanes of less living and estate." However, the MacKinnons are an ancient clan who track their lineage to St. Columba (yes, the one from the phrase

"St. Columba's bones") and the ancient kings of Scotland. Their battle cry, *Cuimhnich bàs Alpein,* means "remember the death of Alpin." The Alpins and MacAlpins are historically seen as the first kings of Alba, a land now known as Scotland. Historical research shows a strong likelihood that MacAlpin, the first King of Scots and Gael, actually descended from Pictish kings. The clan's coat of arms depicts a saint's hand holding a cross. That, along with numerous MacKinnon abbots on the Isle of Iona, are the foundation of the clan's claim to be linked to St. Columba.

This rather lengthy lesson in genealogy is useful to understand the clan rivalry and alliances among the Hebrideans. Clan MacNeacail, also known as Clan MacNicol, once dominated the Isle of Lewis, but the MacLeods steadily pushed them from that island. The MacNeacails resettled on the Isle of Skye, but it may go without saying that they were not fond of their new neighbors, the MacLeods of Skye. While many of the Hebridean clans either attempted to remain neutral or joined Robert the Bruce's cause during the Wars of Scottish Independence, the MacNeacails notably sided with the English King Edward I—Longshanks, the Hammer of the Sots.

The valiance of Clan MacKinnon during Robert the Bruce's fight earned them increased land holdings on the Isle of Skye, enabling them to claim nearly the length of the center of the island. Needless to say, their neighbors were not eager to see the MacKinnons' increased territory or their preferred status. Their original seat was Dunakin Castle, but with the gift of new territory, their clan seat moved to Dun Ringill. The MacKinnons lay claim to their own interesting legend. It is said that Dunakin was built by a Norwegian princess who married a Findanus MacKinnon, fourth clan chief and the clan name's progenitor. Clan history states he was the great-grandson of King Alpin. His wife earned her moniker Saucy Mary. She collected tolls from anyone who wished to cross through the narrow kyle between Dunakin and the mainland, though Norse ships were exempt. If anyone refused or failed to pay their toll, she would raise a chain to effectively prevent ships from passing without paying.

But the most vivid of legends is that of the MacLeods' of Skye Fairy Flag. It is real. It is a silk square that is now yellow or brown. This may have been its original color, or the result of aging over the centuries. I took creative license in this story about its colors. Yellow or brown didn't feel as though it created as vivid an image as pink and green. To me—and Disney—those feel more like fae colors. There are numerous theories about its origins, which include claiming it was created in the Far East, making it extremely rare and even leading some to believe it was a relic. Others claim it dates to the Crusades and was a banner. It's even said that it was used by Vikings while fighting in the British Isles. Scientific examination suggests it was from the Near East (Syria or Rhodes) and might have been the relic of a saint's shirt. We may never know. But it continues to reside in Dunvegan Castle.

The Fairy Flag likely did originate in the Near East and was possibly brought to Scotland by Harald Hardrada—the Viking who attacked Britain, was defeated at the Battle of Stamford Bridge, and effectively ended the Viking Age—because he was known to have spent time in Constantinople. But that, in the world of storytelling, isn't nearly as exciting as believing it came from the fae.

The Fairy Flag, according to legends, has the power to enact any number of miracles. The legends claim is will multiply the MacLeods' warriors, protect

MacLeods' lives, improve fertility, bring more fish, and rid the clan of plagues, among other things. For my purposes, I relied on the first and second claims. I allude to the flag protecting the clan, both their lives and their strength to ward off enemies.

In this book, I weave in the tale that Titania, wife of Oberan, King of the Fairies, entrusted the flag to the MacLeods' safekeeping. Titania was a *ban-shi*, which comes from Irish folklore and was a woman who heralded impending death—usually through wailing and screaming, hence our modern use of the word "banshee." Supposedly, Titania blessed the Fairy Flag with powers that would come to be if the flag was unfurled three times. However...if the flag was unfurled a third time, both the flag and its flag bearer would be whisked away to the realm of the fae.

I like this legend the best, but unfortunately, it may not hold water since the flag has supposedly been unfurled thrice, but it continues to reside in Dunvegan Castle. According to folklore, the first time was during an unequal battle between the MacLeods of Skye and the MacDonalds. It is said that the Mac-Leods forces mysteriously multiplied tenfold, giving them an advantage they didn't have. The second time was to save the life of the clan's lady, and thus the life of the clan's heir. The man most known for telling this tale was Thomas Pennant, who toured the Hebrides in the 1770s. He claimed it was unfurled for the third time to save his own life. I do not know the events surrounding his need for the fae to save him, but his accounts state that the Fairy Flag was so tattered by the time it was used to rescue him, Titania saw no worth in reclaiming it. And that, I assume, is why it still exists. I choose to ignore that last bit of the story and prefer to think about the flag's mysticism before Thomas Pennant.

As always, I hope this background helps you gain perspective for how I crafted this story. We are fortunate that much of medieval history was recorded and has been further studied in the Modern Age. But there is something to be said for those tales that can't quite be quantified, those steeped in lore. I hope you enjoy *An Angel at the Highland Court.*

Happy reading,
Celeste

ONE

Holy Father, guide me with Yer infinite wisdom and divine inspiration, so I dinna bungle ma interview with the king. Lord, keep me from making an eejit of maself. St. Columba, spiritual ancestor of the MacKinnons, watch over me. Infuse me with yer way with words. Pray for ma soul that I dinna say the wrong thing and embarrass maself and ma people. Oh, and Lord, thank Ye for the blessings of the coming season. May I keep in ma heart and ma mind the season of Advent and the celebration of the coming birth of our only Savior, Yer Son, Jesus Christ. In Yer name, I pray. Amen.

Ronan MacKinnon opened his eyes and realized he was the last person in the church at Stirling Castle. He'd thought to say a few extra words after the morning Mass ended, but his prayers drew out as his nervousness about meeting with King Robert the Bruce increased. Unfamiliar with the castle and life at court, Ronan had never felt more like an islander and less like a Scot in his life. His home on the Isle of Skye felt like a million miles away, a foreign realm compared to life on the mainland. He would have much preferred the constant drizzle and gloom of winter in the Hebrides because it came with the fresh saltwater scent and the sound of crashing waves, the call of seagulls, and the brisk sea breeze. The sights and sounds of Stirling Castle were off-putting to a man accustomed to the wilds of the Hebrides.

Ronan rose from his knees, making the sign of the cross one last time, and turned toward the doors. It surprised to him to see a young lady kneeling with her head bowed several pews behind where he'd been praying. He hadn't heard a sound and believed himself to be alone in the castle's kirk. He was grateful he hadn't spoken his prayers aloud, as he often did at Dun Ringill Castle. He could see little of the woman's face, but he noticed her ebony locks shone like a raven's wing. Her hands were fine-boned, and her fingers showed cleanly manicured nails. Her gown was elegant, but not as ostentatious as those worn by many women at court. He deduced from her age and her appearance that she was one of Queen Elizabeth de Burgh's ladies-in-waiting. When her eyes shifted as he approached, he blinked twice at their color. They were the same greenish blue as a robin's egg. She didn't acknowledge him but dipped her head again and resumed her prayers. Ronan had been unprepared for the shocking contrast between her inky hair and light eyes and the stunning combination it created. Even though she couldn't see him as she prayed, he still nodded as he walked past. If all the women at court were as striking as this youthful one, he would likely trip over his tongue every time he opened his mouth. He would undoubtedly make a fool of himself and the MacKinnons. He wished he could call for his horse and gallop away, never looking back.

Abigail MacLeod first sensed, then saw, the man moving toward her. She'd seen the back of his head when she slipped away from the other ladies-in-waiting, opting for additional time in prayer rather than

2

gossiping with the ladies as they broke their fast. It was a fortnight before Advent started, and the beginning of her third month as a lady-in-waiting. She spent a few extra minutes in prayer after the Sunday Mass to thank God for where her life had taken her after the last few years of turmoil.

Abigail reflected upon the woman she was not so long ago. Her cheeks always grew heated as shame washed over her as she remembered how abominably she acted toward her sister-by-marriage, Maude Sutherland. She recalled the hateful and mean-spirited things she said when her loving and patient sister-by-marriage arrived at Stornoway, on the northeastern side of the Isle of Lewis, as Abigail's older brother's bride. She and her mother had been atrocious because they believed Kieran should have married a woman of their choice, a woman they believed was more like them. They'd ridiculed Maude for her appearance, though now Abigail couldn't fathom what they'd seen as the woman's flaws. She wasn't a striking beauty, but she was pretty in her own way. She wasn't the image of the thin and comely lady-in-waiting that Abigail's older sister Madeline had been. But Maude made life better at Stornoway Castle, and she was a model wife, mother, and chatelaine. But in the beginning, Abigail and her mother had only seen what they'd believed were Maude's flaws, and blamed her for Madeline's banishment to an abbey. They refused to accept Kieran's decision to send Madeline away because of Abigail's sister's disgraceful choices at court.

Abigail prayed for thanksgiving that Maude survived an animal attack that nearly killed her and could have killed the twins Maude carried. It had been a devastating and eye-opening experience to see Maude fight for her life and the toll that fear took on Kieran. It caused Abigail and her mother Adeline to re-evaluate their perception of Maude and the dreadful way they treated her. While the two women turned over a new leaf, Kieran initially hadn't been as forgiving as Maude. He'd threatened to send Abigail to court as Madeline's replacement among the ladies-in-waiting, or to marry her off to an old toad still in need of an heir. She was grateful that she had wound up as a lady-in-waiting after a failed yearlong handfast. Abigail forced herself to set aside thoughts of her doomed trial marriage. She didn't wish to ruin a beautiful morning or her concentration by remembering *him*. She finished her prayers and left the kirk to find the other ladies and the queen.

Ronan swept his eyes over the Great Hall filled with courtiers and visitors as they settled at tables and waited for the evening meal to begin. He'd been at court for three days, but he still found the Great Hall and the evening meal to be a jarring experience. He spotted the table where his guards sat chatting with guardsmen who wore the MacLeod plaid. He recognized the red pattern and knew the conversation was genial. Had it been the blue MacLeod plaid, he feared a fight would have broken out. His clan was on amicable terms with the MacLeods of Lewis, but there was constant strife with the MacLeods of Skye, who were less than thrilled to share the island with the MacKinnons. The Bruce had rewarded the MacKinnons with more land after the Battle of Bannockburn. Ronan's family had lived at Dunakin Castle for generations, but with the royal gift came a new castle. His home was at Dun Ringill, the place he longed to be.

"Strathardale," a booming voice called out. Ronan wanted to cringe. He held various titles, but

"MacKinnon of Strathardale" grated on his nerves when used in public. Ronan supposed it came from not wanting to alert any MacLeods of Skye that their enemy lurked among them. Ronan much preferred to go unnoticed. It allowed him to observe, rather than take part in conversation.

The deep voice belonged to John MacDonald of Islay, Lord of the Isles. Ronan wanted to cringe again. The man was as powerful as he was ambitious. He'd inherited his title of Lord of the Isles, but he was ambitious enough to have pursued the title "King of the Isles" if not for his loyalty to Robert the Bruce. While the MacDonald lived at Loch Finlaggan on Islay, his clan had Armadale Castle on the Sleat peninsula of Skye. It made them neighbors, but fortunately they were a full day's ride apart. Ronan wished the ride took the three days that separated Dun Ringill from Dunvegan, the MacLeod of Skye stronghold. With such proximity to Armadale, Ronan hosted John more often than he liked when the man came to Skye. The Lord of the Isles boasted that Ronan's cook was better than the one at Armadale, but Ronan wasn't fooled. John MacDonald was simply nosy.

"John of Islay," Ronan returned the greeting, knowing the lesser title irritated the man. But Ronan refused to call the man "Lord of the Isles" when he stood before him. It was too pretentious for Ronan's taste, and it annoyed him. The MacKinnons descended from the first kings of Scotland. They weren't minions to Clan MacDonald. The two men clasped forearms, and Ronan sensed when John capitulated in their silent power struggle.

"MacKinnon, it's good to see you among the splendor of court. You so rarely get off the island," John sniped.

"Why leave when it's God's gift to Scotland?"

Ronan grinned. He could match John's snide comments. "The king summoned, so I came. I'm uncertain why he did, but here I am." Ronan wasn't certain, but he suspected it had to do with the ongoing troubles with the MacLeods, and King Robert's wish to see him secure an alliance through marriage. Ronan didn't oppose marriage; he just hadn't met a woman who didn't madden him with frivolous talk. He would never understand why their mothers raised them to believe it was expected of a lady. He'd rather not talk at all.

"MacLeods still giving you trouble? We're getting along these days."

"Aye. And you're getting along because the MacKinnons keep you both on your sides of the island while we're trapped in the middle," Ronan grumbled.

"If Skye is God's gift to Scotland, then you're God's gift to Skye. You keep those upstarts from claiming they should be Lord of the Isles. They're no more than a gnat buzzing aboot," John smirked.

Ronan hardly agreed. The MacLeods of Skye were a powerful clan that held influence throughout the Hebrides, and they outnumbered the MacKinnons. But they didn't outnumber the MacDonalds, who had two branches on the island: those in the north and the MacDonalds of Sleat in the south, which John claimed as his branch. They also had the MacQueens on their side, and Clan MacNeacail strongly allied with the MacDonalds of Sleat. There was no love lost for the MacLeods of Skye after the MacLeods of Lewis pushed Clan MacNeacail off that isle. The MacKinnons often felt like little more than a buffer, as their land ran through the middle of the island, separating the MacDonalds of Sleat from the MacLeods of Skye.

John took Ronan's silence as an invitation to continue speaking. "If King Robert doesn't want to discuss the MacLeods with you, what do you think he wants?"

"I shall find out when I'm called for an audience with him," Ronan demurred. "I understand you were in Lochaber again not too long ago. How do things fare there?"

"Bluidy hell! Ever since the Mackintoshes convinced the Shaws and the MacThomases to join them in that ridiculous plot to attack the Camerons, it's been a right bluidy mess for the MacDonalds. Hardwin decided that once Artair died—had a crazy bitch for a wife, that one—he wouldn't allow another MacDonald to sit as chieftain at Inverlochy. Now he has one of his own as the guardian."

"But your people still live at Inverlochy, don't they?" Ronan hoped they could remain on this topic rather than shifting back to him. He suspected he might spend the entire night listening to John's tale of woe about how people thwarted his ambition.

"Aye, but Hardwin—really his wife Blair—renegotiated the levies again. She might look like a saint, but her mind is as sharp as the devil. The banalities and pannage will keep that branch from ever prospering," John frowned. Ronan knew the MacDonalds at Inverlochy were doing just fine with the portion of land the Camerons gave them. He also knew that John wanted Inverlochy to belong to the MacDonalds outright, so he would have more sway in the western Highlands. He considered Lochaber to be his, never mind the several other clans who had rightful claims to that land. Ronan wished for at least the tenth time that day that he could return to Dun Ringill, even if he didn't see the king. He was a Hebridean, not a Scot.

Ronan muttered his excuses and slipped over to the table where his men sat with the MacLeods of

Lewis. He joined the conversation in time to hear that the laird and lady were preparing to celebrate Christmas with a larger feast than usual to celebrate both their bairn and their twins' saint's day.

"I wonder if the laird's sister will join them," one of the MacLeod guardsmen mentioned.

"I doubt it. It's too far to travel as is. The weather has been foul, and I doubt it will improve," another MacLeod commented. "And the laird willna want to leave our lady and the bairns to fetch his sister. I ken I dinna want to travel in this."

"I feel a wee bad for the lass after everything that happened last year. I mean, she could be aboot as sweet as pickled herring, but she and Lady Adeline came around to Lady MacLeod. She was even friends with Lady MacLeod before she left Stornoway. The lass deserves a chance to see her family. She's a different woman these days," the first guardsman stated. Ronan only partially paid attention as he chatted with his own men. The evening meal progressed, but as soon as the servants cleared away the tables, Ronan made his escape to his chambers.

TWO

How am I lost again? Ronan looked to his left and his right, but he couldn't orient himself in the passageway. He was attempting to make his way to the lists, but he couldn't tell which side of the castle he was facing or how to find the doors that would take him to the bailey. The one time he needed someone milling about to give him directions, every passageway was empty. He continued in the direction he'd been walking, hoping he would find an arrow slit to look out of to determine where he was.

"You can't be here," a woman's voice hissed from behind him. Ronan spun around and came face-to-face with the woman from the church the previous morning. He hadn't seen her again until now. Her bright blue eyes scrutinized him, and Ronan suspected she wanted to tap her toes as she waited for him to respond. But he had no idea why he couldn't be wherever it was that he stood. "This is the wing for the ladies-in-waiting," she confirmed. "This entire passageway until the end is where our chambers are. Men aren't allowed here."

Ronan and the courtier exchanged a look, both knowing that while men might not be allowed in the chambers, that didn't stop them from visiting. Ronan cleared his throat as he attempted to come up with an excuse. He decided that honesty would make him less foolish than devising a lie.

"I'm not familiar with the keep, and I find myself lost while trying to make my way to the bailey. I intend to go to the lists, not pay a call to anyone," Ronan explained, proud that he'd said more than one sentence without tripping over his words. She'd appeared attractive in the chapel, but now her robin's-egg blue eyes mesmerized him.

The lady-in-waiting huffed as she glanced back over her shoulder as though she expected someone to appear. When she looked back at Ronan, she nodded. "I can take you most of the way, then point where you're to go. Follow me."

Ronan noticed that her last words were imperious, but her soft voice made them less commanding. She hadn't spoken loudly, but Ronan was certain he detected an accent from the isles. Her wariness and silence made Ronan think she didn't want to draw attention to them as they moved into more crowded sections of the castle. When they reached a part of the castle Ronan recognized, he was sure he could find the lists.

"Thank you, my lady. I'm certain I can make my way from here," Ronan offered softly, unsure if there was more that he should say. Part of him wanted to bolt before he made a fool of himself; another part wished he could think of a reason to linger.

"Very well," the courtier smiled. "Stirling is an exceptionally large and confusing place at first. You aren't the first or last person to become turned around. It took me a fortnight before I was certain I wouldn't get lost. Good day." She dipped a curtsy and turned away before Ronan could ask her name.

Ronan was certain she had a Hebridean accent and wished to know from which isle she hailed. Even if they didn't see one another again, he found it reassuring that there was someone else at court who was an islander and not a Scot. He'd given up trying to explain the difference to people not from the Hebrides. The islands shared a heritage that was both Scottish and Irish, and they'd been content to be a world unto their own for generations. They identified more with Highlanders than Lowlanders, but even the Highlanders were more Scots than the Hebrideans. Not that he would ever say that aloud to a Highlander. There was no love lost between the two parts of Scotland.

Ronan stepped into the brisk November air and inhaled. It made his nose curl. Rather than the fresh, invigorating air from Loch Slapin, the body of water Dun Ringill overlooked, he breathed in the fettered stench of the market town of Stirling. He sighed as he walked toward the entrance to the lists. Once he began swinging his sword and concentrated on sparring, he felt much of the tension slip away. Fighting and training were things he understood, and they didn't require him to converse. Despite the noise of swords clanging, Ronan found the relative lack of voices rather peaceful. He didn't know anyone else who shared that sentiment, but he felt confident in the lists, unlike when he had to speak before people he didn't know. He might be Laird MacKinnon, but to the men who surrounded him, he was just another warrior.

After leaving the stranger by the doors to the bailey, Abigail slipped to a window embrasure and watched as he walked with more confidence once he spied the lists. Although he'd been soft spoken, she immediately recognized his Hebridean accent. He was clearly not a guardsman, both by how he dressed and by his presence within the private wings of the castle. She knew he was a MacKinnon from his plaid, but she was certain they weren't acquainted. He moved with the graceful ease of a warrior, his frame tall and broad. There was self-assuredness in his stride, and while Abigail had to strain, she could see his ease with the blunted sword he drew from the armorer's collection. She abandoned watching the still-nameless man and hurried to the queen's solar. She couldn't deny he was a handsome man, but the two times she'd seen him there was a shyness in his eyes. She wasn't interested in someone who appeared meek and retiring. She already learned her lesson about such men, and she didn't feel compelled to gain a refresher.

Abigail entered the queen's solar and slipped to an empty seat near several other new ladies-in-waiting. Mostly Lowlanders, they'd snubbed Abigail as a Highlander when she arrived at court. When they discovered she was from the Hebrides, they'd gawked as if they'd never met anyone from the isles. It had taken Abigail several days to realize that most of the ladies had never met someone from the isles, and they believed everyone who wasn't a Lowlander was a heathen. They claimed Highlanders were barbarians, and people from the isles were barely civilized. Abigail learned the invaluable lesson of biting her tongue and keeping to herself.

Two more experienced ladies, Emelie and Blythe Dunbar, took pity on her and befriended her. They had known her older sister, Madeline. The sisters had arrived at court several years before Abigail, replacing their older sister Isabella when she married. They were quiet and tended to prefer one another's company. But they'd been kind to Abigail and welcomed her.

"Good day, Lady Abigail," one lady greeted her, but there was no warmth in the greeting.

"Good day to you, Lady Sarah Anne," Abigail smiled. Sarah Anne Hay was the self-appointed leader of the younger members of the queen's entourage. When Abigail arrived at Stirling, it was assumed that she would join Sarah Anne's ring and fall in line with the vindictive woman's expectations. In fact, there had been whispers that Abigail might be enough like her sister that she would oust Sarah Anne. But Abigail never had an interest in cattiness for its own sake, and she'd arrived at court resolved to be a better person than she had been in the past. But when Sarah Anne and her older sister Margaret made Abigail their target, the courtiers soon learned that Abigail had no problems defending herself when necessary. A scathing assessment of Sarah Anne and Margaret's characters made both sisters avoid Abigail most of the time. Abigail tried to sound sincere, but when Sarah Anne turned her nose up, Abigail found she didn't care.

"Lady Abigail," Emelie greeted her as she moved closer to the light from the window embrasure near which Abigail sat. "Have you had any more news aboot Maude's weans? Blythe and I are eager to hear aboot the lass."

"I'm afraid not. If I hear aught, I will surely pass it along promptly," Abigail reassured. Emelie nodded, returning to her own sewing now that she had more light. Abigail knew neither Emelie nor Blythe had been close to Maude, but they'd both been happy when the former lady-in-waiting found a love match much like their sister Isabella had.

Abigail picked up the embroidery she'd left behind the previous day and continued stitching the tunic she was making for her nephew. A toddler now, he had a cherubic face with perpetually rosy cheeks.

Abigail finished her older niece's tunic a few weeks prior, so she was confident she would finish the matching set she was making for the twins before Christmas. She'd embroidered the edges of a sheet to embellish what Maude could use to carry the babe strapped to her front and eventually on her back. While Maude's younger daughter now toddled, Maude often carried her, so they could both keep up with the twins. They were all practical gifts, but she hoped her family liked them. She'd forgone the lavishness she'd once expected, even demanded, before her brother married. When Abigail looked back at her life before Maude arrived at Stornoway, she felt as though she watched someone else's. It was only within the past year that she felt she'd grown up.

She'd handfasted with Lathan Chisolm and become Lady Chisolm, albeit temporarily. She'd thought him so handsome and charming when they met. She was eager to become a clan's lady, and she believed she was ready for the responsibility. But she was woefully unprepared, despite the intensive training Maude offered and the duties that fell upon her shoulders while Maude was injured. Abigail had still expected servants, particularly the cook and the housekeeper, to shoulder much of the work while she floated around the castle supposedly keeping an eye on everyone.

In truth, she'd been useless at keeping the ledgers and living within a budget. The clan was fortunate that the housekeeper, the cook, and Lathan were knowledgeable, or she would have failed completely. By the end of the year and a day, she admitted she was still more like her mother than she was her sister-by-marriage. She was still immature.

"His name is Ronan," Sarah Anne whispered—though none-too-quietly—to her sister Margaret. "He's braw and handsome. His clan is prosperous too. Just what a bride wants." Abigail dipped her head to hide her smile. She'd sounded so much like Sarah Anne not long ago.

"We just need him to notice us," Margaret replied. Abigail sighed as she tuned out the women's conversation, uninterested in the man they discussed.

The Chisholms welcomed her, but she soon realized it was for the dowry and the lands in Assynt that she brought to the handfast. Despite her failings, the clan was kind and patient with her. But when she thought back over her time there, she suspected their kindness was more from pity than anything else. She hadn't understood Lathan's determination to secure her dowry until their wedding night. They consummated the handfast, but before he spilled his seed, Lathan withdrew. That became the norm for when they coupled. He wasn't a selfish lover, and he taught her how to enjoy intimacy, but he never climaxed within her. He'd refused to answer beyond the vaguest of explanations at first. But by the time three months had passed, Abigail understood Lathan didn't want to sire a child with her so he could more easily repudiate their handfast. It wasn't until she overheard a conversation between Lathan and his brother that she understood how unwanted and manipulated she had been.

Lathan intended to continue the handfast until the end, all the while searching for a more advantageous match on the mainland. He had a leman in the village, and he had already sired three illegitimate children with her. Abigail encountered them the first week she was there. She'd wished that Lathan would come to care for her and decide to remain faithful to her. She'd hoped that he wouldn't want to end their trial marriage, but as she looked back, she knew in her heart that he never intended to keep her as Lady Chisholm. It wasn't until she overheard the conversation that she understood he'd never been faithful to her. She learned that he frequently left her bed and the keep, spending the night with the other woman.

Margaret's voice intruded upon Abigail's thoughts again. "If he notices us, then we'd be forced to live among the savages. Mayhap he's better to just look at."

"There's still a fortnight before Advent. I intend to dance with him every night. He's bound to kiss me," Sarah Anne preened.

Abigail tried not to roll her eyes and resumed her introspection. Once she'd put all the pieces together, Abigail was heartbroken that her life with Lathan was more a figment of her imagination than reality. She'd attempted to slip missives to Kieran to warn him of Lathan's plan, but after five failed attempts, Lathan grew so angry that Abigail feared for her life. She'd wondered if she could escape and make her way back to Lewis, but she was unfamiliar with all the clans that surrounded her. She knew no one among the Mackenzies, the Frasers of Lovat, or the MacDonnells. Abigail knew Cairstine Grant was once a lady-in-waiting, but that was before Abigail arrived at court. Abigail had even wondered more than once if she could escape all the way to Dunrobin and seek shelter with the Sutherlands. In the end, Lathan had unceremoniously dumped Abigail on the steps of Stornoway while Kieran, Maude, and their children were visiting Maude's family. With only her mother to greet her, there had been no way to stop Lathan.

"I'll run a stake up his arse and leave him dangling from his curtain wall!" were Kieran's first words when he returned from Dunrobin to find Abigail pale and underweight.

It enraged Kieran to learn of Lathan's actions. For all Abigail's faults, Kieran was livid that she'd

16

been disgraced and mistreated. He'd been beside himself with guilt when he learned about the fear that became part of Abigail's daily existence. He petitioned King Robert, whose mandate compelled Lathan to return Abigail's dowry and lands, less the amount he felt his clan was owed for housing and feeding Abigail for a year. Maude rarely made it known—or took advantage of the fact—that she and her siblings, along with her Sinclair cousins, were all King Robert and Queen Elizabeth's godchildren. But after Abigail's return home, Maude requested a place for Abigail among the ladies-in-waiting.

Five months later, and Abigail still gave thanks every day that she no longer suffered through her handfast. She didn't miss Lathan, but her heart ached for the missed opportunity for happiness. Her mother, along with Kieran and Maude, agreed that she returned to Stornoway as a more introspective and mature young woman, but Abigail wasn't wholly convinced. However, she knew she was a better person than when she'd left the Isle of Lewis for her handfast. After three months at court, Abigail wondered if she might ever meet someone who would wish to marry her. No longer a maiden, with a failed handfast to her name, she was a less-than-desirable candidate.

"Who was that mon you were walking with?" Blythe asked as she sat between Emelie and Abigail. "I haven't seen him before."

Abigail shrugged, not giving it much thought as she peered at her embroidery. "I don't know, other than he's a MacKinnon. He was lost, and I showed him how to get to the lists. We didn't say aught else." Abigail's attention returned to those around her after tuning out the other ladies-in-waiting while she reflected upon her doomed handfast.

"You mean you didn't introduce yourselves?" Emelie's brow furrowed.

"Nay. He strikes me as rather shy. We both needed to go our separate ways, so I pointed him in the right direction, and we parted." Abigail shrugged again, but the nameless MacKinnon and his rugged attractiveness played through her mind for the rest of the day.

THREE

Abigail kept her head down during the Sunday Mass. She was supposed to be paying attention to the Latin being recited by the priest, but her mind drifted toward the MacKinnon warrior she kept noticing around the castle. She caught sight of him during meals, but he always disappeared as soon as he'd eaten. She assumed he spent his days in the lists or with his men. He didn't strike her as a courtier or an advisor to the king, so Abigail thought he must be a visitor.

Abigail hadn't dared ask anyone who he was, since the last thing she needed were more rumors circulating about her. Her arrival caused a stir after Kieran removed Madeline from court. Her brother had heard several of the hateful things she spewed about Maude while they both served Queen Elizabeth de Burgh, and her lack of tact threatened their clan's standing. People expected Abigail to be just like Madeline, and while Abigail knew she'd been on the path to becoming like Madeline, she'd mended her ways.

As she thought about her sister's near-consecration, Abigail's lips twitched. Kieran not only dragged Madeline away from court, he sent her to Inchcailleoch Priory, an abbey on "the island of auld women." The priory was known for its austerity and rules of silence. Madeline had been so intimidated by the nuns upon arrival that she did whatever she was told to avoid extra hours of prayer, a hair shirt, and self-flagellation. It hadn't taken long for Madeline to realize that behaving herself and being kind took less effort than being hateful. She'd found peace and grace during her time as a postulant and novice.

Madeline had spent four years at the abbey and had been prepared to take her vows of chastity, poverty, and obedience; but despite her reformation, the Mother Superior knew the monastic life wasn't Madeline's vocation. She'd recommended that the order release Madeline from service, and Kieran accepted the nun's suggestion. Now Abigail's older sister had a blissful marriage and was preparing to one day become Lady Grant.

"Amen," Blythe hissed as she elbowed Abigail. Her head whipped up, and Abigail noticed that the congregation was standing for the final hymn. She hadn't realized her thoughts drifted so far and for so long. She rose and joined in with the rest of the con-gregants. A rich baritone floated to her ears, and she was certain she'd never heard the voice before. It wasn't loud and overzealous—in fact, it was just the opposite. The man's voice was rich and subtle, but she felt like it coated her in warm honey. It was smooth and would stick with her. Abigail did what she could to shift and look back over her shoulder inconspicuously. She failed to go unnoticed when the singer smiled at her, the very same man she'd given directions to and seen in the kirk the previous week.

I canna keep thinking of him as "that mon" and "him." I should learn his name. But why? What does it matter what he's called? He'll leave court, and I'll likely never see him again. I'm too curious. I should find better things to pay atten-

tion to. Like Mass. Dammit. Och, sorry, God. The service is over, and I'm keeping the others trapped in the pew because ma mind is drifting. Again.

Abigail slid from her pew and turned toward the back of the church. She offered the stranger a nod before continuing down the aisle. When she was nearly at the rear of the nave, she slipped into a pew and kneeled. The other ladies were accustomed to her routine, and as a very devout woman, Queen Elizabeth never begrudged her more time in prayer. It was the week before the start of Advent, and Abigail recited her usual litany of thanksgiving. She tried not to think about how much she would miss richer foods, music, and dancing while trying to show her newfound selflessness to God.

I suppose nay one's perfect. I mean, other than Jesus. I suppose Ye understand, God, why sometimes I slip back into ma auld way of thinking. But it is through Yer bountiful mercy that I have seen the error of ma ways and ma many sins. I strive to be better each day, and Ye have given me another chance for both happiness and to prove I am a worthy servant to Ye, Lord God. Thank Ye for the many blessings of this life and those who I love and care aboot. Guide me with Yer presence even when I may nae think of Ye. I place ma trust in Ye, Lord. In all things and in all ways, in the name of the Father, the Son, and the Holy Spirit. Amen.

Abigail glanced at the hanging crucifix and the altar beneath it one last time before rising. She genuflected as she left the pew and turned around to see the same man, with his fair hair bowed in prayer, just as he had been the previous week. This time he sat in a pew behind hers, so it was she who passed him. She offered a slight smile as she walked past. Ronan dipped his head, and the corner of his mouth twitched before he returned to his prayers. Abigail wondered what he prayed about, and why he needed more time than the Mass allowed. She knew why *she* wanted more time, but she was curious about him. She reminded herself that other people's prayers were none of her business.

Ronan was lost again. He was certain it was at least the thirtieth time since he arrived at court nearly a fortnight earlier. He seemed to find fresh places to get lost each time he ventured from his chamber or the Great Hall. He'd waited for an audience with the king, praying over and over that he make a good impression. Now he was late—extremely late. As he rushed along a passageway he believed he recognized, he wished he had a guide who could lead him from place to place. He normally had a keen sense of direction, so getting lost within the castle doubly annoyed him. He found too many of the passageways looked the same, with only closed doors lining each side. He'd grown more confident about finding his way to the lists, but he'd never been to King Robert's Privy Council chamber.

"Are you turned around again?" Abigail called out. Ronan looked to his left and spied a shadowy figure. He realized he stood in the light, which made his appearance clear to her even though he had only her voice to help him recognize her. "Off to the lists again?"

"Nay." Ronan shook his head and waited until Abigail stood before him. "After a fortnight of waiting on tenterhooks, I've finally been called for my audience with the king. I haven't the foggiest notion how to find the Privy Council chamber, and I was meant to be there at least a quarter of an hour ago."

"Oh, dear," Abigail gasped before a corner of her mouth drew down. Her expression showed she knew how dire it was that Ronan was so late. She didn't envy him. "We'd best get you there sharpish. You'll lose your audience, and it could be a moon before the king will risk wasting his time again."

"I ken. That's why I'm in a bit of a dither aboot it. It's been quite some time since I last saw the king, and now I'm late when *he* summoned *me.*"

"You're here on behalf of your laird. Did he not warn you that it could be several weeks before you're granted an audience? The king might summon you by a specific date, but it rarely means you'll be seen in less than a fortnight."

"For my laird?" Ronan's brow furrowed before he smiled. "My lady, I am Laird Ronan MacKinnon."

Abigail stopped short as she rudely looked him over from the top of his hair to the tip of his boots before she caught herself. "My pardon, my laird. I hadn't realized you were who you are." Abigail dipped into a curtsy before grinning. "I'm Abigail MacLeod."

It was Ronan's turn to stare. His eyes opened wide before narrowing as he looked for any plaid in her ensemble. Abigail chuckled, having expected his reaction.

"I'm from Lewis, not Skye. We need not try to run each other through," Abigail's voice was light-hearted despite her embarrassment in thinking that Ronan was a clan delegate rather than the MacKin-nons' laird. She held out her hand while offering him a shallow curtsy. Ronan's fingers barely grazed the underside of her fingers as he leaned over to kiss the air just above her hand. Abigail stepped away and began guiding Ronan to his destination.

"I suppose I should have introduced myself the last time you guided me, but I'm afraid I forgot my manners in my frustration to find my way out of this maze," Ronan explained.

"It's quite all right. I recognized your plaid and your accent. I should have introduced myself as a neighbor," Abigail replied.

"I knew you were a Hebridean, but I didn't guess a MacLeod."

"From Lewis," Abigail teased.

"Aye," Ronan returned her grin. "My men and I have sat with your guards each evening."

Abigail waited for Ronan to continue, but when he said nothing more, she glanced at him. It seemed as though he'd used all of his words and wasn't sure what to say next. It reminded Abigail that he'd appeared shy the previous times she'd seen him. They carried on in companionable silence until it became awkward walking together as though the other didn't exist. Abigail didn't want to prattle, but she felt like she needed to fill the quiet.

"Do you plan to remain long at court?" she asked.

"Nay." Ronan looked down when he realized how abrupt his answer sounded. He smiled sheepishly at Abigail. "I intend to be home before Christmas, my lady."

"I miss Christmas at Stornoway. It's festive here, but it's not the same as being with family," Abigail admitted. She glanced up at Ronan, but he only nodded, his eyes staring ahead of him as the doors to the Privy Council chamber came into view. Abigail stopped, and Ronan nearly walked past her. "The Privy Council is just ahead. You must make your presence known to the guard who will summon the chamberlain. He will admit you or turn you away. I wish you luck that you didn't miss your audience."

"Thank you, Lady Abigail."

Ronan and Abigail stood looking at one another, neither sure who should take the first step. They both stepped in the same direction, but when each of them tried to alter course again, they stepped in the same direction once more. Abigail pointed to her left, and Ronan nodded before pointing to his left. They stepped around one another, and Ronan carried on toward his meeting. Abigail glanced back and caught Ronan doing the same thing. They exchanged another smile before going their separate ways.

FOUR

Abigail found herself in no hurry to join the other women in the queen's solar. She wasn't looking forward to the dull hum of voices while the ladies gossiped, or the monotonous tone of someone reading one of Thomas Aquinas's treatises the queen preferred. Abigail would have been content with just harp music, but she knew that would likely only be in the background. She considered her latest exchange with Ronan MacKinnon.

He was so outgoing one minute, and then he wasna. It was as though he realized he was being congenial, and it was too much. He wasna rude, but it was odd. Mayhap worrying aboot meeting King Robert distracted him. Or mayhap he really is shy. But how can a shy mon govern a clan as large as the MacKinnons in a place like Skye? Is he weak? Is that why they have so much trouble with the other MacLeods? A weak mon has nay place as a laird. I wonder if that's why the king wishes to see him. To determine if he's fit to be laird.

Whatever the reason for his meeting, I wouldnae want to be him right now. King Robert willna have any sympathy for him getting lost. Though he said he's been here a fortnight, and I was still getting turned around that soon after I arrived. It was closer to a fortnight and a half before I figured things out. I still wonder if he's a good laird. He strikes me as a powerful

27

warrior, but I dinna get if he has the backbone for being laird. Och, it's none of ma business. Let St. Peter pass judgment on him. Or at least the Bruce.

Abigail entered the queen's solar to exactly what she predicted. Harp music, chattering, and the droning voice of someone reading. She wanted to turn around and run away, but she couldn't. Blythe and Emelie waved her over, and she took a seat near them. She listened to them discussing women Abigail only knew by name, women who had been ladies-in-waiting before her arrival. As Blythe and Emelie reminisced, then speculated on their friends' marriages, Abigail was reminded that she might remain a spinster.

Mayhap a convent would be good for me. I could take ma vows just as the nuns prepared Madeline to. Though I'd rather be at a Franciscan abbey as they're nae as austere and dogmatic in their lifestyle. But I dinna think I'm really called to that. For all Lathan's faults, and mine, he did teach me to enjoy the sins of the flesh. Do I really want to resign maself to a life of chastity? Nae if I dinna have to. Nae yet at least.

But what if nay one ever offers for me again? I'll live a life of chastity anyway. Nae necessarily. If I stay here long enough, I'll be seen more like a matron or a widow. It's nae secret I was handfasted. I could take a lover someday. Bah! Kieran would kill me. He'd do more than send me to a convent. He'd string me up by ma toes. And I dinna just want to couple. I want something real. I want someone who cares aboot me for more than a roll in the sheets. I need to stop fashing and let life happen.

Abigail continued listening to Emelie and Blythe talk, and their conversation turned to the upcoming Christmas feast.

"We have the entirety of Advent, and then the festivities can begin. I can't wait to have meat again." Emelie practically licked her lips. "I will miss it, and the season hasn't even begun yet."

"Cheese," Abigail chimed in. "I will miss cheese. I'd even like a mug of milk if it meant I could have dairy again."

"I will miss the music after the evening meal," Blythe sighed.

"You miss dancing with Michail MacLeod," Emelie teased. Abigail couldn't help but smile as she listened to the Dunbar sisters. Michail, a MacLeod of Assynt, was a distant cousin to Abigail. He would become chieftain after his father's death. But Blythe's face went blank, and she notched up her chin. Emelie heeded Blythe's silent warning and shifted the conversation. "I wonder what I will wear for the Christmas feast. I shall miss wearing bright colors. All I can say, though, is at least it isn't Lent. We may do without our favorite foods, dancing, and music, but we don't have to spend hours upon hours in prayer. My knees are grateful. I'm too young for my knees to ache as much as they do when I kneel on the stone floor."

"That is true. They creak like an auld woman's," Blythe giggled. "And you sigh as you lumber to your feet."

"Lumber?" Emelie pretended to be indignant. "You should help an auld woman since you are so young and spry. I must be too feeble to carry my sewing back to our chamber. Would you be a dearie and do it for me?"

Blythe snickered as she shook her head. Abigail enjoyed the banter between the two women, and it helped pass the time until the ladies left the solar to prepare for the evening meal. Abigail wondered if she would catch sight of Ronan once again. She had to admit he was handsome, and she enjoyed his appearance, but she wasn't sure what else drew her. She wondered if it was more morbid curiosity to see if he was the hesitant laird she suspected. Or was she trying to be optimistic that he wasn't? *Mayhap he's just reserved around strangers. He doesnae ken me, and he learned I'm a MacLeod today. Mayhap he's being cautious and doesnae trust me. That's reasonable.* Abigail hurried to change her attire before entering the Great Hall with the other ladies.

Ronan stood in the passageway outside the Privy Council chamber, watching the posted guards who stared at nothing and everything. The chamberlain had been even smugger than Ronan feared when he introduced himself. The man looked down his nose at Ronan despite being nearly two heads shorter than Ronan. He'd sniffed, then ducked back into the chamber. Now Ronan tried not to fidget as he waited to learn whether they would turn him away. As he surreptitiously glanced at the other people who tarried, he wondered what brought them to court. He looked at each person and tried to guess how long they'd been waiting.

It was the middle of the afternoon, the air oppressive in the passageway, by the time the chamberlain bid Ronan to enter the king's meeting room. *Dinna bungle this, mon. Ye represent every MacKinnon. Think before ye speak. Think twice at least. If ye muck this up, it'll nae only be yer head on a platter, but it may be the MacLeods and MacDonalds gaining yer land. Then what?*

"Laird MacKinnon, King Robert has found time for you," the chamberlain smirked. Ronan stood to his full height and pushed his shoulders back. The chamberlain scurried to take a step away from Ronan as the Hebridean laird glowered at him.

Ronan approached King Robert's throne and bowed deeply to his sovereign. He knew enough not to speak until spoken to, and only if it was a question that necessitated an answer. He was uncertain how long he should bow, so it relieved him to notice the Bruce flicked his fingers for Ronan to rise. The King of Scots ran an assessing gaze over Ronan, and the only time the laird felt more scrutinized was earlier that morning when Abigail discovered who he was. He forced his mouth not to twitch as he recalled her surprise. Her expression told him more than she realized. He knew she would doubt his strength as a laird because he tended toward being quiet and was generally very reserved. He'd predicted her response because it was the same one he received when he made any new acquaintances. Most people underestimated him, and he used his introverted nature as a weapon. In politics, it served him well since few expected his dogged tenacity, but he found he didn't care for the idea that Abigail might think less of him for it.

"Laird MacKinnon, I take it you are still getting turned around in the castle," King Robert mused. Ronan canted his head and nodded. "And who was your tour guide this time? Lady Abigail again?"

The king's observation took Ronan aback. He never suspected that word would reach the king that Abigail helped him twice. He swallowed and trod carefully, unwilling to endanger the young lady's reputation. "I was most fortunate that Lady Abigail took pity upon me twice and steered me in the right direction."

"Even though she's a MacLeod?" King Robert pressed.

"It was only upon meeting her for the second time that I learned she is a MacLeod. Of Lewis," Ronan explained.

"And there is a difference?" King Robert persisted.

"Mayhap not by blood, but there must be since she didn't run me through," Ronan attempted to jest.

31

He relaxed for a heartbeat when King Robert laughed.

"Underestimate none of the ladies at court, particularly my wife's attendants. They are a spirited lot, and most are braver than any mon I ken." King Robert sobered and narrowed his eyes before continuing. "And how did Lady Abigail react to learning you are Laird MacKinnon?"

"Lady Abigail recognized my plaid and already knew I was a MacKinnon. It may have surprised her to learn I am the laird."

"Surprised?" King Robert pretended bewilderment, but Ronan understood that the Bruce was using Abigail as an excuse to assess what he'd surely already heard about Ronan.

"My mother raised me to ken children are to be seen and not heard. As an adult, I've realized that such an approach allows one to learn far more than by monopolizing a conversation."

"And what have you learned since arriving at Stirling?" the king asked. Ronan was prepared for the question.

"I've learned that I prefer sea air, Your Majesty," Ronan said with a straight face. King Robert guffawed and nodded his head.

"I shall think you're being diplomatic. Tell me, have you seen aught of particular interest to you while in Stirling?"

"Aye. But I keep getting lost, so I never find the same mural twice," Ronan answered. King Robert blinked owlishly before he recovered and chortled.

"Laird MacKinnon, your mother did a fine job raising you. Just bear in mind that some people don't care for evasiveness," King Robert warned. Ronan nodded. "Do you know why I've summoned you?"

"Not with certainty, Your Majesty. But I suspect it has to do with the climate on Skye," Ronan hedged.

"That is why I requested your presence. But there is more to it than recounting how many sheep the MacLeods and MacDonalds raided from you this year." King Robert waited to see if Ronan would respond. When the young laird remained quiet, King Robert sighed. "Yours is an ancient clan, but your territory is not ideally located. The MacLeods dominate both Skye and Lewis, while the MacDonalds gain more influence throughout the Hebrides. Both clans want dominion over the outer islands, and you are trapped between them. The MacLeods would set you adrift while John of Islay would drink and eat you out of house and home, then claim it for himself."

Once more, King Robert waited for Ronan to speak, hoping the man would offer his opinion. But the Bruce understood Ronan was hesitant to overshare or overstep the rules of decorum. He rose from this throne and gestured for Ronan to join him before the fire. There were two chairs placed at the hearth, and Ronan waited until the king sat before taking his seat.

"You may speak freely, Ronan. I am not trying to corner you or trick you," King Robert kept his voice low. "You need to secure your clan's position on the isle."

"You wish me to marry," Ronan stated.

"That would be the most ideal method to recruit new allies," Robert nodded.

"Who do you intend for me to wed?" Ronan came straight to the point, but an image of Abigail flittered through his mind. It relieved him to watch the king shake his head.

"There are many eligible ladies here at court, or you can pursue other daughters and sisters if there is a clan you prefer," King Robert offered.

"When do you expect my decision, Your Majesty?" Ronan held his breath.

"After Epiphany. That gives you a little more than a moon," King Robert answered.

To find the woman I'm to spend the rest of ma life with. Bluidy hell. If there were a woman I kenned of that I wanted to shackle maself to, I would have already inquired or done it. Doesnae leave any time to get to ken the lass. She may show up on the steps of ma keep, or me on hers, and have the wedding that vera day. I canna even stay here that much longer. If I dinna leave soon, I'll likely be snowed in here. I amnae spending Christmas among people I dinna ken.

"I'll begin thinking of possibilities immediately, Your Majesty. When I've secured a betrothal, I'll be sure to inform you." Ronan prepared for the king to dismiss him, but King Robert held up his hand.

"It's not that simple. You will inform me of your choice, and I will decide whether to grant you permission. The situation is too tenuous to create an alliance that will only inflame things on Skye and within the Hebrides. John of Islay may be a loyal servant, but he can be worse than a rotting tooth awaiting the blacksmith's tongs. I know he wanted to be King of the Isles. That's no secret. I fear he will attempt to gain control of all the islands. I can't afford that. I need at least Skye or Lewis to remain free of his control."

"Aye, Your Majesty. I will bear that in mind while I consider my options," Ronan conceded. King Robert dismissed Ronan, and he didn't dawdle as he left.

FIVE

"My laird," a young page came to stand beside Ronan as he collected his belongings near the lists. "His Majesty wishes to see you."

"Now?" Ronan looked down at the mud that had splattered on his leine and caked on his legs and boots. He was in no condition for an audience with the king, and it had been less than a sennight since King Robert made his decree that Ronan should marry. He'd spent more than a fortnight observing the women at court with the intent of approaching them. But each time he considered one of the younger maidens, she would do something to grate on his nerves. A shrill laugh would set his teeth on edge. He listened to their inane conversations about clothes, their gossip about various lovers, and their estimations of various men's worth—in coin and in bed. This all served to alienate him from the younger women.

Several matrons—married and widowed—approached Ronan, but it was always an offer for a tryst. He wasn't interested in that or bringing any of these women home to his clan. The only woman who continued to draw his attention and didn't make him want to ride away was Abigail, but he didn't approach her considering the way the younger women gossiped about one another. He wished to keep himself and Abigail free of the unwanted attention and comments.

"Without delay, my laird." The page scampered away before Ronan could say anything else. Ronan spotted two of his men and said a prayer of thanksgiving that they were similar in size to him. He signaled to them and explained that he needed to borrow a fresh leine and plaid. He followed them to the barracks and quickly scrubbed away as much dirt as he could, making himself barely presentable. He hurried through the passageways, finally remembering the way.

Now what? What did I say the other day that has him summoning me back? Did I say aught I shouldnae have? Did I let something slip that I didna realize? If all were fine, why would he want me back? Think before ye speak, Ronan. Dinna make a fool of yerself. Take a deep breath, calm down, and dinna be an arse.

The chamberlain was no less disdainful than when Ronan attempted to gain entry the first time. The man turned his nose up at Ronan before disappearing within. However, this time Ronan entered immediately. He noticed the Privy Council chamber was abuzz with people working. Some poured over documents and maps, while others talked in small groups by the walls. Ronan suspected the Bruce wanted some ideas as to who he would pursue. But discussing his nuptials and any alliances in front of so many people was unappealing.

"Laird MacKinnon, good of you to come," King Robert nodded as Ronan bowed, as though he'd asked Ronan rather than ordered him to appear. "You may approach."

Ronan crossed the chamber and took the seat offered to him at the table in the center of the room.

King Robert cast a speculative eye over Ronan, but he forced himself not to shift under the king's assessment.

"It has been four days since last we met. Have you news to share?" King Robert inquired.

"I have considered a few potential brides, but I have yet to decide," Ronan admitted.

"And who is on your list?"

"Laird MacNeill has an eligible daughter, but she's a wee younger than I would prefer," Ronan began. With a frown and a nod, the king agreed. "Laird MacDonald of Clan Ranald's sister is also unwed, but much like the MacNeill's daughter, she is still younger than I am comfortable…"

A pointed look from Ronan communicated that he would not consider a child bride, not even one in late adolescence. Robert nodded before saying, "You know that means you are nearly out of options among the clans of the isles."

"Laird MacLean has three daughters who might be of interest. I don't know if any of them are spoken for, but they are of a more acceptable age to me." Ronan watched the king, who observed him with skepticism.

"Come to the point, MacKinnon. Who really interests you?"

"Lady Abigail." Finally, Ronan had admitted it. He'd observed Abigail in the days since his last meeting with the king. He sat where he could see her during meals, and he timed his walk to the lists to coincide with the queen's morning constitutional around the gardens. She was fair of face, but she seemed intelligent and not given to unnecessary chatter. Ronan witnessed that she often listened more than she spoke, and he recognized the same guarded demeanor as he possessed.

But Ronan remembered that, while quiet, Abigail

had been outgoing and polite during his few encounters with her. He'd intentionally crossed paths with her at least once each day, at different times and when she was with different people. Each time, she greeted him warmly and inquired about his day. He knew they were the banalities of decorum, but they had seemed more than just pro forma.

During each of these exchanges, Ronan had pushed himself to be outgoing. He returned Abigail's interest in his days and found that, unlike the ladies who bored and irritated him with their banal twittering, he didn't mind listening to Abigail tell of morning strolls and time spent in the queen's solar. He'd even gone so far as to ask her to dance more than once. But to avoid causing unnecessary chatter about his attention toward her, he forced himself to dance with some of the other ladies as well.

"She's a fine choice, but—" King Robert glanced around before rising. He ushered Ronan back to the chairs where they'd previously sat. "Are you aware she handfasted with Lathan Chisolm?"

"I hadn't heard," Ronan responded cautiously.

"You ken that means she isn't a maiden," King Robert continued.

"How long ago did the handfast end?"

"Going on six moons," King Robert answered.

"And she bore him no children? Is that why he repudiated it? Or did she?" Ronan realized he'd asked too much and leaned back.

"You are right to ask such questions. He repudiated the trial because he wanted her dowry, but not her. He intended all along to send her back to Stornoway and find someone on the mainland to marry. He was lucky that the MacLeod settled for demanding redress through me rather than flaying the mon alive. He took precautions not to sire any children, though he has three—nay, four—illegiti-

38

mate children who live in his village with his mistress."

"Was Lady Abigail aware of this—er—arrangement before entering the handfast?" Ronan's chest tightened as he thought about the humiliation and pain Abigail must have suffered. He didn't know Lathan Chisholm, but he was certain he would despise the man on sight.

"Nay. He approached Kieran, and Kieran allowed his sister to choose between marriage or service to the queen. She understood it was a handfast but chose Lathan, anyway. From what I understand, she learned of the mistress and the intended repudiation by accidently overhearing a conversation between the laird and his brother. When she attempted to let Kieran know, Lathan began threatening her and made her a virtual prisoner within the keep. The bluidy bastard waited until the last minute when he kenned Kieran and his wife Maude were visiting her family, the Sutherlands. He rode into Stornoway, pulled Lady Abigail from her horse, tossed the reins to one of his men, and rode out."

Ronan forced himself not to grimace or clench his hands. He was angry on Abigail's behalf. While he couldn't imagine being such a cad, he knew plenty of men who didn't think twice about treating women as little better than livestock.

"It was a Chisholm guardsman who unfastened her chest from a packhorse and explained his laird's intentions. They left Lady Abigail and her mother, Lady Adeline, stunned." King Robert sat back, his eyes keenly fastened on Ronan's face, observing his expression. When nothing flickered within Ronan's eyes, King Robert wondered how the young laird had learned to hide his emotions and reactions so well. He'd expected his news to shock Ronan, make him shake his head and refuse the lady.

39

"If Lady Abigail is amenable, I would like to get to know her and see if marriage to me might interest her," Ronan announced.

"Her past doesn't bother you? You don't mind that she's not an innocent?"

"From what you told me, she's innocent. It's the mon she trusted who isn't. He manipulated her and took advantage of her faith in their agreement." Ronan nodded and held up his hand. "I ken that's not the innocence you mean. As long as she isn't bearing another mon's child, then it is of little consequence to me that she isn't a virgin. I see her as being in a position little different from a widow. It wasn't immorality that stole her maidenhead. It was a conniving bastard."

The Bruce considered Ronan's comments and eventually nodded his head. The memory of how Abigail's older sister Madeline treated his goddaughter Maude was still fresh, despite the years and Madeline's own personality changes. He recalled how Abigail refused to welcome Maude when her sister-by-marriage arrived at Stornoway. But he also considered the woman he'd seen over the past three months and what his own wife had shared with him. He was confident that Abigail had matured during her time away from Stornoway, both as a wife and as a lady-in-waiting.

"I think you will find Lady Abigail is an excellent choice. Besides the obvious political benefits, she's a woman I think you will appreciate. I will not force a betrothal on you, but I would advise you send a missive to her brother as soon as possible. I believe she intends to return to Stornoway for Christmas."

"She will travel to the isles during this time of year?" The news surprised Ronan. Even he didn't want to travel north in early December.

"The lass is an islander. You should ken she's

hardier than she looks," King Robert grinned. "And if it wasn't life on the isles, then surviving Lathan and life among the other ladies here that has thickened her skin."

"With the queen's permission and Lady Abigail's agreement, I would ask for opportunities to spend time with Lady Abigail," Ronan requested.

"I am sure that can be arranged. When will you speak to her?"

Ronan considered that and forced himself not to shrug. "Truthfully, Your Majesty, I don't know. I can't count on her to appear if I get lost. And I wouldn't be so presumptuous as to approach her in front of others."

"Come to my antechamber by the Great Hall before this evening's meal. I will ensure Lady Abigail meets with you, and you may discover if she's interested," King Robert stated. Ronan said his thanks and bowed when the king dismissed him. He spent the rest of the afternoon trying to decide what to say.

SIX

Abigail broke away from the ladies moving toward the Great Hall and made her way to the royal couple's antechamber. She'd received notice that her presence was expected by the king and queen before the evening meal. She must have appeared terrified because Queen Elizabeth cooed and reassured her that she had caused no trouble; in fact, the queen alluded to a potential suitor. As Abigail drew closer to the doors, she wondered who awaited her. She thought of Ronan and how they'd briefly encountered each other throughout the four days since she led him to the Privy Council chamber. She wondered if it was by design or merely coincidence.

Abigail realized the man Sarah Anne and Margaret Hay had gossiped about the previous week was the man who kept crawling into her mind. He was courteous each time they met, but he was still so much shyer than she was used to. It was clear to anyone that he was muscular and agile, and he carried himself with the ease of someone able to defend himself. But Abigail wasn't interested in a man who couldn't match her resolve and fortitude. She didn't want a man who couldn't hold his own against her should they disagree.

But his handsome face and that body make up for quite a bit. He's braw and looks like he could carry me to bed any night. Would he? Or would he whisper his request and then retreat while he waits for me to decide? I dinna want a mon like Lathan, who used his size to intimidate me, but I dinna want to feel like I'm—what? What is it that I dinna want to feel? Too dominant? I suppose I want to feel like he wouldnae hesitate to rush into the fray to protect me. I want to feel feminine beside him. But I also want him to hear me, really hear me, and respect me. I dinna bluidy well ken what I want. Or at least I dinna ken how to say it even to maself.

Abigail waited for a guard to open the door for her, then stepped inside. She blinked several times as she glanced around the room. Ronan stood near the fireplace, one arm leaning against the bricks above the fire. He peered into the flames as his arm supported his weight. Other than two guards, there was no one else in the chamber. She felt her unease grow as she realized her only chaperones were the guards. Did people assume that because she wasn't a maiden, she no longer required a chaperone? She didn't fear Ronan. She realized that she knew within her bones that he would never hurt her, but that didn't mean her reputation wouldn't be in tatters. On silent feet, she walked further into the room. Abigail couldn't tell if Ronan sensed her or she moved into his peripheral vision, but he straightened and turned to her. They stood staring at one another.

Ronan knew he must speak first, but he found himself unable while Abigail stood before him. He'd seen her attired in her evening finery before, but he'd never paid attention to the intricate beading on her clothing. Now he absorbed every detail. Her beauty overwhelmed him, and he found himself unsure that anything he could say would appeal enough for her to agree to at least courting. As the seconds dragged on, Ronan's mind warred with itself about whether he should pursue Abigail. When he feared she would turn around and walk out if he didn't speak, he stepped forward and held out his hand for her to place hers above. When her palm hovered over his, he made the brazen decision to wrap his fingers and thumb lightly around the sides and bring her hand to his lips. He pressed the lightest and briefest of kisses to her skin, but they both felt it.

"Lady Abigail, I will confess that your appearance leaves me speechless," Ronan admitted. He'd decided the first time they met he would be honest with her rather than make excuses. Now, he figured if she were to consider ever marrying him, she should know who that man was. He wouldn't deceive her like Lathan Chisholm did.

"You're very kind to say so, my laird," Abigail whispered. She once again glanced around the chamber before bringing her eyes back to meet Ronan's. Even though she had seen him numerous times, she had never noticed his unusual coloring or masculine build. She found the contrast of his blond hair and brown eyes intriguing. She realized it was the same contrast of her own features but reversed. She'd been in a hurry to take him to his meeting, and the crowded Great Hall didn't afford him space to stand with his shoulders back. Watching him from a distance hadn't done his physique justice, either. She'd failed to notice how broad his chest was or how much taller he was than her. Her eyes shifted down to where Ronan's hand still held hers. He released it immediately, but not before Abigail considered how his large hand dwarfed her own. But no one had ever touched her so gently. Their eyes met again, and Abigail felt her left eye twitch as she fought not to narrow them as she studied him.

"Is there something aboot me that you didn't expect, my lady?" Ronan's voice rumbled from his chest as he spoke in a hushed tone.

"You're much—I'm a lot—we are very different in size." It was Abigail's turn to stumble over her words. *Ye're much bigger than me. Aye. And just what is so large that I might be referring to? I dinna need him thinking I'm thinking aboot his rod. Though I am now.* Abigail forced herself to keep from looking down.

"Aye, my lady," Ronan replied. He struggled not to let his mouth twitch as he watched Abigail attempt to back her way out of what could have been an awkward comment. *She may be shorter than me, but there is naught small aboot her breasts or her hips. I wonder what it would feel like to touch them.*

Abigail waited for Ronan to say more, but once again, she sensed he'd used all that he had to say. She searched for something to talk about, otherwise there would be no reason for them to linger. Just as she began to panic, Ronan spoke up.

"Lady Abigail, I've never had this conversation before, so I am at a loss as to how to begin." Ronan paused, but Abigail's raised eyebrow and small nod prompted him to continue. They didn't give him confidence, but they compelled him to speak. "I've observed you several times since we first met, and I'm intrigued by you. You're an attentive listener, and not given to needless chatter."

Abigail canted her head before replying, "Thank you, my laird." But she wasn't certain what she was thankful for. It didn't feel like a compliment, but she suspected he meant it as one. Did he not like women who talk? It seemed odd to arrange a rendezvous for just the two of them if he didn't want her to talk.

"You have a lovely smile," Ronan plowed along. "And you seem to possess a jovial sense of humor. From what I've observed, the other ladies like you well enough."

Another bluidy backhanded compliment. He doesnae even realize that they arenae what a woman wants to hear. Am I supposed to thank ye for nae thinking I'm a simpering and blathering eejit? Should I appreciate that ye noticed I amnae the pariah ye must assume?

Abigail kept her expression neutral, a feat she'd learned while living among the Chisholms, but perfected once she came to court. Ronan glanced away and bit his upper lip for a moment before returning his gaze to Abigail.

"I'm afraid my compliments—at least that's what they're supposed to be—sound much better in my head than they do out loud. I'm not a talkative mon by nature, and I often fear saying the wrong thing." He smiled ruefully. "Much like I am this evening. But I find you hold my attention, Lady Abigail. I will always be straightforward with you. That you may trust. The king has suggested that I marry soon. I have until Epiphany to consider my choices and present my decision to the king. You are the only woman who holds any appeal to me."

Ronan blurted out the last sentence after feeling as though his previous words made it sound like he considered her because King Robert was forcing him to marry. Abigail didn't move, but Ronan noticed her pulse flutter in her neck. It seemed rapid, but he admonished himself for wishful thinking.

Abigail didn't know what to say as she listened to Ronan. He made it sound as though he wouldn't have noticed her were it not for the king's order. As though reading her thoughts, Ronan clarified his words.

"Lady Abigail, I find myself attracted to you and, as I said, intrigued. I thought that before the king mentioned marriage. I don't want you to think I'm speaking to you because I'm rushed to pick someone, anyone. I may have until Epiphany to give King

47

Robert my answer, but I won't hurry any woman into marrying me. I confess the king's directive has spurred me into action, but I'd like you to consider allowing me to court you because it is my own wish to become better acquainted. And perhaps there is some small interest on your part, too."

"You are rather straightforward, my laird," Abigail murmured. She inhaled deeply as she considered the man standing before her. He was so opposite of Lathan that she almost agreed to marry him on the spot. But she still wasn't certain that she wanted a soft-spoken husband, even if he was almost too blunt. But she couldn't deny she was physically attracted to him, and he intrigued her too. He was a puzzle to reason out, she decided. She nodded. "Laird MacKinnon, I would like the opportunity to learn if we suit."

"Thank you, Lady Abigail. I won't court you, though, without asking your brother's permission to marry you if you become amenable. But neither will I write to him without your permission. I will proceed with what you feel is best."

Abigail frowned. She appreciated the consideration, but Ronan's deferential manner was so at odds with the men she knew. She also knew there would be no point in sending a missive to Kieran, and she wasn't sure how Ronan could even court her with only four weeks left before Christmas. "My laird, a missive to ask Kieran's permission may not be possible if you must answer to King Robert by Epiphany. You may not want to present me as your choice. I'm leaving at the end of the sennight to return to Stornoway for Christmas. It's my nieces and nephew's first Christmas that they are all auld enough to enjoy the festivities. I'm going home and won't return until after Epiphany. I imagine you don't plan to spend Christmas here."

"I do not. I confess, court is the last place I want to spend Christmas. Too much fuss with too little meaning. And I belong among the isles, not in a mainland town like Stirling," Ronan said as he looked toward the window embrasure.

"You prefer the quiet of the Hebrides?" Abigail realized she genuinely wanted to know.

"Always, my lady. I miss the ruggedness of our landscape, the freshness of our air, the birdsong. Even the smell of fish! It's better than what I can smell from the town."

Abigail chuckled as she nodded her head. "I have missed that too. They say Stirling straddles the divide between the Highlands and the Lowlands, but with so many Lowlanders at court, it never feels much like the Highlands. The year I spent on the main—" Abigail snapped her mouth shut. She swallowed as she realized she would have to tell Ronan about her past. *This may vera well be over before it begins. He doesnae strike me as the type who wants another mon's leftovers. He will want a maiden bride, nae one who was returned like a bad penny.*

"Lady Abigail," Ronan whispered as his eyes darted to the guards. He gestured for her to stand alongside him as they peered into the fire. "I ken aboot your handfast. I don't ken too many details, but I ken Laird Chisholm was dishonorable in his intent and that he didn't treat you properly." Ronan turned his head toward Abigail and waited for her to look at him. "I ken you're not a maiden. That doesn't matter to me."

"Why not?" Abigail blurted.

"I don't see it as much different from you being a widow. Your first husband is gone and won't come back."

"My first husband," Abigail mused. "You seem certain there will be at least another one."

"I hope it'll be me," Ronan smiled. "Abigail, you are your own person. One I'm drawn to. But I will never keep you prisoner in your home. I will never treat you like a possession to be coveted, then returned. I ken the law says a woman becomes a mon's possession like chattel, but I like my horse, and I can bed a tavern wench."

Abigail spluttered as she laughed. "I don't even know what to say aboot that. But you are so serious, and your comparison is so blunt. I can't help but be amused. I'm sorry. I ken I shouldn't laugh, but please know it's your turn of phrase and not you that I'm laughing at."

"I'm trying to say that your lack of virginity is unimportant to me. We both made choices before we met each other. To be honest, whether you lost your maidenhead to a previous husband or a lover, I don't care. I will pledge fidelity to you, and I expect the same in return. If you can live with that, then your past is your business." Ronan waited for her to respond.

"I've never, ever—*ever*—heard a mon say that, especially not a laird."

"I think people put far too much store in believing women should be virgins on their wedding nights while men should bed every whore in sight before his," Ronan replied. Abigail stared at him as if he were an aberration. He supposed he was.

"I—thank you, Laird. I confess that puts me at ease. I wish that I could undo that year of my life, but I can't."

"You don't sound bitter or mournful. Perhaps regretful. Do you think you came out a better person for it? Even if it was dreadful?" Ronan asked.

"Aye." It was Abigail's turn to be brusque. "I learned much, and I believe I am better for it." She

50

didn't want to delve deeper than that, so it relieved her to see Ronan nod his head.

"I hope worrying aboot finding a mon who will accept you is no longer part of why you wish you hadn't handfasted," Ronan's voice once again softened.

"It isn't anymore," Abigail smiled. A bell ringing in the distance signaled the evening meal was about to begin. "I don't know that we came to any conclusion, my laird."

"We didn't," Ronan shook his head ruefully. "May I ask that you to allow me time with you until you are ready to leave? Then, if you're willing, my men and I will travel with you. We're headed in the same direction, and with the weather likely to change at any moment, it would provide better protection to us all to travel in a larger group."

"If you are returning to Skye and intend to remain there, then it should be possible for us to see one another before Epiphany."

"I would like that very much, my lady," Ronan smiled and dipped his head to her. He gestured toward the door and offered her his arm. He guided them to the door that led toward the passageway rather than directly to the Great Hall. "I will wait until you are inside before I enter," Ronan explained.

Abigail nodded, but she felt disappointed that Ronan didn't want to escort her into the evening meal. If they were to court, people would see them walking and talking together. She wondered why he was unwilling to be seen with her. *Perhaps he is too shy. But can he nae be brave just this once? Abigail! He's clearly a warrior. Ye shouldnae doubt his bravery. That wasna right. But what is it, if nae cowardice? Does he fear ruining ma reputation? He's the one who wanted to court me.* She cast her eyes up at Ronan and found him watching her.

"I don't like crowds," Ronan stated.

"A widow here doesn't like them either. She says she feels the walls closing in. It makes her heart race, and she fears swooning," Abigail offered. She hoped to reassure him, but when Ronan's gazed hardened and his mouth pressed into a fine line, she realized she'd misread his meaning. And she realized she'd just compared him to a fainting woman. She opened her mouth, then snapped it shut.

"I don't fear crowds. I dislike them," Ronan clarified. "I dislike coming up with things to say. I find it tiring having to think aboot every word that comes out of my mouth to ensure I represent my clan as a laird should. And I'm not particularly interested in most of what people have to say. At least not what these people at court have to say. I find it awkward and tedious if you must know. You need not fear I will collapse, my lady."

"Ronan," Abigail stopped and turned toward him, then realized she'd addressed him by his given name. Her cheeks radiated heat, and she feared they would set her collar ablaze. "I beg your pardon, Laird MacKinnon. It seems it is I who should think aboot every word that comes out of my mouth."

"I prefer Ronan," he stated. Abigail waited for him to say more, but there was nothing forthcoming. Once again, it was as though he had no more words left to spare. She studied his eyes, and he didn't appear to retreat. He just had nothing more to say.

"I prefer Abigail," she replied. They stood gazing at one another. As the seconds drew into minutes, neither was ready to step away. Abigail found herself leaning in, wishing Ronan might kiss her. With such slowness that Abigail wanted to grab his hand and hurry him along, Ronan brought his palm to Abigail's cheek. She turned her face into it, feeling the rough skin. It was the hand of a man who spent his life swinging a sword. There was nothing cowardly about its feel. She tilted her head back in invitation, and she waited to see if he would accept.

Ronan watched as Abigail's eyes grew heavy lidded, and her lips parted. He understood what she wanted, what she offered, and it tempted him. But uncertainty warred within him.

I ken she wants me to kiss her. And ma bollocks are screaming for me to do it and far more. But what happens when she realizes I dinna ken what I'm doing? What if she laughs at me? What if she rejects me and thinks I amnae mon enough for her? But isnae it better she learns now than after I court her? If I'm going to disappoint her, I may as well do it now.

Ronan rested his other hand tentatively on Abigail's waist as he lowered his mouth to hers. His lips brushed hers, and she opened for him. He understood what that meant, but he didn't know what to do. Her soft breath whispered across his mouth, and he brought their lips together. He was hesitant at first, unsure how to take the lead, but not wanting her to give up on him and pull away. As their mouths fit together, Ronan eased his tongue past her lips. He wanted to groan as lust spiked through him. The feel of his tongue sweeping across the satiny recesses of Abigail's mouth made him want to devour her. When she stepped closer, Ronan's arm pulled her against him of its own volition. But his worry eased when she snaked her arms around his neck and turned her head to offer him more.

He doesnae ken what he's doing! Has he never kissed before? Or has he never kissed a woman before? Merciful God, does he prefer men? Abigail's mind swirled with thoughts as she realized Ronan wasn't just being respectful and not moving too quickly. He didn't know how to kiss. She couldn't wrap her mind around the notion, but she found his efforts endearing. And she found them arousing. She slid the fingers of one hand into his hair as the other rested at the base of his neck, the heel of her hand over his collarbone. When he pulled her against him, she didn't bother stifling the moan that escaped. Ronan pulled away, uncertain if the sound Abigail made was a moan of pleasure or pain. He lifted his head, but her hand tugged his hair. She went up on her toes and brushed her lips against his.

"Dinna stop yet, Ronan. Let me show ye," Abigail whispered before drawing him in for another kiss. She took the lead, pressing her tongue into his mouth, encouraging him to twirl his tongue with hers. When he grew more confident, he slid his tongue into her mouth and nearly spilled when she sucked on it. His hardened length had a mind of its own, and it knew what it wanted. He knew he would have no skill nor any finesse, but he wanted to lift Abigail until her legs came around his waist and thrust into her until they were both satisfied. A soft clearing of a throat broke them apart. They both looked in the direction of the guard who studiously avoided looking at them but had sounded the warning.

Ronan opened the door and led Abigail through it before either of them could speak. They walked the few feet in silence before another set of guards opened the doors to the Great Hall. Abigail stepped within and waited for Ronan. She remembered he'd offered to wait until she entered before he would, but she'd hoped after their kisses that he wouldn't be so hesitant anymore. She moved toward the table where she normally sat, but she glanced back at the door several times, expecting Ronan to walk through. She took her seat and accepted a trencher, but Ronan didn't appear. She was halfway through her first course before she accepted that he wasn't attending the evening meal.

SEVEN

R onan stood naked in his chamber, sipping a dram of whisky by the fire. Despite easing the ache in his bollocks by taking himself in hand, his body clamored for the feel of Abigail pressed against him. He remembered every moment, every sensation as though it were happening again.

"Dinna stop yet, Ronan. Let me show ye."

He replayed her few words over and over in his mind. His inexperience hadn't repulsed her. She hadn't taunted him or mocked him. She wasn't smug either, flaunting knowledge he didn't have. But he couldn't stop wondering if the choice he'd made years ago had been the wrong one. His father's voice echoed in his head, taking turns with Abigail's.

I wish I could have spared yer mother so much pain and embarrassment. She was gracious and stoic, but I ken it hurt her every time she encountered a woman I'd bedded. They had this knowing, condescending gleam in their eyes. Almost possessive even though I never returned to their beds once I wed yer mother. They flaunted ma past with them. She understood it was to make them feel superior to the graceful lady come to marry the laird, but it hurt her and shamed me.

Ye will marry one day, Ronan. What welcome, what home do ye want to offer yer bride? One where at every turn she finds

55

a woman who used to climb all over ye? One where she meets yer bastards before she does her servants? She will be an inno-cent, and she will expect ye to ken what ye're doing. But she will fear she doesnae live up to yer past. She will wish there were something special between just the two of ye. Even if ye're never a love match, she will want to feel like yer wife, nae an-other whore. If I could only go back, lad. If only.

Ronan took a sip from his mug. His parents were an arranged marriage, but from the beginning, they respected one another. His father never ceased to re-mind him of the wonderful woman who raised him and how fortunate they both were to have her in their lives. Ronan wasn't convinced they'd ever fallen romantically in love, but they loved one another. His father would never have hurt his wife intentionally, so Ronan understood why his father held regrets.

As Ronan became a man, and women took no-tice, his father had taken him into his solar, poured him his first dram of whisky. He'd explained all the unnoticed duties and expectations that came with being laird. Ronan recalled being told that everyone would expect ten times as much from him as they would anyone else because he was the heir and would one day be the laird. His father stressed upon him how every choice and action he took reflected and affected his clan. Ronan knew it was that conver-sation that made him fearful of saying the wrong thing, made him dread crowds and attention. But he'd worked every day since that one to serve his clan with honor, dignity, and loyalty.

Now he feared it might cost him Abigail. It was clear, even if he hadn't known about her handfast, that she was more experienced than he was. He hadn't thought it would be an issue until they kissed. He wasn't ashamed of his choices or even regretful, but it embarrassed him. He'd assumed he would marry a virgin, and they would each be as lost as the other. He even looked forward to learning the pleasures of the flesh alongside his bride. Now he worried he would disappoint his future bride, be it Abigail or someone else.

He threw back the rest of his whisky before climbing into bed. He stared at the ceiling in the dark for a long time, but eventually the strain of meeting with Robert the Bruce, asking Abigail's permission to court her, and their kisses overcame him. He drifted off to sleep, but his eyes snapped open with the first rays of sun. He felt as if he hadn't slept at all. It would be another interminable day.

Abigail tripped and nearly fell down the stairs as she made her way to join the other ladies for the queen's morning constitutional. She couldn't stop thinking about her conversation with Ronan the night before or, more specifically, their kiss. She'd surprised herself with how much she wanted him to kiss her. At first, she thought she wanted it because the opportunity was there, and she missed the intimacy. In fact, her body often craved release and the feel of a man within her. But she'd soon realized that she wanted Ronan, not just any man, to kiss her. It took her aback completely when she understood that his hesitation wasn't from trying to keep from overwhelming her, but because he didn't know what he was doing. Something in her heart melted as her body ached for him to touch her.

But she couldn't reason through why he didn't have experience. She kept going back to wondering if he preferred men. She'd never heard of such a thing until she arrived at court. It had left her aghast to hear a woman and two men discuss their planned tryst. She was aware that men sometimes shared a

57

woman, but she'd been unprepared for what the men said they wanted to do with one another.

Is he just another Lathan, even if he swears he's nae? Does he want to marry me to keep people from kenning his real preferences? Is it a sham? Would he confess if I asked? I dinna want to enter another marriage based on lies, and I dinna want to be made a fool of again. But he seemed to enjoy it? Mayhap he is like those men and likes both men and women. Does he have someone he already loves? Already wants? Is that what he's doing? Protecting them by using me as a distraction?

Abigail's mind was aswirl with unanswered questions as she walked across the bailey. A shout drew her attention toward the lists, and she watched as Ronan hurled himself toward a man, knocking them both off their feet. In the blink of an eye, Ronan had the man pinned beneath him and unable to move. Ronan quickly rose and helped the man up. He backed away before motioning for another man to step forward. This time it was his opponent who rushed toward him. Ronan twisted, caught the man's waist, and brought the man over his shoulder before he landed on top of his opponent. Once more he stood, held out his hand, and helped the man up.

As Abigail struggled to take everything in, she noticed that none of the men wore MacKinnon plaids. There were her guards, who she knew Ronan and his men spent time with. The others were from various clans or the king's men. She inched closer, not noticing her feet carried her toward the entrance of the lists. She couldn't hear Ronan's words, but she watched him give orders to the men, who followed his commands without pause. He instructed them into various battle stances, some with weapons and some without. He had clearly prepared them, so when he motioned for them to begin, it came together in violent synchronicity. Abigail noticed he called out comments as he walked around the men.

She couldn't tell what he said, but she could see the almost immediate corrections.

Abigail was in awe. She'd watched her brother train with his men, and she'd caught sight of Lathan many times while he sparred. But nothing prepared her for what she'd seen when Ronan bested his two opponents, or how the mock battle seemed almost perfect as he coached the men. It was obvious to anyone that Ronan was comfortable in the lists and among fighting men. Abigail suddenly understood that what she had thought of as moments of weakness were not even shyness. Ronan was reserved, an observer. And Abigail witnessed how he used that to his advantage.

Nay mon who commands such respect and trust from men that they dinna even realize how they follow him is a weak mon. I have so misjudged him. At least aboot his abilities as a laird. I thought I'd become a better person, but I did to him just what I did to Maude. I judged him based on what I thought I saw. What is wrong with me? Will I never learn? Ronan doesnae deserve a wife who doesnae have complete faith in him.

Abigail heard the ladies gathering at the entrance to the gardens, so she made her way there. But she felt ill. Her conscience nagged at her for misjudging Ronan—for judging him at all. She might not have understood him, but she knew she was being far too quick to assume the worst. She was angry at herself for behaving just as she used to. She thought she'd become better than that.

"You don't look well," Emelie whispered as she walked beside Abigail. "Are you all right?"

Abigail nodded, then kept her chin tucked down. She hoped it looked as though she was shielding her face from the wind when she was trying to avoid crying. Her heart felt heavy enough to pull her off her feet. She looked back over her shoulder in the lists' direction, but she could no longer see within the walled training area. She faced forward and watched the ground as she walked.

"Did something happen?" Emelie asked. Abigail recognized the suspicion in Emelie's voice meant she felt protective. Abigail shook her head, unwilling to share with anyone what she'd thought about Ronan or their conversation from the night prior. She certainly wouldn't share any details about the greatest kiss she'd ever experienced.

It really was the best. I only have Lathan to compare with, but even the most heated kisses with Lathan were naught like with Ronan. It was sweet and tender, but it was lusty and arousing all at the same time. I ken I want to do it again. But I canna lead him on. He deserves a wife who doesnae doubt him.

"Abigail?" Emelie broke through Abigail's thoughts. "Abigail, you're not listening. Why don't you go back to your chamber and rest? If anyone asks, I'll say you got your courses. No one will ask aught more after that. You don't look well."

"Hmm?" Abigail looked at Emelie blankly as she tried to work through the snippets she caught from Emelie's comments. "Aye. I don't feel so well, to be honest. Thank you."

Emelie nodded, and Abigail drifted to the side of the path and watched as the distance grew between her and the group of women. She turned away only to come nose-to-chest with Ronan. She stumbled backward, but his hands shot out and caught her upper arms. He righted her, but his gentleness made her eyes mist. She couldn't bring herself to look at him.

"Abigail?" Ronan murmured. "You look very peaky. Are you unwell?" Abigail shook her head, then nodded, then shrugged. She didn't understand how she felt other than conflicted. She knew Ronan waited for her to look at him, but she couldn't. Wave after wave of shame rolled over her as she chastised herself for passing judgment on Ronan.

"Excuse me, please," Abigail whispered. She tried to step around Ronan, but he hadn't let go of her arms.

"I'm sorry." Ronan murmured.

Abigail's head jerked up as she pitched backwards. Once again, it was Ronan's grip on her arms that kept her upright. "You're sorry? What on earth for?" Abigail blurted. She glanced around, relieved they weren't drawing unnecessary attention.

"For disappointing you so many times," Ronan answered. "Perhaps it would be better if I didn't pursue a courtship with you."

"You don't want to court me anymore?" Abigail choked around the gorge in her throat. This confirmed her feeling that Ronan deserved better. "Wait. What did you say? You disappointed me? Nay."

"You don't have to pretend on my account, Abigail. I ken you think I am weak. And after what you must have figured out last eve, I suppose you don't think I'm the mon for you. Not enough of a mon for you," Ronan finished on a whisper.

Abigail looked around once more. She reached up and pulled Ronan's hand from her arm and took it in hers. "We can't stand out here. It's freezing, and someone will hear us. Come with me."

EIGHT

F lurries had begun falling since Abigail walked outside, and her toes tingled in her boots. She also didn't want anyone listening to what should be a very private conversation. She hurried them inside and led him along several passageways until she pushed open a door to a library. She glanced around, then opened the door wider for Ronan to enter. She glanced back into the passageway, ensuring no one spied them from either direction.

While she locked the door, Ronan began a fire in the hearth. It was clear the room hadn't been used for some time, and it was nearly as cold within the chamber as it had been outside. Despite the chill in the air, Abigail ripped her arisaid from over her head and pushed it off her shoulders. She came to stand beside Ronan by the fire. His earnest expression did her in. She grabbed a fistful of his leine and plaid and tugged him toward her. She went up on her toes as she met him halfway. She pressed her lips to his, her tongue flicking against the seam of his lips. When he opened, she pushed her tongue past his teeth. Her kiss was both patient and demanding. She encouraged Ronan to explore their kiss, but she refused to relent in her need to fuse their mouths together.

Ronan struggled to keep up, then he struggled to keep from mauling Abigail. Years of repressed lust and curiosity demanded an outlet. He wanted to sink into Abigail and discover what it felt like to be with a woman. He feared he'd be useless at pleasuring her, but he wanted to know what it would be like. He'd never wanted a woman as much as he did Abigail. Her aggressiveness triggered something primal within him. The image of her clinging to him with her arms and legs wrapped around him flashed before his closed eyes. His hands slid down Abigail's back until they cupped her backside. When Abigail made a sound of impatience and frustration, Ronan needed no more encouragement. He lifted her high off her feet, and Abigail wrapped herself around him. He stepped to the wall beside the hearth, pressing Abigail's back against it. His mouth explored her neck and the exposed skin of her chest while her hands roamed over his back and through his hair. When he made his way back to her mouth, she sighed.

Abigail was drowning in need, and it scared her. She'd been prepared to walk away from Ronan, but now wild horses couldn't drag her from him. She thought she'd experienced desire during her handfast, but it seemed more like child's play than the intense longing and deep ache that she felt now. She wondered if a man who preferred members of his own gender could ever kiss a woman as Ronan did her. She wondered if it even mattered to her. Just as it came to her that it didn't, Ronan's mood shifted, and he pulled away. Abigail blinked several times before realizing Ronan was setting her back on her feet. He stared at her, as though he expected her to speak first since she had been the one to kiss him. Her mind felt too fuzzy to do more than stare back at him.

"I don't think I want you to stop courting me," she announced when she finally pulled her thoughts together.

"Even now that you know?" Ronan shot her a skeptical look.

"What is it that you think I know? Because my mind has come up with two explanations, but I don't know that either is right. Or mayhap they're both right. Or—mayhap you should just tell me before I stick my foot in it."

Ronan studied Abigail for a long moment before nodding. He led her to a bench, and they sat angled so that their knees brushed.

"You believe I'm a weak laird. You wonder how I can lead my people. You wonder how I could be a suitable husband to you. I would venture a guess that you either fear I prefer men, or you've deduced that I've never been intimate with anyone before." Ronan waited for Abigail to answer, or at least nod her head. But she did nothing for so long that Ronan wanted to squirm.

"You believe me to be a fair and reasonable woman," Abigail began. "You think I would make you a good wife. But I'm still as quick to judge as I ever was. I'm no better than I was when my sister-by-marriage arrived at Stornoway. No better than I was when I met Lathan. No better at all." Abigail felt tears prick behind her lids. "I did judge you. I don't know how you knew my thoughts, but you were right aboot it all. I did wonder if you were too shy and too weak to be a good laird. I did wonder if you prefer men. I did wonder why you're inexperienced."

Abigail furrowed her brow and bit her top lip then her bottom. She inhaled deeply then sighed. "I don't understand how a mon as braw and desirable

as you are can be so—so—innocent. Unless you—"
Abigail couldn't say it out loud, but she was certain
Ronan understand what she implied. "And if you can
kiss me like you did, then do you, or rather can you
—mm—both?"

Ronan smiled at her discomfort even though he
knew he shouldn't. At least he wasn't the only one
embarrassed by their conversation. He swung his leg
over the bench and took both of Abigail's hands in
his as he slid closer. He ran his thumbs over the back
of her hands as he considered how to answer.

"Nay. I do not prefer men. I have never been
with a mon. I've never been with anyone. I thank you
for the compliment aboot my looks, and it's not from
lack of offers." Ronan shifted his gaze for a moment
as he collected his thoughts and his memory jumped
to the conversation he had with his father. "When I
was six-and-ten, my father noticed I had a healthy
interest in the lasses, and they were interested in me.
He took me to his solar, and we had a lengthy conversation. He explained his regret over choices he
made before he married my mother. I dislike admitting anyone in my clan has flaws, but they do."

Abigail nodded with encouragement, genuinely
curious about his explanation. Ronan drew a deep
breath before proceeding.

"Women my father bedded before he married
were catty and vindictive to my mother, never
missing an opportunity, in the beginning, to remind
her that they were just as intimately acquainted with
my father as my mother was. If not more acquainted. I'd never known that. Those women had
moved on by the time I was auld enough to notice
aught like that. But my father warned me aboot dal-
lying with women before marrying. He warned me
that while I might enjoy rolling around with whores,
wenches, and widows, my wife wouldn't appreciate

having to live alongside those women. His words made a very lasting impression on me."

"You're a virgin?" Abigail whispered. "Did you ever kiss anyone before last night?"

Ronan nodded. "A few pecks here and there, but I always stopped it before it became aught like last night or just now. It didn't seem fair to kiss a woman knowing I had no intention of doing aught more when that's what she wanted or expected."

Abigail swallowed. "I'm your first kiss?"

"Aye, lass. You are. Do you think me less of a mon for not having the experience other men my age do?"

Abigail vehemently shook her head. "Not at all. You are a far better mon than most. Your reasons are so selfless and honorable. Were you never tempted?"

"Of course, I have been. Couldn't you tell? My body reacts just like any other mon's. I have the same desire and wants as any other mon my age. But I have never indulged in them. I feared the cost too much." Ronan hesitated once he heard himself say the word fear.

"I don't think you're a coward for that, in case you're wondering. I didn't understand, and I rushed to judge. If your greatest sin is not tupping every woman who makes you twitch, then you are a far better mon than any other I ken. You deserve a wife who has unfailing confidence in you. And I've failed." Abigail looked away.

"Because you don't know me? Because you didn't know enough to understand me or my life? Because you handfasted with a maggoty piece of shite who probably makes you wonder if all men have secrets and are untrustworthy? You haven't failed, Abigail. You've been human."

Tears leaked from Abigail's eyes as she shook her head. "You don't understand. If you were the only

67

person I'd prejudged, then mayhap I could forgive myself. But you're not. It's what I do. I took one look at my sister-by-marriage, Maude, and decided on the spot that she wasn't good enough. She wasn't thin and beautiful like my sister, like I believed I was. I thought my family was too good for an ordinary, plump woman to be a part of. I was horrid to her. Horrid. So horrible that had she not intervened on my behalf—more than once, mind you—my brother would have sent me to a convent, or sent me here years before I came. Anywhere to have me away from Maude. I was so vain, so self-centered, so petty and frivolous, just so wretched. But I thought God gave me a chance to redeem myself when Lathan showed an interest."

Abigail struggled to swallow the lump in her throat and to keep the tears to just a steady stream rather than sobs. She wiped her cheeks on the plaid covering her shoulders as she looked down to where Ronan still held her hands. It surprised her that he still held them after what she admitted. She doubted he'd still be holding them when she finished.

"Lathan was handsome, charming, and attentive to me when he came to Stornoway to arrange to meet me. I was certain that I was ready to become a clan's lady, despite never having taken an actual interest in learning to be a chatelaine. I thought Maude's hurried lessons and some extra responsibilities while she was injured would be enough. I didn't wait to get to know Lathan better and accepted his offer because I based my decision and my judgment on appearances."

Abigail glanced up at Ronan, expecting judgment and disdain in his gaze. But she found none. Instead, he waited patiently for her to continue.

"What did it get me?" Abigail laughed harshly. "A mon who lied from the first words out of his mouth. A year of wishing I could be anywhere but with the Chisholms. I failed as a chatelaine. I swanned around in the beginning as though my only duty was to watch other people work. I thought Lathan wanted a life with me, wanted a family, but we both know that wasn't the case. In the end, he frightened me so much after he learned I tried several times to write to Kieran, that I remained in my chamber except for meals. He stopped visiting me and made no effort to hide his leman. She dined to his right while I dined to his left."

"He brought his mistress into your home and made you break bread with her?" Ronan didn't realize how hard he was squeezing Abigail's hands until she flexed her fingers. He glanced down as he relaxed his hold. "I'm sorry. I just can't believe he would treat you in such a way. Do you think he would have made good on his threats, or was he satisfied with just intimidating you?"

"I think the latter. I don't think he dared lay a finger on me to abuse me. He feared word would reach Kieran, even if I wasn't the one to send the missive. He knew Kieran would tear him apart if he hurt me. For all my faults, my brother still loves me."

"Abby," Ronan paused as he tried to work through what he wanted to say. Abigail was so intent upon what Ronan would say that she didn't notice the diminutive. "You may be a little quick to judge, but I think you understand now when you make that mistake. Did you realize when you were being judgmental in the past?"

"Not really. Not until after things went poorly with Lathan. That's when I started thinking aboot those who were good to me and how he wasn't. I thought aboot how forgiving Maude always was and how wonderful she is, but I judged her as unworthy. I thought Lathan was better than he was. I was certain

I would have a perfect life with him because he was charming and handsome. Turns out he was a toad. I thought aboot how my mother and sister behaved, their pettiness and spitefulness, and I realized I was far more like them than Maude. That's when I realized that my rush to judge people seemed to never be right. I thought I'd convinced myself to leave judgment to God and St. Peter. But that fell apart when I met you. I reverted to the auld me, and I'm ashamed of it."

"You met a quiet mon who appears shy," Ronan began. "Then you learned I'm a laird. You wondered how a shy and reserved mon could lead an entire clan. You doubted me, but you aren't the first, and I'm certain you aren't the last, to do that. Abigail, I am quiet, and I tend to be cautious aboot what I say and do because of the weight of responsibility. But you've only seen me at court. You haven't seen me at home, among my people. I know no one here. I'm only visiting. And I represent my entire clan. I'm not a mon to boast and draw attention to myself when I'm somewhere new and don't know the people around me. I'm not scared, I'm cautious. My clan depends upon me for everything. Our livelihood and our security. While being reserved makes many men underestimate me, it gives me the chance to learn a great deal aboot others."

"That's wise, Ronan. I didn't think aboot it like that. No one has ever had to rely upon me for aught. I was too unreliable and immature for anyone to trust me enough."

"During that same conversation with my father, he warned me that the expectations placed upon me would always be daunting and heavy. He made me realize that I am not only the face of the MacKinnon clan, I am the first and last defense my people have. Ever since then, I have been cautious aboot what I say and do in case it reflects poorly on my people. That's why I'm so reserved. I fear saying the wrong things and jeopardizing my clan's reputation, our alliances, our trade agreements, our position with the king. I keenly feel the weight of my duty, and I take it seriously. I don't want to fail." Ronan swallowed as he admitted his greatest fear. He would rather ride into battle naked with no weapons but his fingernails than do something that could harm his clan.

"You fear failing," Abigail whispered. "Your father was wise to explain so much aboot life to you. I wish my mother had done so. But I wish you'd walked away from that time with your father without doubting yourself. I think the fact that you are so dedicated to your people shows you are the furthest thing from a failure. Is worrying you'll say the wrong thing why you will suddenly go quiet?"

"Aye."

"Och, Ronan." Abigail cupped his face. "Do you fear that your mouth gets too far ahead of your mind and suddenly you panic and need to stop speaking? It sounds like you fear enjoying talking to people."

"Aye. But it's not like that everywhere or with everyone. Only those who either hold sway over my clan or those who I want to respect me." Ronan's open expression pulled at Abigail's heart. She leaned forward and pressed a gentle kiss to his mouth.

"Am I one of those people? You get quiet around me," she whispered.

"Very much," Ronan admitted. Abigail shifted close enough to lean her forehead against his.

"Do you realize that you've said a great deal to me since we entered this chamber, and you haven't run out of words yet? Your mouth hasn't run faster than your mind. I think everything you've said has been thoughtful, and I respect you even more." Abigail sat up straight. "And that makes me feel even

71

worse. I was so quick to judge. Ronan, I'm sorry. I still think you deserve a wife who—"

"Abby, I want you," Ronan interrupted. "Do you still have the same impression of me as you did before this conversation?"

"Nay. Not at all," Abigail shook her head.

"Do you feel like you know me better now?"

"Very much."

"Do you like who you now know me to be?"

"Very much," Abigail whispered. It was Ronan's turn to cup her face. He brought his mouth to within inches of hers and stopped. Their eyes met before both sets slipped shut. The kiss was tender and slow. They explored the recesses of each other's mouths, discovering what they liked until desire overtook the kiss. Abigail leaned back at the same time as Ronan lowered his body over hers. He pushed his sporran out of the way, and Abigail moaned as she felt his weight and his hardened length press against her. "I want you, too. And not just like this."

Ronan's hand ran along her ribs, up and down, until he slid his hand to cover her breast. He waited for Abigail to push him away, to laugh at his uncertainty, but she arched her back, moaning once again. Her arms pulled him down to rest more of his weight against her, but he was hesitant, worrying he would hurt her.

"Abby, this can't be comfortable for you. This bench is too narrow, and it must be too hard with me squashing you. I don't want to hurt you."

"Then put me on the table," Abigail suggested. She watched the surprise, then the lust, flare in Ronan's eyes as he scooped her up and laid her on the table. She locked her ankles behind Ronan's thighs and slid her hands beneath the neckline of his leine. His hand kneaded her breast once again as the other gripped her hip.

"I don't know what to do," Ronan admitted.

"I think you do. You must because what you're doing feels amazing. I—" Another moan leaked from Abigail's mouth as Ronan's cock pressed against her mons. She shifted her hips to gain more friction. "That, Ronan. Rub your cock against me. It feels so good, but it makes me want you so much more." Ronan obliged and thrust his hips forward, and he discovered just how good a woman's body could feel, even though they were still clothed.

Ronan felt Abigail's mood shift as she grew restless. Her hands found his backside and squeezed as she pressed him against her harder. Her hips flexed with the rhythm of his thrusts. He watched as she tilted her head back, the chords in her neck straining. Ronan had never brought a woman to climax, but he knew what he was watching. He rocked his hips harder and faster as Abigail's nails bit into his backside. It was only a moment later that Abigail's breath hitched, and her body went stiff. Her hands gripped his upper arms as she coasted through her release. Ronan stepped back, thinking he should give her room to breathe. He was unprepared for her hand to dive beneath his plaid and wrap around his cock. She stroked him thrice before he shuddered, and his seed coated her hand.

Ronan sucked in deep lungfuls of air as he watched Abigail pull her hand free. When she reached for her arisaid, he caught her wrist and shook his head, wiping her hand with his own plaid. As his mind cleared as more oxygen reached it, he blushed to his roots.

"I don't usually—I mean it's not always so—" Ronan was embarrassed yet again.

"I'm glad it didn't take long. I find it incredibly flattering. Mayhap there will be other times when it takes longer, but it makes me feel good to ken you desire me as much as I do you," Abigail shrugged.

"Are you saying that to make me feel better?"

Abigail scrambled to kneel on the table, so they met at eye level. "You have been honest with me each time we've talked. I've been honest with you. Why would I start lying now? You lasted longer than I did." Abigail pressed her body against his as she leaned her head against his shoulder. "Ronan, I will do my best never to compare you to Lathan. But I will this time. You make me feel more desirable than any mon ever has. My body *never* reacted like this, and he never made me feel this way."

"You're not repulsed that the mon who wishes to woo you is less experienced than you? You're not disappointed that I don't know how to pleasure you?" Ronan whispered. Abigail sat back on her heels, her expression incredulous.

"You told me you don't care that I'm not a virgin. I was confused, but I never judged you for being one. Now I understand what you meant last night." When Ronan looked at her quizzically, she explained. "I didn't get the implications, but I will always remember every word. You said, 'I think people put far too much store in believing women should be virgins on their wedding nights while men should bed every whore in sight before his.'"

"I don't remember saying that, but I meant it." Ronan grinned. "Besides, someone should know what they're doing in the dark."

"Dark? Oh, no. I intend to see every inch of you." Abigail's eyes went wide, and her nostrils flared as she realized she'd spoken her thought aloud. "I mean, if we marry," she finished lamely.

"I understood what you meant. Abigail, it will always be your choice whether we couple. I don't expect us to join without marrying just because I know you're not a virgin. It's your decision when and if."

"How are you so wonderful?" Abigail mused.

"Because I want to be good enough for you," Ronan confessed. "At least good enough for you to consider me."

"Holy Mother! Ronan, it will never be a question of whether you're good enough for me or any woman. You are. You absolutely are. Better than most of us could ever deserve. It's whether we find we suit besides our physical attraction."

"I'd like to find that out too," Ronan said before kissing Abigail's forehead. "Aren't you expected to be with the queen?"

Abigail bit her lip as she shook her head. "I saw you in the lists. I saw how those men followed you, how they trusted you and didn't even realize how they obeyed your commands. I realized I'd grossly underestimated you. I felt—still feel—horribly aboot that. It was unsettling. One of the ladies noticed I wasn't acting the way I usually do. She offered to make my excuses, so I could return to my chamber. That's when my nose ran into your chest," Abigail grinned.

"Abby, I don't want you to worry aboot that anymore. Nay, I don't like the idea that you thought I was weak, but I did naught to change your opinion. I wasn't trying to manipulate you, but I have learned to use that impression to my benefit in politics. I hope you understand that I will never be as outgoing as some, and I will never feel comfortable in crowds of people I don't ken. But I'm not weak. I can promise you that."

"No one else calls me that," Abigail murmured before she realized that wasn't the most important thing Ronan said. "I know you weren't manipulating me. I find that now that I understand, I rather like that you prefer a more sedate—shall we say—life. It suits a mon of the isles. I never doubted your ruggedness or your obvious strength as a warrior. Tall, blond, and brooding is incredibly attractive."

Ronan grinned. "Is it?"

"Aye," Abigail breathed. "Would you kiss me again? Please."

Ronan nodded before lifting her so Abigail could uncurl her legs. He came to stand between her thighs as their kiss sparked into passion. Abigail tugged at Ronan's leine until her hands could slip beneath the fabric and touch the smooth skin at his waist. She trailed them up his abdomen, then froze. She pulled back from their kiss and snatched her hands from beneath Ronan's shirt. He blinked several times.

"I don't want you to think I'm a whore," Abigail blurted. "Just because I'm not a virgin doesn't mean I've been with other men. Others besides Lathan."

"I never thought you had. Abby, just like it flattered you that I didn't last very long," Ronan chuckled ruefully. "I'm flattered that you want me." He leaned forward, but a noise at the door made them both look in its direction.

"No one ever comes here," Abigail whispered. She slipped from the table and tugged Ronan's hand as she pulled him toward a tapestry that hung in the shadows of the chamber. They hid just as the door opened. Ronan backed into the corner and wrapped his arm around Abigail's waist. As she leaned back against his broad chest, Ronan's arm brushed against the underside of her breasts. She didn't make a sound, but Ronan felt her inhale. His other hand rested on her shoulder. The temptation to slide his hand beneath the neckline of Abigail's kirtle made Ronan want to groan.

"Oh, Stuart," a woman's voice moaned. "I

thought you'd never get the door open. I can't wait any longer."

Ronan and Abigail peered around the edge of the tapestry as a man lifted the woman onto the table, much like Ronan had done to Abigail not that long ago. Except this woman pulled her skirts to her waist while the man pushed down his leggings. At their grunt as he entered her, Abigail's fingers dug into Ronan's forearms. She hadn't realized they rested there until she felt the muscles tense. Ronan's arm tightened around Abigail, and her backside brushed against his sporran. She reached back and pushed it out of the way, her bottom now rubbing against his cock. As they watched the couple thrust against one another, Ronan gave into his impulse and slid his hand beneath Abigail's gown, his fingers finding her taut nipple. Abigail gathered handfuls of Ronan's plaid as her head tipped back against his chest. With each moan from the woman laid spread-eagle on the table, Ronan rolled and pinched Abigail's nipple. They could feel each other's rapid breathing, and it heightened their desire.

"I ken we shouldnae watch," Ronan whispered, his voice thick with lust. He hadn't noticed he slipped back into his burr. "But I ken I canna look away."

Abigail nodded her head. She guided Ronan's hand to cup her mons. He pressed his fingers between her legs at she clutched his thighs, pulling herself tighter against his body. They continued to watch in silence, but the couple finished nearly as quickly as they began. The woman righted herself as the man pulled his breeks back into place. With a giggle, the woman pushed her breasts back into her gown and hopped down from the table. Without a kiss or a fare-thee-well, she walked to the door and left. The man didn't dawdle and left only moments later.

Abigail didn't know what to do. She wanted to turn around and beg Ronan to toss her skirts like they'd just witnessed the unknown man do. But another part of her thought they should slip away now that the unexpected show had ended. Ronan squeezed Abigail's breast and mons before withdrawing his hands. Abigail felt the hesitation and nearly held them against her.

"If we marry," Ronan whispered. "One day— preferably many days—I will take you like that on my desk."

"Take me?" Abigail pushed away the tapestry and stepped out. She held it back for Ronan. "That implies I wouldn't want it. I'd come willingly." Both grinned at Abigail's double entendre.

They stood staring at one another at a loss for what to say after their conversation, their tryst, and their spying. Ronan took Abigail's hand, and they walked in silence to the door. Ronan put his finger to his lips as he eased the door open. He stood looking in both directions before stepping forward.

"Could we go for a walk this afternoon, if the queen permits it?" Ronan whispered over his shoulder.

"I will see that she does," Abigail replied. Ronan left the chamber without looking back, but Abigail watched his hands open and close, knowing he wanted to but didn't dare. She slipped from the chamber moments later.

NINE

A bigail slipped into her chamber before pressing the door shut and leaning back against it. She shut her eyes, trying to visualize the time she spent in Ronan's arms. Like the fine Sutherland whisky Maude's family sent to them, Ronan's kisses had the power to make heat suffuse every fiber of her body, going straight to her head. She felt giddy while at the same time her limbs felt heavy. Her breasts and core ached for more of his attention. She'd moaned when his hand slipped beneath her kirtle and pinched her nipples. She wanted to rip the material from her shoulders and hold her breasts up in offering. She'd felt Ronan's shaft pressed against the crease between her bottom cheeks, and it aroused her in a way she never imagined. All she wanted was more time in his arms, more time to explore how their bodies fit together.

But more time alone would only make the temptation too great—at least for her. She supposed Ronan would restrain himself, just as he always had, but she didn't know that she could. She feared she would beg Ronan for his kisses and his touch, making a fool and a harlot of herself. She respected Ronan's choice of abstinence, and she didn't want to put him in a position where he might abandon his resolve because of her. But Abigail found doing the right thing to be deeply unfulfilling.

Since the queen wouldn't expect her for the rest of the morning, Abigail lay down on her bed. She would have to make an appearance at the midday meal to prove she was well enough to go for a walk with Ronan that afternoon. She would suffer through hours of off-key harp music if it meant she could spend time with Ronan away from the keep. She closed her eyes and imagined what Dun Ringill looked like. She'd been to the MacLeod's stronghold Dunvegan on Skye, but not since she was a child. She recalled Ronan saying his home looked out over the water. She supposed that, as an island much like Lewis, there were few fortifications that wouldn't sit on the coast. They would be the first line of defense against an attack, blocking the aggressors before they could move inland.

As she pictured Dun Ringill, she pictured Ronan's chamber. If it were anything like her brother's, it would hold a massive bed. She wondered if she and Ronan might be like Maude and Kieran, sharing a chamber and a bed every night. As more images of Ronan's chamber formed behind her closed eyelids, she hitched her skirts to her waist. Remembering the sensations Ronan's kisses and touches stirred earlier, she slipped her fingers along her seam, finding dew collecting between her thighs. Her fingers sought the bundle of nerves that were still stimulated despite the release she'd found in Ronan's arms. She rubbed in slow circles as she imagined Ronan stripping her bare. In her vision, they tumbled onto the bed, both naked. As Abigail pictured Ronan's lips scorching a trail along her body, she bit her bottom lip to keep from crying out. As she rubbed faster and harder, her breathing became more labored. As need coiled tightly in her belly then released pleasure throughout her body, Abigail's breasts ached for Ronan's touch. Satiated and breathless, Abigail drew in deep breaths of cool air before feeling calm. She pushed her skirts back into place.

Abigail's thoughts turned to what it would be like as Ronan's wife. She considered her duties beyond his or her bedchamber. She tried to imagine herself as Maude. She imagined sitting down with the cook and planning the week's menu, checking with the housekeeper to ensure there were plenty of candles, oil, and the servants remained industrious. A picture of Abigail sitting beside Ronan materialized as she imagined them sitting together in the Great Hall once a month as they adjudicated disputes among clan members. Ronan would rule over disagreements between men, while Abigail would oversee the women.

Surprisingly, Abigail found she looked forward to those tasks she had previously dreaded. She wondered if she would tour the villages with Ronan when he went to check on their inhabitants as spring arrived, when the fall harvest was upon them, and in preparation for winter. Abigail discovered she wanted to learn how she could help the MacKinnons. She felt ashamed that she'd never had that calling for her own people, but she supposed developing a sense of duty was better late than never.

The morning drifted away as she daydreamed, and Abigail startled when the bells rang to alert everyone that it was time for the midday meal. She stuck her feet back into her slippers and made her way to the Great Hall. She cast her gaze toward where she knew her guardsmen sat, and she found Ronan watching her. She offered him a brief, almost timid smile before she looked at the ladies'-in-waiting tables and wanted to groan. She made her way to her peers, wishing she could sit with Ronan instead.

"Lady Abigail, you're looking remarkably well, considering you are indisposed," Lady Sarah Anne smirked.

"I rested and now feel quite recovered. Your concern is—noted," Abigail nodded as she took her seat. She reminded herself that if she hadn't anything nice to say, she would do well to remain quiet.

"We saw you walking into the keep with Laird MacKinnon," Lady Margaret winked conspicuously at her younger sister.

"Aye. I wasn't feeling well, and he offered to escort me out of the chill weather. It was gracious of him, considering that he had somewhere else to be." Abigail wouldn't say that the somewhere else was locked in a library with her as they nearly coupled against a wall and on a table. She maintained a neutral expression, even though it was a feat she couldn't believe she accomplished. She desperately wanted to look in Ronan's direction and grin.

"That's interesting because Lady Margaret and I were concerned and went to check on you. You didn't answer when we knocked on your door." Sarah Anne bore a matching smirk to her sister's.

"Aye. One can't answer the door when one isn't awake in the chamber." Abigail wouldn't lie, but neither would she give away the truth.

"You were sleeping?" Lady Margaret asked skeptically.

"What else would I be doing if I was unwell?" Abigail asked innocently.

"Perhaps you were—sewing," Sarah Anne answered, but her expression implied far more than her words.

"And I suppose you put your ear to the door to check," Abigail narrowed her eyes. She'd seen both

82

women do it at other ladies' doors when they wished to find gossip. In response, Sarah Anne turned her face away from Abigail. When Margaret opened her mouth to continue, Abigail cocked an eyebrow, daring her. Opting not to enter a battle of wits with Abigail, Margaret reached for her chalice instead.

The meal continued, and Abigail spent it chatting with Emelie and Blythe. She kept her head down as she ate but glanced from under her brow in Ronan's direction. She found him doing the same thing and struggled not to blush or smile. But she nearly bounded from the table when the meal finished. She maneuvered so she would be the last one of the ladies to leave the Great Hall. With everyone else's back to her, she slipped toward another exit, hoping Ronan saw the direction she headed.

"I've already asked your guards to join us, lass," Ronan's rich baritone drifted to her ear, and Abigail wanted to sigh. She recalled how he sounded when he sang in the pew beyond hers. "I see you have your arisaid. Are you ready to go now, or would another time be better?"

"Now."

Ronan chuckled. "That's what I hoped you would say." He led them out to the bailey and signaled to his men. One of them ducked into the barracks and returned with the MacLeod guards. With the MacKinnons in front, and the MacLeods behind them, Abigail was nearly hidden by the mountain of men surrounding her. She pulled her plaid over her head and kept her head down. In part she wished to keep the wind from her face, but mainly she sought to avoid anyone seeing her going for a walk with Ronan. She knew her plaid would give her away, but she didn't feel the need to be brazen about it.

"Please don't think I'm hiding and ashamed to be seen with you," Abigail murmured.

"I wasn't thinking any such thing," Ronan replied. "I think you're being circumspect, and I appreciate the discretion."

"It's hardly discreet, being the only woman among more than a dozen warriors, but I suppose I'm well hidden." Abigail canted her head and turned her face toward Ronan, grinning ruefully.

"Where would you like to go? Would you care to stroll through town?"

"Not at all. There are paths leading toward a meadow and one into the woods. I'd rather move toward the fresh air rather than away from it."

"I'm relieved to hear you say that. I was dreading a stroll through the littered streets."

Abigail studied Ronan for a moment before she smiled shyly. "But you would have if I'd asked, and if I didn't know you for an islander, I wouldn't have been able to tell you hated it."

"Is that why you've suggested going another route?"

"Hardly," Abigail laughed. "Birds, trees, and grass. I much prefer that over refuse and the rotting of God only knows what. The only thing missing is—"

"The sea," Abigail and Ronan said in unison. They both chuckled as Ronan wrapped Abigail's arm around his. She shifted so their upper arms rubbed together. They fell into companionable silence until they passed the last cottages of the village, which lay west of the center of town. When Ronan cleared his throat, the MacKinnon and MacLeod guards fanned out, maintaining a protective barrier around the couple but not within earshot if Ronan and Abigail kept their voices low.

It amazed Abigail that a simple sound conveyed an order to not only Ronan's men but men from her clan, who owed him no obedience. But she supposed that wasn't true; as a laird, they would show him deference.

"I asked them to give us some space once we were away from the keep," Ronan explained, guessing at what made Abigail furrow her brow. "They do not read minds."

Abigail sucked her cheeks in before casting a rueful grin at Ronan. "They may not, but you already seem to have a habit of reading mine." She found she didn't mind that Ronan already understood many of her thoughts. In fact, it intrigued her to guess what else he might perceive.

"I don't read your thoughts, Abby," Ronan said, returning her grin. "I watched the confusion on your face as you watched the men spread out. It was easy to tell what you were wondering. As for this morning, I told you. You're not the first person to make assumptions aboot me. I haven't been divining your thoughts."

To Ronan, Abigail's expression seemed indulgent, bemused, and skeptical all at once. It made her startling eyes twinkle while the brisk air brought color to her cheeks. She was breathtaking, and Ronan couldn't look away. He adjusted their arms, so Abigail's forearm rested over his rather than around it, making it possible for him to hold her hand without drawing attention. Her arm brushed his once more, and Ronan felt a little added pressure as she leaned toward him. He wanted nothing more than to wrap his arm around her, but she'd only agreed to consider him the night before. Despite their tryst that morning, he didn't want to make her fear he expected more.

Abigail inhaled the fresh air as they crunched over the dusting of snow that had settled from that morning. There was little wind compared to what she lived with on the Isle of Lewis during winter.

With no gusts coming from the sea to nearly knock her over, Abigail felt like she could spend forever outdoors with Ronan. She was in no hurry to return to the keep, so when Ronan didn't object, she guided him and their men across the meadow and toward a stream that turned into a surging river in spring. If they'd been riding, she would have urged them to ford the waterway and climb the far embankment to gaze at the vista. They would have seen mountains in the distance, a sign that the Highlands beckoned them.

A thicket came into view, and Ronan squeezed Abigail's hand. When she looked up, Ronan raised his eyebrows. She nodded, and they continued toward the trees. Bursts of sunlight around the canopy of trees made the snow twinkle. It was thicker where the sun hadn't melted the last dusting they received. As they entered the tree line, the guards fanned out further, giving the couple privacy. Abigail didn't doubt Ronan knew where every man stood, but she couldn't see any of them. They came to a stop in one of the patches of sparkling snow.

"Abby, there is so much I wish to know and to ask you, and it feels as though there is so little time to get to know you."

"I feel the same. We have a sennight before we depart. I still have duties to the queen that I can't neglect no matter how much I want to. What will you tell the king?"

"The truth. You have agreed to let me court you, and we intend to travel together to the Hebrides. We haven't come to an agreement yet, but I will hold to my word and inform him of who I choose by Epiphany." Ronan watched as Abigail cast her gaze aside, uncertain what to make of his final comment. He nudged her chin up. "Abby, you're the only woman I'm considering. If we find we don't suit, then I will have to choose someone else. But until we decide one way or another, there is no one else. I ken it only gives us a moon, since I must dispatch a messenger at least a fortnight before Epiphany. It's the only way for the mon to arrive back here in time."

"That isn't long, but it's longer than most couples have. Do you have to be wed by Epiphany or merely betrothed?"

"I have to make my choice by then. The king didn't say aught aboot being betrothed or married."

Abigail bit her bottom lip. More than a moon's time gave her more time to get to know Ronan than she'd taken to become acquainted with Lathan. But she'd never considered needing to get to know Lathan. She'd assumed everything would work out perfectly merely because that's what she wanted to happen. As she stood with Ronan, she realized in the space of a day, she knew more about Ronan's character than she likely knew about Lathan's during the first six months of their handfast.

"Abby?"

"I was thinking aboot how I feel like I ken you better after a day than I did—*him*—after the first six months there. I want to get to know you, which I hadn't considered the last time. And I feel like you'd let me. I don't feel like you're keeping me at arm's length—" Abigail smiled guiltily. They both knew neither was keeping the other physically at an arm's length. "I believe you'd like me to know you better. I don't think you'd hide aught from me either, or at least, you wouldn't play me false in what you let me see."

"I may not always be able to tell you everything when we both might wish, but I won't purposely deceive you to hurt you. The only time I will be less than truthful is if I believe you or our family is in danger."

Abigail focused on Ronan's earnest gaze, and she knew the man before her had too much integrity to lie to her. She understood it wasn't about her or how he felt about her. It was his ingrained sense of honor and duty that guided him. She knew that he wouldn't fail her, because to do so would be a failure he couldn't live with. He'd admitted that was his greatest fear. She stepped forward and wrapped her arms around Ronan's waist. He returned her embrace, and she rested her head against his chest.

A sense of security and peace washed over Abigail, one that she hadn't felt since she was a child and her father embraced her. As the youngest, he'd spoiled her, and she'd always gone to him when she hurt herself. Just as her father made her feel as though the world couldn't reach her, Ronan offered her the same solace. As a woman fully grown, pressed against the man she desired, she wished she could show how she appreciated the comfort he offered.

Abigail inhaled deeply before releasing her breath gradually. One hand fisted the back of Ronan's leine as the other glided over his ribs and swept over his chest. She strained to kiss the bare skin at his collar. She inhaled again, the fresh scents of mint and musk filling her nostrils. Ronan's scent hadn't been unappealing that morning, even though he'd come from the lists. But Abigail knew he'd cleaned up before going to the midday meal. She found she'd happily grow accustomed to the mixture of smells if it meant she was near Ronan.

"Abby?" It was the second time Ronan had to bring her thoughts back to their conversation.

"I'm sorry. I confess, I was enjoying standing here with you."

"So am I. I wasn't sure if I said something that made you withdraw."

"Ronan, I'd climb inside your clothes to be closer to you right now." Abigail jerked backed, once more shocked at what she said aloud. She winced as her cheeks went up in flames.

"I'd rather we both took all of our clothes off," Ronan teased.

"You didn't say aught wrong. I realized I'm truly content being here with you just as we are. I could— want to—get used to it."

Ronan kissed Abigail's forehead before she tilted her head back, her need reflected in his whisky-hued eyes. She would happily drown in them if she could stare at him all day. He lowered his mouth to hers, and their kiss began softly. Abigail mused silently that Ronan was a quick study. He'd moved past his tentativeness and hesitation. He led this kiss, coaxing Abigail to open to him, cradling her skull and positioning her head, so he could devour her. His hand slipped beneath the yards of wool wrapped around her and grasped her backside. When her hips rocked forward, he tightened his grip. Abigail was ready to maul him, not caring who watched. The hand that already grasped the back of his leine tugged with impatience, while the hand that rested on his chest slid up to cup his jaw.

Abigail's cool fingers against his scorching flesh made a heady contrast. Ronan reminded himself that they weren't truly alone, and it was far too cold to ruck up Abigail's skirts and take her against a tree, despite how the thought made his cock pulse. The feel of her lush backside in one of his hands while the other cupped her breast nearly made him cast aside his honor in favor of delicious sin. There was no doubt in Ronan's mind that they were suited physically, but even before they kissed among the trees, he'd had little doubt that their personalities complemented each other.

They both panted as they pulled apart and gazed at one another. Soft smiles playing on their lips, a shared secret of what passed between them. Abigail closed her eyes once more, locking away the moment as a memory she would cherish until she was too old to remember. Ronan cupped her jaw and rubbed his nose against hers before dropping a tender kiss on her lips.

"I would remain out here forever, but you shall freeze, Abby. Then we won't be able to enjoy aught."

"I certainly don't want that. I'm not eager to return to the keep, but now that you mention the cold, I must admit my toes are rather chilled." Abigail cast him a flirtatious expression before she whispered. "But most of me is surely overheated."

"I'm surprised I'm not melting the snow around us," Ronan murmured. "I'd like to go for a walk tomorrow if the weather holds. Not just so we can do this, though I hope we do. I'd like time to talk. I want to know more aboot your life on Lewis and Stirling. I'd like to get to ken what you expect in a husband, a marriage, and life in a new clan."

"I'd like to ken the same—I mean what you expect in a wife," Abigail chuckled. "I want to learn aboot the MacKinnons, and I want to learn more aboot you. What I already know has convinced me —" Abigail snapped her mouth shut before she gave away how she felt.

"That we already suit?" Ronan provided. "And not just like this."

"Aye." Abigail nodded, relieved Ronan didn't appear to think her foolish or disagreed.

"I still wish to know you better, Abby. But I want that because I believe we are well matched, because I think what exists between us already is the basis for something more."

"I feel the same, Ronan. I want it to be more."

"As do I." Ronan brushed his lips against hers before they turned toward the tree line. Ronan whistled, and the men materialized like apparitions. They chatted as they walked back to the keep, sharing what they liked most about the island upon which they grew up and what they missed most about it. They chuckled when they finished one another's sentences, their sentiments mutual. By the time they arrived at the keep, they were both certain they were more than halfway to being in love.

TEN

A bigail smiled as she watched Ronan joke with the man who rode beside him. She'd spent the rest of the week between their interlude in the library and their departure from Stirling enjoying Ronan's company. It surprised her how accommodating the queen was. They'd been able to go for walks when the weather permitted, and they'd even gone riding one afternoon. They'd stopped to take in the vista, but with their horses shielding them from their guards' view, their chatting soon turned into kissing. But when Abigail's nose turned red and her eyes watered, Ronan hurried to take her back to the warmth of the castle.

Now she rode in the center of the party of riders headed to the Hebrides. It was the sixth day of their journey, and they'd encountered excellent weather despite traveling north. It was cold with frequent flurries, but no heavy snow. Ronan took turns leading their group and riding beside her. She encouraged him to ride at the front, where one would expect to find a laird, but he'd pulled her aside their first night and made it clear through his touches and kisses that he wanted to be near her as much as he could.

Under the guise of guarding Abigail when she needed privacy as they made camp, they slipped away together. But they knew they couldn't linger too long. Between the weather and their guards, much more than kisses and running their hands over one another wasn't possible.

Ronan looked back over his shoulder and shot Abigail a knowing look that heated her from the inside out. They had a week's worth of travel left before Abigail would reach Stornoway. They'd agreed that Ronan and his men would travel to the Isle of Lewis, so Ronan could request permission to court Abigail in person. She also suspected that he was nervous about her traveling with only a handful of guards in winter. She watched him say something to the surrounding men before he let them pass him on either side. Abigail rode up beside him.

"How're you faring, Abby?" Ronan asked softly. "Your eyes are very glassy."

Abigail pulled the scarf from her mouth and nose to speak. "I'm well. It's just the wind." She smiled warmly as Ronan's brow furrowed. She could tell he wanted to disagree, even order them to stop early for her sake, but he nodded.

"What are you most looking forward to the moment you step inside? Other than getting warm," Ronan chuckled.

"Besides speaking to Kieran and making him understand why you've come? I'd say playing with my nieces and nephew," Abigail shared.

They'd spoken at great length over their six days on horseback, telling each other more about their childhoods and lives on their islands. It surprised neither of them how similar their experiences were living among the Hebrideans. They shared stories of their clan history, and it fascinated Abigail to learn that the MacKinnons believed they were descendants of St. Columba and the earliest kings of Scotland, the Alpins and MacAlpins. The folklore Ronan shared made Abigail believe in the validity of the MacKinnons' claims.

Abigail retold the legend of the Fairy Flag and how it protected the MacLeods of Skye. When Ronan smirked and nodded his head, Abigail hissed and warned him that the fae would come after him. The MacLeods of Skye and Lewis believed Titania, the wife of Oberan, the king of fairies, was a *"ban-shi"* and warned the clan about impending attack and death. The MacLeods of Skye were the protectors of the *"Braolauch shi"* and could rely upon it in times of danger by unfurling it and summoning the fae to aid them. But if they unfurled it a third time, both the flag bearer and flag would be swept away to a mystical land of the fae. With her earnest expression and serious tone, Ronan relented and agreed it was possible. She'd broken into a wide grin and struggled not to laugh. She admitted she believed some parts of the legend, but not to the extent that the MacLeods of Skye did.

As morning passed into afternoon, Ronan watched the sky darken with thick clouds that looked ready to burst. He feared a blizzard awaited them. They approached Glencoe Pass, and he considered whether they should push through before the storm began or try to seek shelter in a cave. He feared keeping Abigail exposed to the elements when she already looked to be struggling, but he didn't want them trapped if the blizzard snowed them into a cave. They would all freeze. He glanced at Abigail, whose eyes crinkled at the sides. He knew she was smiling beneath her scarf. He swept his eyes over the men who accompanied them and knew he didn't have long to decide. There were a dozen guards along with the couple. If it started snowing, even lightly, it would slow their train of riders as they wound through the pass and into the glen.

"We need to make haste," Ronan called out. "To a gallop."

They'd been cantering at a comfortable pace, but a diagonal shadow from one cloud told him it had already begun to snow on the other side of the pass. The clouds moved toward them. The group spurred their horses, and Abigail tucked her head to hide her face from the wind. Ronan was proud of how Abigail made no complaints about the weather or the hard travel. He knew she didn't dare since her men traveled because it was her wish to go home. He still admired her hardiness. As they entered the pass, the wind whipped around them, making Abigail struggle to stay upright. The flurries gathered on her eyelashes, and she feared her eyes might freeze shut. It could be slow going in many parts of the path, where the uneven ground forced the horses to trot in a line lest they take a wrong step and go lame.

"Laird MacKinnon," a MacLeod guard called out. Ronan looked back over his shoulder to see his fear realized. The guard's horse limped with each step. Ronan looked at Abigail and could tell her strength was draining faster than anyone else's.

"Halt," Ronan called out. He pulled a spare plaid from his saddlebag and snapped it open before wrapping it around Abigail. He swung down from his saddle and crunched through the accumulating snow until he reached the warrior and his horse.

"I dinna ken what happened, ma laird. He followed the other's hoofsteps, but suddenly he began hobbling." The guard ran his hand along his horse's leg and lifted it to look at the hoof. "Bluidy hell! Begging yer pardon, Lady Abigail. Look, ma laird." The man pointed to where the shoe was loose and had slid across the hoof. The nail had ripped part of the sole. The weight of a rider could have permanently injured the horse.

"Have you a spare plaid?" Ronan asked. He glanced again at Abigail, who watched him. He noticed her lips were turning blue as she fought to not let her teeth chatter. He turned back to the MacLeod guard. "Can you get the shoe off? It would be better than that nail tearing his hoof. Either way, wrap the hoof in the plaid until we can get him to a farrier."

"I dinna ken if he will make it that far, Laird."

"We can't stay here much longer. I'm sorry, but you must decide. We aren't going faster than a trot. Guide him and walk with him. But if he can't go on, know that I won't leave you behind, and I can't stay here with Lady Abigail. She's already freezing."

The guard nodded as he lifted the horse's injured hoof and worked to pry the shoe loose. Everyone breathed a collective sigh when it came free. A MacKinnon helped wrap the horse's hoof before mounting his own horse. The MacLeod grabbed the bridle and nodded. Ronan ordered them on, but they'd barely taken a handful of steps when the injured horse whinnied. With coaxing, the horse continued, and so became the pattern for the next half-hour. An angry whinny and cajoling. Ronan didn't blame the horse or the man, but it frustrated him that the delay continued to expose Abigail to the elements.

Ronan looked at Abigail for at least the hundredth time, but his heart pounded as he noticed her eyelids were growing heavy and her body leaned forward. It was more of a slump than trying to avoid the wind. He was running out of time to get her warm.

"We must press on," Ronan called. He turned to Abigail and whispered, "What's your guard's name?"

"Douglas."

"Douglas, mount with one of the other men. Bring your horse if you can, but we must move faster."

"Nay, ma laird. I'm nae leaving ma horse to freeze. I canna do it," Douglas answered.

Ronan turned in his saddle as they stopped again. "Douglas, I don't want you to leave your horse either, but I can't have you or Lady Abigail, not to mention the rest of the men, freeze in favor of a horse. If you must, put the steed out of its misery, but we can't wait any longer."

"We can move off the path and shelter in those trees," a MacLeod suggested. There was an opening in the pass with a copse of trees not far in the distance.

"Nay. It's still too exposed, and there's too great a chance this pass will become untraversable by morning," Ronan shook his head.

"Ye and yer men may go on, Laird MacKinnon, but we will seek shelter with Lady Abigail in the clearing," the MacLeod guard commanded.

"Dennis," Abigail hissed, her eyes wide open. She'd always taken the advice of her guards when she traveled, but it stunned her to hear her guard disagree with Ronan.

"She's our responsibility," another guard named Daniel spoke up. "Ye do what ye must, but we will protect Lady Abigail."

Abigail watched a hardened stare take hold of Ronan's gaze as he turned his horse so he could look at the men in front and behind him. She held her breath, terrified of what would happen to her men for disagreeing with Ronan. She knew his temper was fraying when his brogue entered his voice.

"I dinna ken if ye make a habit of disagreeing with yer laird or ye just reserve that for me. I dinna give a shite. The only thing I am concerned aboot right now is getting Lady Abigail through this pass. She is nae going to freeze to death because ye get her trapped in this pass until the spring thaw." Ronan dismounted and walked between their horses to stand next to Abigail. Keeping his voice low, he asked, "Ye ken what I think, but what do ye wish to do? If ye want to stop in the clearing, we will."

"I trust you, Ronan. Whatever you think is best."

"Lass, if I didna worry that it would slow ma horse too much, I would have ye ride with me. I am sorry for yer mon, but there are thirteen other people and fourteen other horses to consider," Ronan explained.

"I ken. May I speak to him?"

"Abby, ye dinna need ma permission. He's yer guard, and ye're an adult," Ronan frowned.

"I ken, but I won't if you fear spending more time here."

"Just a minute or two. Do ye want me to help ye down?" Ronan offered.

"Aye, please." Ronan lifted Abigail from her horse and gripped her elbow as they walked to where Douglas patted his horse's broad nose. "Douglas, I ken you don't want to leave your horse behind. But I would never forgive myself if I agreed to letting you stay back or if we slow down, and someone perishes because of it. I don't want to explain to Kieran why I'm missing a guard rather than just a horse. Laird MacKinnon speaks sense. We can't wait any longer, and I agree with the laird that staying in the clearing isn't wise." Abigail had pulled her scarf down to talk and offered him a kind smile. Her genuine sympathy was easy to read in her expression. Douglas nodded.

"Have two of the men take yer saddlebags and

add yer saddle to the packhorse. Nae ideal, but the lighter weight may buy ye more time with yer horse," Ronan ordered.

"That's a good idea," Abigail nodded. But she turned to face two of her other guards. Her eyes narrowed as she stepped toward Daniel and Dennis's horses. "I ken you are looking out for your brother, and I believe you are trying to do what you think is best for me, but if I ever hear you speak to a laird like that again, I will be the one with the lash. You can make your disagreement known, but you will do it with respect. Am I understood?" Abigail stood to her fullest height, which was inconsequential compared to the men she traveled with, but her position of authority was clear.

"Aye, ma lady," came two deep voices. Abigail glanced back to see Douglas's horse only had a plaid over its back and another wrapped around its hoof. Douglas mounted on the back of his brother Daniel's horse, riding pillion with him. He held the reins to his horse. With a double rider, Daniel's horse struggled to plod along, but they were all surprised when Douglas's horse no longer complained. The injured steed limped behind the others, but they made their way clear of the pass. When they entered the meadow, Ronan breathed easier. The open space was just as dangerous and exposed to the elements, but he didn't worry about them becoming trapped. The snow fell faster and heavier, but they found shelter once visibility was almost completely gone. Just as they had the previous nights, Abigail lay down on her bedroll near the fire, and Ronan lay near her. Once the steady snores of the men filled the air, Ronan slid behind Abigail and wrapped her in his arms. In her sleep, she nuzzled closer and burrowed into his warmth. Ronan was back where he lay down as the camp came awake, but he knew every man was aware of what he did, since they surely saw him during their turn at watch. But they understood he did it to protect Abigail in the below-freezing night air, and none said anything to keep her from embarrassment. While neither said it aloud, Ronan and Abigail discovered neither wanted to sleep without the other, even after their journey was through.

ELEVEN

"Abigail!" Maude MacLeod rushed to greet her sister-by-marriage. Maude wrapped her arm around Abigail's shoulder as she propelled her toward the fire. She glanced over her shoulder and nodded at the stranger who entered the keep with Abigail's arm wrapped around his.

"Ronan MacKinnon," Kieran's voice traveled across the Great Hall. "Ye must be turned around. Ye came to the wrong isle." The two lairds came to stand before one another, sizing each other up before sticking out their arms to shake forearms. Ronan looked at Abigail, who peeled off the MacKinnon plaid, then her two extra MacLeod ones before she reached the MacLeod plaid that served as her arisaid. She kept that one on and pulled it tighter around her shoulders. Abigail looked at Ronan, then down at his plaid, which she'd worn as an extra layer for the past week. Reflexively, she pulled it against her, fearful someone might snatch it from her.

"Come to ma solar. I see we have much to discuss," Kieran grumbled. Ronan nodded, but he hadn't stopped watching Abigail. He didn't care for her apprehensive visage. Kieran reassured, "She's nae going anywhere."

"That isn't what I'm worried aboot," Ronan mumbled. He turned his palm up and raised his hand just enough for Abigail to see the offer. She nodded, thrusting her MacLeod plaids at Maude, but clinging to the MacKinnon. She rushed to take Ronan's hand. "You should be part of this conversation too."

"Maude?" Kieran asked. He growled when he noticed the grin on his wife's face. When Maude stepped beside her husband, he wrapped his arm around her waist and lifted her off her feet as he walked. Abigail couldn't hear what Kieran told Maude, but Maude snorted and shook her head. Kieran scowled, and Maude laughed harder as he set her on her feet with such care it belied the strength he'd just used to carry her.

They entered Kieran's solar to find a cheery fire in the hearth. Ronan led Abigail to the fireplace and, without thought, took her hands in his and rubbed them to get the blood flowing again. The exhaustion in Abigail's eyes concerned him as he pushed hair back from her face.

"If you're too tired, then we can have this conversation after you've rested. It can wait," Ronan offered.

"It can't. It's nearly Christmas, and you must go to Skye."

"There's still close to a fortnight. That's plenty of time, Abby," Ronan reassured.

"Not to have the banns read before you go," Abigail whispered.

"Banns?" Ronan swallowed.

"Aye. A Christmas wedding?" Abigail whispered, and Ronan saw the hopefulness in her eyes.

"Aye, aught for you." Without considering their audience, they leaned into one another and shared the most tender kiss they'd ever had.

"Get yer bluidy tongue away from ma wee baby sister's mouth," Kieran roared. Ronan tried to push Abigail behind him, but she swatted at him. She noticed Maude was still grinning, and she shot her sister-by-marriage a pursed lip and exasperated glare.

"Kieran, cease. We both ken there is no reason I can't kiss the mon I'm marrying," Abigail announced. She intended to get all the shock and arguing done with as soon as possible.

"Ye're nae marrying a MacKinnon," Kieran crossed his arms and shook his head.

"I am," Abigail countered. "You ken that's why you invited us in here. Laird MacKinnon—Ronan—and I met at court, and he asked my permission to court me. He didn't want to begin until he could write to you, but there was no time to send a messenger ahead of us before we both planned to leave Stirling." Abigail left Ronan's side with a placating pat on his arm. She walked to stand before Kieran, but she looked at Maude. "I've made a lot of mistakes, and they've hurt a lot of people. I thought I'd become a better person by the time I arrived at court, but for reasons I won't share, I misjudged Ronan. I nearly missed my opportunity to find a mon who cares aboot me, flaws and all. Someone who is patient and helps me to be a better person while accepting me for who I am at this point. I can't explain how we understand one another's thoughts, but we do. It became more obvious over the past fortnight of travel. Kieran, I think I can have with Ronan what you have with Maude. That thought never even entered my mind the last time. But now I can see it's within reach."

Maude stepped beside Abigail and whispered, "Ye love him, dinna ye?" Abigail turned her head to look at Maude, and she found such kindness that her heart once more ached for how she'd treated Maude when she first arrived.

"I believe I do," Abigail responded. Maude nodded her head and took Abigail's hands.

"Ye need to forgive yerself. I did a long time ago, Abigail. Ye are different, and anyone who kens ye can tell." Maude looked at Kieran, a pointed expression on her face. Kieran gazed at the woman who stood before him. He remembered her as a sweet child, always excited to see him. Then she'd grown into a spoiled and uncharitable young woman. But she was changed once again. He recognized much of the sweetness that had once been part of Abigail had returned. He saw conviction where there had once been frivolity. He noticed self-assurance that was once pridefulness. When he shifted his gaze to Ronan, he recognized the concern, protectiveness, and even desire that he was certain were in his own eyes any time he spied Maude.

"Go stand with him, if ye must," Kieran grumbled. Abigail didn't hesitate to hurry back to Ronan's side. Ronan wrapped his arm around Abigail's shoulders, raising his chin in challenge. Kieran frowned but nodded his head. "We'd better settle the contracts if the priest's posting the banns tomorrow."

The two couples spent the rest of the afternoon shut away in Kieran's solar. By the evening meal, both women were confident that the two lairds wouldn't tear one another apart. They'd drafted the betrothal contract, and Abigail, Ronan, and Kieran signed. The portion Kieran allotted for Abigail's dowry pleased Ronan. The amount surprised him after hearing about Abigail's last dowry. Ronan hadn't expected the land in Assynt or the gold that would come with Abigail. He'd assumed Kieran would be too wary to offer so much, or that there hadn't been such a generous amount left after settling with the Chisholms.

Kieran introduced Ronan to the clan during the meal, and there were several stunned expressions since it was no secret that the other branch of the MacLeods were not on friendly terms with the Mac-Kinnons. But it took only the space of one meal for people to whisper about how enamored the couple was with one another. Maude didn't know where to look when she suggested a chamber on the guest floor above the family's chambers. Abigail giggled knowing that Maude couldn't meet their eyes since she was attempting not to laugh herself. Once she ceased laughing, Abigail assured Maude that a separate chamber was an appropriate offer. Ronan could only stand and watch the women in silence. They appeared much like sisters, and he hoped that Abigail would realize Maude cared for her despite their rocky past.

TWELVE

Abigail understood why Maude offered Ronan the chamber she did. It was above hers, and no one would hear them moving around. With no one else staying on the guest floor besides Ronan, there was no one to notice how long it took them to say goodnight. Abigail followed Ronan into the chamber and pressed the door shut behind her. She waited by the door, uncertain what Ronan would want. They'd grown close during their journey, and their desire certainly hadn't abated, but Abigail didn't want to make any assumptions.

Ronan turned back to find Abigail waiting by the door. He worried that she was uncomfortable being in a bedchamber with him, but the way she raked her eyes over him made his cock harden. He stepped before her and rested his hands on her waist before pulling her toward him. Their mouths crashed together as they clawed at one another. It had been more than a fortnight since their tryst in the library and the copse of trees, and they'd left both with unspent lust coursing through them both.

"Ronan, I've missed touching you. I want to feel every inch of you," Abigail mumbled between kisses. "I want you."

"Christ's bones, Abigail. I don't ken that I can last long enough to do more than look at you," Ronan confessed, a touch of his brogue flavoring his speech.

"Then don't," Abigail dropped to her knees and pushed Ronan's plaid out of the way before taking Ronan's cock in her hand. She stroked him before licking his rod, making the heated skin slick. Her hand glided up and down as her tongue swirled around the tip of his cock.

"Abigail." Her name came out on a strangled groan as she slipped the head of his cock into her mouth.

"You must ken a woman can pleasure a mon like this." The intimacy of their conversation brought out the hints of Abigail's brogue.

"Just because I haven't done it doesn't mean I don't ken what a mon and woman can do. But you don't have to do this," Ronan choked as Abigail slid her mouth down his shaft.

"Why not?" She asked as she pulled back. "Does it disgust you? Do I disgust you?"

"I ken you ken the answer to both questions, Abby."

"Do you think me a whore for going down on my knees for you?" Abigail continued to stroke Ronan.

"Of course not. I just..." Ronan trailed off, and Abigail froze. She looked at Ronan's pained expression, and she knew it wasn't from a physical ache. She came to her feet and wrapped her arms around his waist. Slowly, his arms encircled her, and she laid her head against Ronan's chest.

"Do you worry you won't ken what to do?" Abigail whispered. At Ronan's shuddering breath, she knew she'd guessed correctly. "Ronan, you can't disappoint me. I want whatever you are willing to give. I

110

want it so much that naught short of never touching you again could disappoint me."

Abigail stepped back and looked up at Ronan. She read the doubt across his face, and she wished she could rip his father from his grave and shake him. She doubted the man intended to create so much anxiety that Ronan never bedded any woman, but that was the outcome. She took his hand and walked to the foot of the bed before turning to look at him.

"I want to do this to you—for you—with you. However you look at it. I want to, Ronan. I don't expect aught in return. If you don't like it, I'll stop." Abigail promised as she reached back to undo the laces to her kirtle.

"You ken I'll like it," Ronan whispered. Abigail reached up and unfastened the brooch on his shoulder, holding out the pin which he took and dropped in his sporran. Ronan lifted the sword strapped to his back and leaned it against the foot of the bed as Abigail loosened his belt. He leaned forward and quickly shucked off his stockings and boots. Abigail's hands trailed along his thighs as she inched his leine higher. When she reached his waist, she wrapped her hands around his cock and stroked as Ronan tore the leine off over his head. Abigail froze as she watched the muscles across Ronan's chest and abdomen bunch and release. She'd thought Lathan was attractive with and without clothes, but she had no idea a man could look like Ronan. Fine scars marked his bronzed skin, and some were deeper than she wished to learn about. She continued to stroke him with one hand as her fingertips ran over the planes and ridges.

"You are so beautiful," Abigail whispered. "I don't mean that in a womanly sense. I mean as in perfection."

She released his rod and skimmed both of her

hands over him before walking around to run her fingers over his shoulders, back, and buttocks. She was in no hurry, exploring what she could reach as her eyes gorged on his form. He was unlike anything she ever imagined. When she came to stand before him again, Ronan saw how she marveled at his body. He was certain his cock grew as her gaze heated his bollocks. Abigail found she couldn't speak louder than a whisper. It was as though his physique demanded quiet reverence.

"Am I the first woman to see you bare? I mean, other than a healer?" Abigail looked up, then regretted the question. She didn't want to know if there was a woman who bathed him at his keep.

"Ye are," Ronan's burr slipped through as he pushed Abigail's gown down the length of her body until it pooled on the floor.

"I don't ken that I'll ever be able to explain what that means to me. But I think I understand now why men demand virgins. There is something intoxicating kenning that a mon as perfectly crafted as you are is for my eyes only." She glanced up to meet his eyes before she once again feasted on him. "You have bestowed upon me a gift that I swear never to take for granted."

Ronan cupped Abigail's cheek in one hand as he eased her against him. His cock pulsed between their bodies, and Abigail resumed stroking as their kiss heated to a frenzy. She nudged him toward the bed before once again sinking to her knees. She slid her mouth over Ronan's cock and moaned as the head brushed the back of her throat. She calmed herself, fighting against her instinct to gag. She would do nothing that made Ronan fear she didn't enjoy every moment of what they shared. She'd performed the same act for Lathan countless times over the course of their year together, but never had she longed to feel a man's rod fill her mouth. Her eyes drifted closed as she focused on the groans and sighs Ronan made as she did everything in her repertoire to please him.

"Abby," Ronan hissed. "I'm too close. I canna stop." He tried to pull back, but Abigail's lips clamped around him as one hand stroked what she could no longer manage and the other swatted him away. Her piercing glare warned him that she had no intention of relenting. He grasped the bedcovers in both hands as his hips thrust, and his seed filled Abigail's mouth. Their matching sighs made them smile as Abigail licked her lips, then patted the corners with her fingertips. Ronan stood and helped her to her feet before pulling her into his embrace. He'd fantasized for years about what having a woman's mouth wrapped around him would feel like, but he'd wholly underestimated the melee of emotions he experienced as he watched Abigail. He understood it was only partly physical. The woman who stood before him was an enchantress, but she was kind and patient. She introduced him to the pleasures of the flesh by giving rather than taking.

Ronan lifted Abigail off her feet, and she squeaked. Abigail had never seen a more handsome face than when Ronan grinned. She cupped his cheeks, her fingers barely touching his bristly skin. She kissed him with all the tenderness she could muster. She was driven to ensure he understood what she felt wasn't just lust. Ronan lay Abigail on the bed, and as she scooted back toward the pillows, he prowled toward her. He pushed her chemise up her thighs until he found the thatch of black curls. She eased her thighs open, and Ronan spied the promised land for the first time. In theory, he knew exactly what to do, but in practice, he still feared failure.

"Ronan, please don't make me wait. I just need you to touch me. Please," Abigail begged. Ronan looked into her eyes and knew she wasn't encouraging him out of pity. The desire in her eyes and strain across her face told him that her impatience and need were real. He kissed along the inside of her thigh until he reached the juncture of her leg and hip. His fingers ran through the ebony curls and along her nether lips as his other arm slid beneath her thigh to grasp her hip. He could feel the dew that drenched her entrance. He glanced up and met her eyes. "I really need you, Ronan."

Spurred on by her words and her body's telltale signs that she wanted him, he slipped his middle finger into Abigail and kissed the hollow where her leg and hip met. He slid his finger in and out, unsure of what else he was supposed to do. He watched Abigail writhe with growing frustration, so he slid a second finger into her. It mollified her, but only for a moment before she once more squirmed with impatience. He tentatively flicked his tongue at her entrance, and Abigail moaned deeply.

"Please," she panted. Ronan would have gladly indulged, had he known what to do. He laved his tongue across Abigail's heated skin and found the pearl hidden within her folds. He noticed that touching the bud made her clench her hands in the sheets, so he continued to focus his attention there as his fingers slid in and out. He wondered if Abigail expected him to do more, but he hadn't a clue what that would be. Her heels pressed into the mattress as she lifted her hips in offering. He continued as he had, but as he watched Abigail's expressions, he realized she wasn't enjoying his ministrations as he had hers. Rather than moving toward completion, she appeared to be straining with frustration.

Abigail felt when Ronan began to withdraw. His

fingers moved slower, and his tongue no longer applied the same pressure. She looked down at him, her eyes stinging from the sweat that dripped from her brow. A maelstrom of need, impatience, and eagerness held her in its clutches as she reveled in the feel of Ronan touching her. But she realized that he didn't understand how his touch both tormented and pleasured her. She deduced that he was self-conscious and worried that he was failing her. She didn't dare offer suggestions, but at the same time, she didn't want to pretend that she climaxed if she didn't. She wouldn't lie to him, but neither did she want to embarrass him. She considered her phrasing before making her request.

"Ronan, you're bigger than just your two fingers. I need more. I can't stop imagining what you'll feel like, how you'll fill me," Abigail explained. But she realized she'd said the wrong thing when Ronan's expression shuttered.

Och hell. He doesnae want to be reminded that I amnae a virgin, that I ken what it feels like to have a mon inside me. That did naught to reassure him. Sard!

Ronan struggled with what to do. He'd practically spilled the moment Abigail looked at his cock, let alone touched him. But it was obvious he was nowhere near satisfying Abigail as she had done him. He didn't know if he should give up or continue to bungle along, praying that he touched her pleasingly. He obliged and slid a third finger into Abigail's sheath, and her head fell back as her arms gave out. Her hips undulated, and he grew hopeful that his ministrations were finally bringing her closer to the brink.

Without thought, Abigail reached between her legs and grasped Ronan's hand, guiding his thumb to her pearl to rub in circles. She was too close to release, but the more she strained, the more elusive it felt. Ronan followed her lead, but he noticed her expression became pinched when she let him touch her without her guidance. With a groan, she brushed Ronan's thumb out of the way, using her own fingers to create the pressure she needed. When he moved to withdraw his hand, she grabbed his wrist and pressed his fingers deeper with a feral scowl that warned him not to stop. Her moans intensified until her body went rigid, and he felt her core tighten around his fingers. She went limp with a sigh, her eyes resting closed.

Ronan withdrew his hand, unsure if he'd failed or marginally helped, but he knew he hadn't succeeded in his attempt. He stood and went to the stand with the ewer and pitcher. He cleansed himself before bringing the damp cloth to Abigail. She sat up and reached for the cloth, but when Ronan hesitated, she sighed and leaned back. Her eyes once again closed. Ronan assumed it was an invitation, so he swept the linen square over her seam, surprised when Abigail moaned again. When he was through, he returned to the washstand, his back toward her. He didn't hear her approach and jumped when she ran her fingers up his back then down to his waist where she wrapped her arms around him. She leaned her head against his back and squeezed before planting quick kisses over his heated skin. She pulled at his upper arm, wanting him to face her. When he wouldn't budge, she walked around him and moved the washstand. She strained to kiss him, but with his chin held high, she couldn't reach.

"Please don't do this," Abigail whispered. "Don't shut me out. I need to kiss you as much as I needed you to touch me."

Ronan glanced down and noticed the tears in Abigail's eyes, and he felt contrite for being cold after they shared their first true intimacy. But he waited too long, and a tear trickled down Abigail's cheek as she took a step back. Ronan's arms shot out and brought her against his body with such force that she puffed out her breath. He swept his thumb over her cheek to catch her tears.

"I never want to make you cry, Abby. I'm sorry," Ronan apologized. "This is aboot me, not you. And I ken it's selfish without saying it out loud."

"You didn't do aught wrong. I was enjoying it, and that's why I grew impatient. But, Ronan, do you ken how I kenned what you liked?"

"Experience?" Ronan blurted. Abigail's eyes widened, and she stepped away. Hurt made her wrap her arms around her, her shoulders came up to her ears, and her face crumpled.

"You say that as though I am a whore. You swore to me not being a virgin wasn't a problem. Obviously, it is. That wasn't what I was thinking at all, but now I ken how you really feel."

"What am I supposed to assume?" Ronan straightened to his full height, defensive when he knew he should have been consoling.

"That I care a great deal aboot ye and that ye're the only person I want to be intimate with." Abigail's anger made her courtly accent fall away. She turned to find her gown. She looked over her shoulder as she stepped into the gown and yanked it up. "I was going to say—even though ye dinna seem to be interested —that I could tell what ye liked because ye twitched, then groaned when it was something ye enjoyed. And aye, I do ken that when a mon is pleasured, he spills his seed, but I kenned that before I lost ma maidenhead. I could taste ye. I would have said that makes it a far sight easier for a woman to ken she's getting it right than any sign she can give a mon. But what does any of that matter, since I'm just a whore?"

Abigail thrust her arms through her sleeves, not

bothering to pull the laces tight. She searched for her stockings and shoes, but before she could slip her second shoe on, Ronan scooped it up and held it away from her. If he hadn't caused her anger and pain, he would have thought that Abigail's fiery temper was mesmerizing.

"I thought I was failing. Again," Ronan admitted, his own brogue coming back. "And ye are nae a whore. That isnae what I thought. Ye made that assumption as much as I made mine."

"That's a pile of shite. Did I look like I wasna enjoying maself? Did I say stop or did I ask for more? Ye're angered because I participated in ma own pleasure. Ye're bent out of shape because I ken what I like. Men arenae the only ones who can find release on their own. Mayhap that's how I ken."

"But is it?" Ronan demanded.

"It is. At least when it comes to that. I figured that out on ma own."

"How can that be? Lathan wasna a virgin when ye married."

"Nay, he wasna," Abigail's laugh was brittle. "Eejit that I am, it took me three moons before I learned he had a mistress and three weans. A fourth on the way by the time I left. I'd said he was vera much nae a virgin."

Ronan opened his mouth, then snapped it shut. He hadn't thought before he spoke. Not only had he hurt Abigail by insulting her, but he'd reopened a wound that hadn't even healed. He felt like an arse and admitted as much.

"I'm being an arse, Abby. I'm sorry. It's none of ma business what happened in yer past. Ma words have cut ye deeply, and instead of telling ye that I care aboot ye deeply too, I was defensive."

"Ronan," Abigail sighed. She sat at the foot of the bed and patted the spot beside her. "Let's have this out right now. For all his faults, I enjoyed bedding Lathan. He made sure our coupling satisfied me, but I ken now that he did it to keep me content and out of his life beyond ma chamber. He encouraged me to learn what I preferred, so that's how I discovered what I like. But all of it—absolutely all of it—was manipulation and deception. I felt so stupid for being naïve and thinking he might one day love me. He used coupling to control me in the slyest of ways. He got a good tumble but never spilled his seed to avoid having a legitimate child. He bedded me to keep me occupied and to make me think I meant something to him."

Abigail inhaled deeply as she pulled at a thread on the cuff of her sleeve. She forced herself not to cry as she finished speaking. "Ye didna really make me feel like a whore. He did. I said it because I was hurt and angry."

Ronan held out his hand, and Abigail took it without hesitation. With a gentle tug, she moved closer, and he lifted her onto his lap. "Ma fear of failing is ma shortcoming, nae yers. I need to move past it, but it's hard when I would do aught to keep from disappointing ye." He paused as he gathered his thoughts. He had an idea that might solve their problem of his inexperience and anxiety. He cleared his throat. "Mayhap I should visit someone, so I ken what I'm doing on our wedding night. I wouldnae be nervous, and ye would enjoy the pleasure ye deserve."

Abigail jumped off his lap like a scalded cat. She narrowed her eyes at him as she spat, "Ye better fuck every one of them because I ken each of them, and I dinna want to figure out who fucked ma husband before me. In fact, fuck them over and over again because ye arenae ever fucking me." She snatched her shoe from where Ronan dropped it and hobbled to the door. "Ye waited all these years finally to bed a woman because ye wanted to honor yer wife. Ye have a woman who loves ye and wants to marry ye, but ye'd rather hump a whore."

Ronan was across the room in three strides. He pulled Abigail's hand from the handle and spun her around. His enormous body imprisoned her against the door, but she didn't fear him. She even wished he'd lose control if it meant he'd act on impulse rather than calculating and worrying about everything.

"I dinna want a whore any more than I want a toothache, but there is naught I wouldnae do to make ye happy, Abby," Ronan growled.

"Happy? Ye telling me ye want to bed someone else is supposed to make me happy? Ye're cruel and daft," Abby spat.

"I love ye too, Abby," Ronan swore before pressing his mouth against hers with a ferocity that took Abigail's breath away. As they kissed, she pulled her gown off, and Ronan pulled the ribbons loose from her chemise. When they stood naked, Ronan's hands slid to her backside and squeezed until Abigail moved her mons restlessly against his cock. "The bed."

"Right here," Abigail demanded. Ronan lifted Abigail, and she wrapped her arms and legs around him, locking her ankles to keep her in place. Ronan's cock found her entrance as though her sheath were a lodestone. He pressed into her, and it took all of Abigail's willpower not to sink onto his rod in a rush. She wanted Ronan to enjoy every moment of his first time—their first time. Abigail dropped her head to his shoulder as his excruciatingly slow pace made her want to scream. "Naught has ever felt as good as this. Christ's bones, Ronan. I will spend before ye're all the way in me."

Abigail shifted, and Ronan thrust the rest of his length into her. He shuddered as Abigail's nails sank into his shoulders. She shifted again, the friction between their bodies causing just enough pressure to send her over the edge. She tightened her thighs as her core clenched around Ronan's length. She cupped his face and gave him a savage kiss, enticing his tongue into dueling with hers. When he thrust his into her mouth, she sucked it in. Ronan grunted, remembering how her mouth felt earlier, knowing that was why she did it.

"I'm sorry. I couldnae wait," Abigail panted. At Ronan's confused expression, she grinned. "I already climaxed once. It just took ye finally being inside me."

"That's all?" Ronan was incredulous. He was teetering on the edge, wrestling with his control. He'd been determined not to finish embarrassingly fast his first time and without at least trying to bring Abigail to release.

"I told ye I needed ye. But dinna stop. I want to feel it over and over," Abigail murmured against his lips as she pressed hers to his and rocked up and down his length.

"Ye can do that? More than once?" Ronan wondered.

"Aye. A woman can, and I wi—" Abigail's body exploded, making her first release pale in comparison. She trembled as she strained to draw out the waves of sensation. Abigail pleaded, "Take me to the bed. I want to touch ye without having to hang on."

Ronan walked them across the room, Abigail's weight barely registering with him. He climbed onto the bed and lay her against the pillows with such gentleness that Abigail's heart melted. "I love ye, Ronan. I regret I didna tell ye that properly the first time. I said it recklessly, but I mean it with ma whole heart."

"I understood that. I didna ken that ye felt that way. I love ye, Abby. I do. That's why I will do aught for ye. I just want to be the mon ye can keep loving." Ronan confessed as his hips rocked against Abigail's. When she stopped moving, Ronan's brow furrowed. He feared he'd done something wrong.

"Stop. Stop right now. Ye didna do aught wrong. And dinna look so surprised. I ken how ye think. I just need ye to hear me." Abigail brushed the hair back from his face and gazed into the eyes of the man she couldn't imagine ever living without. It was unlike any emotion she'd ever experienced. She finally understood her brother's fierce loyalty and drive to protect Maude at any expense.

"Ronan, if I must, I will spend every day for the rest of time reminding ye that ye are all that I want. Ye are a mon I respect and admire. I grievously underestimated ye in the beginning, and I will always wish I hadnae been so judgmental. Yer father may have been earnest in his conversation with ye, but ye havenae said aught that makes me think he judged ye as hard as ye judged yerself. Nay one thinks ye're a failure but ye. I will do what I can to reassure ye, but ye must decide for yerself whether ye will let go of this. I ken it's easier said than done, but ye must try. We canna be happy together if ye fear aught ye say or do is wrong. Think aboot this: if ye were such a miserable failure, why would I have fallen in love with ye?"

"I dinna ken. I hadnae thought of it like that."

"If ye were such a miserable failure, would I have been begging ye to touch me more? Would I have climaxed with just the feel of ye? Would I have climaxed again as soon as ye moved within me? To me, ye succeeded." Abigail grinned as she flexed her hips and grasped his buttocks. "Let's see if I can be such a success."

Ronan lowered himself onto his forearm, his free hand kneading her breast before suckling it. There were only gasps and brief words of encouragement until they leaped over the precipice together. Abigail blinked several times as her body registered the feel of a man spending within her. They kissed languidly as Ronan settled himself on her, careful not to suffocate her with his greater mass. He brushed away hair that stuck to Abigail's temples.

"Will ye let me stay?" Abigail asked softly.

"Ye willna be out of ma arm's reach until at least midday tomorrow. And I may reconsider and insist ye remain until the new year," Ronan teased as he kissed the tip of her nose. Abigail bit her bottom lip as she glanced at the door where they'd begun their lovemaking, then at the bed.

"I hope ye dinna regret nae waiting until our wedding. I should have thought better of it and left. Nae in anger, but from respect."

"Abby, we signed the betrothal documents. Ye are ma wife. We just consummated our marriage. We can have a kirking if ye wish, but it isnae required." Ronan hoped it wouldn't upset Abigail to realize that they'd—albeit without intention—became husband and wife.

"I'm really yer wife?" Abigail beamed so brightly that Ronan was certain she illuminated the entire chamber.

"And I'm yer husband," Ronan nodded. "Assuming yer brother doesnae kill me."

"Bah," Abigail wafted her hand. "Maude wouldnae let him. She chose this chamber because it's over mine. She kenned before we did how this eve would turn out. She kenned nay one can hear us."

"I pray ye're right. I dinna wish to leave ye a widow before the sun sets," Ronan smiled ruefully.

"If it's all right with ye, I'd still like to have our kirking on Christmas," Abigail asked tentatively, but she gained more courage as she noted the joy in Ronan's eyes. "But I dinna plan to act like yer betrothed while we wait. I intend to enjoy every wifely duty I have."

Ronan rolled over when Abigail pressed upward. She straddled his hips as she began to move. Ronan's sword slid back into her sheath, and Abigail spent the rest of the night showing Ronan each of those wifely duties.

THIRTEEN

A bigail stretched and reached her arm behind her to wrap around Ronan's neck, his warm body pressed against her back. She knew he woke before her, but he hadn't moved to avoid disturbing her. As she shifted, she felt his cock brush against her backside, then rest between her globes. She recalled how it felt when it did the same thing as they hid behind the tapestry in the library, but now there were no clothes in the way.

"Ronan," Abigail moaned as the hand that rested on her belly slid up to cup her breast. She arched, pressing her breast against his palm and her hips back against his. Ronan was propped up on his elbow, watching each of Abigail's reactions to feeling his touch. He'd woken hard as a pike, more so than any other morning of his life. He was tempted to wake Abigail, but they'd gotten nearly no sleep that night. He feared Abigail would be sore, but her arm lowered from around his neck until she could reach back to grab his buttocks. She rocked against him, and his intuition told him the next way they could couple.

Ronan lifted Abigail's leg until his cock slid

against her entrance. When she mumbled, "mmm-hmm," he pulled her back as he angled himself to thrust into her. The arm that propped him up slid beneath her to cup her breast as his other hand caressed her mons. She'd taught him what she liked, so he found the button filled with thousands of electrified nerves. He rubbed as he rocked into her. But it wasn't long before they both grew unsatisfied with not looking at one another, holding one another. Ronan pulled back as Abigail twisted around. He eased his weight above her as her knees squeezed his hips. It was with a shared groan that he entered her again.

"Abby, I'm glad I waited. I'm glad you're the only woman I'll ever share this with."

"Please believe me when I say the past feels so long ago that it'll be easily forgotten. You fill every one of my senses, and these are the only memories I want."

"I love you, and I'm overwhelmed by that. I never imagined I would love a woman like I do you, love any woman."

"I thought I understood love. I thought I knew. I've seen Maude and Kieran. But now I get it. Now I'm certain. Make love to me."

Ronan increased the force and speed, making Abigail grow breathless as she met each of his thrusts. Their bodies grew slick, sliding against one another in unison. Ronan held Abigail against him, and he felt them breathing in time with one another. He wanted to believe their hearts beat the same rhythm. As he gazed into Abigail's eyes, he knew he would do anything to keep his wife happy that they'd joined their lives together. He silently pledged to show her every day what it meant to have a husband who valued and appreciated her. When her body tightened, and her hands gripped his backside as she ground her mons against him, he spilled into her once more. There was no going back. They were married, and neither would let the other go.

"I suppose we should make an appearance belowstairs," Abigail said around a yawn as Ronan gathered her in his arms. She now lay sprawled across his chest. His fingers danced along her spine.

"No one would fault you for having a lying in. It was an arduous journey in winter. They'll understand that you're fatigued."

"And when a strapping warrior like yourself doesn't show up?" Abigail looked up and grinned. She ran her hand over the peaks and troughs of his abdomen.

"Do that some more, and they won't see us until February."

Abigail winked as she moved to lay her narrower body over his, but a knock at the door interrupted them. She smiled unremorsefully as she huffed, then she put her finger to her lips. She would wait out whoever was rude enough to interrupt her love nest.

"MacKinnon, I ken ye're in there with ma sister. I wouldnae come within a league of this door if a messenger hadnae arrived for ye." Kieran pounded on the door again. Ronan sighed, wishing with more conviction than he ever had that he wasn't a laird. It was rare that he had that sentiment, but knowing he had to climb out of bed and away from Abigail made him want to abdicate that very moment.

"Go," Abigail whispered. She had no fresh clothes or robe in the chamber, so she donned her chemise and pulled Ronan's spare plaid around her shoulders while Ronan wrapped his plaid around his waist. He forewent his leine, seeing no point to pretending he had been dressed. He glanced back at Abigail before opening the door a crack.

"I have nay intention of looking," Kieran grumbled. "She's yer wife now. But do one thing to upset yer wife, and I will kill ye."

"Kieran," Abigail scolded.

"What? Ye dinna think Lachlan said the same thing to me aboot Maude?" Kieran chuckled. Maude's older brother Lachlan threatened far worse when there were no female ears within hearing. He thrust a parchment out to Ronan and yanked the door closed as soon as Ronan held it. Abigail waited quietly as Ronan took a seat before the fire. He reached out an arm to Abigail, and she perched on the arm of the chair. Ronan unfolded the parchment and held it so they could both read it, but Abigail shook her head.

"It was meant for you. It might be private."

"Private now means you and me, Abby. You're not only my wife, you're Lady MacKinnon. Whatever affects me and our clan affects you too."

"That doesn't mean I was intended to read it. I think you should read it first. If you believe it's aught I should ken, then I'll read it."

Ronan frowned but decided the matter wasn't worth their first argument as a married couple. He scanned the missive and grinned. "It's naught more than our seneschal, Angus, complaining that John of Islay showed up and expects our hospitality. Angus tried to insist that MacDonald couldn't stay since I'm not in residence, but he had to relent when MacDonald snarled at him." Ronan laughed louder and shook his head. At Abigail's bewildered expression, he explained.

"Angus's father was my father's seneschal. Angus never took an interest in keeping the ledgers and pled with his father to train in the lists rather than my father's solar. His father compromised, allowing him to train with a sword *after* he trained with parchment and a quill. He agreed to be my seneschal because I trust few others. But Angus is enormous. He's one of the biggest men in our clan. If you think I'm tall, I look like a wean next to him. He's nearly a head taller than me and twice as wide. He's ten years my senior, and I've avoided sparring with him as often as I can. He terrifies me. So to hear him back down from MacDonald makes me laugh."

"If you look like a wean next to him, then I'm sure to look like a bairn. I shall be a pea to his mountain."

"Aye. His wife is your size. As much as Angus terrifies me, Bethea is scarier. She also happens to be our housekeeper. I have never seen Angus move so fast as when she's after him. She's as mild as a lamb until she's pushed too far. I suspect Angus does it often just so they can make up. They have seven children!"

"Merciful saints. I shall be careful where I trod," Abigail grinned.

"Bethea will adore you. As I said, she's mellow except with Angus and her children. She'll help you become acquainted with Dun Ringill, and she'll make it easy for you to become chatelaine."

Abigail bit her bottom lip, a long pause before she nodded. "Ronan, there is still much I need to learn aboot being the lady of a clan and running a keep. I ken more than I did when I left here the first time, but I'm not adept enough yet to do it properly. She'll wonder what kind of lady you've married."

"Abby, you can tell Bethea that you didn't take an interest in learning. Or you can say your mother was alive while you were here, you had an aulder sister, and then a sister-by-marriage. It's understandable why you'd be inexperienced."

"And when people learn I was handfasted before I met you?"

Ronan shrugged. He didn't have an answer to

that or all it would imply. He pushed the matter aside when it came to mind, but he would have little choice but to address it to his clan when they arrived. They could attempt to hide it, but the truth would inevitably come out at some time during their lives. It would be better if they were direct about it.

"It's still your choice how you wish to present yourself to Bethea, but we will have to tell the clan you were handfasted."

Abigail rose from the chair and moved toward the fire, suddenly chilled. She'd been ashamed of her failed handfast long before she met Ronan. But knowing that her shame would be shared with a third clan, even after the entire royal court learned of it, felt overwhelming. Ronan came to stand behind her and eased her around to face him. Cupping her elbows, Ronan dipped his head until she met his eyes.

"Ronan, I don't want to embarrass you."

"Chisholm would have repudiated you even if you were the greatest chatelaine to ever live. He wanted your land and your money. I loathe pointing that out. But he was set on gaining that and a mainland bride to increase his holdings. He wanted to have it all. He ended up with very little. That was never your fault. It still isn't. That's easy enough to explain. What islander doesn't understand mainlanders trying to gain land that isn't theirs?"

Abigail offered a wobbly smile, knowing Ronan was right. The Hebrideans would have been content to remain unto themselves rather than being dragged into the fray with the rest of Scotland. But men like John of Islay, Lord of the Isles, made that impossible. Ronan's words reassured her that her new clan members would understand at least that part. But she still felt uncomfortable with Bethea, or anyone else, realizing how inexperienced she was for her age and her position.

"I will make an effort to work with Maude until we leave. This time, I'll truly pay attention and actually practice what she shows me."

"I ken you will. But Abby—" Ronan squeezed her arms gently then eased her chin up, so he could brush his lips against hers. "I'm already proud of you."

Abigail wrapped her arms around Ronan and inhaled his pine and musk scent. They stood together, enjoying the calm of one another's presence. Eventually, they both knew that while they'd jested that they wouldn't leave their chamber until at least midday, they had to make an appearance.

"Are you going to train with Kieran?"

"Aye. Are you going to find Maude?"

"Yes. With all that I need to learn, I will be her shadow when I can. Otherwise, I'll be playing with the weans."

"You were incredibly good with them last eve. They adore you."

"I adore them. But I wish I weren't such a stranger to them. They warmed to me, but they're too young to understand I'm family, even though I'm not here."

"You can be as often as you wish. I will bring you here whenever you want to visit."

"Thank you. That means a great deal to me."

"And don't think that you'll need to ask me if you can invite them. Dun Ringill is your home now."

"You ken that was exactly what I was thinking. You say you don't read my mind." Abigail pursed her lips, then smiled when Ronan pulled his in sheepishly. "I rather like it. I like kenning you ken me."

"I'd say I ken you quite well now, lass." Ronan's smile grew wolfish, and he waggled his eyebrows.

"That you do." With a quick peck, they dressed

and left the chamber, Ronan headed toward the lists and Abigail to her chamber to change.

FOURTEEN

R onan swung his sword at Kieran, who ducked, spun, and blocked the next swipe. Ronan side-stepped as Kieran thrust his blade at him, the flat side of his own sword coming to push Kieran's away from underneath. The two lairds had been sparring the entire morning, the battle of wills only somewhat casual. Ronan knew Kieran was testing him, and he was determined to prove himself to Abigail's brother. He was intent upon reassuring Kieran that Ronan could protect Abigail. It was important to both men.

"Will ye return to Dun Ringill before Christmas?" It was the first time either of them spoke after silently battling one another for hours.

"I dinna have a choice." Ronan fought not to sound out of breath. The effort it took to regulate his breathing and to fight Kieran left none for Ronan to think about how he sounded. "I'll have to go back at least once if for nay other reason than to be sure Abigail's home is ready for her."

Kieran drew up short and stepped back. It was the first time he'd heard anyone refer to somewhere other than Stornoway as Abigail's home. They'd never thought of Stirling as her home, and he'd realized soon after Abigail returned from the Chisholms that no one referred to their keep as Abigail's home. It was jarring to think Abigail would no longer claim his home as her own. When he'd taken Madeline to Inchcailleoch Priory, he'd been so furious that he couldn't imagine Madeline ever calling Stornoway home. She'd lived at the priory for nearly five years before marrying Fingal Grant and moving to Freuchie Castle. He lowered his sword and studied Ronan. The MacKinnon laird matched him in size, and he knew Ronan's reputation as a warrior and just leader. He had to admit that he was happy for his sister, even if he was unprepared.

"Kieran, I love Abigail," Ronan spoke in a reassuring tone. "I hope ye can grow to trust me with her happiness and her safety."

"I ken ye do. Maude said ye spent the entire night looking at Abigail the same way I look at her. If ye feel even an ounce of what I feel for ma wife, then ye are a blessed mon. Abigail hasnae always been an easy woman to get along with, but she's matured a great deal in the past two years. Promise me ye'll have patience with her. She isnae an experienced chatelaine."

"I promise ye. Abby and I spoke aboot that this morn. She's nervous, and she intends to work with Maude while we're here. Our housekeeper, Bethea, will take Abby under her wing."

"Ye refer to everything as ours. She hasnae even stepped foot there."

"What is mine is hers." Ronan shrugged. It seemed simple to him.

"And what will yer people say when she doesnae arrive immediately prepared to take over running the keep? When they learn she wasna a maiden?"

Ronan looked around and tilted his head toward a space where no one else fought. He would admit what most of his clan had figured out years earlier.

The two men walked to the wall encircling the training field.

"We both ken the expectations are different for women than for men. But until last night, I—" Maybe it wasn't so easy to admit out loud that he had no experience. Ronan shrugged again and gave Kieran a look he hoped could communicate his meaning.

"Ye hadnae?"

"Nay. I hadnae. Dinna fear it doesnae work. It's just fine. But I'd taken to heart something ma father told me aboot ma mother's welcome to Dunakin, her first home among the MacKinnons. I didna want ma wife, whoever she might be, to have the same experience if there were a cast of women already acquainted with me."

Kieran nodded, his lips drawing in. "Maude had a single experience with that while still at Stirling. I would have protected her from that if I could."

"I told Abby once she figured out that I wasna experienced. Her lack of maidenhead means naught to me. We've talked aboot it more than once. I likened her to being a widow when the Bruce told me. Her first husband is gone and nae coming back. She's worried aboot what people will think, and I admit I've worried aboot what ma own people think aboot me. I'm certain most ken. But I will stand by her side nay matter what anyone says, and I will defend her honor till ma last breath. I willna tolerate anyone speaking against her, especially for something that she believed was honest and legitimate."

"I've kenned yer reputation and ye for years," Kieran replied. "I trust ye with ma sister, but if ever ye break that trust—if ever ye break her trust—I will make yer death so long and painful that ye will beg the Lord to take ye. But I willna let ye go. I will torture ye in ways I havenae even come up with. I will make sure ye meet the Devil with little more than yer bones."

"Is that what Lachlan told ye?"

"Something like that. But he cursed far more. I would too if yer wife and mine werenae so close."

Ronan turned to find Abigail and Maude huddled together as they approached, their arisaids pulled over their heads. He felt the cold air, but it didn't bother him. He knew his larger frame and bulk made it easier for him to withstand the temperature, but he wasn't keen on Abigail remaining outside after nearly a fortnight of travel. He looked back at Kieran and nodded. "If ever I fail either of ye, ye willna have to catch me. I will turn maself over to ye."

Ronan looked back to see Abigail's eyes widen at his words before her brow furrowed. As Kieran stepped forward to bring Maude into his arms and shield her from the wind, Ronan did the same for Abigail.

"It's too cold out here, lass," Ronan said as he rubbed Abigail's back.

"It is a wee brisk," Abigail nodded. "We came out to tell ye we're headed to the village. Maude has a family she needs to visit. Two of the weans were injured playing, and she'd like me to watch how she tends them."

"Will ye take at least two of ma guards?"

"If they dinna mind company. Kieran willna let Maude out of the walls without at least a dozen."

"Half a dozen, if ye dinna mind," Kieran grumbled. "Ma wife tends to put her life at risk to help others. I canna fault her, but I can try to keep her alive."

"One time, Kier. One time," Maude reminded him.

"Aye. That was one time too many."

Maude sighed and shrugged before she nodded. Abigail smiled up at Ronan and nodded too. Ronan signaled to his men and selected a pair to accompany Abigail. He watched as his wife and sister-by-marriage left the lists and made their way to the postern gate, surrounded by guards.

"Ye'll never like it. But ye'll learn to live with it." Kieran clapped his hand on Ronan's shoulder.

"There is something I wish to discuss that I havenae spoken to Abigail yet. It's a matter best fit for only two lairds to ken."

"Ma solar and ma whisky, I suppose." Kieran led the way into the keep and poured Ronan a mug of whisky before they took seats before the fire. Both men stretched out their long legs, knees apart to allow the toasty air to billow up their plaids.

"We've been having more trouble than usual with the MacLeods. I havenae said aught aboot it to Abigail because I dinna want her to fear I will hold that against her or yer people. And I dinna want her thinking to intervene because she shares a clan name with them."

"Reiving?"

"That and sailing far too close to Dun Ringill. They're encroaching upon our fishing while stealing our cattle. They've lost several men while I havenae lost any. Ye would think they would learn that they are coming out the losers. But they're persistent." Ronan took a sip of his whisky, swirling it in his mouth and savoring the flavor before it burned a path down his throat. He appreciated that Kieran dropped his refined speech when he married Maude. They'd abandoned pretention, allowing Maude's Highland accent and Kieran's Hebridean one to dominate their speech. It meant Ronan could too while he chatted with Kieran. "I'm nae telling ye this because I have any wish to involve ye. I'm telling ye for two reasons: ye have a right to ken the situation yer sister enters and to warn ye that ye are likely to hear from yer distant relatives. They willna be pleased to ken ye let one of yer own marry me."

"Cormag MacLeod and I arenae close, as ye ken. I canna stand the bastard. He would gladly claim himself as the only MacLeod laird, and I am naught but an inconvenience. Ye share ma concerns. I needed to see for maself this morn that ye can protect ma sister. Cormag will be a raging arse when he discovers I've allied the MacLeods of Lewis with ye. I dinna put it past him to use ma sister as his first target. I hadnae heard of his latest antics. He's a fool. He believes that because he outnumbers ye that he will defeat ye. He forgets that ye have most of the island as yer land. If ye wish to press him, he has naught but the loch and the sea at his back."

"A loch ma ally can sail into." Both men knew Ronan posed a question, even if he made it sound like a foregone conclusion.

"Aye. A vera good loch for yer ally. Ken, though, until I'm certain ma sister is accepted and happy with yer people, I do it for her, I dinna do it for politics."

"I never want it to be aboot politics, Kieran. I didna marry yer sister for the alliance. King Robert may have pushed me to marry soon, and he may have wanted an alliance that would help me against the MacLeods. But I married Abigail because I love her. If ye come to ma aid, it's because ye come as family. The king may believe this is a strategic joining, but it isnae for ye. I ken I'm putting ye in the middle whether ye like Cormag or nae."

"That is true. And ye married ma sister anyway."

"I did."

The two lairds looked at one another, assessing the situation and the merits of their newly formed alliance, both political and kindred. It would enrage the MacLeods of Skye. It would be inconvenient for Kieran, but it would be dangerous for Ronan. But he'd assessed the risk when he first took notice of Abigail. He was confident that his clan could not only weather the storm, but triumph against their neighbors.

"Call on me, and I will come." Kieran extended his arm to Ronan, who grasped his forearm. They shook, and it felt like this conversation solidified their agreement more than the contracts they'd both signed the day before.

Abigail.

FIFTEEN

The next fortnight was a hive of activity as the
MacLeods prepared for Christmas and Abigail's wedding. The clan noticed the difference in
Abigail from when she left for Stirling. The clan remembered her as a spoiled young woman before she
handfasted with Lathan. Then they recalled the
heartbroken but resolute woman who returned to
them. A more loving sister and aunt could never be
found, but the peace and maturity that emanated
from Abigail since returning with Ronan made many
secretly smile. The blustery winds trapped them in-
doors many days, but when they could venture outside, people spotted them walking hand-in-hand
along the headland.

Abigail marveled at the difference in height and
took advantage of leaning her head against Ronan
during their walks. They tried going for a ride one
morning, but the brisk wind left Abigail with watery
eyes and wind-chapped cheeks. They went into the
village several mornings, where Abigail introduced
Ronan to the villagers. Inevitably, they walked past
the tavern, and Abigail's heart pinched as she surreptitiously watched Ronan from the corner of her eye.
He was in the midst of explaining the layout of his

keep and never turned his head, though Abigail was certain he was aware of the wench standing in the doorway. She could tell it wasn't that he ignored the woman; he just didn't notice, his attention solely on Abigail.

Neither enjoyed the two brief trips Ronan made to Skye during the weeks leading up to their wedding. It was inevitable that he had to return to his clan after spending more than a moon away, and Abigail encouraged him to go. But neither was eager to part, even if for only three days each time. Ronan assured Abigail that his clan was eager to meet her, and none held any animosity toward her as a MacLeod of Lewis. Abigail was only half-jesting when she said she would be sure to wear the MacKinnon plaid she would receive on their wedding day and tuck away her MacLeod one in their chamber.

Abigail sensed the strain Ronan experienced upon his return both times. He insisted all was well, but he didn't elaborate. His evasiveness made Abigail worry, and her mind leapt to various conclusions.

"Why won't you tell me, Ronan? You promised not to keep secrets from me, but now you change the subject or try to avoid answering me. What happened that is making you no longer trust me?"

"I trust you implicitly, Abby. That hasn't changed. I'm weary from being away from you each time. I confess that I sulk while I'm home without you, and it takes a little while for it to wear off."

"Now you really are lying to me," Abigail huffed.

"I am not." Ronan sighed as he sat on the edge of the bed they shared each night. He watched Abigail pick at her cuticle, a nervous habit he'd noticed. It was clear he was upsetting her when all he wanted was the opposite. He could guess the various scenarios playing out in her head, and they were all worse than the truth. He patted the bed beside him as he scooted into the middle. He'd shed his boots, stockings, and plaid when they entered since they were splattered with mud from his journey. He stretched out in just his leine.

Abigail hesitated but climbed onto the bed next to him. He lifted his arm to wrap around her, expecting her to lean against him like she usually did. But she sat cross-legged, looking at him. "Abby, there is no great mystery. There's no illness sweeping through the clan, there's no famine, there was no attack, and there isn't anyone else."

Abigail wanted to breathe a sigh of relief, but she scowled instead. If there was no grave situation, she was even more frustrated that he wouldn't tell her what happened. And it still disconcerted her that Ronan read her mind, but she'd grown just as proficient at reading his. It's why she knew he hid something.

"I haven't said aught yet because there hasn't been much to say. The MacLeods are trying to cause trouble, but that's naught new. They're growing bolder, sailing closer to our shores and fishing where we do. There have been some terse encounters between our fishermen and theirs. They've reived further into our territory than they have in at least a decade, just because they can. They don't need our cattle. I'm frustrated that I have to deal with that when I'm home. There isn't enough time before—"

"Before you have to come back here," Abigail interrupted.

"No. That is not what I was going to say," Ronan snapped defensively, frustrated on her behalf, even if she was the one frustrating him. "This isn't aboot you or the time I spend with you. There isn't enough time before my men raid them to move all the outlying villagers further into our territory. We need the cattle back before there's a snow too heavy to herd

143

them. The MacLeods are likely to retaliate, even though they began this. They won't come all the way to Dun Ringill. They'll take it out on our villagers."

"Has this been going on long? Is it because you married me?"

"It was happening before I went to Stirling. It's part of why the Bruce wanted me to marry. It's grown worse while I've been away, but I don't think they ken yet of our marriage."

"Have they hurt anyone?"

"Aye. Not killed anyone, but more than one farmer's been injured trying to defend his flock and herds."

"So they've taken cows and sheep?" Abigail asked.

"Aye. They take whatever they find."

"And the king did naught?"

Ronan rolled his eyes. "As long as our infighting doesn't get in the way of him sitting on his throne, he cares little aboot what happens on the islands. I have a leg to stand on though, because all our animals are branded. Even if the MacLeods shear all our sheep, they can't remove the brand. It's obvious they aren't theirs."

"Do you think raiding them will be enough? Won't you lose men?"

"I likely will if it comes to a fight, which seems likely. But my men are well trained, and I don't expect heavy losses. I would avoid any death, but the MacLeods have made that impossible to avoid. I just hope we kill—" Ronan snapped his mouth shut.

"That we kill more of them than they do us." Abigail reached out her hand and took Ronan's. "I'm not naïve. I ken how this works. And I ken it makes you uncomfortable because I shared the same clan name as them. But I feel no connection to the Skye MacLeods. It would be different if this were between you and Kieran, but it's not. I don't wish death upon anyone, and I certainly wish you could spare your men, but Cormag knows what he's doing. He knows he's sentencing his own men to death."

"Thank you for understanding, Abby."

"That's why you didn't want to tell me. You feared I would be upset with you."

Ronan nodded. "I know you know this isn't a new development between my clan and theirs, but it's the first time you're faced with me fighting your clansmen."

"They aren't mine. I was a MacLeod of Lewis, and now I'm a MacKinnon of Skye. At no time was I ever one of them. They're distant relatives several generations removed. We've been rivals just as often as we've been allies. Currently, we're not much of aught to one another. Kieran may not want that rivalry to flare again, but neither does he consider Cormag an ally or a friend. He trusts the mon as little as you do."

Abigail crawled over to lean against Ronan, just as she usually did when they lay on the bed to talk. She felt the heavy weight of his arm around her like a shield. The steady thud of his heart made her eyes drift closed.

"Are you going to fall asleep again?" Ronan murmured.

"I could, but no. Just enjoying it. Ronan, I don't know that I can offer any help, but I would if you asked or if there was something I could do."

"I ken. I'm sorry I left you to fear the worst. I told you I would never lie to you to hurt you. I would only do it to protect you. I may not have lied, but I was purposely selective in the truth I told you. I was trying to protect you."

"I ken. That's why I was frustrated, but not angry." Abigail sat up and looked at Ronan. "Though I confess one thought frightened me."

"There's no one else, Abby."

"I know. But when you wouldn't be straightforward, it was one of the things I imagined. The thought lasted but a moment, but it shook me. I admit that. But I ken, Ronan, that if ever you fall out of love with me, you will still be faithful. If not for me, then for your honor. I don't fear you straying."

"I never will. And I pray we will love each other until the end."

"Me too." Abigail settled back against Ronan. "Shouldn't you lead the raids? If you're worried aboot raiding before the worst of the snow arrives, doesn't that need to happen now?"

"To reive cattle, no. I stopped going when I became laird. My people can't afford to lose their laird because I went chasing cows. I'll lead my men into battle when the time comes, and I hate admitting that it will. But as much as I want our animals back, it isn't the right risk to take."

"That must be frustrating," Abigail mused.

"It is. Incredibly. But I can't be shortsighted."

"Is this a lesson your father taught you?" Abigail felt Ronan tense, and she wondered what she'd said wrong.

"Indirectly. He died insisting on revenge against the MacNeills for raiding us. He led a raid that went afoul. He returned draped over his horse, wrapped in his plaid. He refused to let me go."

"Do you feel guilty for that?"

"I did for many years. It was the reason I became laird. I'd always figured he would grow auld before I took on the role. I never pictured inheriting the lairdship because he died in battle, even if I always knew it was more likely than auld age. I argued that I should go in his stead, but he'd wanted revenge, not

146

justice. I know why he took it personally. The Mac-Neills crossed far onto our land and attacked my mother and her guards while she was out riding. They didn't hurt her, but they killed her guards and stole her horse. They left her to make her way back to Dun Ringill alone as night approached. My father was incensed."

"I'm surprised you let me leave the keep with only two MacKinnon guards," Abigail said softly.

"That's only when you go to the village. I ken the men on the wall can see the entire village, I ken Kieran has ample men escorting Maude when you go with her. When we leave together, all my men come with us. Two won't be enough when we arrive on Skye. You will have a larger detail, Abby."

Ronan's tone of voice told Abigail that he would brook no argument, and she had none to make. She understood better these days why Kieran was as protective of Maude as he was. It wasn't merely because he loved her. She was the mother to his children, one of whom was his heir, and she was chatelaine to the keep, where their clan depended on her. While his love for her might be the strongest reason for his protectiveness, practicality also guided Kieran's choices. She knew Ronan would be the same.

"I'll follow your guidance, Ronan. But please don't fear telling me things. I need to know if I'm to help defend our home and our people. I must know who I can and can't trust and why."

"I ken. I just don't want you dreading going to Skye."

"Dread it? Because Cormag is a greedy bastard? I don't dread it. I feel like we should go back sooner. Should we?"

"Nay. I believe things are in hand for the time being, though I do need you to ken it's a possibility.

But I want you to have Christmas here with yer family. I want you to have your wedding among your family."

"I do, too. But you ken that I know that isn't more important, don't you?"

"I do." Ronan kissed Abigail's forehead, and she snuggled closer. They lay together in silence until they went belowstairs for their meal.

When it was time to retire each evening, Abigail made the pretense of going to her chamber, but she never stopped on the second floor. She went directly to Ronan's chamber and waited for him. He waited long enough to appear as though they observed the rules of propriety, but both were certain everyone knew that they spent every night together.

"You may as well get used to sleeping next to me, Abby. There won't be separate chambers unless you wish for them. Even then, I would just spend every night in your chamber," Ronan explained.

"And if I like the lady's chamber better than the laird's, would you move into mine?" Abigail teased.

"Yes." Ronan's response was so deadpan that Abigail snorted. Ronan tickled her as they lay in bed together. Separate chambers never came up again as they reminded each other of the benefits of sharing a bed.

While Ronan trained in the lists or dealt with correspondence that arrived from Skye, Abigail trailed Maude like a second shadow, absorbing everything her sister-by-marriage did as chatelaine. Abigail hadn't realized how little attention she paid the last time Maude attempted to train her until she genuinely attempted to learn. She feared her head would burst with what she learned in such a short amount of time, but she felt prepared to take on the role of a responsible chatelaine.

Abigail accompanied her sister-by-marriage on trips to the village, learning how to evaluate thatching that needed repair. Maude showed Abigail how to look at the soundness of cottage walls. She pointed out how to tell when a family was underfed but refused to admit it. Maude explained the daily schedule for all the servants in the keep, along with her own duties. She ensured Abigail understood why certain tasks were done on certain days and in a certain order.

Maude encouraged Abigail to plan the weekly menu with their cook and to assist in taking inventory with their housekeeper. It wasn't long before Abigail could point out supplies that needed replenishing, estimating their cost and how long it would take. Maude beamed at her sister-by-marriage, telling her frequently that Abigail impressed her. It pleased Abigail to hear the praise, and she believed its sincerity. It gave her confidence that she hadn't previously possessed. Ronan noted the difference and couldn't keep the pride from his eyes and voice when he talked to her. It filled Abigail with warmth, and it made the effort feel worthwhile.

Abigail and Maude stood together in the kitchens when Ronan and Kieran returned from goose hunting wet, muddy, and cursing. But both women praised their men for ensuring the clan would have a Christmas feast thanks to their skill. The men scowled when they left the kitchens and heard the uproarious laughter that drifted to them. The women were in the kitchen assisting the servants as they baked dozens of mince pies to serve on each of the twelve days of Christmas. While Abigail had been disinterested in all other duties as an adolescent, she had enjoyed time in the kitchens. She sneaked a mince pie to Ronan on Christmas Eve, even though he shouldn't have eaten meat. He swore that he would have married her just for her cooking.

SIXTEEN

Abigail leaned against Ronan's shoulder with their fingers woven together beneath the folds of Abigail's gown. The candles twinkled in the wall sconces of Stornoway's chapel. The music of the Christmas Eve vigil filled the high ceilings. She closed her eyes as years of childhood Christmases celebrated with her family floated back to her. While some clans and their clergy preferred "troping" during the service, Abigail was happy that the length of the service wasn't increased by the congregation and clergy taking turns repeating verses of prayer and songs. She much preferred the MacLeods' of Lewis tradition of a Nativity play. With a young lass in the laird's family, the manger held a toddler to play Baby Jesus that year. Abigail, along with everyone else, fought to stifle their laughter when one of the Magi leaned over the manager to present his gift and was greeted with a loud belch. It was soon followed by more sounds of gastric distress, and Maude rushing forward to retrieve her daughter.

Abigail listened as the clan's priest and three men performed *The Prophets* play. She enjoyed the priest's interviews of Jeremiah, Moses, and Daniel as part of the celebration of Christ's birth. She always felt Christmastide began when the congregation sang "*In Dulci Jublio.*" As a child, Abigail thought the sweet rejoicing meant the service was nearly over. As an adult, it gave Abigail pause to consider the blessings her prosperous clan enjoyed. As though thinking the same thing, Ronan squeezed her hand as the last verse began. She glanced up at him, and her heart melted from the love that shone in his eyes.

With each night that they made love, they grew closer as they shared their bodies. But their conversations as they lay abed together brought them a connection that forged their relationship in steel. Abigail had never felt as understood and accepted as she did with Ronan. He encouraged her lightheartedness and easy cheer while he often remained a quiet observer. She drew him out of his shell with each night that they spent among her clan. She wondered how she would feel when she was introduced to the MacKinnons. He chuckled as she rattled off question after question, but he welcomed her excitement and curiosity. When news of three successful raids reached them, they agreed to remain at Stornoway through Epiphany, and Abigail showed her gratitude the night Ronan suggested they stay through the second Christmastide feast. She whispered a suggestion from what she'd overheard the day she stumbled upon the trio planning their *ménage à trois* at Stirling. Ronan eagerly embraced the new position they tried, and both fell asleep, exhausted but satiated.

Christmas morning shone brightly with a layer of snow on the ground when Abigail and Ronan awoke. Neither was in a hurry to begin the day, but they both looked forward to the festivities, knowing they would marry on the steps of the kirk at sundown. Then the clan would celebrate their nuptials and the birth of Christ with a feast that would last well into the next day.

"Are you ready to be known as Lady MacKinnon?" Ronan asked as he stroked her back while Abigail lay nestled against his side.

"Very much, my laird-husband. I ken pride is a sin, and today of all days I should probably strive not to sin, but I am so immensely proud to be your wife. I want the entire world to ken how much I love you and want to be married to you."

"I think your entire clan kens after those lads caught us in the hayloft. You aren't very quiet," Ronan teased.

"I'm not very quiet?" Abigail snorted. "I wasn't the one bellowing like a stuck boar. They came to investigate your noises, not mine."

"Are you excited, Abby?" Ronan asked quietly. Abigail rolled onto her belly and propped herself up with a forearm on Ronan's chest.

"Ronan, we both ken we're already married, but aye. I'm extremely excited to be officially married. It's not the feast I look forward to. It's not the wedding night—though I can think of a few things I would like to try again. I'm excited because as much as I join your clan today, you join my family. I may be Abigail MacKinnon now, but you are part of the MacLeods' family." Abigail chuckled. "At least the good MacLeods. Those on Skye won't be jumping to call you kin."

"I love you, Abby MacKinnon," Ronan nuzzled her nose. Their affection sparked into desire, just as it always did. They missed the morning meal. Again.

Abigail froze midway down the stairs, Ronan walking ahead before he realized she had stopped. He looked back and caught Abigail's awed expression. He came back to stand beside her and swept his eyes over the Great Hall below them. Maude and the servants had transformed it into a Christmas wonderland. Abigail covered her gaping mouth with her hands as tears came to her eyes. Her clan always celebrated the Savior's birth with both reverence and exuberance, but never had she seen the keep so decorated. Someone had draped garlands of evergreen and holly over the hearths and over the doorways. Servants had festooned the laird's table with garlands and sprigs of mistletoe. The fresh rushes smelled of pine and lavender, her favorite scents. There were fresh candles in every holder, and the silver sparkled. She watched as people continued to move about, setting out more garland. Delicious and rich scents wafted to her from the kitchens. She covered her stomach as her belly rumbled.

"Mayhap we shouldn't have missed the morning meal after all," Ronan winked. He took Abigail's hand and led her down the stairs. She looked around the castle that had once been her home. Memories of past Christmases danced before her eyes. She had a moment of sadness that her mother was no longer alive to share in the festivities. Adeline had died just before Abigail left for court. Her mother's death spurred her to leave and make a fresh start at court. But now, as she stood beside Ronan, she had only happy memories of the holiday. Abigail knew Maude's family celebrated Christmas and Epiphany with great fanfare, but Adeline had always been especially attentive to Christmas. She'd argued that Epiphany may have been when the wise men visited Jesus, but there wouldn't be any point if Christ hadn't been born. Abigail smiled to herself as her heart warmed. She glanced up at the rafters as though she might see through them all the way to Heaven.

Maude approached with her twins grasping each hand, and her younger daughter tied to her back with the embroidered sheet Abigail gave Maude. She hadn't been able to wait when she saw her niece tied to Maude's back with an older plaid.

"I still have much to do," Maude explained. "Abigail, would ye take the twins, please? Ronan, the men are aboot to leave to chop down the Yule logs."

Ronan dropped a kiss on Abigail's forehead before he hurried across the keep, his plaid swishing around his legs. Abigail's mind jumped to what she knew hid beneath his plaid.

"Ye will have plenty of time to ogle yer husband this eve after ye run away from the feast," Maude teased.

"Run away? We won't be rude and leave early," Abigail assured.

Maude's peal of laughter made her daughter stir with an angry gurgle. "I've seen yer gown, Abigail. Ronan willna be as interested in the roast goose as ye may think. And I suspect seeing him in his formal dress will make ye just as impatient. It may have been a few years ago, but I still remember being a bride. Just ye wait and see, sister."

Maude laughed again before cooing to her daughter. Abigail took her niece and nephew up to the nursery, where she sang and read to them and sat on the floor surrounded by their toys. She welcomed the midday meal of soup along with leeks and onion porray, her favorite type of stew, since her belly continued to rumble. The scent of roasting meat made her mouth water after a month of going without.

She'd feared she would collapse if she had to wait until after the wedding and Christmas Mass to eat. Once she was called down for the meal, the hours sped by until it was time for her to prepare for the wedding.

SEVENTEEN

Ronan forgot the cold the moment Abigail stepped into his view. He was certain it was an angel floating toward him rather than a mortal woman. Her blue gown was trimmed with wool along the collar, sleeves, and hem. She'd chosen the embellishment for its practicality. She knew she would have to stand before the church in December, so she added it to help her keep warm. She wore a MacKinnon plaid as her new arisaid. Her eyes had watered when Ronan presented the plaid to her at the midday meal. She'd nearly toppled them over in her exuberance to thank him. She'd held onto the plaid Ronan lent her while they were traveling, and she still wore it often. But it came as a surprise when Ronan presented her with a plaid made with the laird's family's formal pattern rather than the hunting one, and it was the right length for a woman. More than one randy comment was called out to re-mind her how to show her appreciation.

Her greenish blue eyes were a close match to her gown's fabric, and they sparkled in the late afternoon sun. The soft tones of the approaching dusk did little to dim how her raven locks shone, and the berries in her mistletoe crown distracted him with thoughts of how he wished to kiss her. Ronan was certain only a celestial being could be so perfect.

Abigail rued her short stature as she attempted to peer around and between people to catch sight of Ronan. Her breath hitched when her clan members parted, and she saw the full length of him. Dressed in a saffron leine befitting a laird, Ronan wore a freshly pleated plaid with his laird's brooch polished until it gleamed. His freshly washed hair was still wet at the ends, and he was clean-shaven. She didn't mind when his beard grew in, but she was happy to have an unrestricted view of his face. Her lips twitched as she thought about how much taller Ronan had appeared compared to the courtiers at Stirling Castle, but among the Hebridean men of her clan, he looked merely average.

There is naught merely average aboot any part of him. Aye, ladies, feast yer eyes on what ye can see, and I shall feast ma mouth on what ye canna. Abigail struggled to fight the smug smile that pulled at her mouth as she watched the women stare at Ronan. She didn't bother stopping her salacious thoughts. When she came to stand even with him, he offered her his hands. He didn't notice as the priest bound their wrists or laid a swath of MacKinnon plaid over them.

"M 'aingeal." My angel, Ronan whispered reverently. "You have saved me from myself, and surely any place beside you is Heaven."

Abigail swallowed the lump in her throat as she tried to think of something as equally endearing to say, but her mind was blank. She managed to whisper, "I shall love you, on Earth and in Heaven."

They recited their vows, hurrying from excitement along with the cold. While the priest normally would have held the wedding Mass for only the couple's family, the clan followed them into the kirk to celebrate both their marriage and Christmas. The service passed in a blur as Abigail and Ronan kneeled, their arms brushing against one another. When their hands weren't clasped in prayer, they were clasped together. Before Abigail realized it was over, the church bells pealed, and Ronan helped her to her feet. Neither cared that their kiss was far too long for a church setting. Ronan swept Abigail into his arms and carried her to the Great Hall.

Abigail sat beside Ronan as course after course made their way to the tables. The servants presented a roasted boar's head that sat in a place of prominence on the laird's table. Dishes of trout, herring, and eel made up the fish course. Roasted mutton and veal accompanied the boar that Ronan killed. Maude patted Kieran's shoulder and gave him a gentle kiss when the geese arrived, and Kieran's contribution was half the size of the fowl Ronan caught. Kieran playfully pouted and none-too-quietly reminded Maude that she would console his bruised feelings later.

Abigail knew she overindulged in the cheese brought out for dessert, but she'd missed her favorite food. Ronan fed her thick fruit custard, while she was slow to draw her fingers away when she placed figs in his mouth. The clan made toasts of good health and prosperity throughout the meal, and more than one woman reminded Abigail that the mistletoe she wore in her hair would aid with fertility. Abigail blushed and thanked them for their well wishes.

"We shall have to see if they're right. I think I shall strip you of your very fetching gown and take you to bed with just that halo on," Ronan whispered. His warm breath made her shiver. When she turned to look at him, their lips brushed.

"It's not a halo," she smiled.

"It is to me. I was serious, Abby. I have never

been so confident as I have been in the past weeks. I've enjoyed my time among your people and haven't feared saying the wrong thing or misstepping. It's been freeing and heavenly. I have you to thank for that."

Abigail reached up and nudged Ronan's face toward hers before pressing a lingering kiss. The couple ignored the cheers and wagers about whether their autumn babe would be a lad or a lass. They danced thrice, then slipped away to Ronan's chamber, where Abigail had taken up residence since their arrival. Ronan was true to his word; they landed on the bed without a stitch of clothing, and Abigail only wore her mistletoe halo. The MacLeods only spied the newlyweds for meals between Christmas and Hogmanay.

EIGHTEEN

R onan and Abigail emerged to spend the new year with their family and clan. Abigail toiled beside Maude and the servants as the ashes were collected from every hearth and the Great Hall and chambers were scoured in preparation for the coming year.

While locked away in their love nest, if they weren't filling their time making love, the couple sat playing chess, Nine Men's Morris, backgammon, and cards. Both discovered that they had keen minds for strategy, and both had a competitive steak that led to cheerful ribbing and the loser divesting their clothing.

Abigail defeated Ronan at a particularly challenging game of chess, and the boon she requested before they began was that Ronan would strip naked and run into the sea if she won. Despite trying to distract her with tasks and an afternoon tryst, Abigail insisted that he take his arctic plunge before the bells tolled at midnight to ensure he cleared his debt to her. Their tryst happened afterward while Abigail helped take the chill from Ronan's bones.

After celebrating for several hours around bonfires, the clan gathered in the Great Hall for the "first stepping" tradition while a clan elder banged on the doors to the keep. The dark-haired older man entered to cheers celebrating the first minutes of the new year. The "first stepper" moved toward a table and set down his sack. He pretended to rummage within before he pulled out the expected lump of coal, piece of shortbread, jug of whisky, a jar with a few granules of salt, and a black bun. Kieran toasted to his clan's health and prosperity in the coming year.

"What do you think the coming year will hold, Abby?" Ronan asked before handing Abby her own dram of whisky.

"I don't know. I pray for acceptance among my new clan, grace and humility as I become Lady Mac-Kinnon in practice. Mayhap a growing family," Abigail shrugged at the end.

"Do you ken something that I don't?" Ronan held his breath. He realized he liked the thought of having a baby with Abigail. He recognized many of the same qualities in Abigail as he'd seen in his own mother. He'd watched Abigail with her nieces and nephew, and she had a natural way with children. Stern but always kind and patient, Ronan looked forward to building a family with his bride.

"Nay. It's too soon to ken aught, and I don't think I am. But I would very much like to see you as a father. I've seen how you are with the wee ones here and how they cling to you for stories and games. Mayhap you won't have time for such jocularity once we arrive at Dun Ringill, but I've enjoyed it."

"Abby, I will always have time for you and our bairns. It might not be at the very moment I wish, but I had two loving parents who raised me, and I intend to see our children have the same." Ronan wrapped his arm around Abigail as she stepped into his embrace. "I swear to put you and our family ahead of all else whenever I can. Know that when I can't, it's not because I don't want to. Know that it's only duty that prevents it."

"I ken, Ronan. Is it wrong of me, though, to hope it takes a little while before I get with child? I'll already have to share you with the clan, and my time will be shared with them as well. I'd like to spend what time I do have with just you for a while. Weans will undoubtedly pull me away even more. I would never begrudge our children that, but I confess to being greedy and wanting you to monopolize my attention as much as can be."

Ronan swept Abigail into his arms, leaving the Hogmanay celebration behind as they made their way to their chamber. "I shall monopolize your time, your attention, and *all* of your energy," Ronan promised. They entered their chamber and didn't leave until Maude discreetly reminded Abigail that she'd promised to watch the children while Kieran and Maude visited the older and poorer members of the clan.

The feast of Epiphany signaled the end of the twelve days of Christmas. It also signaled their last day at Stornoway, and Ronan promised Abigail that they would celebrate with such merriment that she would sleep the entire boat ride to Skye. While some clans celebrated Epiphany for eight days, duties at Stornoway and Dun Ringill made it impossible for the MacLeods of Lewis or the MacKinnons to prolong the festivities.

"I'm looking forward to more than one chaliceful of *la mas ubal*," Abigail confessed as they left their seats in the laird's pew after the Mass. Lambswool was a hot apple punch often served alongside Wassail. The clan gathered in the orchard to hang toasted pieces of bread soaked in cider from the branches. When Ronan looked dubiously at the trees' decorations, Abigail asked, "Do the MacKinnons not do this?"

"Nay. And I'm not sure what it is we're doing. Why hang bread?" Ronan's voice held all the skepticism and some of the disbelief he felt.

"I don't know why the tradition started, but we shall sing to wish everyone good health in the new year," Abigail explained. "And it's an excuse for more cider." Abigail winked as a servant brought around trays of the warmed drink. The kirk had been freezing despite the people packed inside. A heavy snowstorm the day earlier dumped several inches on the isle, and the wind remained blustery.

Much like Christmas Day, a feast awaited everyone when they entered the Great Hall. Abigail heaped food on Ronan's side of their trencher, always astonished at how much her husband ate while remaining svelte. But she would remind herself of what she saw when she caught glimpses of him training in the lists. Her husband was never idle, and every muscle she reveled in touching and watching while they made love was hewn from his training.

Ronan kept his promise, and the couple ate, drank, danced, and made merry until a couple of hours before dawn. It was with bleary eyes that they joined the villagers by the fields for the sunrise plough races. A riotous way to return to the routine laboring in the fields, the plough races signaled the end of the three most festive holidays of the year. Abigail and Ronan returned to the keep to break their fast with Kieran and Maude, their children still sound asleep. As they finished their meal, Ronan's men checked their horses' saddles and prepared the birlinns for their departure. Maude and Abigail clung to one another as Kieran and Ronan clapped one another on their backs.

"I dinna suspect ye shall ever want to leave Ronan's side, but if aught should ever happen, come here," Maude whispered. "Kieran told me he taught ye how to sail as a lass. A birlinn isnae easy in foul weather, but ye can manage it with a steady breeze. Ye have a home here nay matter what, always. Abigail, I wish ye happy, and I believe ye will be."

"Thank you, Maude. You have been so good to me, and I appreciate your faith in me, even when I haven't earned it," Abigail kissed her sister-by-marriage on the cheek.

"Abigail, we're family," Maude said it as though it explained everything. And Abigail realized that to Maude, it did.

"Take care of Kieran and the weans," Abigail whispered as she hugged Maude one last time before Kieran tugged her away for his own embrace. Abigail nodded as Kieran whispered nearly the same thing to Abigail as Maude had. She squeezed her older brother before turning to take Ronan's hand. They walked to the dock where four boats waited to ferry them from the Isle of Lewis to the Isle of Skye. With sails raised and oars in the water, Ronan and Abigail drifted into the current. As Stornoway faded into the distance, its disappearance signaled the end of Abigail's life as a MacLeod but marked the beginning of their lives together as Laird and Lady MacKinnon.

"I love you, Lady Abigail MacKinnon," Ronan murmured against her hair before kissing her temple.

"And I love you, Laird Ronan MacKinnon." Abigail turned her face toward Ronan's before adding, "You can kiss me better than that." Always willing to accept Abigail's challenges, Ronan did just that until they were both breathless and smiling. They stood together as they sailed toward Skye, the water calm and the sky a shade that matched Abigail's eyes. Abigail thought for a moment how the time between meeting Ronan and their boarding the boat was like a fairy tale. Her stomach clenched for a moment, recalling that most fairy tales had a monster before the characters found their happily ever after. With another kiss from Ronan, she reminded herself monsters weren't real, but her happily ever after with Ronan was. She sighed as she leaned against him.

"To our future, Abby," Ronan whispered as they gazed at one another, joy evident in both of their smiles.

"To our future."

NINETEEN

A bigail huddled beneath her own plaid, as well as the extra ones Ronan wrapped around her. Only twenty minutes into their voyage the wind shifted drastically, blowing against the MacKinnon birlinns as they attempted to cut through the icy water that sprayed over the side. The wind whipped around Abigail as she sat in the stern and prayed that they didn't capsize. The waves had grown rough, the sea seeming angry that they left the Isle of Lewis. Since Stornoway sat on the northeastern coast of the isle—which comprised two parts: Lewis to the north and Harris to the south—they would sail south and around the western tip of Skye to reach Dun Ringill. It was only meant to be a six or seven-hour sail, but with the weather against them, Ronan feared it would be well after sunset before they arrived home. The dropping temperature concerned Ronan; he was freezing, so he could only imagine how miserable his wife was.

Ronan glanced back at Abigail from where he stood at the bow. He'd moved to the front of the sailboat to survey the open water of the Minch. They would enter the Little Minch as they neared Mac-Leod fishing territory. Clouds hung low over the water, making it difficult to see the coast to their right or what lay ahead of them. An aggressive swell, intent upon overturning them, nearly knocked Ronan off his feet. He clutched the rail of the boat and looked at the three other birlinns bobbing alongside him. The horses on all four boats grew more agitated; his men struggled to control the animals while trying to brace themselves against the gale. Ronan could only be grateful that there was no precipitation. While the cloud cover nearly touched the water, none looked pregnant with rain or snow. Ronan stumbled his way back to Abigail and eased to the deck, pulling her into his embrace.

"We can put ashore on Harris and wait this out," Ronan offered.

"Where would we stay? Knock on the Morrisons or the MacIvers' doors? The only people the Morrisons hate more than the MacLeods are the MacIvers, and they have nay love for us either. We can't go to any of their strongholds without them kenning who I am. My hair and eyes are too distinct, and my features look too much like Kieran's and Madeline's. Even if I'm a MacKinnon now, they won't welcome you. Better yet, the MacLeods of Harris. They're likely to send someone to Skye ahead of us and tell Cormag exactly where you are. I don't ken which is more dangerous: the sea or the clans."

"We may have no choice but to remain on the ships, but there are coves where we can anchor and shelter," Ronan reasoned. Abigail nodded, and Ronan noticed for the first time that her lips had a blue tinge. Recognizing how cold Abigail truly was made his decision easy. "We put in at the cove between Grimshader and Ranish!"

Men from all four boats nodded their heads, relieved that they would move out of the crosswinds and hopefully calm the horses, that whinnied and tried to rear. Ronan had never seen these experienced warhorses, who had sailed countless times, become so agitated. He believed strongly that animals sensed danger well before humans, and the horses' behavior increased his nervousness. Based on the wind's direction, which pushed them backwards and side-to-side, Abigail guessed that the trip south to where Ronan wanted to stop—usually a five-minute journey—was still at least a half hour away. Abigail reminded herself that she had survived a year with the Chisholms and nearly four months at court. A minor storm would not get the better of her. She watched as the men slid oars into the water, fighting against the surging tide until they finally neared the inlet.

"We drop anchor here. Even our shallow bottoms can't risk running aground." Ronan ordered his men as they dropped the anchors. Abigail dreaded having to wade ashore. It was only a few yards, but she was certain her toes would be numb by the time she was above the shoreline. Ronan reached out his hand to Abigail and pulled her against him. "Once I'm in, I'll lift you over. Keep your skirts tucked in your lap."

"Tucked in my lap? No, Ronan. The surf is too rough for you to carry me. I can walk, just like the rest."

"And unless you intend to pull your skirts over your head, there is no way that you'll make it without the current trying to drag you away. The fabric will become your anchor."

Abigail drew in a deep breath and nodded. She saw the sense in what Ronan said, even if she feared she would cause them both to fall over. She watched as the men lowered the ramps into the water and led the horses off. The water was nearly waist-deep on most of the men. She knew they normally would have ridden them ashore, since the horses' hooves touched the bottom, but the added weight and height in current conditions would only endanger man and beast.

Ronan clenched his teeth to keep from grimacing as the frigid water swept his plaid up to his waist. He braced himself and reached for Abigail, who had wrapped her skirts around her legs, then tucked the extra length into the belt that kept her arisaid in place. She hobbled to the rail and sat upon it before swinging her legs over the side. Until she released her skirts, she had little space to move her legs. She pushed off from the rail and was immediately caught in Ronan's brawny arms that held her high against his chest. He didn't wait to turn toward the shore, since one of his men was already guiding his horse.

Abigail looked around, noticing there was little shelter in the way of trees where they'd stopped, but they were no longer on the rolling and pitching boats. Driftwood brushed the sand before the tide pulled it back out, only to send it back toward shore. There was no point in gathering any, since it would never catch fire. Abigail couldn't see any other way for them to generate heat, to warm themselves, or to cook. She wasn't even certain there was anything to catch to eat. It surprised her to see several men working to drill oars into the sand in order to tether the horses. One after another pulled dried beef and fruit from their saddlebags, and then they piled their saddles high enough to drape tarps over them and climb underneath. Abigail realized that if she hadn't been traveling with the men, Ronan would have been the first to go ashore. He would have scouted before allowing his men to make camp, but with her aboard, Ronan waited until other men signaled it was safe to bring Abigail onto the beach. She also realized that Ronan moved slower than he could have to keep water from splashing onto her. By the time Ronan lowered her to her feet and she unwrapped her skirts, the men had built the makeshift lean-to as far out of the wind as they could. She looked around, but none of the men entered the tent. She looked up at Ronan, her eyes widening as she understood that the men erected it for her. And none would use it while she was there.

"No, Ronan. I'm not sitting there by myself while your—our—men freeze. I'm no princess. I will not take that and leave them to suffer. Either they share with me, or I won't go in. And if you think to drop me in there, I will only climb out." Abigail's brilliant eyes warned Ronan that she would fight him until he relented. It wasn't worth the battle, since he would welcome the entire Isle of Harris if it meant Abigail was out of the elements. Ronan called out three names and told them to build a second shelter behind the first, since they only had spare plaids to use for that one. The first lean-to would buffer the wind for the second. "Go inside, Abby. I need to check the animals and send men out to hunt."

"Ronan, they must go inland at least a mile before they find trees either for firewood or wildlife. I don't know how far north and east the MacIvers send scouts. If they should find MacAuleys, they should tell them I travel with you. They're the only ones who get along with us. The Mackenzies can go either way, but we aren't on good terms with them."

"Who are you on good terms with?" Ronan chuckled, creases forming at the corner of his eyes.

"The MacLeods." Abigail pursed her lips.

"There is one MacLeod I'm happy to be on vera good terms with, lass," Ronan said with a wink. He knew the clan dynamics as well as Abigail; in fact, it was likely he knew them better, since she'd been away from the island for more than a year. But he appreciated her concerns for her new clansmen, and it relieved him that she understood the gravity of being discovered by rival clans. He hoped his voice sounded lighthearted enough to ease her worry, but as her eyes continued to sweep the water and the surrounding land, he knew she would remain as vigilant as all the men. "Try to rest, Abby. I'll join you as soon as I can."

Abigail nodded, knowing that there was no more she could say. She trusted Ronan would tell his men her preference that they share the cover, but she also understood the confined space with their new lady would make them uncomfortable. Honor and chivalry dictated they give the tent to her alone, but she refused to make any of them suffer for the sake of decorum. She also knew they were on edge from being in an unfamiliar location with little but one another to guard their backs. Abigail crawled under the shelter and sighed. While she once again had to huddle, the wind no longer gusted against her. She anticipated the warmth Ronan would bring when he sat beside her and engulfed her in his embrace. She knew his soaked plaid had to be freezing. He and the other men stomped their feet whenever they stood in place, trying to keep their circulation going. The only thing Abigail could imagine to make their situation worse was snow. She gazed at the sky and prayed that now that they were off the rough seas, they wouldn't face Mother Nature's wrath any longer.

It wasn't long before Ronan had his men organized into watch shifts and hunters. He climbed under the tarp with Abigail, wanting to lift her onto his lap to save space, warm her, and to hold her. But he knew his still-wet plaid would only soak her gown. He settled for pulling her tightly against him and kissing her cheek. She leaned against him, curled tight within her layers of plaid and her wool gown. Hesitantly, despite her welcoming smile, four men

172

came to share the shelter with Ronan and her. She remained quiet, too tired to speak and worried that she would annoy the men if she chattered. It wasn't long before her eyes drifted closed, warmed by Ronan enough to relax. He kissed the top of her head and leaned his cheek against her crown.

TWENTY

R onan didn't want to alarm Abigail, but his men reported signs of patrols three miles inland. They returned with wood and a collection of rabbits and squirrels that hadn't been easy catches in early January. He knew all his men needed heat from a fire to keep them from suffering damage to their feet from stockings and boots that were still wet. Neither could they eat the ground animals raw. But he didn't want to alert anyone nearby. He ordered a fire made to the right of both tents, keeping the camp small and tightly gathered. He had to accept the risk of being spotted over losing his men to the elements. He would have preferred neither risk since Abigail was with him.

When it was Ronan's turn to stand watch, he eased Abigail onto her side on the unforgiving ground, wishing he had more to protect her from the frost that developed during the night. He instructed the men within their lean-to to remain there. If Abigail needed privacy, they were to take her no further than one hundred yards, encircle her, and turn away. He wouldn't risk anyone sneaking up on his wife. He stood his two hours' sentry, softly whistling every quarter hour and listening for his men to return the call. When he eased back into the tent after one of his men relieved him, he found Abigail sleeping peacefully. He wrapped his broader frame around her, making a cocoon, before falling asleep. They awoke to a clear sky and calm seas.

Abigail inhaled the fresh saltwater scent as the sun peeked over the horizon. The inclement weather from the day before might have been a figment of her imagination were she not standing on a beach rather than on a birlinn or within the walls of her new home. With the tide out as they boarded the ships, the men weren't in the water for as long—or at the same depths—as when they arrived. Abigail began to argue that she would wade out on her own, but Ronan's scowl cut her short. She nodded, knowing he was being the sensible one, but she felt guilty nonetheless. With the waves lapping against the hull rather than crashing against the wood planks, the horses were quiet once the anchors and the sails were raised. Just as they'd started their journey the day before, Abigail and Ronan stood together at the bow. Ronan's wide shoulders kept some wind and spray from Abigail as she tilted her head back to feel the sun against her skin.

It was still the middle of winter, but with no gusts assailing them and no snow in sight, it felt tolerable. Abigail felt excitement building as they sailed closer to the Isle of Skye. The worst of the journey was behind them, and everyone expected the rest of the journey to be uneventful. It was nearly midday when the tip of the Isle of Skye became a fuzzy outline to the south. Abigail grinned as she considered what her distant cousins would think when they discovered she had married the very man they lived to antagonize.

With nearly no wind that day, Ronan ordered the men to the oars. Abigail looked back over her shoulder from her place at the bow as she watched Ronan take his turn. Even with his leine on and a length of plaid crossing his back, Abigail could still see the powerful muscles bunch and strain beneath the layers. She bit her top lip as lurid images of running her fingers over his back danced before her eyes. She recalled how she had circled Ronan the first time she saw him naked, mesmerized by his perfect physique. She knew many women at court shied away from the colossal Highlanders when they arrived, preferring the average-sized men who spent their days as courtiers. But Abigail couldn't picture bedding any man who lacked a warrior's build and strength. As she thought about it, she couldn't imagine that any man could meet the standard Ronan now set. While the ladies-in-waiting might have tittered over him, she was the one who shared his bed.

As Abigail turned back to watch as they approached the headland while keeping a safe distance from it, she tried to imagine what Ronan's chamber looked like. They'd already agreed that there would only be a shared chamber, neither wanting to prowl along passageways, even if the lady's chambers were next door to the laird's. Her cheeks grew warm as she recalled confessing to Ronan how she'd passed the afternoon between their time in the library and their walk. She'd admitted that she'd daydreamed about his chamber while pleasuring herself. His response had been immediate—and lasted well into the night.

Abigail already knew there was no bed in the lady's chamber and that Ronan's mother had used it as a solar. Ronan's parents, despite never being in love, had shared a chamber since early in their marriage. Ronan had blushed to his roots when he told Abigail that. His cheeks hadn't pinked when he'd told her about his father's regrets about his actions before he married. But admitting that his parents shared a bed every night—the bed Ronan now slept in and would that night share with Abigail—made him flustered.

Shading her eyes from the sun overhead, Abigail squinted as shapes materialized and inched toward them. She leaned forward until her toes were nearly off the deck. Her stomach dropped before it heaved upward and settled in a knot. She turned toward the men and eased her way to Ronan's bench. Keeping her voice low, she leaned over to whisper, "There are seven MacLeod birlinns moving toward us."

Ronan checked over his shoulder, not wanting to believe Abigail's observation. He nodded before he drew his oar in and rose to his feet. His men, still rowing, strained to look at him as he followed Abigail to the bow. Uttering an oath, Ronan led Abigail to the bench closest to the stern. "When the attack starts, get beneath this bench. It's the only way to protect you from arrows. It won't keep them from spotting you, but it will make you a harder target to hit."

Abigail nodded, looking at the man who sat beside where they stood, continuing to row but listening to every word. Ronan didn't mince words with Abigail, refusing to pretend that anything other than violence awaited them. She knew as well as Ronan, and every man now aware of the impending attack, that they would not pass quietly by the MacLeods. Ronan prayed that the MacLeods would leave them alone if they moved away from their rival's fishing lanes. But as the MacLeods sailed closer and the steel of their swords caught the light, Ronan signaled to the other boats. All oarsmen pulled as the four birlinns attempted to steer away from the approaching boats.

Ronan ordered his men to point toward shore. He would get them as close to land as he could, praying that some—most importantly, Abigail—would make it ashore. He didn't doubt his men would fight valiantly, protecting Abigail as their top priority, but he would prefer to stand against the MacLeods on land. If the enemy forced them to defend themselves on the boats, the MacLeods would encircle them and then overwhelm them by sheer numbers. If they made it to shore, he would abandon the boats and lead his warriors and Abigail overland on horseback.

With the wind at their backs, the MacLeods' progress was far faster than the MacKinnons'. When time ran out for them to reach the coast before the MacLeods reached them, Ronan and his men drew their swords. Abigail slid beneath the bench, her back to their attackers, shielding her organs from the arrows Ronan warned her about. It felt like the minutes were hours as Abigail waited for the first battle sounds. She desperately wanted to turn over to watch Ronan, but she knew he would want her to protect herself before all else. She heard the orders drifting from their enemy, at times, drowned out by Ronan's commands. She knew the moment the MacLeods recognized Ronan and made him their primary target.

The impact pushed her onto her belly, smashing her face against the deck, when one of the enemy boats rammed the MacKinnons'. The boat shuddered and pitched precariously to port, and Abigail felt herself slipping. She struggled to roll over and grab the bench above her. She clung to it as the sound of metal striking metal rang around her. It was just distant enough for her to know the enemy boarded one of the other boats, not hers.

Abigail's body ached from the tension in her taut muscles. She kept expecting to feel the vibration of men jumping onto the deck, the echoing sound of swords clashing near her ears, even hands dragging her from beneath her bench. But none came. Instead, another jarring impact pushed the boat back to port. Her head pointed toward the side that dipped toward the water's surface, and she felt herself sliding again, despite hanging on. It was her legs being pushed toward her chest as the boat keeled.

"Abby!" Ronan glanced back in time to see Abigail's body slam into the port bulkhead. He swung his sword over and over as he fought to keep the enemy from boarding his boat. He was unrelenting in his drive to keep their attackers away from his wife. She would be dead before she could convince the MacLeods she was one of them. She wore only her MacKinnon plaid, and Ronan doubted any of them would recognize her by sight alone. Abigail had told him she hadn't been to Skye since she was a child. Unlike on Lewis, where people would at least be aware of the various lairds' family members, Ronan couldn't guarantee the MacLeods of Skye would believe her claims.

A third crash made Ronan fall backwards as one of the MacLeod birlinns continued to push against his boat in an attempt to capsize it. No longer able to remain on his feet, his clansmen struggling too, Ronan scrambled to reach Abigail. But he was only halfway along the deck when the boat finally capsized. Ronan tumbled toward the water, his eyes on Abigail as he fought to get to her. He knew her heavy skirts would cause her to sink, and the freezing water would sap her strength and steal the air from her lungs. He plunged into the water, but the birlinn flipped over him, trapping him and several other men with a pocket of air. But Abigail's head never surfaced. He didn't know if the sea had already dragged her under or if she bobbed on the other side of the boat. He kicked and circled his arms until he came to where he'd last seen her. He ducked under the rail that floated beside him and came up free of the boat. He twisted and turned as he looked for Abigail.

"Abby!" Ronan called out to her, just as he had when he watched her crash against the wall of the boat. "Abby!"

The only sound that reached Ronan came from the fights that raged on his other three birlinns. When Abigail didn't answer his cry, he dove beneath the surface, the saltwater like shards of glass against his open eyes. They'd traveled close enough to land that the water was shallow enough to kick to the bottom. He looked around, moving his hands in front of him, but he could see nothing but rocks and sand. Forced to surface for a breath, he dove again, swimming back under the boat but toward the sea floor. Just as he had before, his hands searched the seabed as his eyes struggled to focus. But just as before, he found nothing. Moving beneath the surface for as long as he could, Ronan continued searching until his lungs screamed for air. His head emerged in time to see the hull splinter where the wood finally succumbed to the impact of the MacLeods ramming the boat three times. A hole now released the bubble of air beneath the boat, and the vessel sank.

Ronan continued to look for Abigail among the many heads bobbing in the water. He recognized most as his men, but there were some MacLeods among them. All his men could swim, and they were struggling against the current to reach land. But Ronan wouldn't abandon his search for Abigail. He called out to her over and over to no avail. He felt his strength draining and began to panic, knowing that if he was growing tired, Abigail would already be exhausted. He lunged to catch a piece of driftwood from his boat before the tide carried it away. He pushed it beneath the surface and draped his arms over it. When the wood forced its way back up, he used it to keep him buoyant. Ronan knew he would die in the water before he gave up hope of finding Abigail. He kicked away from the wreckage, but his legs no longer had the power they did when he first entered the water.

Letting the water pull him further from shore, he struggled to make his way to the far side of the boat farthest out to sea. The fighting had ceased. The MacKinnons were dead or swimming toward shore. His gaze swept over the MacLeods celebrating their victory, unaware that he'd survived. He could only assume that either they hadn't recognized his voice, or he hadn't been as loud as he thought. If the MacLeods thought he lived, they would either capture him or taunt him until they watched him slip beneath the surface for good.

"Ro," a feminine voice hissed at him. He watched as a pair of robin's-egg blue eyes bore into his. Abigail floated halfway on her belly, her hand grasping an opening for an oar. He was closer than he realized. He'd looked in her direction as he came around the side of the boat, but he was certain she hadn't been there. When a voice drifted closer, he watched as Abigail dipped underwater, her fingers barely wrapped around the wood. He followed her example, releasing the board he'd used to help him float. Beneath the waves that broke on the surface, he propelled himself toward his wife. When he felt her fingers seeking his, he squeezed in response. Together, they eased their heads out of the water until their noses were clear. They stared at one another, neither daring to make a sound, the situation still too grave for smiles. But the intense look they exchanged communicated more than words could.

"Ho-ho! And here is where the great Ronan MacKinnon shall meet his grave." A booming bass crowed from above the couple. Ronan glared at Donovan MacLeod, Laird Cormag MacLeod's youngest brother. "Though honor demands I save the lass."

Ronan's brow furrowed as he watched Abigail's free hand move below the surface. He couldn't see more than the barest hint of her knuckles, so he was unprepared when she launched her own attack. Donovan reached over the side of the boat and grasped Abigail's underarms. As he lifted, she pushed down with the hand that still held onto the boat. Her other arm swung from the water, droplets falling from a blade that shone in the sunlight. It entered Donovan's neck just as he spotted it flying toward him. He'd twisted his head to see, giving Abigail the perfect angle to slice his jugular. Blood spewed forth, and Donovan dropped Abigail. With nothing to hold on to and the weight of her skirts pulling her, she floundered as she tried to grasp the boat again. Ronan yanked a handful of her bodice upward as he slipped beneath the surface. He looked up as he felt Abigail being lifted once more. Strong hands fisted his leine, dragging him up and over the side of the birlinn. They dumped him on the deck beside Abigail, who still clutched her dirk. A man grabbed for her arm and came away with a gash across his palm.

Ronan scrambled in front of Abigail, snatching the knife from her hand. She released it immediately, shrinking behind her husband's wide back. It was Ronan's turn to slash at anyone who reached toward him. Praying his legs would cooperate and support him, he pushed to his feet, stunned by his own agility after so many minutes in the freezing water. Despite facing men with swords, Ronan kept them at bay after he drove the knife into the hollow at the base of a MacLeod's throat. Ronan recognized the knife he wielded as one he'd given Abigail before they set off, intended for the purpose of defending herself. While he rued the need for it, he was reassured that he had thought to arm Abigail. He knew she'd carried a *sgian dubh* at court, and if she still wore her boots, it was tucked beside her ankle. She had strapped the knife he held now to her outer thigh. He'd slid it into the sheath attached to the garter the morning before.

"Knock him out and bind him. Gag the woman, and for Christ's sake, make sure she hasn't any more weapons." Abigail turned her head to lock eyes with Gordon MacLeod, the middle brother named for his mother's clan. She saw no flash of recognition in his eyes, but she'd seen it in Donovan's just before he turned his head and she thrust the knife into him. She wondered how badly she erred to kill the only man who seemed to know who she was. A strip of MacLeod plaid—blue rather than her branch's red —appeared before her eyes before a warrior forced it between her teeth. Hands ran over her arms and body, lingering too long on her breasts and eliciting a feral growl from Ronan as he fought his captors. They ran over the top of her skirts, but none of the men thought to check her boots.

Abigail silently scoffed at them as she took in the various knife handles protruding from the men's boots. She watched the MacLeods strip Ronan of most of his, but she knew where he kept a few they didn't discover. She feared his sword, an heirloom from four generations back, was lost to Ronan forever. Gordon raised it in the air as if he were assessing its quality, but Abigail and Ronan knew he did it to mock the MacKinnon laird. Abigail was powerless when Gordon used the hilt of Ronan's own sword to bash him against the temple and watch him crumple to the deck. She turned a loathing glare on him, only to be met by his derisive laughter.

TWENTY-ONE

Abigail shivered as she pulled her knees to her chest and watched Ronan's chest rise and fall. He'd come around as the MacLeods dragged them from the boat, but a man struck Ronan on the opposite temple before he could get his bearings. Now they were locked together in a cell within Dunvegan Castle. Guards thrust them into the stench and filth an hour earlier, and Abigail grew frightened when Ronan didn't wake as easily as he had the first time they knocked him out. She'd done what she could to make him more comfortable, but it was difficult with their hands bound behind them. She'd managed to nudge him onto his side, careful not to bang his head but keeping his weight from trapping his arms. Frozen and terrified, Abigail cared not that her back and hair brushed against the grimy wall. But when she grew too tired to remain upright, she curled up facing Ronan. She let her eyes close, but she kept her mind active enough not to fall asleep. Until she was certain Ronan would wake, she couldn't relax.

"Abby." Ronan opened his eyes to find Abigail resting with hers shut. He watched as she shivered, and he tried to scoot closer, but it was awkward. Her eyes flew open when she heard his voice, and she inched her way toward him. Their cracked lips pressed together; their kiss soft as relief overwhelmed them both. When they drew apart, Abigail's weak smile worried Ronan. "Are ye hurt?"

"Nay. Just cold and tired."

"Did ye tell them who ye are?"

"I didna have a chance. They removed ma gag just before they left, but they talked over me when I tried."

"Do they ken ye're ma wife?"

"They figured it out. Ma plaid is the laird's pattern, and I have a ring on ma finger."

"Did they threaten ye? Mistreat ye?"

"Nae at all. Nay one talked to me once we came on shore, and Gordon warned me that talking would only kill ye sooner. Quite the incentive to remain quiet." Abigail pushed herself closer until her head fit beneath Ronan's chin. "None of them touched me, either. Even though they checked me for weapons, after watching me stab Donovan, I dinna think any of the men trust getting near me. I think they all believe I'm a bampot or a banshee."

"Would that ye could convince them ye're a banshee. Mayhap they'd think Queen Titania sent ye."

"They'd believe that as much as they'd believe ye're King Oberan. Ma husband, aye. An ancient king, nay." Abigail chuckled as she rested her cheek against Ronan's chest. "Ronan, I'm sorry I scared ye earlier. I heard ye calling to me, but I didna dare answer. I just kept praying and praying that ye would swim around to where I was."

"As soon as I saw ye, I figured as much. Ye were smart to nae bring attention to ye until I was with ye. It may nae have done either of us much good, but it means we're together."

"I ken there are plenty of other things I could want, but until we're away from here, all I want is to be with ye."

"How long have we been down here?"

"Probably two hours."

"That long?" Ronan tried to rub his temple with his shoulder.

"The mon who hit ye when ye woke the last time did it much harder than Gordon. I feared ye wouldnae wake at all."

"I'm nae giving up ma life with ye when it has just begun. I dreamed of ye while I was unconscious. I was fighting to get back to ye. I'll always fight to get back to ye." Ronan leaned back until he could see Abigail's face. She tilted her head away from his chest before they exchanged another tender kiss. Both were too exhausted for more, and relief was stronger than passion as they lay looking at one another.

"What do ye think they will do? Will they ransom us back to our people?"

"Most probably. But I dinna think Cormag will be in a rush. I think he'd rather I languish here for as long as he can keep me. I can only hope his wife, Cecily, learns that he has a woman imprisoned down here. She'll rail at him until he takes ye out of here. She's as greedy as he is, but she's also the most pretentious woman I have ever met. She'll nag him about how improper it is to keep a woman down here, and how she's too good to live in a keep with savages who keep women locked away."

"How can ye be so sure?"

"Because that's what she did when Cormag kidnapped MacNeacail's sister."

"Kidnapped?"

"More like bride stealing. MacNeacail arranged

for his sister to marry a northern MacDonald chieftain. Cormag refuses to accept any alliance between them because he kens they'll partner against him. He stole the woman, intending that Donovan marry her. But he didna ken she was already with child—from a mon in her own clan. Neither marriage happened."

"But Lady MacLeod intervened?"

"Only so much as to get Lady Katherine into a chamber, for appearance's sake. She didna care what happened to Lady Katherine once she thought she'd protected her own reputation."

"I'm nae leaving ye down here, Ronan."

"Ye will if ye can."

"Nay, I—"

"Abby, if ye can get out of here, ye will. I dinna want ye in this filth. I dinna want ye falling ill, if ye arenae already going to. Ye're still soaked. Cecily will give ye something to wear, and she might even let ye have a bath. Dinna count on being invited to their table, but ye're safer up there than ye are in here."

"But, Ronan, ye might die down here. I amnae leaving yer side."

"They willna let it come to that. There is money to be made off ma head. If I'm dead, our clan willna pay a ransom for me. Same for ye. If aught happens to ye, there'll be nay ransom. Cormag is impetuous and greedy, but nae entirely stupid. Killing me in his own keep rather than in battle will only anger the Bruce. Yer MacLeod plaid is somewhere at the bottom of the Little Minch, but if ye can convince Cormag that ye're Kieran's sister, he willna touch ye. If he kens he'll cause a rift between the branches, he'll think twice. Yer brother could overrun the MacLeods of Harris if yer branches from Raasay join Kieran. Cormag willna let yer brother have the entire island nor dominate members of his own branch."

"Do ye think there is any way to get a message to Kieran?"

"I dinna ken aboot that, but Cormag willna need vera many reminders of what will happen once Kieran learns he captured ye."

"Us. Captured us. Ye're a MacLeod now, whether Cormag acknowledges it. I told ye that when we exchanged vows at the kirk. I may bear yer name now, but ye're part of ma family as much as I'm now a part of yers. Our marriage contracts bind Kieran as yer ally, even if he didna already like ye and think of ye as a brother."

"That's a wee stretch."

"It's nae. Ronan, I ken what I saw. He's the same way with ye as he is with Lachlan, and he considers Lachlan to be his brother, even if it's only by marriage. For all our faults, Kieran is vera protective of his family, especially if Maude learns of this and it upsets her."

"I'd rather ye were well away from here, preferably at Dun Ringill, before the MacKinnons or the MacLeods of Lewis attack. I dinna want ye caught in the middle."

"Cormag may have already made that decision for ye."

Abigail and Ronan turned their heads toward the door when they heard the heavy thud of boots approaching. Ronan glanced at Abigail and cocked an eyebrow, telling her this might be their chance for her to leave. He wouldn't allow her to remain. She frowned at this, but nodded. She swore silently to herself that if she got free of the dungeon, she would get free of the keep. She would get them both away from Dunvegan, then sit back and watch as Ronan and Kieran rained holy hell down upon Cormag. The moment the MacLeods attacked, they had sealed their fate. Even if Ronan and Abigail didn't survive, the MacKinnons and MacLeods of Lewis held the combined strength to suppress the MacLeods of Skye. It would create a fissure between the two MacLeods branches that wouldn't be reconciled in the lifetime of anyone who drew breath now.

"Dinna drink aught but watered ale or water. Better yet, naught but water. Dinna eat aught with a sauce," Ronan hurried to whisper. "Naught that they can tamper with and ye wouldnae taste. Be careful that nay one spots yer *sgian dubh* if they give ye a bath or a change of clothes. Tell every lie ye can think of if Cormag or Gordon demand information and ye even suspect it might protect ye. I love ye, Abby."

"I love ye, Ronan. And dinna think for a moment that I will let ye die down here." Abigail pressed a swift kiss to Ronan's lips, her tongue flicking out against his lips. They pulled away all too soon for either of their wants, but the key in the lock told them their time together was likely over.

"Lady MacLeod is eager for a lady companion," one guard announced. Abigail looked at Ronan, barely able to see his cocked eyebrow in the dim light. She knew he was thinking "see." She dipped her chin in agreement. Rough hands once more grasped her underarms and yanked her to her feet. She kept her eyes on Ronan as they dragged her from the cell. She watched as the cell door slammed shut and another guard locked the door.

As the guard steered her forward, Abigail caught sight of several MacKinnon guards languishing in their cells. Some were unconscious, but some watched her pass by. She hoped they understood her determined expression and didn't think she was abandoning them. Her eyes swept over the area where the guards sat watch. She observed the guard with the massive keyring hang it on a hook beneath a tabletop, hiding it from sight. She'd counted the number of cells and the number of men she could see. Only half of the men they set out with were present. Grief for their families swept through her, and it strengthened her resolve to get Ronan and the MacKinnons free.

TWENTY-TWO

Abigail complied with all the orders given to her, hoping to appear too frightened and over-whelmed to fight back. It didn't match how she'd fought earlier that day, but she was determined to make the MacLeods think she was complacent and unsuspecting. She also needed the dregs of her strength to survive whatever would come next. With a guard shoving her in front of him, and one on each side flanking her, she made her way abovestairs to the third floor. A maid led the way to a well-appointed guest chamber that already had a steaming tub awaiting her. Abruptly, her hands were freed as a dirk sliced through the rope binding them. Another shove pushed her into the chamber. Appearing to flee from the guards, she moved around the far side of the bed. Her long gown hid the boots she wore, but they were loose from the time spent in the water. She toed them off and slyly kicked them under the bed, hiding the *sgian dubh* sheathed in her right boot.

"Lady MacLeod ordered me to help ye," the maid sneered. Abigail raised her chin and cast as imperious a glare as she'd ever managed toward the maid. She sniffed and turned up her nose. She wouldn't cower before servants, knowing the woman would report to Cecily, if not Cormag. If they thought her already cowed, they would ignore her. She needed as much information as she could gather. The young brunette stood beside the bath once the door closed, waiting for Abigail to approach. Abigail stood her ground, refusing to follow the woman's silent command. The standoff lasted several minutes before the woman huffed and muttered something about having better things to do than wait on a bitch. Abigail nearly asked if that was to wait on another bitch, namely Lady MacLeod.

Once the maid stepped behind Abigail and wrestled the matted and knotted laces, she helped Abigail peel the damp, salt-encrusted gown from her arms. Free from her kirtle and chemise, Abigail stepped into the tub. She knew the maid was assessing her, but the temptation of the steamy water grew too strong. She eased her body beneath the surface, but she didn't dunk her head. Instead, she leaned her head back, never taking her eyes off the maid. The maid reached for the soap and a linen square, but Abigail was faster.

"I'd rather you find me some clothes. Please." Abigail's tone made it a command, but she conceded to a basic curtesy. She worked quickly to scrub her hair while the maid stared at her. She poured the clean ewer of water over her head herself, still watching the other woman. When the maid didn't budge, Abigail released a mirthless laugh. "Very well. But I doubt Lady MacLeod will appreciate me turning up before her husband bare as a tavern whore because we both ken the laird will demand to see me. Your head, not mine."

Abigail lazily ran the soapy cloth over her arms as she grinned at the maid. The woman paused, pursing her lips before nodding. She went to the door and rapped on it once. Abigail slipped further beneath the water, draping the cloth over her breasts and bringing her knees up to hide her mons. She knew guards remained in the passageway, and she wouldn't offer any of them a peek. Gruff voices confirmed what she knew, but the door closed and the lock clicked. She hurried to finish her bath, wrapping a drying linen around her waist and another around her chest. She draped the third one over her shoulders, covering as much as she could. She moved to stand behind where the door would open, once more refusing to allow the men to see her. When the door swung open, it nearly hit her, but she recognized that Cecily intended to make a grand entrance. She watched the woman enter the chamber and look around. Abigail pushed the door hard enough for it to slam, making Cecily jump before she turned to look at Abigail.

"Holy hell."

"Thank you for welcoming me to your home," Abigail returned. She would not curtsy to the woman. Now that she was Lady MacKinnon, they were of equal social status. Abigail didn't know if the rude greeting was because of her appearance or due to recognition. She had her answer soon enough.

"You're Madeline's sister. Bluidy hell."

"I believe I shall agree that I'm in hell, but I see you recognize me. I'm Lady Abigail MacKinnon. I take it you know my sister."

"We were ladies-in-waiting together briefly. I married a month after she arrived. You could practically be twins. And you have the look of your brother, too."

"So I've been told. Perhaps you could convey that to your husband."

Cecily nodded before she looked at the gown draped over her arm. She held it up, surveying whether it would fit Abigail. With a nod, she laid it, along with a chemise and a pair of stockings, on the bed. Abigail eased across the chamber until she stood beside the bed where she'd hidden her boots. She reached for the chemise and tugged it on before letting the linens fall to the floor. She grabbed the stockings but pretended to drop them. She snagged her blade from her boots as she bent to pick up the clothing. With a haughty glance at Cecily, she turned her back to don the stockings. Fortunately, they were tight at the top even without a ribbon to cinch them.

Neither the maid nor Cecily noticed that one of Abigail's ribbon garters was exceptionally wide and held a sheath. She slipped her dirk into place before turning back around. She bent again and picked up her boots. She placed them before the fire, hoping that by the time she left the chamber, they would be dry. Cecily watched in silence as Abigail returned to the foot of the bed and pulled the kirtle on. It laced at the sides, so Abigail didn't need help.

"Are you going to tell Cormag who I am?" Abigail's lack of deference by using the laird's given name was purposeful, and she knew she hit the mark when Cecily's eyes widened a fraction. Their disdain matched one another.

"Aye. I suppose I must."

"And just what do you think he'll say when he discovers he had Kieran's sister in his dungeon?"

Cecily flinched before she nodded. She glanced at Abigail's boots and huffed. "A moment." Cecily went to the door, knocking just as the maid had. The door opened, and Cecily gave a whispered command to someone Abigail couldn't see. Abigail strained to look past Cecily and into the passageway, but broad shoulders that nearly met blocked her view. However, it allowed her to learn that two men guarded her door. When Cecily turned back toward Abigail, she had a pair of satin slippers in her hand. Abigail gratefully took them, a hint of a genuine smile tugging at her lips. It relieved her that she wouldn't have to traverse the freezing stone floors in just her stockings. She knew many servants did just that, and she could have, but she'd dreaded it. The slippers were a little loose, but she was confident she wouldn't step out of them.

"Come with me. The evening meal will be served soon," Cecily announced. Abigail hadn't realized so much time elapsed between the attack that came shortly after midday and when she left the chamber. It surprised her that Cormag would allow her to leave the room. She followed the guard who walked in front of Cecily, painfully aware of the two guards who walked behind her. They made their way to the Great Hall, where Abigail took in everything she could see. She spotted the doors leading to the bailey and to the kitchens, a dark passageway she assumed led to storage rooms, and a door she guessed was Cormag's solar. She swept her gaze over the two enormous fireplaces, the swords and shields hanging above them, and the tapestries that covered the walls. She noticed the fresh rushes over a floor that needed scrubbing. She finally looked to the table on the dais. Cormag and Gordon sat together talking, a chalice in either of their hands. At her appearance, both men stared at her. She moved toward the dais along with Cecily.

"Husband, I would introduce you to Lady Abigail MacKinnon," Cecily announced.

"I'm Kieran's sister," Abigail blurted before anyone could say more. She locked eyes with Cormag, daring him to respond.

"Shite."

"I'd say that's exactly what you're up to your eyeballs in," Abigail replied to Cormag. She turned her gaze to Gordon. "Perhaps you shouldn't have been so quick to gag me."

Gordon rose from his seat, his hands on the table as he leaned forward. With a menacing glare, he snarled, "And perhaps you shouldn't have been so quick to kill my brother."

Abigail shrugged one shoulder. "Don't lead an attack if you're not prepared to die."

"You've got the same bollocks as Kieran," Cormag broke in.

"The three of us inherited them from our mother." Lady Adeline MacLeod had a reputation for being a vain spendthrift, but people also knew her for her iron will and sharp tongue. She was certain her sister Madeline's reputation was also well known, both from her time at court and her steadfast insistence that the Grants rescue her husband after they lost Fingal during battle. Kieran's loyalty and protectiveness of Maude was known throughout the Highlands. "Release my husband and our men, and mayhap this will slip my mind in my next missive to my brother."

"Or mayhap your husband's clan and your brother's will spend a pretty penny to keep your head on your shoulders," Cormag countered.

"You really are as big a fool as they say at court," Abigail muttered, but she made certain those on the dais and around her heard.

"Care to say that with some courage?" Gordon tested. Abigail grinned, making Gordon grimace.

"You really are as big a fool as they say at court," Abigail repeated loudly enough for most of the Great Hall to hear. Gasps, coughs, and a few quiet chuckles met Abigail's ears. She shrugged again. "You asked."

"You don't seem to value your life," Cormag mused.

"I can tell you exactly how much value my life

holds. And it goes up significantly if you kill me. Between the MacKinnons, the MacLeods of Lewis and Raasay, and the Bruce, I'd say it's far more than you can afford. Add an unprovoked attack, then holding hostage and attempting to kill a laird? I'd say it'll only take the time for the Bruce to learn the news before the MacKinnons own most of this island. Is there room for you all on Harris? I doubt there will be by the time Kieran's done." Abigail exaggerated her examination of the Great Hall, turning all the way around. "I haven't seen Dun Ringill yet, but I can see myself tossing out those rags on the wall and replacing them with the MacKinnon colors. I think Ronan will look quite intimidating in your chair come spring. This will make a fine MacKinnon stronghold."

"You talk a lot," Gordon growled.

Abigail grinned, wrinkling her nose. "I know. Kieran tells me that all the time. But he also says I come up with the most novel ideas."

"My idea is to toss you back into that cell with your bastard husband," Cormag barked.

When Abigail shrugged yet again, Cormag banged his fist on the table, but it didn't stop her. "One more tale of woe to tell King Robert. I'm certain Queen Elizabeth will make it known to her husband how aggrieved she is to learn aboot her lady-in-waiting's mistreatment. She can be very convincing."

"Take your seat, eat your meal in silence, and pray I don't have my wife sew your lips shut," Cormag ordered. Abigail decided she'd antagonized him enough for one evening. But she understood her posturing held the same significance as what passed between lairds before a battle. She wouldn't appear weak and servile to any of these MacLeods. She would remind them that she was equal to all the laird's family, and that her captivity could only result in their loss. She took her seat beside Cecily, who sat to Cormag's left, while Gordon had taken his seat once again to Cormag's right.

She heeded Ronan's warning, drinking none of the wine placed before her and eating only the food that was served to the laird first, preferring bread and cheese over the rest. When Cormag leaned forward and smirked, she knew he recognized her tactic. She raised her eyebrows as if to ask him if he could blame her. For a moment, Abigail thought she saw respect flicker in his eyes before his expression became mocking once more. She spent the rest of the meal in silence, eager to return to the chamber they had given her. She slid the *sgian dubh* under her pillow and fell into a light sleep. She woke each time the guards switched at her door.

TWENTY-THREE

R onan's teeth chattered as he pushed himself to sit up. He'd tried unknotting the rope at his wrists, but he'd only chafed the skin. His shoulders burned from his arms being bound behind his back. His belly's rumbling echoed in the cell, but he doubted Cormag would order him fed. He expected to go days without food since his clan wouldn't know where he and the other guards went. They expected him to return with Abigail after the new year, but they would accept that foul weather might delay them. It could be at least a sennight before they became alarmed, and then they wouldn't know where to look. His men would form search parties to travel along the shore and likely even to Stornoway, but none would know to look for him at Dunvegan. He hoped they would grow suspicious of the MacLeods quickly and assume he was a captive here.

Ronan's mind constantly returned to Abigail and his consuming fear that Cormag already ordered her death or was abusing her. While he wanted to believe Cormag possessed enough sense to see the danger in harming Abigail, he didn't hold the same faith for Gordon. The man had a reputation for being brutal on and off the battlefield. Ronan easily imagined what Gordon would do with a beautiful and spirited woman like Abigail. Gordon would attempt everything he could think of to bend her to his will, and Ronan knew Abigail would not snap easily.

Just after they took Abigail from his side, he whistled his call, saddened to only hear a handful in return. The guards threatened them, but his men knew he lived, and he knew how many survived. He hadn't been able to see if any swam to shore. If any men made it to land, they would find themselves in Mac-Leod territory. It would be a miracle if they could traverse their enemy's land, let alone cross most of the island on foot after nearly drowning. But it was Ronan's only hope that word would travel to Dun Ringill to guide their rescue.

With no way to free his hands and no way to predict what the next day held, Ronan allowed himself to sleep. He knew resting his mind and body would be his only defense in the days to come. His head still ached from being bashed on both sides. His last thoughts and all his dreams were of Abigail.

"Lazy bastard."

Ronan opened his eyes to the sound of voices and the lock turning. He couldn't be certain, but he suspected it was morning. He pulled his feet in and pressed his back against the wall, prepared to push onto his feet if he needed to defend himself. But a piece of bread flew toward him and landed in his lap. "Good luck eating that. Mayhap I should watch the mighty Laird MacKinnon eat like a dog."

Ronan didn't move. His legs remained prepared to stand, but he would wait out the guard's interest in him. When he didn't respond to any of the man's barbs, the guard grunted and pulled the door shut, leaving Ronan alone again. Just as the guard stated,

Ronan felt like a dog as he bent forward and grasped the heel of bread with his teeth. He dragged it higher until it rested between his knees and chest, and where he could gnaw on it. It was nearly too hard to eat, and he suspected it was more than a day old, but it was food. If it was all they would give him that day, he wouldn't turn it down. His belly was so empty that the stale bread made it churn.

Once his stomach calmed, recognizing the bread as fuel for his body rather than poison, Ronan felt some of his strength return. Able to stand without growing dizzy, Ronan rose and slid his back along the wall as he made his way around the cell. The feel of sludge seeping through his leine made bile burn the back of his throat, but he lived with his disgust when he found a spot on the wall jagged enough to saw the rope against. He knew it would be slow going, and any time he heard a guard approach, he dashed back to where they'd last seen him sitting. He would give them the notion he'd given up and accepted his imprisonment.

It took him hours of working on the rope before it began to fray. His wrists were raw, and the rough stone left several nicks from when Ronan tried to adjust the angle at which it cut through his bindings. When he whistled to his men again, he did so to learn if they were together or in separate cells. He grinned to learn that they were in pairs. Most warriors could communicate through birdcalls and whistles, but their meanings were unique to each clan. It kept their messages secret even when surrounded by the enemy. The pairs would sit back-to-back and loosen each other's ropes. He suspected they were already free of them while he had to work on his alone. But he much preferred solitude if it meant Abigail was out of the cell.

It surprised him when a guard with a waterskin

returned just before evening. He entered with three men to protect him. He laughed at the man, mocking him for not coming in alone if Ronan was still restrained. But he knew his men did the same when they entered any prisoner's cell, always expecting a hidden weapon or the captive finding a way out of his bindings. When they stripped him of his weapons earlier, they found those sheathed in his boots, in his wrist bracers, and the three hanging at his waist. They even found the one strapped to his thigh, but they hadn't lifted his plaid high enough to see the two sheathed beneath his belt and the wool. Nor had they found the *sgian dubh* sheathed at the small of his back. That blade was his sharpest, but it was also the shortest, no longer than the width of his belt.

He wouldn't make a move against his captors until he learned where Abigail was and whether his men still carried any of their dirks. He complied when the man put the waterskin to his mouth and tipped it to drink. Ronan expected any number of liquids, but he hadn't expected fresh water. He drank his fill, turning his head before he drank enough to make himself ill. The guard grunted before putting the stopper in it and tossing it beside Ronan. He supposed it was the only concession to his status. He doubted his men received the same mercy. The four MacLeod men retreated from Ronan's cell in silence. As desperate as Ronan was to learn about Abigail, he would wait until the guards genuinely believed he'd accepted his captivity. They would give him information to mock his loss of freedom and inability to save her. But it would be knowledge, nonetheless.

Ronan's mouth felt parched despite struggling with the waterskin as the guards watched him the previous night. He hadn't touched it, wanting it to last until the next day, but the guards returned to harass him. He had to continue pretending that his hands weren't free, leaning sideways to pull the stopper out with his teeth then lift it with his lips sealed around it. But he drank the rest of the water without dribbling any. The guards entered his cell and retrieved the waterskin, making certain he'd drained it. Leaving him throughout most of the next day without water was now their form of torture. They'd tried to raise his hope only to slash it away, but since Ronan hadn't bothered to hope for food or water, there was no disappointment.

His mouth could no longer produce saliva, and his lips were chapped and cracked. His belly once again filled the cell with echoing grumbles. However, despite his discomfort, he could hear the low voices of his men talking to one another. It reassured him that they hadn't sapped the last of their strength. When guards arrived that day, he suspected it was already late afternoon, and his second night in the cell approached. He let his head loll to the side, his eyes half shut.

"Nae so mighty now," one guard scoffed as he kicked Ronan's boot. It forced the man close enough to Ronan that he could have pounced, once more prepared to lunge. But he reminded himself that he wouldn't enact any plan to escape until he knew about Abigail.

"Ma wife?" Ronan didn't have to pretend to make his voice croak.

"The daft bitch nearly drove the laird mad last night. Yer cock in her mouth must be the only thing that keeps her quiet."

Ronan held his breath, keeping himself from

snarling as the man's vulgar reference to Abigail. He shifted his gaze when another man spoke.

"Haughty wench, crowing on aboot how her bluidy brother will come to yer rescue, how the king will be angry. Nay one's coming to get any of ye lot." The man's laughter reverberated against the walls, and the others soon joined in. "She's lucky all the laird did was lock her in her chamber today. Softer prison than ye have, but a cell all the same."

Ronan expected taunting and more crude comments, but he'd gained the information he needed. If Cormag or Gordon had abused her, it would have been the first thing the men would have crowed about, knowing it would drive him mad. He was confident Abigail drove home the significance of her relationship to Kieran and her time as a lady-in-waiting. He prayed it bought her peace for the time being. He relaxed his tense muscles as his heart slowed. He was still on guard, but much of his anxiety eased.

"She just better keep her gob shut at the evening meal, or Gordon's likely to shut her up the same way ye do," another guard mused. Ronan's clenched his jaw, forcing himself to not take the bait, even if it enraged him to think of Gordon forcing himself on Abigail. He wished for at least the hundredth time that she still had her longer dirk on hand. When the man's comments didn't get a rise out of Ronan, the four MacLeods trailed out of the cell, slamming the door extra hard, reminding Ronan of exactly where he languished.

TWENTY-FOUR

$\mathbf{A}$bigail glanced at the sun, knowing she'd sat in the window embrasure for at least four hours. They had given her a tray for her morning and midday meal. She suspected neither Cormag nor Gordon wanted to hear from her, and she assumed Ronan had been right about Cecily. She'd turned her nose up at Abigail throughout the previous evening's meal. She appeared as pretentious as Ronan described, happy to have another lady at her table and to claim she'd rescued Abigail. But Cecily had looked down her nose at Abigail and had no desire to engage her in conversation. For her own part, Abigail didn't miss Cecily's company, much preferring to be alone in the chamber.

As Abigail sat and looked out of the window, she watched the guards move along the battlements. She'd counted the sentries and estimated the timeframes when they switched positions. She strained to make out any distinguishable features or appearance among the men; she easily recognized the captain of the guard. He was an ox who barreled along the wall walk. Even from across the bailey and at her elevation, Abigail could tell the captain barked orders.

When he turned his back, none of the men jumped to follow his command.

Abigail observed the clan members moving around the bailey. She spied the blacksmith's workshop, the laundresses, a small fruit tree grove, and several storage buildings. The only things that interested her were the barracks and armory, but they were outside her line of vision. She could only guess how many warriors were at Dunvegan, even after she counted how many stood watch throughout the day and tried to count the men training in the lists between the inner wall and outer barmekin.

With nothing else to do, Abigail lay down to rest, soon falling asleep. Her strength was still diminished from the ordeal of the previous day. The fear during the attack, the physical strain of being in the water, and then the anxiety of waiting for Ronan to wake exhausted her. She'd turned away the porridge and eggs that morning, trusting neither offering. She'd settled for bread and butter with a chunk of cheese and an apple. When the midday tray arrived, she picked at it, only trusting the neeps and tatties. She didn't care for turnips, usually skipping the neeps. But she was ravenous, so she ate them along with the potatoes. She devoured her second serving of bread and butter. She longed to try the apricot tart, but she didn't trust it. She sipped at the watered ale, taking at least two hours to finish a single mug. She looked forward to the evening meal only if she sat at the dais and watched the servants offer Cormag and Gordon the same dishes before her. She would suffer their company for a hearty meal.

She woke with a start as the same maid from the day before shook her shoulder to rouse her. She sat up so quickly that she nearly bumped her head against the maid's. The woman jumped back as though scalded, which was fine with Abigail. Distance between them meant the woman couldn't stab her. The maid watched her through squinted eyes, suspicious of Abigail even though she was still groggy.

"Evening meal," the maid mumbled.

"I'll just use the pot," Abigail said as she jutted her chin toward the screen that hid the chamber pot. She would use it as an excuse to put her knife back in her boot. Her shoes were dry now, but no one had returned her kirtle to her. She hoped it was being laundered, but it wouldn't surprise her if they never returned it. Borrowing clothes from Cecily would keep her indebted to the woman. She would wear her boots in silent rebellion and because they fit better and hid her *sgian dubh* within easier reach than the top of her stocking. Abigail rose from the bed, turning back to straighten the sheets and retrieve the knife from beneath her pillow. She palmed the blade along her leg as she moved behind the screen.

Abigail knew using the chamber pot forced the maid to retrieve it rather than lead her out of the chamber. While the maid turned her nose up at the task, it gave Abigail time to grab her boots and slip the blade into its sheath. She laced and tied her boots with no one watching. When she was ready, she knocked on the door, and a pair of guards escorted her belowstairs. She maintained the same air of cool superiority that she'd shown the night before when she approached the dais. She didn't wait for an invitation to sit at the table, taking the same seat she'd been offered the night prior. She pulled her chair close to the table and folded her hands in her lap. Her right leg crossed over her left in a most unlady-like manner in order to bring her knife within easy reach. Fortunately, the table covering hung to the floor on the other side, keeping her posture hidden from the rest of the diners.

"No blathering on this eve?" Gordon asked as he looked past his brother and Cecily. Abigail offered one of her shrugs that seemed to irritate Cormag.

"There's no one I wish to talk to."

"I prefer your silence," Cormag snapped before taking a long sip from his chalice. Abigail offered him the practiced smile she'd used countless times at court, but her eyes spoke a different tale. They challenged Cormag, her loathing clear. She watched as the servants placed food in Cormag and Cecily's trencher first before moving to Gordon's then hers. She watched as the three ate each item before she tasted hers. She wouldn't put it past them to poison a dish and know not to eat it, while duping her into thinking it was safe. Like the night before, she avoided the wine that already sat in her chalice. Unwilling to drink it, she never received a drink from the same pitcher that refilled the others' chalices. Cormag smirked, just as he had the night before. "Either Kieran or Ronan advised you."

"Or I ken how to survive living alongside King Robert and Queen Elizabeth." Abigail glanced at Cecily. "I wonder if you found your time as a lady-in-waiting as filled with intrigue as I did." Cecily turned a disdainful look at Abigail.

"It was sophisticated and entertaining," Cecily said archly. Abigail didn't care how the woman responded. She'd made her point to the laird and his brother. She reminded them of her connection to the royal couple and that she'd survived living at the royal court, a place where poison wasn't foreign. "Your sister was the most entertaining part."

Abigail turned to look at Cecily squarely, running her eyes over the woman's appearance, sniffing much as she had the day before. "Madeline has a way with words. I have never known her to be wrong." Abigail wouldn't defend her sister, trying to persuade them that the former lady-in-waiting turned postulant cum Lady Grant-to-be had reformed her vicious tongue. Instead, she would use that reputation to her advantage. "People say she and I are much alike."

Abigail watched as Cecily retreated, both from the conversation and into her chair. The woman leaned back, abandoning the food before her. Abigail thought Cecily was prudent not to test her. But it left Cormag with an unobstructed view. He leered at her and licked his lips. She offered him a sardonic gaze before glancing at Cecily and cocking an eyebrow. It wasn't difficult to see there was no affection between the couple, but she suspected Cecily was possessive and territorial about her husband. Either he conducted his affairs discreetly or he didn't dare to have any. Either way, Abigail was confident he wouldn't make advances while Cecily was nearby.

"Three sennights should be an appropriate length of mourning." Gordon shifted the conversation to him. "Convenient as that is how long it takes to post the banns."

"You think to force me to marry you." Abigail's disgust rang in her tone. "Kieran will think it odd that I should remarry so soon considering he knows my feelings aboot marriage and my husband." She was careful not to admit how much Ronan meant to her. She knew the brothers would use it as leverage against her when the threats of torture came next.

"As a widow, you'll be expected to remarry. It doesn't take long to rip each finger from a mon's hand or to stretch his limbs so far that they tear from his body." Gordon was entirely predictable. "Mayhap you will watch, so you understand the type of mon you're marrying."

"No priest in Scotland will marry an unwilling woman. Kill Ronan, and there is naught but a guaranteed war. Since the Lord of the Isles favors my

213

husband over you, and Kieran would undoubtedly make me a widow a second time, I wouldn't do that." Abigail turned her mouth down in a mocking frown. She broke with decorum and placed her elbow on the table and leaned her chin against her palm as though she were settling in to gossip with Cormag. "Did you forget that John of Islay wanted to be called the King of the Isles? I mean, he and the Mac-Donalds now control most of the Hebrides."

Abigail leaned further forward and lowered her voice conspiratorially, letting go of her ladylike tones. "Dinna tell, but I think King Robert will give Islay whatever he wants if the mon will leave the Bruce alone. So, when the MacDonalds of Sleat march alongside the MacKinnons, I bet ye'll spot the royal livery in there too. Imagine that. Do ye have enough birlinns to get yer entire clan to Harris?"

"Dunvegan is impregnable, well you know it," Gordon snarled.

"Only if ye wave yer wee Fairy Flag," Abigail mocked. She watched as Gordon and Cormag's expressions grew guarded. While Abigail didn't believe the folklore, it was clear the men did. Or at the least, their expressions gave away the existence of the fabled banner. Abigail turned back to her food, biting into a dried apricot. If she couldn't have the tart, she could at least have a piece of the fruit. Neither Cecily nor the men spoke to her again. Abigail preferred they ignore her. It meant she'd be left alone that night, which was perfect.

TWENTY-FIVE

A bigail listened at her door until the keep beyond her chamber grew silent. She'd wasted no time when she returned from the evening meal and ran her hands over all the walls, sweeping them high and low until she found what she searched for. She wiggled the loose brick and pressed down, finding the inconspicuous door that led into the hidden tunnels. Cormag was a few years older than Kieran, but Donovan had been close to her own age. When she'd visited as a child, Donovan bragged about how much more impressive Dunvegan was than Stornoway. Proud of their home, Abigail and Madeline argued with their distant cousin. In an attempt to prove his claim, Donovan not only admitted to the sisters that secret passageways existed, he'd also shown them parts of it.

Abigail hadn't remembered in time to tell Ronan, but she knew the tunnels led throughout the keep. At least one tunnel led down to the dungeon, one to the laird's chamber, and one to the laird's solar. She recalled Donovan leading them through a tunnel from the laird's solar to the sea gate while the tide was low. She'd seen the metal gate that blocked the archway that led into the underbelly of part of the castle. She closed her eyes, trying to picture the docks they'd arrived at the day before. She recalled the docks were adjacent to an outcropping of boulders that hid the sea gate. When the tide was high, it submerged most of the gate.

As she remembered her childhood tour, she visualized the cavernous outlet, seeing a wooden door to the back of the dark space. She pictured crossing the bailey from the postern gate at the top of the path from the docks, then the external door they'd passed through before she and Ronan were dumped into their cell. The door they'd used to lead her up a flight of stairs and into the Great Hall took her to the midpoint of the ground floor. The laird's solar wasn't far from where she entered the gathering hall.

When Donovan led them through the tunnels to the sea gate, they'd entered close to a wood door in the back of the cave. She suspected that was the door that led to the dungeon. She knew she needed to do two things: get the dungeon door open and get the sea gate open. How she would accomplish that, she wasn't certain. She'd seen where the dungeon guard hid the keyring. There'd been more keys than cell doors, so one likely led to the bailey door, one to the cave door, and one to the door within the keep. If she could get to that ring, she could free Ronan and their men, then get them into the cave. But she didn't know where the key to the subterranean gate was, and she couldn't guarantee it would be on the dungeon keyring. She would need to ensure she could get the gate open before she tried to rescue Ronan.

Now that the keep settled for the night, she opened the secret hatch and felt around. But she didn't find a torch, making her groan. She pulled a fresh log from the pile and lit the end, hoping it would remain lit and that it wouldn't burn too quickly. She felt along the walls inside the tunnel until she found the latch that would release the door and gain her reentry to her chamber. She prayed the MacLeods left her alone like they had the night before. She and her aspirations of freedom would be doomed if anyone discovered she left her chamber, especially if they realized she'd done it via the secret tunnels. She pulled the door shut, crossing her fingers that the latch she found worked once she was sealed into the dark passageway.

Holding the torch in front of her, Abigail held her skirts above her ankles and eased her way along the pitch-black corridor. She moved silently, uncertain how sound might carry from within the tunnels. She followed it as it turned and sloped downward. At the bottom, she considered where the laird's chamber likely was, since she was sure she was on the second floor. She'd spied his door when she passed along the second-floor landing. She turned left and glided along until she heard muffled sounds. She leaned the side of her face against the wall and listened. It didn't take much to deduce she heard a man and a woman coupling. The female moans didn't sound as if they would come from Cecily. Either she'd found Gordon's chamber, or Cormag did have affairs. Abigail ran her hand along the wall until she found a latch. She did nothing to it, instead turning to face the other wall. She kept her hand at the same height as where she found the first latch and soon discovered a second. Listening at that wall only brought snores to her ear.

Abigail turned back the way she came and followed the passageway as it led her down another floor. She spied light flickering through the wall. She crept until she could find the crack where the light shone through. She peered through it, finding both Cormag and Gordon in the chamber. She drew back, trying to figure out who she'd heard the floor above. Could the feminine moans have been from Cecily? Did she have a lover? Who was the person snoring?

"Will you send a missive to Lewis?"

"At some point, but not yet."

Abigail listened to Gordon's question and Cormag's answer. The laird's response didn't surprise her. He had learned nothing from her, and he likely had learned nothing from Ronan. They were still useful. He wouldn't free them or kill them yet. She put her ear to the crack rather than her eye as the men continued to talk.

"How did he seem when you went down there?" Cormag asked Gordon.

"I didn't go. I remained outside his cell, listening. He asked aboot his wife, but that's it. He didn't respond to aught the men said, nor did he ask for aught. He didn't even make any threats. Brandon said he whistled to his men a few times, but he didn't know what they meant. Each of the men answered, though. I suppose he was checking to see who survived."

"Where are the men you gathered from the beach?" Cormag's question made Abigail's brow furrow. She'd been there an entire day. If there had been other survivors, she didn't understand why they hadn't taken them to the dungeon too.

"Still in the storage building. I don't want the bastard kenning he only lost two men. A few are injured, but none mortally."

"Fine," Cormag responded. "I'm to bed."

"What aboot Lady Abigail?"

"One meal a day is all I can manage without wrapping my hands around her throat."

"That's not what I meant, Cor."

"I ken. She just annoys me." When Cormag paused, Abigail shifted to look through the crack.

She watched Cormag run his hand over his face before gulping what she assumed was whisky. "Keep her in her chamber during the day, mayhap even take her to see her husband after you've roughed him up. But I'm warning you, Gordy, stay away from her. She's not far off from what will happen if she's harmed. Donovan may have predicted that MacKinnon would return to Dun Ringill this sennight, but none of us kenned he married the chit or that she'd be aboard. She complicates everything. Killing him would be easy. But if she dies, she brings a giant's helping of trouble to us."

"But the banshee killed Don."

"I ken that as well as you. He was our baby brother, but you both sailed out to fight. I never wished him dead, and I suffer my own grief for our loss. But he underestimated a woman who'd survived nearly a half hour in frigid water. From how you described her, he should have known she wasn't weak. If she'd looked half-dead, her attack might have been a surprise. But neither she nor MacKinnon were going to go with you willingly. They would have perished together. Punishing her, making her beg for her life is what I want more than aught—more than the MacKinnon—but it doesn't serve our purpose. At least not yet."

"Fine." Abigail could hear the disagreement in Gordon's tone, but he didn't argue with his brother. She watched the men rise from their chairs. Cormag used the poker to spread the logs in the fireplace so the flames would die. The brothers crossed the chamber together. Then Abigail heard the door close. She turned and rested her back against the wall beside the crevice. She would search the solar, but she would wait to ensure neither man returned.

Abigail leaned against the wall for what she figured was nearly ten minutes before she eased the hidden door open. She'd found a sconce in the tunnel and left her torch there, using the dying fire to illuminate the solar. She hurried to the massive desk that sat at the far end of the chamber, positioned so that Cormag's back would be to the wall across from the secret entrance. She grinned when she discovered Cormag locked none of the drawers. She pulled one after another open, withdrawing parchments, some folded and some rolled. She skimmed each of them, finding nothing she considered useful. She was careful to return everything exactly how she found it. She surveyed the books along the wall beside the door leading to the main floor. A flash of memory returned to her as she recalled Donovan leading them into the tunnels on the other side of the chamber from where Abigail entered that night. Abigail hurried to retrieve her torch before she searched near the bookshelf for the other door. It popped open with a creak, making Abigail wince. Once more holding her torch out before her, she slipped through the darkness.

TWENTY-SIX

R onan sighed as he waited out yet another night in his cell. He would try to never reveal to Abigail that this wasn't his first stay in a dungeon. He knew it would only upset her, and it was likely to reignite feuds when she demanded vengeance. His lips twitched as he thought about his petite bride. He thought back to how he'd assumed she wasn't talkative and how that was the type of woman he wished to make his wife. He recalled how stricken she'd looked the morning she ran into his chest as she left the garden, how ashamed she'd been as she confessed her shortcomings. But he also remembered their first burst of passion and how he'd never wanted a woman more before that day.

His rod twitched as he thought about Abigail's arms wrapped around him as they lay together in bed during their stay at Stornoway, the feel of her hand wrapped around his length as she stroked him before she took him into her mouth or into her sheath. He leaned against the wall with his eyes closed as he watched one erotic scene after another play behind his lids. Some were memories and some were fantasies, but they all involved a woman with raven hair and startling green-blue eyes. With nothing else to do, Ronan reached beneath his plaid to ease the ache. He didn't doubt Abigail thought of him, and he knew she could find her own pleasure after she'd taught him multiple ways to pleasure her with his hands. He wondered if she had touched herself while they were apart. He grinned and shook his head as he continued to stroke his length. His wife was lusty, but he doubted she'd agree that their situation could involve any pleasure. But Ronan figured it passed the time.

He stifled his groan just as a whistle drifted to him. He wasn't sure he'd even heard it, but rather imagined it. It was the call he'd taught Abigail in case she ever became separated from him or their men. He rose and crossed the cell, his hands hidden behind his back but holding a dirk in case it was a trick. When he heard it a second time, he was certain it was Abigail. He put his face to the bars in the rectangular opening and whistled back. Once he did, a few more whistles sounded. He couldn't understand how Abigail was within the dungeons without guards dragging her, or how she could be at the opposite end from where they'd entered and where they'd taken her.

Silence filled the air, and Ronan wondered if someone pretended to be Abigail to fool him. As he backed away from the door slim fingers, one adorned with an emerald ring, slipped between the bars. The top of a dark-haired head and a pair of bright greenish blue eyes appeared. Ronan reached for Abigail's hand, crushing her fingers in his eagerness to touch her. He knew she stood on her toes when the rest of her face appeared. She glanced away from him and toward where the guards sat together. They could both hear the low rumble of the men's voices.

"I'm all right. Are ye?"

Ronan had never heard a more welcome sound

than Abigail's whisper. "Aye. They never searched me for more weapons, so I still have three. I got ma hands free, but they dinna ken. I suspect the others did too, but they've kept it hidden. What're ye doing here, Abby?"

"Secret tunnels."

"That's how. I asked what," Ronan hissed.

"Making sure ye're still alive. Now I ken how to get into the dungeon from within the keep. I believe there's a way out of the dungeon and into the cave beneath the keep. There's a sea gate there."

"Nay more exploring, Abby. Ye're likely to get caught. Please."

"I've found all I dare for tonight."

"Nae just tonight." Ronan didn't miss how Abigail hedged.

"Unless they chain me in here or in ma chamber, I will nae give up searching for a way to get ye out."

"Abby, if ye can get away, then get away. Dinna wait for me. Just go while ye can."

"Daft mon," Abigail scoffed in a whisper.

"Nay, Abby. Dinna perish alongside me."

"I heard Cormag and Gordon in the laird's solar. Neither of them is going to do aught to either of us. They ken harming me isnae worth the consequences. By extension, they ken that means ye too. The only danger we're in is if they receive a ransom but dinna let us go. They'll likely kill ye then." Abigail kept Gordon's threat of marrying her to herself. It wouldn't do either of them any good to both be upset, and Abigail believed, at that point, it was still a hollow threat.

"Go back now, Abby, before the guards find ye. I canna protect ye behind a locked door. They willna have the restraint Cormag or Gordon have if they catch ye. Please," Ronan begged.

"I ken. Do ye swear ye're all right?"

"Aye. Hungry and filthy, but hale. I love ye, Abigail."

"I love ye, Ronan." Abigail strained to rest her chin on the opening. Ronan leaned forward, but it was too wide from their lips to meet. But they squeezed one another's fingers before Abigail slipped back into the darkness. Ronan listened, hearing Abigail's muffled whistle, letting him know she'd found her way out.

Abigail spent her second and third full days at Dunvegan with little more to do than pace in her chamber. After her explorations during her second night at the keep, she barely made it into her bed before the door opened. She kept her lids lowered, but she watched Gordon enter her chamber. She clasped the handle of her dirk beneath the pillow, but he did nothing more than look at her. She feared Gordon suspected her of traipsing through the tunnels, so she didn't dare go exploring the third night of her captivity. While no one entered her chamber that night, she heard voices outside her door more than once.

But on the fourth night, Abigail was resolved to wait no longer than it took for the keep to grow quiet. She slipped into the tunnels, more confident now than the first time. She hurried to the laird's solar, but there was no one inside. The tunnels didn't go around the chamber, so she had no choice but to enter the room and exit through the other hidden door. She slipped into the dungeon, but as much as she wanted to see Ronan again, she only whistled to let him know she was still safe. She was determined to discover the cave. Once she left the door to the dungeon, she retraced her steps until she came to a fork in the tunnel. She turned down the one she hadn't explored.

The decline was much steeper than any Abigail had traversed yet, but it was still familiar to her. She remembered Donovan grunting in annoyance when both Abigail and Madeline grabbed his shoulders to keep from slipping. Abigail trailed her hand along the wall to brace herself. She was still a dozen feet from the end when she heard the lapping waves and barking seals. She grinned as she recalled the stories about selkies her father used to tell. He'd teased Abigail and Madeline that they might each be one with their dark hair. He would ask if they'd cast a spell over him, shedding their seal skins to come live amongst humans as his daughters. Abigail's heart pinched as the memory became stronger as she approached the cave.

Abigail held her torch down and away from her as she eased her way to the opening. She heard no voices, nor any movement, but she didn't know if the clan posted guards at the gate at night. If anyone breached the gate, they could overrun the keep. With a deep breath, she risked her life yet again and stepped into the cave. Unlike when she was a child, there were crates and barrels stacked beside the walls. She lifted her torch, sweeping her arm back and forth as she looked for a key that would open the gate. She didn't spy one, and she nearly wet herself when she heard the distinct splash of oars just outside the gate.

"Who's there?" A deep voice barked. Abigail cursed to herself, realizing that the goods lining the walls were leaving the keep, not arriving. She gathered her skirts and turned back the way she came. She heard the same voice again. "I saw light, but where are the men to open the gate if they're in there?"

Abigail didn't wait to offer an answer or to discover what the men would do if they found her. She stomped out the flame, even spitting on it, before she traversed the black corridors back to her chamber. She heard no one behind her, but she couldn't be certain they didn't move silently. She tossed the log into the fireplace and kicked off her boots as she tugged at the kirtle laces she'd kept loose. She slipped into bed, her heart thumping as she waited for men to burst into her chamber. She stared at the ceiling, convinced men would drag her from the bed and dump her before Cormag or Gordon. Eventually, she relaxed and drifted off to sleep.

Discussion at the evening meal about the next night warned Abigail that shipments were coming and going from the keep. While no one said that the sea gate was where the loading and unloading would happen, Abigail opted not to test her luck again. For that night and the next, she settled for checking on Ronan from afar, then returning to her chamber. Her sleep was restless each night, growing more and more worried about Ronan and the other men suffering in the dungeon. Unable to withstand the need to see and touch Ronan, she slipped back into the dungeon the seventh night they were at Dunvegan. After a sennight in the cell, Ronan's eyes were sunken, and his cheeks were hollow.

"Ronan, ye canna stay down here much longer. We must get ye out. I must," Abigail whispered.

"Get yerself out, Abby. Get free of here and send someone for me, but dinna wait for me."

"I'm nae leaving ye behind," Abigail refused.

"Ye're more likely to die trying to free me."

"Then what? Roam an island I dinna ken? I

226

dinna ken how to get to Dun Ringill. It's more likely someone else will capture me before I can send men to rescue ye. I amnae leaving this hellhole without ye."

"Abby—"

"Nay," Abigail snapped. She softened her tone. "I'll only go if I'm certain I can get ye help. I willna abandon ye. I'd rather be in that cell with ye than in that bluidy chamber alone. Tell me the truth, are they torturing ye? Ye tell me ye're all right, but that isnae what yer face tells me."

"I havenae seen Gordon since they tossed us in here. Cormag hasnae been once. The guards kick me once in a while, but I dinna fight back. It's still nae the right time for them to ken I can. It's too dark in here for them to notice ma hands are free, and it's nae as if they change the chamber pot."

"That first night I spied on them, I heard Gordon say that more of yer men are in the storage buildings in the bailey. They're the ones who made it ashore. It sounded like they rounded up the survivors and stuck them in there, so ye wouldnae ken that ye only lost two men."

"Only two?"

"That's what they said."

"I still didna travel with enough men. Even with the extra guards that came to Lewis with me after ma last trip home, there werenae enough to protect ye."

"Dinna say that, Ronan. I'm in better shape than ye. Ye and yer men kept the fight off the boat. I would have surely died if any of them reached me. Ye protected me." Abigail's adamance was clear despite her whisper. "Ronan, I'm scared for ye. The longer ye're down here…"

"Shh, Abby. I ken. I wish I could make this all go away. Just ken that I, and the others down here, are still alive. Hungry, but alive. Abigail, I love ye."

"I love ye just as much, Ronan." Tears pricked at the back of Abigail's eyelids. Ronan only used her full name when he wanted her to understand how serious he was. Each time he said it, she feared it was the last time she would hear it.

"Ye must go."

"I ken. I dinna want to, but I ken. I love ye." Abigail strained even more than the last time she'd kissed Ronan through the bars. This time their lips brushed, and Abigail couldn't stop her whimper.

"Wheest, Abby. We'll be gone from here soon enough, and then ye can scrub ma back as I wash yer hair. Then I'll spend a moon making love to ye before we leave our chamber."

"Two moons," Abigail countered with a weak smile. They squeezed each other's fingers before Abigail slipped back into the darkness, a soft whistle her goodbye.

TWENTY-SEVEN

Abigail's seventh full day at Dunvegan passed, and she was ready to climb the walls. She'd continued to watch the guards on the wall and the people moving about the bailey. She knew people's daily routines, and she could even predict which dishes would be served at the evening meal. But she couldn't escape the keep, and she couldn't free Ronan.

Cormag allowed her to go outside for an hour that day. Cecily demanded she only be allowed in the grove, and Gordon insisted four guards trail her. After watching her attack Donovan without a flinch, he was the least trusting. What none of them seemed to realize was letting her outside when most were eating their midday meal meant she could watch food being delivered to a storage building. Abigail realized that her hour-long reprieve coincided with when the MacKinnon warriors could leave their prison and sit outside. The moment she saw them, she whistled. One of her guards shoved her away, but it wasn't before she heard a MacKinnon respond.

She slipped into the dungeon that night, relaying her observations to Ronan. She still couldn't believe how she hadn't been discovered. When she pointed that out to Ronan, he mused that it spoke to the quality of men Cormag led. Abigail had to agree, remembering how men reacted to the captain of the guard. During her time outside, she heard the guardsmen on the battlements and clearly saw their expressions. She thought it childish how many sneered and mocked the captain when he turned his back, but it showed their sentiments about the man. She noticed Gordon elicited more respect from the men, and that only frustrated her. It was obvious they were loyal to the middle brother and, Abigail could only assume, to their laird. But she wondered if they were as lazy as the men assigned to the dungeon. When she spoke her thoughts aloud, Ronan grinned and pointed out the men on dungeon duty were likely assigned there for a reason.

After nearly being caught in the cave, Abigail had halted her midnight exploration, hoping no one had grown suspicious about the unexpected light. She knew they kept her chamber door locked, and at least two guards stood in the passageway throughout the night. From the grove, she saw out the postern gate when it opened. The MacLeods had a large fleet of birlinns; at least twenty were within sight that day. Abigail gazed at them, watching the fishermen unloading their catches as they returned at midday. Then she watched them sail away, wishing she and Ronan were aboard. The glimpse of freedom only increased her anxiety as she thought about Ronan locked in his cell.

Ronan promised her during each visit that he was well and that he could manage if she were safe. As the days dragged on, Abigail lost her appetite for everything and could only eat enough to survive. Her fear of being poisoned lessened, but it didn't disappear. She felt ill thinking about food when she knew Ronan had nearly none. She smuggled food from her morning and midday trays down to the men, dropping bread, fruit, and cheese into the cells.

When a week of captivity went by, Abigail could no longer wait. She was determined to free Ronan or die trying. While conversing in a whisper, they had a heated disagreement about what Abigail should do. She suggested she should free Ronan and his men, so they could overpower the dungeon guards. They could agree on that, but where their thoughts differed was how to escape while leaving none of his men behind.

Ronan knew neither he nor any of the men in the dungeon could get to those locked in the storage building without being seen. There was no way for Abigail to do it, since Cormag had only just allowed her outside that day. She suggested that she sneak across the bailey and release them at night, but Ronan refused to entertain the risk. None of the MacKinnons had swords, and Abigail knew she couldn't gather them from the armory unseen. She suggested freeing Ronan and taking him through the tunnels, so he could see the inner bowels of the keep and the cave with the sea gate.

"And how will ye get the keys to do that?" Ronan hissed.

"I can try the tip of ma dirk."

"And when it scrapes the metal, ye'll bring the entire guard down on ye. Cormag's good intentions will go to hell. Right now, ye are free to gather information. If he locks ye in yer chamber or down here, then it really will be impossible to escape. I dinna want ye down here, Abby. I can bear it, but it's cold and disgusting. Ye'll fall ill."

"And why are ye so certain ye'll survive? Because ye're bigger than me?"

"Because I've done it before," Ronan snapped. He flinched at Abigail's gasp. He hadn't intended to reveal that, but his constant fear for Abigail frayed his patience. He feared her being caught and thrown into a cell, perhaps with him, but probably without. He worried every moment that he didn't know where she was, fearing what the MacLeods might do to her. He lived with a constant headache and stomachache from too little food and water. His clothes were always damp, and the stench made him want to heave any time he was awake.

"When?" Abigail's voice was more a puff of air than a sound.

"I spent time in the MacNeacails' dungeon when I rode out on ma first sortie. I didna pay enough attention, and I learned ma lesson for it. I spent nearly three sennights there before they sent a ransom to ma father. He thought I was dead. I found maself in the MacNeills' dungeon just before ma father died. I led a raid to retake cattle they stole. I was the decoy while ma men herded them toward our land. I was too far behind them as I raced toward our border. They captured me before I crossed over to MacKinnon territory. It wasna long after that the MacNeills attacked ma mother and ma father rode out instead."

"Ronan, do ye blame yerself?" Abigail could hear the anguish in Ronan's voice.

"He would be alive if I hadnae failed to teach the bastards a lesson. Instead, they held me captive, then left ma mother to die alone as she tried to find her way home. He couldnae trust me to do the job right, so he went himself."

"Dear God, Ronan. That's why ye're truly afraid to fail."

"Aye. And if I agree with any of yer suggestions, I'll be a widower *and* an orphan. I willna agree to aught that risks yer life. Remain here, unmolested and safe, Abby."

Abigail remained quiet, shocked at what Ronan revealed. She suspected he meant to keep his previous captures a secret, and she was certain he hadn't intended to tell her about his parents while they stood together in a dungeon. She didn't doubt he would have shared their fates, but they were hardly in the right place for such a grief-laden story.

"Abby, I didna mean to tell ye that," Ronan confessed.

"I ken, *mo chridhe*. I ken. But ye having experience in a dungeon doesnae make me any less scared for ye being in this one. Mayhap ye ken what to expect, but that doesnae mean I do. I want ma husband to hold me in his arms far, far away from here." Abigail called Ronan "my heart" and meant it. She didn't think it could beat without Ronan.

"Abby, I will. As soon as I can. Our clan kens by now that something happened. Men have likely sailed to Stornoway, and Kieran will ken now too. They'll search Skye and the coasts of Lewis and Harris. I ken ye hate being in yer chamber all day, but ye'll see when yer clan or mine arrives. Even if Cormag and Gordon lie, ye'll be able to call down from yer chamber."

"True." Abigail nodded, knowing the value of what Ronan said, but she still wanted a way to free him rather than waiting with uncertainty.

"I have ma hands free, so ma arms arenae sore any longer. If I must defend maself, I can. But I willna let the guards ken until I'm certain I can get ye and ma men free from here without risking yer life or theirs." Ronan squeezed Abigail's fingers through the bars in the door "Ye've been down here longer than usual, Abby. I dinna want ye to, but ye need to go."

"I ken. I love ye."

"I love ye." Ronan and Abigail pressed their lips together before Abigail darted toward the door, hearing a guard's boots approaching. She waited in the dark, but no one called out. She waited until the boots retreated before letting herself out. She moved along the tunnel, intending to return to her chamber, but when she reached the floor with the laird's chamber, she paused. She'd followed Cormag and Cecily up the stairs that evening, and she'd seen which doors they entered. Abigail's mouth nearly dropped open when she realized the sounds she'd heard her first night came from Cecily's chamber. It confirmed the woman had a lover, but Abigail had no idea who. She still didn't know who she heard snoring since Gordon was unmarried. She crept along the passageway until she came to the chamber with the unknown occupant. She listened against the wall, once more hearing light snores.

Abigail felt around for the hidden latch and pressed down with just enough pressure to make it click. She kept the lever down but waited for someone to discover her. When nothing happened, she eased the door open an inch. There was still no movement, and the only sounds were snores. With her heart pounding in her ears, Abigail pushed the door open enough to look inside. She spied an old woman sleeping in the bed, her white hair pulled back in a long braid.

Edina. I didna ken Cormag and Gordon's mother was still alive. She was a kind woman. I wonder if she still makes the meat pies she used to give us. Is she too frail to join the evening meal? Why havenae I seen her?

Abigail shifted her weight, accidentally pushing the door open wider. It creaked, and Abigail froze. Her eyes widened as the woman sat up in bed and looked in her direction. Abigail doubted Edina could see her behind the door and in the dark. She didn't dare move.

"Who's there?" The reedy voice shook, and Abigail felt guilty for terrifying the woman. "Have ye come to take me to our Lord?"

Abigail held her breath. She didn't want the woman to think an assassin lurked in the tunnel. She wanted to groan when Edina pushed back the covers. She made to pull the door shut, but Edina's next words stopped her. To hide her torch flame, she slipped it into the sconce beside the door.

"Dinna go. I'm ready to join ma Henry. He's been gone too long. If ye be an angel or a devil, I dinna care. I would be with ma Henry again." Edina swung her legs over the edge of the bed and stood. She wobbled as she reached for a plaid folded at the foot of the bed. "Ma weans dinna need me anymore. They dinna even care aboot me. I'm ready."

Abigail's heart broke as she listened to the old woman wish to reunite with her long-dead husband. But as she thought about it, it struck Abigail as odd that Edina appeared so aged. Cormag was older than Kieran, but she didn't expect Edina to look so much older than her own mother Adeline had when she passed.

"Annalily? Lass, I ken that's ye playing in those tunnels again. Yer da will skelp ye if he learns ye've been exploring back there again. Ye ken he doesnae want ye getting lost."

Abigail's brow furrowed as she recognized the name of the youngest MacLeod child. The girl had been younger than Abigail and died when sickness swept through the Skye branch. The girl had been dead for nearly twenty years, yet Edina spoke as though she were still alive.

Her mind's gone. Mayhap that's why I havenae seen her. Do they keep her locked away?

Abigail watched as Edina hobbled toward her. When the older woman stumbled, Abigail didn't hesitate to slip past the door and catch Edina. She chided herself the moment she touched the crepey skin of the older woman's hands. If Edina told anyone that she'd had a dark-haired woman visit her in the middle of the night, they would know Abigail used the tunnels.

"That's a sweet, lass. Annalily, fetch me ma shawl."

Abigail didn't know what to do. Keeping her voice to a whisper, she said, "Mama, ye already have yer plaid aboot yer shoulders." Abigail pulled the woolen blanket tighter around Edina as she led her back to bed. "Let's get ye tucked in before ye catch a chill."

"Och, when did ye start putting me to bed?" Edina's arm trembled as she reached out to touch Abigail's hair. Her eyes widened as she leaned away. "Queen Titania, ye have come to Dunvegan."

Abigail blinked at the sudden turn in conversation. She recognized the fairy queen's name, but she knew of no tale where the mythical woman had dark hair. She remained silent, waiting for Edina to say more.

"Have ye come to warn us?" Edina's white eyebrows lifted expectantly.

"I would see that ma people are well." Abigail couldn't think of anything else to say.

"But ye only come in times of trouble. Have ye come for yer flag?"

Abigail's heart pounded as she listened to Edina mention the fabled banner that was said to summon the fae army to defend the MacLeods of Skye if ever unfurled. She remembered telling Ronan about the legend while traveling to Stornoway. The story went that if they ever used it a third time, both the flag and its bearer would be swept away to the land of the fae.

236

"I would ensure its safekeeping," Abigail whispered.

"We havenae touched it in generations," Edina assured Abigail. "It remains safely hidden just where ye left it last time."

Abigail clenched her jaw. If she could discover the flag's whereabouts and even steal it, it would weaken the MacLeods' faith in their own strength. Fairies or not, the MacLeods would believe whoever stole the prized heirloom would defeat them.

"Are ye sure Cormag hasnae moved it, Edina?" Abigail attempted to sound authoritative in a whisper. She wasn't certain she succeeded.

"Nay. Of course nae. It's still behind ma bed."

Abigail's head dropped forward in disbelief. It stunned her that Edina announced its hiding place without a second thought. Abigail glanced toward the bed, then back at Edina. The older woman squeezed Abigail's hand with surprising strength before leading Abigail to the bed. Abigail examined the headboard, wondering if she could return the next day to retrieve the flag. She needed to learn whether Edina left her chamber during the day. If she did, Abigail would risk traversing the tunnels during the daytime.

"Och, ma queen. I canna move this bed these days. Ye shall have to reach back to pull out the bricks."

"Ye would have me take it from where ye've protected it for years?"

"We must need it if ye've come. Mayhap ye willna tell me why, but ye have only ever come to Dunvegan to warn us of peril."

"That is true, Edina. But I amnae ready for all to ken I am here. I would remain a secret, so our enemy doesnae learn of me or the flag." Abigail said whatever came to mind, hoping to keep the woman from asking more questions. The less Abigail said, the less Edina might repeat the next day. The woman's mind was no longer sound, but Abigail feared she would remember enough to make people wonder who visited the former Lady MacLeod's chamber during the night. When Edina pointed to the headboard, Abigail stepped closer and looked between the wood and the brick wall. She leaned forward and ran her hand over the bricks, her fingers pressing against the mortar until she felt a loose one. She pulled the brick free, catching the one above it as it dropped. Squeezing her shoulders into the tiny space, she reached into the hidey-hole and swept her fingers inside. They brushed across soft material. Holding her breath, Abigail retrieved the hidden cloth.

"Aye, there it is," Edina beamed. "The defender of Clan MacLeod. It is back in its rightful hands, the queen of all *ban-shi*."

"I would return with this and inform the king that yer clan has kept it safe all these generations."

"King Oberan?"

"Aye, Edina. It will gladden him to ken yer clan has done its duty." Abigail slid the bricks back into place before she stepped away from the bed, nodding toward it. "Ye shall return to yer bed and sleep once more. Ye will keep ma visit a secret. The lives of all the fae depend on yer secrecy." Abigail prayed her warning seemed appropriate.

"As ye wish, ma queen." Edina grinned as she climbed back into bed.

Abigail watched her pull up the covers and lie down before Abigail slipped back into the tunnel. She moved away from the family chambers, glancing down at the Fairy Flag in the weak torch light. Rather than returning to her chamber, she turned toward the sea cave when she came to the fork in the tunnel. With the Fairy Flag in hand, Abigail was more desperate than ever to find a means to escape and reach Kieran. Entering cautiously, Abigail discovered there were no more crates and barrels lining the walls. The tide was low, so Abigail inched toward the gate. She walked along a ledge until she could reach the metal bars. She looked around, shocked to find a key just within reach if she stretched. A powerful gust blew through the metal squares and chilled Abigail's face, but she froze with the key in her hand.

It's blowing north. If I can get to a birlinn, this wind will have me back to Stornoway before dawn.

Abigail strained to hear anything on the wind that might warn her if someone was on the docks. She had no idea if she could reach the boats without having to swim. The last thing she wanted was to be soaked. She would die of hypothermia long before she reached her brother. She eased the gate open, shocked but relieved that it didn't squeak. Abigail supposed they kept the hinges well-greased to keep the gate a secret. She dunked her torch into the water, extinguishing it. She watched the tide pull the log out of the cave, then stepped onto a rock outside the keep. She pulled the gate nearly closed, but not all the way. She wouldn't risk it locking until she was certain she didn't need to retreat, even if she held the key.

Abigail took a long, calming breath, enjoying her first moment of freedom. But another gust reminded her of what was at stake. She inched along the rock until she could see the docks, illuminated by torches on the wall walk.

Despite the limited visibility, Abigail could tell that she could inch along the rock face since the tide was out. She wouldn't have to swim. She switched directions and pulled the gate shut, locking it and dropping the key down her bodice. She didn't doubt there were others, but she hoped it would slow the progress of anyone who tried to chase her from the cave. She gathered her skirts, throwing them over her shoulder as she crept toward the docks. She cradled the Fairy Flag in the crook of her arm, holding it against her chest to protect it as seawater splashed the rocks.

Abigail's attention shifted between the guards who could spot her at any moment and her goal. When she reached the docks, she crouched on the rock beside it, watching the men above her. She tried to judge the time and when the guards would shift positions. She prayed the nighttime rotation was the same as the daytime one. When she assumed nearly a quarter of an hour passed, she sighed as the men traded posts. She knew she had another half hour before they would move again. She moved her head to different angles as she considered the birlinn closest to her. It would be the easiest to board, but it wouldn't be the fastest to get into the current. She needed to reach the one at the end of the dock, but even if she was fast, she was likely to draw attention if she sprinted along the floating platform.

Despite the strong wind, the water was calm. Abigail stuck her hand in, shivering from the icy bite. She reminded herself that she'd already survived being submerged in it. As she glanced at her target once more, she knew there was only one choice: run down the docks and pray that she got the boat free and into the current before anyone caught her or reach the farthest boat without using the dock. She didn't doubt she would be spotted, and she didn't doubt the MacLeods would pursue her. Only one of the two options bought her more time. She scrambled to untie her boots before tying the laces together and slinging the boots around her neck. She shoved her stockings into one before pushing the flag into the other. She grinned when she remembered Ronan asking if she intended to throw her skirts over her head. This time she did.

Abigail pulled her gown and her chemise above her waist, the cool night air shocking to her nether region and backside. She draped the material over her shoulder, beneath her chin, and then back over the other shoulder. Before easing into the water, she pulled her *sgian dubh* from its sheath in her boot and put the handle between her teeth. The first step made her suck in a breath through her nose. The second stole that breath. The third made her want to cry out. But by the fourth, her legs were already growing numb. She eased her way along the dock, holding herself as high out of the water as she could manage. The ground dropped away quickly, so she kicked her legs and inched her arms along the wood planks. When she neared the first boat, she had to decide whether she could squeeze between the hulls and the dock or if she would get out. She knew she couldn't make it to the seaward side of the boat and inch along the hulls without getting completely wet.

Abigail accepted the risk that a boat might shift and crush her against the dock. She kept making her way toward the end. She felt the water lapping at the ends of her kirtle that were now above her breasts, but most of her gown and her boots were still dry. Her arisaid was caught within the folds of her gown and protected from the water. As she moved toward her destination, she kept her eyes on the guards on the battlements, certain they would raise the alarm at any moment.

What surely took less than five minutes felt like an agonizing five years. She made her way to the very end of the dock, where the torches on the wall barely illuminated the area. The ramp on the last birlinn was down, connecting the boat and the dock. Pushing with all her strength and kicking her legs,

Abigail pulled herself onto the ramp and crawled onto the deck. She lay on her belly, catching her breath and once again waiting for someone to spot her. When nothing stirred, she hurried to use her skirts to dry her legs and feet. She put her stockings and boots back on before looking around the boat. She placed the flag within the overlapping plaid across her chest.

She'd loved the days Kieran took her sailing as a child. Madeline hadn't enjoyed it, but Abigail begged her brother to teach her to sail. Kieran agreed not only because he knew she enjoyed it, but he wanted at least one woman in his family to know how to sail in case they ever needed to escape an attack on the keep. Maude and Kieran's advice echoed in her mind, telling her to sail home if ever she needed to. She wondered if her brother and sister-by-marriage tempted fate or had the second sight.

Abigail crawled along the deck until she came to the center mast. It would be difficult, but not impossible, to captain the boat alone. She checked the rigging and untied the sail, but she didn't hoist it yet. She would never make it far if she had to row by herself, but she placed an oar within reach on each side to serve as a rudder when she needed it. When she was certain the boat was fit for the open water, she inched back toward the dock. Rather than untying the line on the dock, she untied it on the boat. She used her oar to push herself away from the dock, then used the oar to angle herself into the current. A combination of back paddling and catching the current with the oar's blade pushing against it set her on course. She couldn't believe no one cried out, alerting the keep to her escape. Even if no one could see her aboard the vessel, how could they allow the boat to just float away?

Abigail let the wind and tide push her north

without raising the sail, fearing the movement would be what finally signaled the guards. It wasn't until she cleared the headland and had a head start of a few nautical miles that she unfurled and raised the sail. It caught the wind, and the boat glided along the water. Abigail couldn't see much in the dark, but the stars helped her navigate. Kieran's concession to teaching her to sail was to insist she learn how to navigate by the sun and the stars. Abigail knew Kieran always feared she would try to sail one alone one day and get stuck. He insisted she also learn the geography of the eastern coast of Lewis and Harris. While she didn't want to travel overland at all, she was more confident that she could make it to Stornoway on foot than trying to find Dun Ringill on Skye.

As the birlinn cut through the waves, Abigail considered her route. She couldn't imagine her father or brother ever having reason to tell Cormag and his brothers that she knew how to sail. While they might realize she'd slipped away on their boat, they would assume she was at the mercy of the sea and drifting without direction. She pictured where Ronan and his other three captains shifted course to cut across the Little Minch. If the MacLeods set out to recapture her, they would stay closer to Skye, likely believing Abigail wouldn't know how to steer and would feel safer in friendly waters. With a glance to her bow, she turned toward her stern. There was no movement in the distance, so she used an oar again to turn her bow to cross the sea long before she reached the point that Ronan had. Pointed in the new direction, Abigail pulled the oar in and moved to angle the sail. Cutting diagonally across the body of water proved easier than Abigail expected. The current continued pushing her north even as the wind blew her west.

After two hours on the open water, Abigail didn't lower her guard, but some of her fear abated. She remained vigilant, standing at the bow to ensure she didn't run aground, but frequently looking to the south to ensure no one followed her. She didn't understand why the MacLeods didn't catch up to her, so she could only guess that they continued to sail on the east side of the channel while she sailed along the west. When she spotted the southern tip of Harris, she steered herself back toward the center of the Minch and managed to avoid anyone noticing her. The MacLeods of Harris had a deeper connection to the MacLeods of Skye through heredity, and they would surely recognize one of Cormag's boats. They wouldn't hesitate to turn her over to him rather than Kieran.

TWENTY-EIGHT

Stornoway came into view as the earliest rays of sun peeked over the eastern horizon. Abigail shivered on the bench where she sat to steer the birlinn toward her former home. She'd had to crawl under a bench to block the wind during a particularly rough stretch, but that same wind sped up her progress. Snow began falling two hours earlier. She feared her ungloved fingers would break off. She sat on them and curled her toes within her boots as she shivered, but excitement and relief coursed through her as the first bricks of the castle became visible. She heard the call go up before she could announce herself. She hurried to the bow and cupped her hands around her mouth.

"Get ma brother!" Abigail called out, hoping the wind didn't carry her voice away. She waved her arms over her head as men passed through the gate and ran toward her. She recognized her brother leading the charge. "Kieran!"

"Abigail!" Kieran sprinted along the dock.

"I have nay rope. Throw me one."

Rather than listen to her, Kieran leapt onto the birlinn and swept her into his arms. Another man followed her brother and maneuvered them alongside the other boats. Before Abigail could say anything, Kieran was already racing toward the keep. She watched Maude run toward them; her arisaid wrapped around her head and shoulders but not belted. Abigail tried to press against Kieran's massive chest while twisting toward her approaching sister-by-marriage.

"They have Ronan. He's in the Dunvegan dungeon. Dinna take me inside, Kieran. We must go back."

Abigail feared she was babbling, but she didn't want to wait to return to Dunvegan. Cormag and Gordon would know she was gone by now, and she feared what they would do to Ronan. If she waited too long to make her way back, she was certain they would kill her husband. Once off the dock, Abigail scrambled to be put down, and Kieran lowered her feet to the ground lest he drop her. Maude embraced Abigail, and the reassurance the woman offered nearly broke Abigail's resolve. She never imagined she would find more comfort with Maude than with Kieran. Tears she'd held at bay for over a week finally coursed down her cheeks.

"Gordon and Donovan attacked us as we neared Dunvegan. They had seven boats to our four. They captured me and Ronan. They let me have a chamber, but Ronan and half his men have been in the dungeon the entire time. They locked the others in a storage building in the bailey. They'll ken I'm gone by now and will punish Ronan. If we dinna get to him before today ends, I'm certain they'll kill him. They'll believe he's lying, but he has nay idea I got away. Please, Kieran."

Kieran's long arms engulfed his sister and his wife as he held the two shivering women. Despite Abigail's objections, he and Maude coaxed her inside the keep. While Maude ordered food and the fire lit in Abigail's old chamber, Kieran summoned his second-in-command, Kyle. The men listened to Abigail retell her story. She added details about killing Donovan and finding the secret tunnels. Holding her MacKinnon plaid out to shield her hand, she retrieved the gate key and the Fairy Flag and gave them to Kieran. Neither man said anything, both recognizing the significance of the tattered piece of pink and green fabric.

"I found the flag in Edina's chamber. Then I located the key just inside the cave and let maself out. I crawled along the rocks and then along the dockside. I dinna ken how they havenae caught me. Expect to meet them nae far from here, Kieran. If we make it to Dunvegan without being seen, that will get ye inside. I can lead ye to the solar, the Great Hall, Cormag's chamber, and there's a door to the dungeon inside the cave."

"Ye're staying here," Kieran declared.

"The hell I am. They have ma husband and ma clansmen. I amnae staying here like some wean ye can leave behind. I escaped one keep that I didna ken ma way around, so dinna think for a moment Stornoway can hold me. I want ma husband, and I want to go home—to Dun Ringill. Take me, Kieran, or God bless, I will find ma own way back. Dinna doubt that I will."

"Kieran, take yer sister," Maude's soft tone belied the authority in it. "Do ye want us sailing alone?"

"Us? Ye're nae going anywhere, buttercup," Kieran barked.

"If ye dinna take yer sister, I will. She's nae the only woman in this clan whose brother taught her how to sail."

"Remind me to trounce Lachlan the next time I see him. Ye're a mother. Ye canna leave."

Maude's crossed arms, raised chin, and her defiant glare challenged Kieran to see who would win their battle of wills. Abigail shifted toward Maude, knowing her sister-by-marriage would convince her husband in Abigail's favor.

"Kier, take Abigail. She faced more danger sailing here alone. She can get ye into the keep, whether through the sea gate or the main gate. She and Ronan need to go home with nay more detours."

"I ken," Kieran huffed. He kissed his wife's forehead. "And I ken ye arenae going anywhere. But I wouldnae put it past ye to lead the raid, buttercup."

"As long as we understand one another," Maude grinned before she lifted her chin for a kiss. Abigail watched her relatives, warmed by the obvious love the couple shared, but saddened that she wasn't with her husband to share their own kiss. Maude looked at her with a sympathetic smile. "Let's get ye into warmer clothes and get some hot food into ye. By the time ye've eaten and changed, Kieran will have the men organized."

With a glance and a nod to Kieran, Abigail followed Maude to the stairs. They weren't halfway to the second floor before Kieran barked orders and the massive doors slammed behind him. Abigail didn't dally, accepting Maude's help as she changed into two fresh pairs of stockings, a thick chemise Maude lent her, and one of Maude's heaviest wool gowns. She wrapped her MacKinnon plaid around her, then added a MacLeod of Lewis plaid before belting them into place. Maude had returned with lamb's wool when she brought the extra clothes. Abigail stuffed it into her boots, an added layer of insulation.

Abigail shoveled the food that arrived, starving after barely eating for a sennight. What she couldn't manage without feeling ill, Maude stuffed into a satchel. They arrived belowstairs as Kieran and

Kyle walked into the Great Hall, shaking snow from their heads and shoulders. Maids arrived with stuffed sacks of food. Maude and Abigail embraced, genuine sisterly love passing between them, before Abigail followed Kieran and Kyle back to the docks. Abigail turned and waved at Maude, realizing she'd been at her former home for less than an hour. She stepped into Kieran's birlinn, found a spot to huddle in the bow, grateful for the pair of gloves she found in the satchel. She drew her plaids around her and fell asleep, able to trust her safety to her brother.

"Abigail." Kieran shook her shoulder as she came awake. He helped her to her feet and pulled her into his embrace. She huddled against her older brother, fighting to keep her tears at bay. She feared they would make her eyes freeze, and she wouldn't have any of the men view her as weak. Kieran's massive hands rubbed her back and arms, bringing heat back to the numb extremities. "I need ye to tell me all that happened. Especially how ye wound up with their Fairy Flag."

Abigail nodded her head against Kieran's chest. "I've already told you most of it. Skye just came into sight when I spotted the boats. Ronan tried to steer us toward shore. I'm certain he would have preferred to fight there, but the wind was against us. Gordon and Donovan sailed with the wind. Their seven birlinns surrounded ours. I hid beneath a bench, just like Ronan told me. He and his men kept the MacLeods from boarding, but their boats rammed ours until it capsized. Ronan, our men, and I ended up in the water. The boats were close together, and the fighting distracted the men. I inched ma way around

249

them, even though I heard Ronan calling to me. Kieran, I have never been so cold."

Abigail shivered against Kieran, recalling the misery and fear. His arms tightened around her, and despite the two plaids covering her head, she felt him kiss her crown. Once more, tears threatened to overwhelm her. She swallowed the lump in her throat several times before she could speak again.

"Donovan spotted us just after Ronan joined me beside one of our boats. I had ma dirk in ma hand. When Donovan pulled me from the water, I stabbed him. In the neck. I killed him, Kieran." Abigail felt Kieran tense, but he said nothing. "They still pulled us from the water. Ronan took the knife and killed a MacLeod, but Gordon had Ronan's sword and knocked him out. They gagged me and bound us both. They tossed us into the dungeon in a cell together. They took those of us they found on the boats or in the water to the dungeon. They imprisoned the men they caught on land in a storage building in the bailey. I was only in the cell for a few hours before they gave me a chamber. Lady MacLeod—Cecily—recognized me."

"I can imagine what she had to say aboot that. Bitter woman."

"Aye. But Ronan predicted she'd insist they give a lady—even a captive—a chamber. Her pretentiousness is the only reason she has a sense of decorum. I joined the laird and his family for the evening meal and reminded them of what was at stake if they harmed Ronan or me. Ronan swears they havenae tortured him. They ignored me during the day, which was fine. I ken the guard rotation, Kieran. I ken where they station the least guards and where they nap while they should be on watch. I ken how to get into the keep through the sea gate. I remembered the tunnels Donovan showed Madeline and me. I can get from the sea cave to the laird's solar, the family chambers, the Great Hall, the dungeon, and the chamber they gave me. I sneaked out of ma chamber most nights to visit Ronan."

"Abigail," Kieran hissed.

"I ken. He didna like it either. But we've been there a sennight. I wasna going to go without seeing ma husband if I kenned how to find him. He doesnae ken that I escaped. I left the dungeon last night and was going to return to ma chamber. I remembered hearing snoring in one of the family chambers the first night I explored. I couldnae figure out whose chamber it was. I spied in there last night and discovered Edina, Cormag and Gordon's mother. Do ye remember how kind she was to us? Her mind is gone, Kieran. She thought me a spirit come to take her to Heaven and her husband. Then she thought I was Annalily. When she nearly fell, I went to help her. I couldnae let her get hurt. She thought I was Queen Titania! She told me where the Fairy Flag was. She told me to get it!"

"And ye think to bribe Cormag with it for Ronan?"

"Nay. I think to unfurl the bluidy thing, wave it in their faces until they pish themselves, then toss it into the Minch. Let them fall to their knees and beg ye for mercy. They'll believe the battle is lost before it begins if they see we have their banner."

"Do ye nae fear being swept off to the land of the fae?" Kieran grinned.

"Bah. If I'm Queen Titania, then Ronan is King Oberan. We'll be fine together." Kieran sobered as he cupped Abigail's cheeks. He opened his mouth to speak, but she shook her head. Her gloved hands covered his. "I ken they may have killed him, Kieran. But I had to take the risk. This might be the only way to get him free. Ye hadnae already sailed for Skye, so

251

I ken Cormag didna send for a ransom. But I dinna ken why the MacKinnons didna go to Stornoway to tell ye we hadnae arrived. I fear Cormag's led a raid on Dun Ringill."

"That's possible. Nay one told us ye hadnae made it home. It worried Maude and me that ye didna send a messenger to tell us ye arrived safely. But we thought the weather might have kept Ronan from sending anyone."

"It hasnae snowed much at Dunvegan, but I dinna ken what the rest of Skye is like." Abigail bit her lower lip to keep it from trembling. "The weather turned so foul just after we left Stornoway. We had to spend the night in a cove near Ranish. But the next day was beautiful. The water was calm. The sun shone. The only problem was the wind was against us. I thought the worst was over. Then hell truly began."

"We will rescue Ronan and his men."

"I ken ye'll try." Brother and sister stood together in silence until one of Kieran's sailors called out that Skye was in sight. Abigail sniffled and wiped her face. "What will ye do?"

"I'm putting ye on Kyle's boat. I dinna like it, but ye're the only one who kens the tunnels. Ye'll take him and two boats into the sea cave. Guide him through the tunnels to the dungeon. Dinna go in until Ronan is free. I dinna want ye in the middle of the fighting, Abigail. Promise me. If Ronan kens ye're there, it'll distract him. Promise."

"I canna do that, Kieran. If I can do aught to help Ronan, I will. I willna watch ma husband die."

Kieran sighed. He knew his own wife would argue the same thing. He wouldn't force his sister. "While ye lead the men through the tunnels, I'll go to the main gate. I dinna trust Cormag or Gordon to release Ronan in exchange for the flag. But they will have to listen if I have their clan's most prized possession in ma possession. I'll demand they release the prisoners in the storage building before I consider giving the flag back."

"They outnumber us, Kieran. What if they simply overrun ye and yer men?"

"As long as I'm alive, I can unfurl the flag. They willna do aught that might make me do that. I'll shred the bluidy thing before their eyes. When I ken ye and Ronan are safe, I'll give the filthy scrap back to them and be on ma way."

"If ye dinna demand our release until Ronan and I make it out of the cave, Cormag and Gordon will ken something is off. They'll wonder why ye would return the flag without seeing them free Ronan and me."

"Once ye're free, it willna matter. They can have their fairytale and their Fairy Flag. It matters nae to me as long as ye're safe."

"They'll see us approach. Can ye buy us enough time to get the men from the dungeon before they force ye to fight?"

"Aye. They'll think they have the upper hand. They willna ken ye made it to us. I'll say I havenae heard from ye, and I dinna trust them nae to be involved with ye missing. Once they see the flag, they willna attack, but they will make threats. If I can keep them talking and at least release the men in the bailey, then we might get away with little bloodshed."

Abigail nodded; she was doubtful but willing to trust her brother. Kieran signaled to Kyle, who had his men steer his birlinn alongside Kieran's. He lifted Abigail onto his second's boat and said a silent prayer that his baby sister come out of the ensuing fight alive. He didn't doubt there would be bloodshed. He just hoped the rescue mission succeeded before the larger Skye forces overpowered the Lewis men.

Ten Lewis birlinns cut through the water as Dunvegan loomed on the cliffs above them. Without a word or a signal, three drifted toward the sea gate. Kyle jumped to the rocks and nimbly wound his way to the sea gate. Using the key Kieran had passed along to him, he opened the portal. By the time the three birlinns sailed into the cave, guards were already running into the cave. Abigail remained on the boat until only the men from Lewis stood. Abigail suggested Kyle try the key in the door she believed led to the dungeon, but it didn't fit. In silence and without torches, Abigail led the men into the bowels of the keep, winding their way to the dungeon. Chaos met them when she pushed the secret door open.

TWENTY-NINE

"**Y**our bride won't be so bonnie once—I suppose I should say if—her body bobs back up to the surface." Gordon taunted Ronan as the cell door swung open. "Have you ever seen a body after it's drowned? How bloated it becomes? How the skin turns gray? How the eyes bulge?"

Ronan watched Gordon, remaining silent. But his heart raced. He didn't understand why Gordon suggested Abigail had drowned. Had they killed his wife?

"Och, not a word to say? If only your bride were so wise." Gordon waited for Ronan to respond, but they only stared at one another in silence. "I must commend her on her bravery, even if it was equally stupid. Stole a birlinn and sailed north. Got herself lost at sea."

Ronan raised an eyebrow, but he still didn't speak. Gordon was giving him information without asking, so Ronan would allow Gordon to continue.

"Do you ken how grateful she was when I found her? Do you remember how her mouth felt wrapped around your cock? I always will. But then again, once you're dead, she'll be my wife."

Ronan eased his way to his feet, his arms still ap-

255

pearing to be tied behind his back. He glanced over Gordon's shoulder to the men waiting outside his cell. Ronan considered what Gordon said. Abigail couldn't be both alive and dead. Gordon couldn't keep his lies straight. Ronan didn't believe for a moment that Abigail touched Gordon, but he did believe that she'd set sail for Stornoway. He knew Kieran taught her to sail and that she enjoyed it. Ronan had promised to give her a birlinn when they arrived at Dun Ringill. They'd lay together in bed, their fingers entwined, as Abigail told him stories about how she'd been the one to bait Kieran's fishing hooks when they were younger. She made him swear never to tell that Kieran went a little green every time he had to touch a worm.

"Naught to say aboot your wife sucking my cock until my eyes practically rolled back in my head?"

"I ken my wife would have bitten it off before doing aught else. I ken you're lying," Ronan replied calmly.

"Then you underestimate how badly your wife wants to live, how she'll do aught to keep you alive. She may have cried out your name, but it was my cock she begged for as I made her climax. I don't care whose name she called. It's my seed inside her quim right now. If she lives, she might give birth to a son in nine moons. We won't ken until then whose bairn it is. It might be a MacLeod sitting in the laird's chair at Dun Ringill." Gordon watched Ronan, who didn't flinch. Ronan still didn't believe Gordon. His assertion was too preposterous to consider. "Mayhap I didn't make it clear. She cried out your name, kenning you couldn't come to her rescue. She begged my cock to stop splitting her in half. I loved every moment of her tears, of her screaming for help while my men watched."

Ronan's nostrils flared, but he still wouldn't take

Gordon's bait. He was more apt to believe Abigail was already at Stornoway, seeking Kieran's help, than recovering from Gordon's attack. The man's expression and tone didn't match the violence he described. There wasn't pride or boasting in it. There wasn't malice or joy when he described how he supposedly defiled Abigail. Movement behind Gordon caught Ronan's attention. The sound of one of the other cells opening was the only cue Ronan needed. His men had assured him just that morning that they were hale. They'd abandoned whistles days earlier and called out to one another.

With a roar that shook the walls, Ronan launched himself at Gordon. He knocked the man to the ground, his hand wrapped around his captor's throat. He reached behind him and pulled the *sgian dubh* from the small of his back. Gordon struggled to break free, writhing and thrashing beneath Ronan. Gordon underestimated the strength Ronan would find when the opportunity to escape finally came. He also underestimated the strength hatred gave Ronan.

"I dinna believe ye raped ma wife any more than I believe she is dead, like ye said at the beginning of yer lies. But I watched ye touch her in that boat. I can imagine the hell ye've made her life. Ye took her from me, and now I will take yer life from ye." Ronan slashed the *sgian dubh* across Gordon's throat. While the blade was short and narrow, it was one of the sharpest styles of dirks. Gordon gasped, blood gurgling at his throat. Ronan watched the life fade from Gordon's eyes before he rushed out of his cell. Three of his men fought the three remaining guards. His war cry signaled the men to overpower the guards when they opened their cell. Just like Ronan, some of his warriors had hidden their blades well before their captors searched them. One MacLeod guard already

257

lay dead while the fight continued, three against three.

Ronan went back in his cell, taking Gordon's sword from its sheath. "Bluidy, fucking bastard. Wearing ma own sword." Ronan wrapped both hands around the hilt and drove the sword into Gordon's chest. "Shouldnae have taken what's mine. Ma wife or ma sword."

Ronan joined his men as the last guard fell. The MacKinnons took swords from the fallen MacLeods just as the door from the bailey burst open. More MacLeods streamed into the dungeon.

"Kill them before the Lewis get to them," one guard cried.

Lewis? Kieran's here? Dear God, did Abby really sail to Stornoway on her own?

Ronan raised his sword, taking a defensive stance with his men. "Daryl, find the keys," Ronan ordered one of his men. Their only hope was to get his other men free. Even without swords, it would improve the MacKinnons' odds of surviving. When the first men approached, Ronan went on the offensive, taking the MacLeods by surprise. With the MacKinnon battle cry *"Cuimhnich bàs Ailpein"*—"Remember the death of Alpin," the king the MacKinnons believed they descended from—Ronan charged forward. He swung his sword and strength he'd been certain was gone after a week in his jail surged through him. Ronan cut through a second man just before a draught gusted from behind him, and a war cry of "hold fast" filled the corridor behind him. "Kieran?" Ronan called out.

"Kyle!" A man's voice responded. Ronan recognized the voice and the name as Kieran's second. Men poured in from behind Ronan, ready to clash with those charging toward him.

"Abby?"

"Here, but safe," Kyle answered before he drove his sword into a man's chest.

MacLeods of Skye fell as Ronan fought alongside men sent by his brother-by-marriage. As they pressed forward against the men from Skye, something—or someone—slid past, hugging the walls and cell doors. Ronan's jaw clenched and his eyes narrowed when he recognized the head of black hair that didn't even come to his shoulders. But the sound of metal jangling in her hand as she raced past him told Ronan she'd found the keys. As he continued to fight, he heard her unlock one cell door after another. It wasn't long before he sensed that the fighting force at his back grew. His men picked up swords from the fallen warriors and joined the fight for their freedom. A small hand pressed against his back before wrapping around his belt.

"There's a door ahead that should take us into the sea cave. If we can get there, we can get away."

"Abigail."

"Ye can have ma head on a skewer after we're free."

Ronan knew the men heard them when there was another shift. Rather than remain on the offensive, the MacKinnons and MacLeods of Lewis formed a defensive circle around Abigail. They fought their way forward, but the goal now was to protect Abigail. Men continued to enter the dungeon from the bailey, but the onslaught slowed. When they reached the wall with the door up to the keep and the one Abigail assumed led to the cave, she slipped past Ronan. He whistled, and the MacKinnons and her former clansmen turned their backs to Abigail, facing out to guard her while she tried the keys until she found the right one. She yanked the door open, grateful to see the three birlinns waiting for them.

"Ronan!" Abigail lifted her skirts and ran toward

the boats. More Dunvegan men entered the cave from the keep, but the combined forces that Kyle brought and Ronan led were enough to keep the Dunvegan warriors at bay until everyone was aboard the birlinns. Abigail moved to the stern, as far out of the way as she could. As the men rowed out of through the sea gate, Ronan spun around to find Abigail staring at him.

THIRTY

Ronan rushed forward, and Abigail launched herself into his arms. Their lips ground against one another until it finally seemed real that they were in one another's arms. The kiss continued as desperation and terror eased into relief. When they pulled apart, Ronan looked in horror at the grime now covering Abigail. He tried to release her, but she shook her head.

"I dinna care. I dinna care. Dinna let go." Abigail ran her hands over Ronan's gaunt face as tears streamed down her dirt smeared cheeks. She cupped his jaw and pressed a tender kiss to his mouth. She sobbed, "I was so scared, Ro—so—scared."

"Me too, Abby. I canna let go. I'm too scared I'll lose ye again." Ronan crushed her against his chest as he relished the feel of Abigail in his arms again, knowing she was unharmed and leaving Dunvegan.

"Too—tight," Abigail gasped as she tapped on Ronan's rock-hard pectoral. He eased his hold on her, but still kept her within the circle of his arms. She searched his exhausted but handsome face. She ran her hands over his arms and back. "Did they hurt ye?"

"Nay. Gordon said—"

"Nay. He never touched me. I can only imagine what he said, but he left me alone. Cormag warned him."

"Gordon kenned making me think he'd abused ye was worse than any physical torture."

"Did he torment ye often? I thought ye believed me."

"I did. It was only today that he made claims I kenned couldnae be true. He told me ye escaped. The bluidy eejit started out telling me ye'd drowned, then suddenly, he said he'd caught ye. I dinna think he kenned ye made it to Stornoway."

"I dinna ken if Cormag even kens. Kieran went to deal with him and to get yer men locked away in the bailey." Abigail looked toward the keep as they rounded the headland. She spied her brother's tawny hair covered with snow as he stood outside the main gate, the Fairy Flag still folded but raised above his head.

"Is that—?" Ronan murmured.

"Aye. I stole it," Abigail grinned.

"Bluidy hell, Abigail. Do ye never listen?"

"Sometimes. But only when I hear what I want." Abigail stood on her toes and pressed a smacking kiss to Ronan's lips. "If ye or our family is in danger, I willna give up. There's naught I willna do to protect the people I love. I'll accept the risks if I can save ye. Dinna bother trying to convince me otherwise. Ye'd do the vera same."

"But—"

"Och, if ye even think to say it's different because ye're a mon, or because ye're bigger, or because ye swing a sword, I will dump ye in the drink."

Ronan tried to smother his guilty smile. "I was going to say, but I wouldnae look nearly as good as ye."

"Liar," Abigail laughed as she leaned back

against her husband and closed her eyes. She whispered around the tightness in her throat, "I love ye."

"I love ye, Abby. Always." Ronan felt his heart slowing from its rapid cadence as he stood holding his wife. He didn't know what would come next, but he could face anything now that he held Abigail. He knew the fight with the MacLeods of Skye wasn't nearly finished, but he was free of his prison, and his wife was safe. As they sailed closer to the dock, Kieran's voice drifted down to them.

"Cormag, if ye wish to have yer wee blanket back, release the men in the bailey. Otherwise, the fae will fight at ma back as I claim Dunvegan for ma own. Or mayhap ma wee baby sister would like to spend summers here. I amnae telling ye again." Kieran made to stab the flag with his sword, but Cormag rushed forward. Abigail and Ronan shifted to remain out of sight and behind the sail. Cormag didn't need to discover they were already free.

"Give me back what the fae trusted to my ancestors," Cormag demanded.

"Och, that's *our* ancestors. We are kin as ye like to claim. Mayhap they'd prefer to fight for the branch that doesnae keep using women to fight their battles. Or mayhap they gave ye the flag out of pity. They ken ye canna fight for yerselves, and ye need wee, wee fae to fight off yer scary enemies," Kieran mocked.

"You've got boulders for bollocks, Kieran. I will give you that. You ken as well as I do that my branch can destroy you. Give us back our flag, and I will give you the MacKinnons and let you be on your way. Since we're kin."

"Ye canna have forgotten already why I'm here. Ye kidnapped ma sister and her husband. *Husband*. That now makes the MacLeods of Lewis and Raasay allied with the MacKinnons, who are allied with the

MacDonalds of Sleat. That's just our connections within the isles. That doesnae even begin to include our ties to the Highlands. Ye ken I have septs in Assynt. Ma father-by-marriage is the Earl of Sutherland. Ma uncles-by-marriage are the Earl of Sinclair and the Earl of Ross. Ma wife's cousin married Tristan Mackay. Ma wife's other cousin married the Mackenzie's daughter. Dinna forget ma sister-by-marriage married Hardwin Cameron. The Camerons are the only ones who dinna live along a coast. The Mackays, Sinclairs, Sutherlands, and Rosses all sail, Cormag. All of them. The Minch isnae wide enough to escape us, but it's deep enough to swallow yer entire fleet. I ken Abigail killed Donovan. Since I havenae seen Gordon, I'd guess he's dead now too. That leaves ye. Ye havenae a direct heir left. Mayhap ma wife would like to spend our summers here."

"You blather on and on. Empty threats, Kieran. My branch has always been more powerful than yours. Naught's changed. I'm offering you mercy by considering MacKinnon's release."

Kieran draped the Fairy Flag over the tip of his sword and raised it to the sky. The sun glinted off the sword. "I'd say it's all changed." He waved his sword from side to side.

"Ye dinna understand what ye're doing." Desperation laced Cormag's voice, making his burr pronounced as he inched closer. "Ye dinna want to bring the fae. Ye dinna want to be the one they take back. Ye ken the legend as well as I do. Ye ken we've used it twice and been victorious. Even if they fight for ye, ye willna survive. Think of yer wife and weans. What of them?"

"Ma wife would have already flown this if she were here. Count yer blessings she isnae because yer keep is still standing. Release Ronan and his men."

"Aye. I said I would." Cormag turned back toward the keep and yelled out his orders. Abigail and Ronan, along with the free MacKinnons and the MacLeods of Lewis, watched as Ronan's men shuffled through the front gate. Their wrists and ankles were bound, but they were no longer captives. Some of Kieran's men stepped forward to cut the men free. None looked back as they made their way down the dock. Ronan stepped away from the sail, ensuring his returning men saw that he was with them.

"Wait here, Abigail. I'm serious," Ronan warned. Abigail nodded as she watched Ronan step onto the dock. He raised his sword and pointed it toward Cormag as he hiked the trail until he stood beside Kieran. "I ken ye'll brag until yer last day that ye had me in yer dungeon. But remember this: ye took ma freedom for a sennight, but ma clan took yer brothers and yer flag. Donovan and Gordon are dead."

Cormag looked at Ronan, then Kieran, and back to Ronan. He shuddered as he glanced at his castle before staring at the Fairy Flag. Kieran gave a pitying shake of his head before he took the banner off his sword and held it out to Cormag. The Skye branch's laird inched forward until Kieran could fling it at him. Cormag caught it and pulled it to his chest, defending it like it was his child. But a malevolent gleam came into his eyes as he narrowed them toward Ronan.

"You'll want to be on your way now." Cormag's brogue no longer controlled his speech. As Abigail listened, she thought his pretentious tone matched Cecily's. She figured they deserved one another.

"Lady MacKinnon," one of Ronan's warriors called to her, keeping his voice quiet. "The bastard isnae lying. They attacked Dun Ringill two days ago. We heard aboot it while the men gathered in the bailey. They rode out in the middle of the night. We need to return."

Abigail stared at the man for a long moment before nodding and turning to look at Ronan. He'd told her to wait in the boat, and she wanted to oblige, but she needed both her husband and her brother to cease tormenting Cormag, so they could depart. She whistled her call to Ronan, who immediately turned back to her.

"Dun Ringill, two days ago," Abigail called out. A mask of fury settled on Ronan's face, so terrifying that it made Abigail take a step back. He turned around and charged up the path. His sword was beneath Cormag's chin before the man realized he stood on the brink of being the last brother killed for their attack on Ronan and Abigail MacKinnon.

"What did ye do?" Ronan hissed.

"You won't know until you return to what's left," Cormag smirked.

"Mayhap I should let ye live and allow Robert to decide yer fate." Ronan pressed his sword against Cormag's throat until it punctured the skin. "But ye and I ken that's nae how islanders solve our differences."

"Even if I die, my branch doesn't. My cousin will replace me. We will still rule this isle. You and your people are naught more than flies to be swatted."

"See if ye can swat away ma sword, Cormag. Defend yerself." Ronan stepped back, waiting for Cormag to draw his weapon. "If ye dinna, everyone will brand ye a coward. It willna be murder. I'm within ma rights. But ye willna die with honor. Ye will die the pathetic maggot ma father warned me aboot."

Abigail watched Ronan, but her gazed shifted to her brother as Cormag reached for his sword. Kieran's sword was lowered, but Abigail didn't doubt her

266

brother was prepared. She also knew he wouldn't interfere in Ronan's fight. She clutched her hands together as she waited to see what happened. The moment Cormag drew his sword, Ronan launched his attack. Cormag underestimated Ronan's determination, assuming Ronan would be weak and easily fatigued after being nearly starved for over a week. In a blink of an eye, Cormag lay on the ground, blood gushing from a slash across his chest. Ronan wiped his sword on Cormag's chest.

"I'm letting ye live, so ye can live with the humiliation that one wee woman killed yer brother and stole yer filthy scrap of cloth. Nay fae are coming to yer aid today. Dinna underestimate me or mine ever again, Cormag. Ye may claim to have the fae on yer side, but I'm descended from kings." Ronan and Kieran spun toward the boats and jogged down the path. The boats were pushing away from the dock as the two lairds boarded their birlinns. Ronan's weapon clattered to the deck as he pitched forward, unconscious before he landed.

THIRTY-ONE

It was a three-day ride from Dunvegan to Dun Ringill, or a day's sail, but Kieran ordered the boats to anchor for the night. The combined MacKinnon and MacLeods of Lewis crew left Dunvegan just before midday. Kieran couldn't ignore that men needed their injuries tended, and the freed MacKinnons needed food and rest before they arrived at Dun Ringill for another battle. Abigail sat with Ronan's head in her lap, stroking his hair. She'd fallen to the deck beside Ronan when he collapsed. Her hands roamed over him, searching for any hidden injury he hadn't admitted. When she found nothing, she accepted that Ronan's body could no longer withstand the strain. It demanded rest. As much as she feared what they would find at Dun Ringill, she didn't argue with Kieran when he ordered them to go ashore for the night.

Unlike where they'd sought shelter in the cove on Lewis, the place they found on Skye offered cover from the snow that fell on that portion of the island. There was ample firewood and animals to hunt. They were on MacKinnon territory, even if they had several more hours' journey until they reached Dun Ringill. Kieran carried Abigail ashore, while it took four men to get Ronan's heavy body to land. His dead weight and the rough surf meant he was too much for one man to carry slung over his shoulder. Abigail fought not to laugh as she watched the men lumbering up the pebble beach, offering her an unobstructed view up Ronan's plaid. She doubted he would appreciate her giggles or the humbling position he was in if he were awake.

He roused enough to drink from a waterskin and to ask about his men. Abigail looked around the group and found that most of the MacKinnons were in the same condition as Ronan. Her former clan members built the fires, went hunting, and set up shelters for the injured. A few of the MacLeods and MacKinnons had suffered injuries during the battle in the dungeon. Abigail offered to stitch them up, but Kieran assured her that the most important thing she could do was to stay with Ronan. Kieran's order relieved Abigail. She didn't want to leave Ronan's side for even a moment, but she would have if they needed her sewing skills.

"The horses?" Ronan rasped as he leaned against a tree that his men propped him against to eat.

"We dinna ken," Abe answered. The MacKinnon warrior was a guard who'd been locked in the storage building. "Most came ashore. But when they captured those of us swimming or who made it to land, they didna go after the horses. There were men waiting for us on the shore. It wasna just the seven boats that attacked. They were prepared to fight on the ground too. They herded us to the keep and kept us separated from ye. But we never saw what happened to the horses."

"Lady MacKinnon." Abigail looked at Benjamin, another guard locked in the bailey, as he offered her a rabbit that still sizzled. "Seeing ye that day—hearing yer whistle—made us hold on to hope. We kenned if ye were alive, we couldnae give up. They may have locked us up, but we swore our oath to protect the laird's family and our clan until our last breath. They told us they killed the laird, but we kenned it wasna true. We kenned it when we saw ye. We could just tell, ma lady. Ye were spitting mad, but we didna see grief. Ye gave us a reason to keep going."

"I—" Abigail didn't know what to say. She looked over as Ronan, who'd taken her hand. She swept her gaze over all the MacKinnons. "Thank ye."

The men nodded and resumed eating. Abigail realized she'd said just what the men needed to hear. No flowery speeches or explanations. Just humble gratitude. When Ronan argued he couldn't eat another bite—after Abigail gave him three rabbits and a squirrel—he fell into a deep sleep. Abigail didn't think she would sleep, since she was still worried about Ronan. He looked haggard and ill. But he shifted while he slumbered and wrapped his arm around Abigail. Even in his run-down condition, his body heat warmed her against the freezing night air. Between the warmth and the reassurance of having his brawny arm holding her against him, she fell into a deep sleep.

When the sun rose, most of the MacKinnons continued to sleep. Her fears started anew when she slipped away from Ronan, and he never stirred. He was normally such a light sleeper that she couldn't move across their bed without disturbing him. She found Kieran and tapped her brother's arm. He embraced Abigail just as he had her entire life. Her heart ached for the years they'd been at odds because of her selfishness and frivolity. She knew Kieran didn't hold it against her, but she still regretted it. She drew strength from her brother's solid presence.

"Abigail," Kieran said as he led her away from where the men sat and slept. "The men told me what they could aboot the planned attack at Dun Ringill. The MacLeods left Dunvegan five days ago, so the battle—if there was one—was two days past. I canna predict what we will find. Ronan and these men may be all that's left of his guard. The MacLeods could still be there, or they may have left the keep aflame. Ronan's men thought two score rode out for Dun Ringill. That's less than our combined numbers now, but Ronan and his men need a full day's rest at the vera least."

"I ken, Kieran. They all need a fortnight's worth of rest and meals, but we dinna have that long. If we arrive and Cormag's men are still there, can ye roust them and send them off?"

"Likely. But I doubt they'll leave whether we chase them or give them the chance to leave. They'll have orders nae to retreat. If they're there when we arrive, then that's where they will die. But, Abigail, it's most likely we will find the village and the keep burned. Ronan will want to lead, and I canna deny him that right. I willna deny him that right. But neither can I stay with the birlinns and make sure ye stay put. Abigail, dinna leave the guards I post with ye until we sweep the castle and are certain there's nay lingering threat. And neither Ronan nor I would want ye to see the devastation left behind. Please, Abigail. There is little left for me to do as yer aulder brother, but I would shield ye from what ye're likely to see."

"I understand, Kieran. I'll go or stay wherever ye or Ronan tell me. I dinna ken what we should expect, but ma heart breaks for Ronan and his guards."

"I ken it does. He'll need ye, lass. Whatever we find, in the days to come, he will need yer support. Ronan was a fine laird before he met ye, but he will be better for having ye at his side. I ken I'm better with Maude at ma side. Ye'll get through this as partners. Ye're a MacKinnon now, Abigail, but ye're always a MacLeod of Lewis. Dinna think that because ye sought our help once, ye canna do it again."

"Thank ye, Kieran. I love ye, even if ye're auld and crotchety."

"I love ye, Gail." Kieran winked as he used his childhood pet name for his sister. He'd called her Gail for the first two years of her life until he could say Abigail. She had no memory of it, but Kieran had teased her and said she arrived like a gale, so that's why he thought it was her name. She returned to Ronan's side, concerned that he still hadn't stirred. She roused him to eat several times throughout the day since the MacLeods hunted as much as they could find during the middle of winter. All the MacKinnons benefited from the extra food. Two nights and a full day of rest revived Ronan and his men. It mesmerized Abigail to see the MacKinnons board the birlinns as though they hadn't just recovered from near starvation. They took their turns at the oars as they continued south to Dun Ringill.

❧

"That's Spar Cave," Ronan murmured against Abigail's ear as he pointed to a rock formation just inside the mouth of Loch Slapin. "And there, if you squint against the sun, is our home."

Ronan kissed Abigail's cheek before she turned a warm smile toward Ronan. After her initial surprise wore off from Ronan's rapid recuperation, Abigail enjoyed watching her husband's brawny back and shoulders strain when he sat to row. He took his turn as they progressed south toward her new home. But a MacKinnon took his place as they rounded the headland and entered the last stretch of their journey. Ronan joined Abigail at the rail and pointed out various land features.

Snow fell throughout the day, so Abigail welcomed the protection from the freezing wind when Ronan wrapped his arms around her. His plaid was still filthy, but he'd washed the dungeon sludge from his skin. The MacLeods shared spare leines with the MacKinnons, so he no longer felt revolting. With the extra length of wool pulled over his shoulders and head, the wind wasn't nearly as abrasive as it could be. And holding Abigail always heated his blood.

"What would you have me do when we arrive? I mean, after you are sure I can come up from the docks?"

"I don't ken for sure. My men and your brother's will sweep the castle for any Skye warriors who might be lingering. Once I ken it's safe for you to go inside, I'll see aboot getting a fire lit in my solar. Then I need to check the village. Abby, it may be several hours before I can come back to you."

"I ken. Shouldn't I see aboot having food ready for when you're finished?"

"Abby—"

"You don't ken where you might find bodies."

"Aye. That's why I want you to go to my solar. It'll be safe there for you until I ken the full situation."

Abigail nodded as she looked out toward the west side of the loch that eventually split into Loch Slapin and Loch Eishort. As they drew closer, Abigail was certain she saw fishing boats close to the coast. She glanced back at Ronan and noticed he was as mystified as she was. He glanced down at her and shrugged. When they drew close enough to make out faces, they heard the bells ringing from the battlements on the cliffs.

"That's not a warning. They recognized us and are welcoming us home." Ronan's furrowed brow matched Abigail's. The fishermen waved to them.

"Ye're a welcome sight, Laird." Abigail watched as a white-haired, toothless man grinned at Ronan. "We thought ye ran off with yer bonnie bride and werenae coming back!"

"Linus, what happened with the MacLeods?"

"Ye married one?" Linus looked at the men who didn't wear MacKinnon plaids.

"Nay. MacLeods of Skye. How many people did we lose?"

"Lose, Laird? Ye arenae making any sense."

"Wasn't there an attack four days ago?"

"Nay. Massive snowstorm inland. That's all. Havenae seen hide nor hair of any MacLeods, except for the ones ye're with."

Abigail and Ronan exchanged a glance before Ronan looked back over his shoulder at Kieran, who shrugged. "Linus, what of the keep?"

"Still in one piece." Linus grinned again, flashing his gums. Until Ronan could speak to his second-in-command, there was little more a fisherman could tell him. Ronan needed reports from his scouts and patrols. The bells continued to toll as they inched toward the docks. He lent Abigail his hand as she disembarked and followed him onto land. He wrapped his arm around her shoulders as he steered them along the path to the village that lay outside the retaining wall.

"Naught looks out of place," Ronan observed as Kieran walked to his right.

"I don't think aught happened here." Abigail looked at the buildings they approached and the people milling around. Nothing looked out of the ordinary. It appeared like a bustling village outside a large keep.

"Mayhap the MacDonalds, MacNeills, or Mac-Neacails got to them if Mother Nature didna," Kieran mused.

"Mayhap." Ronan guided Abigail through the main gate and into the bailey, where two couples waited for them. It was clear the women were mother and daughter, but the men didn't look alike. "That's Angus, my seneschal, and his wife and our housekeeper, Bethea. Their daughter, Maisie, is the head cook, and she's married to my second, Clyde."

Abigail hadn't imagined the keep's head cook would be close to her age. She recalled Ronan telling her about how intimidating Bethea could be, but at first she appeared motherly. Then Abigail stifled her laugh when she realized Ronan hadn't exaggerated. Bethea stepped toward them, but when Angus didn't follow, she turned around and yanked on his sleeve. Abigail couldn't hear what she said, but it looked like Bethea scolded the older man. However, her smile was cheery and maternal when she looked back at Abigail.

"Told you," Ronan muttered.

"Laird, Lady, welcome home," Bethea called as she walked past the younger couple, her scowl clear. Her daughter, son-by-marriage, and husband all fell in step with the matriarch. "Och, lad!"

Ronan chuckled as Bethea curled her nose up at him. "I'm glad to be home."

"We'll be just as glad once ye've had a bath. What did ye do to yerself?" Bethea demanded before she blinked several times and looked at Abigail. She sank into a deep curtsy. "I beg yer pardon, ma lady."

"Hello, Bethea." Abigail's voice was soft but warm. She couldn't help but return the older woman's smile after Bethea nodded with approval.

"Bethea, Angus, Maisie, Clyde, meet Lady Abigail MacKinnon."

"Welcome, Lady MacKinnon." Angus's gruff voice matched a man of his size, but his rosy cheeks and twinkling blue eyes didn't match the reputation Ronan told her about.

"Maisie, greet our lady, then scarper off to get a bath ready for our laird," Bethea ordered her daughter.

"Aye, Mama." Abigail estimated Maisie was closer in age to Madeline than her. She had her father's blue eyes, even if her other features came from her mother. "We're happy to have ye join our clan, Lady MacKinnon."

Abigail leaned forward to Maisie and Bethea. "Abigail when no one else can hear." Bethea nodded her approval, and Maisie blushed. Abigail looked at Angus. "When Bethea is ready to sit with me, will you show me the ledgers?"

Abigail nearly jumped at Angus's booming laugh. "So ye told her already, did ye?" He looked at Ronan and laughed again. "Aye, when ma wife is ready, I will show ye whatever she tells me to."

"Hauld yer wheest, auld mon," Bethea snapped, but there was no sting to her words. "Maisie? The bath willna heat itself. Look at the laird."

Maisie nodded and slipped away to follow her mother's orders. Ronan introduced Kieran to the three senior members of his household before he led Abigail and Kieran inside. Abigail looked around her new home, only half-paying attention to Ronan as he talked to Angus, Clyde, and Kieran. She looked at the rafters before glancing at the rail that ran along the second-floor landing. She realized that a sheet would have hung from there if she'd been a virgin. It had hung at the Chisholm keep after her first wedding night—*handfast*, she reminded herself. She wondered if Ronan would regret not having a virgin bride when his clan expected proof of their marriage.

"They ken not to look for it," Ronan whispered as he leaned toward Abigail. "They ken there was a handfast, and they ken we're a love match. That's all they need for now." Abigail nodded, but she still felt uneasy.

"Ma lady, we dinna care."

Abigail turned to look at Bethea, who was watching her. She felt her cheeks heating as she swept her eyes over the walls, taking in the tapestries hanging above the fireplaces and from the rafters.

"Ma lady," Bethea tried again. When Abigail couldn't avoid looking at the housekeeper without being rude, she nodded. She hoped that would be enough, but Bethea's determined expression told her it wasn't. "Lady MacKinnon—Lady Abigail—even a blind mon can see our laird has fallen in love. We all kenned it the first time he returned here from Stornoway. We couldnae believe he intended to marry any MacLeod. He told us a bit aboot ye, and he was vera direct that ye'd had a handfast. Whether ye looked at the laird or listened to him, ye couldnae miss the love. The lad has devoted his entire life to serving our people. He's never asked or taken aught for himself. If ye make him happy, then we dinna care where ye came from or what ye did before ye met our laird."

Abigail's cheeks radiated heat. She appreciated Bethea's reassurance, but it mortified her that the woman said so much in front of four men. She didn't know Angus or Clyde well enough to feel comfortable discussing anything to do with intimacy, let alone what happened between Ronan and her, or what happened in her past.

"Thank you, Bethea," Abigail said. She wanted to melt into the floor. She nearly clapped when she caught sight of Maisie returning to them. She hoped the woman would announce Ronan's bath was ready and they could escape to their chamber. Before Bethea could say anything about Ronan, her, and a bathtub, she asked, "Could you ready a chamber for my brother, please? A bath for him, too?"

"Of course, ma lady." Bethea curtsied and spun around, cutting off Maisie's path to them. Maisie cast a helpless look at her husband, who shrugged as his mother-by-marriage dragged his wife into the kitchens.

"Clyde, there is much to discuss," Ronan said. "But with no swords clanging inside the keep, it can wait until I show Lady MacKinnon her new home."

"And after yer bath," Clyde teased.

Ronan scowled at his closest friend and second-in-command. They were second cousins, and Ronan was the elder by four months. They'd played together as children, entered the lists together as adolescents, and fought side by side countless times. Until Ronan and Abigail had a son, Clyde was also Ronan's tá-naiste. He'd told Abigail many stories about his adventures on and off the battlefield with Clyde. He glanced down at Abigail and found her smiling at Clyde. He could only imagine what she would ask his friend first.

"Is it true that Ronan's scar on his—" Abigail leaned back to look at Ronan's backside before giving him a lascivious grin. "—came from you two jousting with pitchforks?"

"Aye, ma lady. I have one to match. In a far more —delicate place," Clyde grinned.

"Is it true that Ronan dared you to swim out in the loch at night when you were eight, then barked like a seal to make you think a kelpie was coming for you?"

"Aye. But when he came in to search for me, I

pulled him under and made him think a kelpie caught him." Clyde's smile grew as he winked conspiratorially. "For every story he told ye that makes me look like an eejit, I have three to tell aboot him."

"Do you promise?"

"Och, yer wife is a wee too eager to hear aboot all yer blundering, Ronan." Clyde clapped Ronan on the shoulder and squeezed. He leaned close to his laird and whispered. "Ye look like shite, yet ye've never looked happier. Ye look like I do around Maisie. I'm happy for ye."

"Thank you, Cly." Ronan returned his comrade's grin before he reached his hand out to Abigail and glanced at Kieran. "I'll point out your chamber, Kieran. I'd show my wife more of our home." Ronan intended to show Abigail only one place: their chamber.

280

THIRTY-TWO

R onan sighed as he leaned back against the side
of the tub, his eyes drifting closed. The feel of
Abigail's fingers scrubbing his scalp nearly put him to
sleep. He was still exhausted, needing both sleep and
several healthier meals, but he was home with his
wife. A steaming tub was already in their chamber
when they arrived. Ronan insisted Abigail take a
bath first. She'd argued until he threatened to put her
in the tub with her clothes on. She scrambled to get
undressed, reminding him they were Maude's and
needed to be returned. Now she sat with his enormous robe wrapped around her as she helped him
bathe. They had talked little since Abigail got into
the tub. The companionable silence was something
he'd once prayed he would enjoy with a wife, and he
found it peaceful with Abigail.

When his leg twitched, Abigail chuckled. He
opened his eyes to find Abigail standing beside the
tub with a drying linen open for him. He reached up
and found his hair was smooth and soap-free. He
hadn't realized he drifted off while Abigail helped
him wash. He stood, watching his wife's appreciative
gaze sweep over him several times. When it settled

on his lengthening cock, he rubbed the linen over his body then tossed it aside. With a squeak, Abigail landed on an enormous and soft bed, while Ronan prowled over her. He pushed the robe aside before she eased her arms out of it.

"Are you up for this?" Abigail asked, then giggled. "I mean, do you have enough energy for this? I ken you're up for it."

"Making love to my wife? I'll always have the energy for this, Abby. I want to sink into you and never leave."

"Good, because I don't intend to let you go."

Abigail's hands traveled along Ronan's back as he swept his tongue over her pebbled nipple. When it puckered into a tight dart, he ran his teeth against it, drawing it out until he could suckle. Abigail sighed as her legs fell wide, welcoming Ronan as the tip of his cock brushed her seam. Cupping her breast, Ronan swirled his tongue around her nipple before blowing cool air onto it. Once more, his mouth closed around it, sucking with enough pressure to make Abigail arch her back and moan with need.

"Ronan, can I admit something to you?"

"Of course. Aught, Abby. Always."

"I missed you so much, even when I could hold your hand. At night, I imagined you were touching me just as you are now. I can live without coupling, so I don't want you to think me wanton, but I eased the ache while picturing you."

"Och, Abby. How do you think I passed the time?" Ronan grinned. His voice grew husky with his request. "Show me."

Abigail massaged her breast before tweaking the nipple Ronan hadn't attended to while her other hand slid along her belly. Their eyes locked until Abigail's fingers slid through her ebony curls. Ronan watched as her index finger circled her button. She moaned his name as she increased the pressure. He was entranced watching his wife. He reached for his own cock, slowly gliding his hand along his rod. The need to taste and touch tempted him to brush her hand aside, but he marveled at the sight. As Abigail's fingers increased their pace and her breathing became shallow, she reached for Ronan's cock. Her hand took the place of his as she worked their aching flesh.

"Watching you is the most sensual and arousing act I've ever witnessed. I don't know how it could ever have bothered me."

"I understand why. That was different. But I need you to ken I never meant to reject you, Ronan."

"I ken that now." Ronan pressed a hungry kiss to Abigail's lips, sliding his tongue into her mouth. As the kiss became frenzied with passion, Abigail guided the head of Ronan's cock into her sheath. When she released him, he thrust savagely into her, eliciting a carnal moan as Abigail's hips rose to meet his.

"Hard," she moaned. The single word unleashed their combined need. There was nothing tender about this joining. That could come later. This mating was a celebration of survival, their shared physical craving for only one another. Sweat soon made their bodies glisten, as the sound of their bodies slamming together, and the creaks of the bed filled the chamber.

Ronan lifted Abigail's leg over his hip, circling them after each thrust. He watched as Abigail's eyes came alive with hunger and determination. Their brilliance rivaled any summer sky or the deepest parts of Loch Slapin. He was drowning in them but had no thought to call out for rescue. There was only a need to consume.

Abigail was surely drunk from the headiness that came with the feel of Ronan surging into her over and over. His whisky-hued eyes bore into hers, and she reveled in the possessiveness she saw. She was certain it equaled what she felt toward Ronan. She would never accept them being apart, never accept anyone keeping them apart. She moved with him, her fingers digging into his buttocks as she urged him on, matching his hedonistic wildness with each move. The burn and ache in her core exploded into fire as waves of pleasure swept up her body, tightening her nipples and making her breasts heavy before spreading into her limbs. Her toes curled as her head pressed back against the pillow, her throat straining with each breath.

"Dear God, Abby," Ronan groaned as he watched his wife's release. As her core spasmed around his rod, he felt his seed pour into her. His buttocks clenched as he ground himself against her, drawing out her climax.

"You're mine." The unequivocal claim suited Ronan. Abigail's words weren't those of a jealous woman, but they were possessive. They matched Ronan's sentiments as he nuzzled her neck. He settled onto his forearms as Abigail's gestures became tender as she stroked his hair and back. His kisses were gentle now that the frenzy subsided.

"Abigail, I love you. And I'm so proud of you my heart might burst."

"I think that's just from exertion," Abigail giggled.

"There is that." Ronan grinned ruefully. "But I'm serious. You're brave and resilient. A bit more reckless than my heart can take, but you did what I didn't. You rescued us."

"Ronan, I know I took a risk that could have

wound up with us both dead, but I'd do it over again, knowing there was even a slight chance that you'd be free." Abigail tucked blond locks behind Ronan's ear before they rolled onto their sides. She hesitated to ask but pressed on. "Are you bothered that it wasn't you who did the rescuing?"

"I suppose, as the mon, I should be. It's my duty to protect you, to keep you safe, and I didn't do that. But I'm just too damn proud to feel aught else."

"Ronan, if you'd fought alone in your cell, they would have killed you."

"Likely, even with my dirks."

"And even if you found the keys, where would you have gone? You didn't know aboot the sea cave."

"I wouldn't have left my men behind, no matter how much I wanted to be with you."

"Because you're not selfish. Without you as a captive, there would have been no reason to let your men live. They would have killed them if you escaped. You don't put your wants ahead of those you serve."

"I try not to." Ronan kissed Abigail softly, but he couldn't meet her eyes. "My cell door was never open at the same time as the others until that day. I admit I wasn't sure I had the strength to fight. But given the opportunity to get to you—to rescue you finally—I discovered a reserve I wasn't certain I had."

Abigail watched Ronan's expressions. She believed him—mostly. "Ronan? Do you feel guilty that with your hands free that you should have tried, even if you might have died?"

Ronan pressed his lips into a tight line before he nodded. "I wouldn't leave my men behind, but I also couldn't leave without being sure you could come with me. You told me they locked you in at night, and I had no keys to free anyone. Abigail, I would have let us all die before leaving you."

"You know you didn't fail, don't you? Your men were just as free as you, and with at least two of them in each cell, overpowering the guards would have been easier for them than you."

"I'm not bothered that a woman saved me. But each time I've wound up in a dungeon, it's been because of my failures as a leader."

"Have you made the same mistake twice? You can't control everything. Things are going to happen that you can't stop. That doesn't make you a failure."

"I knew the risks of sailing past Dunvegan."

"How the hell were you supposed to get us here without doing that? Ride across Skye after coming ashore on the MacNeacails' land or the Mac-Queens'? Both clans might ally with the MacDonalds, but that only means they're not always your enemy. It would have taken longer to ride. You did what you knew was best, especially in the middle of winter. And if you wish to survive the night, you'd better not suggest that I should have stayed in Stornoway without you. I would have swum."

"I suppose I should stay quiet then."

"You became laird because God made you the son of a laird. You've taken that burden on with un-failing loyalty and duty. But you cannot take every-thing that goes wrong as a personal failure."

"It feels like failure when the one person who means more than aught is in danger."

"Please stop." Abigail cupped Ronan's jaw in both hands. "You protected me when we nearly got trapped in the Glencoe Pass. You protected me by telling me to get under the bench. I would have wound up with an arrow through me if you hadn't. You protected me by not letting any of the Mac-Leods onto the boat. I would have been dead before

Gordon or Donovan decided to take us. You told me Cecily would make sure I had a chamber, and you were right. You warned me aboot the food, and from Cormag's looks during the meals, you were wise to do so. You did the best with what you had."

"The thought of you looking at me as aught less than you deserve is more than I can bear," Ronan whispered.

"Then it's a bluidy good thing you are far more than I deserve, expected, or even hoped for. Now cease, so I can make love to you." Abigail didn't wait for Ronan's answer before she slid down the bed. She glanced up at Ronan as he rolled onto his back. She stroked his thickening cock as she swirled her tongue around the tip. She took its bulbous head into her mouth, her lips wrapping tightly. She watched Ronan's eyes slide shut as she took his length into her mouth. With the first hint of suction, Ronan's eyes opened, and he tucked his arm under his head. He couldn't tear his eyes away. As he watched his wife work his length, a hunger of his own made his mouth water.

"Turn around, Abby."

Abigail's brow furrowed, but she moved to kneel on the other side of Ronan's leg. She yelped when he grasped her hips and pulled them toward him. He arranged her legs to straddle his chest. She was unprepared for the feel of his tongue along her seam. She glanced back at him, enjoying the lusty gleam in his eyes. She hadn't conceived of such a position, nor did she imagine her husband thinking of it. But she'd already discovered that her husband's lack of experience had little impact on his creativity or curiosity. Her eyes drifted closed, concentration and arousal mingling. It wasn't long before the need to kiss and look at one another took hold. Abigail moved to allow her sheath to slide down Ronan's sword, moving them in tandem until she collapsed against his chest, both replete. Ronan wrapped his arms around Abigail's narrower frame and sighed. They drifted to sleep until the bells for the evening meal roused them.

THIRTY-THREE

"The men said they heard at least two score warriors leave Dunvegan with the purpose of coming here. Mayhap the weather got the better of them, or mayhap they've been waiting it out. But we must check on the outlying villages." Ronan sat in his solar with Clyde after the evening meal. He'd already escorted Abigail up to their chamber and tucked his sleepy wife into bed. Now he met with his second to relay the events of their capture and to plan for a defense.

Forty men were hardly enough to lay waste to Dun Ringill, even if Ronan had been away. But it was more than enough to wreak havoc on villages a day's ride from the keep. The force was enough to defeat several patrols, opening the way for a larger army from Dunvegan to march on them. It was foolish to attempt such an attack during winter, but he no longer put anything past Cormag, especially after the death of his brothers.

"I didna hear aught from any of the men, nor is anyone unaccounted for," Clyde pointed out. "But that doesnae mean the MacLeods didna make it onto our land. But I must ask, doesnae it make it difficult kenning ye're fighting yer wife's people?"

"If you'd seen Abby drive that knife into Donovan's throat without flinching, you would ken she doesn't consider them family. Neither does Kieran. They share common ancestry, but they've been rivals on and off for generations. Because the Dunvegan bastards are *Sìol Thormoid*, they've claimed superiority since their branch came first. They don't care that *Sìol Thorcaill* on Lewis all hail from same progenitor—the aptly named Leod." Ronan rolled his eyes. No MacKinnon was impressed with the story of how the MacLeods came to be. Their own clan descended from the earliest kings of Scotland and even kings of Ireland. "You ken once the Lewis branch became vassals to the MacDonalds of Islay, those here on Skye believed themselves untouchable. Never mind that they were vassals too! Bluidy Islay calls both Cormag and Kieran 'the greatest of nobles.' That ridiculous title of Lord lingers on from Islay's days up Edward Balliol's arse. Kieran tolerates Cormag—or rather tolerated the bastard—for the sake of keeping the peace within the islands and keeping our business away from the Bruce and those at court who would argue we Hebrideans must come to heel."

"Will Kieran and his men stay to fight?"

"Only if the fight comes to us before they plan to depart. Kieran said he'd stay for another two days to visit with Abby. I think he's pleased to see for himself that she's settled here." Ronan wished he could lavish time on Abigail and show her around the land surrounding Dun Ringill, but between the winter weather and the potential threat, it was impossible. He hadn't told her that he would likely ride out while Kieran was still visiting. He felt better knowing his brother-by-marriage was in residence while he was away. He trusted Bethea and Angus to manage the keep, and his clan council would lead their people.

But he hated the thought of abandoning Abigail the moment they arrived.

"I can go for ye." Clyde broke into Ronan's thoughts.

"We'll go together. You to the northwest along the coast while I move inland. We ken they rode, but the weather is milder along the coast. They may have taken that route, even if it's not as direct. Or they may have switched course if the weather turned foul."

"It's three day's ride to Dunvegan. Even if we dinna cross into their territory, which I hope we dinna, we're likely to be gone a sennight. That's longer than Kieran is staying."

"I ken. My hope is we're back well within a sennight. If they're anywhere, it would be close to here. I'd be only too happy to discover their carcasses."

"Ye and me both. Does that mean we ride out in the morn?"

"Aye," Ronan said with a sigh. "Go to Maisie while I wake my wife."

"Neither will be happy," Clyde mused.

"Nay, they will not."

The men clapped each other on the shoulder before Ronan made his way to his chamber and Clyde went home to his croft. Ronan dreaded telling Abigail that he would leave in the morning. He knew the fact that he was not fully recovered concerned her, and he loathed leaving Abigail to learn her way around without him. He'd envisioned a different welcome for his bride. He eased the chamber door open, unprepared to find Abigail packing a satchel. His heart lurched thinking she packed her own belongings, but he noticed she held one of his leines.

"You're riding out tomorrow, aren't you?" Abigail said as she looked back over her shoulder.

"I don't want to."

"But you must."

"Aye." Ronan came to stand behind Abigail as he slid his arms around her waist and kissed her neck. She leaned back, her eyes closed, and sighed. "I thought you were sleeping."

"I dozed for a few minutes, then awoke kenning you would be going. I gave up trying to sleep and decided the only thing I could do to help at this hour was to pack your satchel. I suppose Maisie and Bethea will ken what to do in the morn, so they won't need me to pack food for you. How many men are you taking?"

"Four score."

"That many? Is Clyde leading one group, and you're leading the other?"

"Aye. How'd you ken?"

"That's what Kieran would do. Are you going along the coast or inland?"

"I'm going inland while Clyde moves northwest."

"You ken you're the one likely to find the MacLeods."

"Assuming they didn't change their path to avoid the snowstorm Linus mentioned."

"Do you ken how bad it was? Enough to get them trapped or freeze to death?"

"The reports that came to Clyde were that it was bad enough to waylay them, but not bad enough to stop them completely. They might have turned back, but I doubt it. They won't ken that Gordon's dead. They'll not want to face Cormag and Gordon."

"I wonder if they set off after they allowed me outside that day."

"Why?" Ronan wondered.

"I'm wondering if the captain of the guard led the men. Few of them seem to like him, and even less respect him. I could see it from my chamber when I looked out the window. They mocked him and sneered whenever he turned his back. It was even more obvious when I crossed the bailey and could watch them from the grove."

"Did you get a sense of how they felt aboot Cormag and Gordon?"

"Not aboot Cormag, but it was clear they respected Gordon. I saw him with them, but I never saw Cormag. Come to think of it, I don't recall seeing Cormag go out to the lists even when Gordon did."

"Abby, I'm sorry I'm leaving you so soon," Ronan said as Abigail turned in his arms.

"I don't like it either, but duty calls, even for newlyweds."

"I wanted you to meet your new clan with more than a brief introduction at the evening meal. I ken Angus and Bethea will help you adjust, but I worry you'll be lonely kenning no one yet. I don't ken how busy you'll be, and I fear that you'll be left with naught to do and no way to occupy your time."

"Even if that's the case—which I doubt since Maude never sits down—I can introduce myself to those who work in the keep and in the bailey. I can start getting to ken people."

"You're comfortable walking up to strangers and striking up a conversation?"

Abigail titled her head and shrugged. "They're not exactly strangers. I'm part of this clan now, and you've kenned them your entire life. You told me you're not apprehensive aboot what you say or do when you're here. I trust that means your people are kind and respectful."

"They are."

"I'm nervous. I can admit that. But this is what life has given us for the moment."

"You're very philosophical."

"Mayhap I'm finally growing up." Abigail rested

her head against Ronan's chest. She didn't know what the next day or the one after that held. She didn't know how well she would fit in or if there would be much for her to do if Bethea had been running the household for years. But for the first time in her life, she felt prepared to take on the role of chatelaine. She was ready for the work that went with the title; she even looked forward to it. She respected Ronan's devotion to his people, and she wanted to match it. Ronan saying he was proud of her meant the world to Abigail. She knew she'd done little over her life to be proud of or that made others proud of her. She wanted to be worthy of the praise moving forward, not for just one event in a lifetime together.

"Abby, I'll return as soon as I can. I swear it. No dillydallying." Ronan kissed her nose as she leaned back to look at him while he spoke.

"I ken. It's too cold to dillydally."

"Lass, you ken that's not why I'll be eager to come home, but I certainly look forward to you warming me up." Ronan patted her backside before he pulled at the ribbons on her chemise. Once they undressed, they climbed into bed. With Ronan's arm around her waist and his hand on her backside, Abigail draped herself across his chest. They were asleep within moments.

THIRTY-FOUR

Abigail sighed as she watched Ronan lead the troop of eighty men through the gates. He watched her as he rode through as well, waving twice before the path forced him to look where he was going. She welcomed Kieran's arm around her shoulders and leaned against her brother. She'd seen Kieran ride out to fight the Morrisons, and she'd seen Lathan ride out for sorties. But it was different watching the man she loved, the one she wanted to live a long and blissful life with, ride out to the unknown. Maude warned her that it never got easier, even as it became more expected.

"Ma lady," Bethea said as she approached. She'd been comforting Maisie as the men left. Abigail learned that morning that Maisie was expecting her first child and was particularly upset that Clyde was leaving. Abigail couldn't blame the young woman. She was already struggling not to show any signs of emotion to those around her. She couldn't imagine the strain that would come once she and Ronan were parents. "Since Laird MacLeod is here, mayhap ye wouldnae mind me waiting to show ye aboot."

"Bethea, that is a kind way of giving me a few

days to sort myself out." Abigail reached out her hand to Bethea, who squeezed hers. "Thank you."

"Whatever ye need, ma lady." Bethea turned around and called out to the laundresses before moving briskly toward them.

"Abigail, I ken I planned to stay for two days, but I can remain here longer," Kieran said as they walked into the Great Hall.

"I appreciate the offer, Kieran. But I ken you don't like to be away from Maude and the weans for that long, and you have your own duties to see to."

"I dinna like being away, but I dislike being unsure aboot how ye fare even more."

"This isn't like the Chisholms. I can already tell. And even though Ronan took four score men with him, there's still more than that to defend the keep. I'm not trying to shoo you away because I don't like your company. I just don't need you to stay."

"Abigail, ye're a woman to admire and respect."

"I'm getting there."

"I can already see it. Ye're different from who ye were two years ago, and completely different from three years ago."

"You can thank your wife for that. As frightening as being in that freezing water was and being scared for Ronan in that dungeon, I still think waiting for Maude to wake from her injuries was more terrifying. Watching you while we waited. It tore my heart and Mother's. It gave us a great deal to think aboot, and I was so scared that Maude's only memory of me would be as a spiteful child. I didn't want that. I might have already been a woman, but I didn't act like it toward her. Knowing she might die from trying to protect someone else's children—I realized how admirable she is. I wanted to be more like her. But I was a long way away from that. I realized that the last time I was supposed to run a keep. I want to be someone others enjoy being around and someone who gives rather than takes."

"Ye are, Abigail. Ye, Mother, and Madeline didna bring out the best in one another. But ye all turned around before Mother shed her earthly coil. Life made ye and Madeline grow up. It did for me, too. It came to me in the way of ma lairdship. It came to Madeline in a convent. For ye, it was an unfortunate arrangement and time at court."

"It was those things, but it was really losing Mother. Once she was gone, the frivolity and indulgences that were so important before seemed even more petty when there was no one to share them with. Even though she didn't prepare me for my future as a clan's lady, she was a devoted mother to me and Madeline. I just wish she'd been that way for you. But no longer having her as a role model made me look at Maude and other women as better guides. My judgment of Ronan before I knew him could have cost me the same love you share with Maude. Having seen you two and seeing a glimpse of what I hope my life will be, I'll do aught to have that with Ronan."

Kieran embraced his sister despite the awkwardness of the chairs where they sat at the dais. "I believe ye will thrive here, little sister. I believe the MacKinnons are fortunate to have ye beside Ronan. I wish ye the love and happiness I have with Maude. I never imagined it was possible before I met her, and I doubt I could ever have it again with someone else. I'm certain I couldnae. I feel better aboot returning to Lewis. But I meant what I said before ye left Stornoway and when ye returned. Ye can always come back if ye need us, and just because ye did once, doesnae mean ye canna any time."

"I know, Kier. That was part of what got me through. I don't know that I would have believed that when I was with the Chisholms. I don't think I would have believed I deserved it. But I came to you because I needed you to help Ronan. It wasn't because my life was in jeopardy."

"I ken. Either way, ye did the right thing. And I'm proud of ye for that."

Abigail beamed at her brother. He was the second person in two days to say he was proud of her when she'd never heard anyone tell her that. It offered a sense of peace along with purpose. The siblings spent the rest of the day meeting various people who worked in the bailey. Abigail was tired when she fell into bed, but it was several hours before she fell asleep, her hand resting over Ronan's side.

"It's time for you to turn toward the coast," Ronan said with a nod in that direction. He, Clyde, and their men spent the morning riding together, but the road split just ahead of them. The sun shone in Clyde's direction, but pregnant clouds hung low inland. Ronan was certain it would snow before they made camp. He wanted to groan, but it wouldn't be his first night bedding down during a storm. He thought about how he would prefer to be tucked under the covers with Abigail, a cheery fire in the hearth.

"Three days, aye?"

"Aye. Regardless of what we find, we meet here in three days," Ronan confirmed. "If you're not here by nightfall, my men and I ride out to find you."

"The same for us."

"I pray we're here waiting for you before the sun sets tomorrow. Let's pray we find them dead, but if we don't, let's put an end to this quickly."

"I'm all for that." Clyde extended his arm, and

he and Ronan clasped forearms. The two forces split, heading in opposite directions. Ronan nudged his horse forward, wishing that his trusted destrier were beneath him. But none of the horses they lost had made their way home. Ronan didn't expect that they would. Someone else would have rounded them up.

Despite moving at a canter, their progress felt slow to Ronan as the wind howled around them. By midafternoon, heavy snowfall forced Ronan and his men to dismount and guide their steeds. The snow accumulated rapidly, making it impossible for them to continue. They sought shelter their second night in a conifer forest, the thick needles keeping the snow out. The men gathered piles of needles before unrolling their bedrolls onto them. They served as insulation against the frozen ground.

By morning, the snow was mid-calf. Ronan considered ordering them to abandon their search until spring, but he knew Cormag's men wouldn't return in disgrace, having to admit that they never reached Dun Ringill. He told his men they would search until late afternoon before making camp. If they hadn't found the men from Dunvegan by then, they would turn back in the morning. It was the only way they would make their rendezvous with Clyde. He didn't want more of his men trekking through the snow. Even if it snowed near the coast, the heavens wouldn't dump on them like they had inland. He strongly suspected the MacLeods wouldn't travel along the coast because it added significant distance to their journey, as they had to weave around bays and inlets. He'd sent Clyde that way because it was a possibility, but he wanted to keep the father-to-be as far out of harm's way as he could.

"Laird!"

Ronan shielded his eyes from the snow, his lashes already caked with ice. Two of his scouts were jogging through the snow, their knees high with each step. The men were breathless when they reached the rest of the men, their horses snorting puff of steams.

"Did you find something?

"We did. The snow's covered most of their trail, but the charred ground shows where they camped probably two days ago. There was more than one fire."

"So their numbers remain large. We've encountered no one. Do you think they turned toward the coast?"

"Sort of. We found a few snapped branches showing which direction they left. They're headed to the Fairy Pools."

"Bampots," Ronan muttered before he looked at his men. "Seems their flag isn't enough to protect them." The men made camp the night before at the foot of the Black Cuillins near Glenbrittle, and Ronan sent out scouts before dawn. They would have to travel through the Glen Brittle forest to reach the pools, but the pools laid halfway between where Ronan was and where Clyde would be. The pools were a breathtakingly pristine blue in summer with waterfalls pouring into them. While still bone-chilling in the warmest of weather, they were mystical places to swim. But in winter, they would be little more than ice. As spectacular as the landscape was, there were no ancient legends that involved the fae or the Mac-Leods of Skye. It made little sense to Ronan why their enemy headed there.

The MacKinnons would approach from *Alt Coir' a' Mhadaidh*—appropriately named "the burn of the wolf's corrie" since the wild animals hunted there throughout the day and night—and attempt to pursue the men along the River Brittle. This would either push them to the coast or trap them with

Clyde and his men blocking their escape to Loch Brittle. It was less than five miles from the pools to the coast, but with the deepening snow, it would be slow for the large number of men in his contingent. It would give Ronan's scouts time to get ahead and look for Clyde. They changed course as they pointed toward their new destination.

Abigail stood in the same spot to wave goodbye to Kieran as she had when Ronan rode out. This time she watched Kieran, Kyle, and her former clansmen walk along the docks until they boarded their birlinns. She'd enjoyed her two days with her brother, sharing stories from court that she hadn't told during her time at Stornoway. She listened as Kieran regaled her with more tales about his children's antics, always the boastful father. He'd taken her out on his birlinn to explore the loch, but they hadn't ventured far. She didn't ask to venture away from the keep on horseback. She didn't welcome the risk, and she knew Kieran would refuse. Her brother trained in the lists with the other men each morning, and Abigail used the time to get to know Bethea and Angus. She was enchanted with the couple, fully appreciating Ronan's fond warning that Angus enjoyed antagonizing his wife so they could later make up. It was no small wonder they had so many children; the couple was as lusty as Ronan and Abigail. But they were endearing and kind to her.

Bethea was maternal in a way Adeline never had been, although Abigail had always considered herself close to her mother. Angus reminded her of her father, who'd been overindulgent with his wife and daughters. Abigail never considered manipulating and browbeating Ronan's seneschal like she had

Kieran's. Despite losing most of her belongings to the Minch, she didn't ask for anything more than the wool she needed for four pairs of stockings and two sturdy winter gowns. Only a few years ago she would have demanded the finest material for an entirely new wardrobe. She wouldn't have considered the cost, but now considered each coin spent on her was money taken from clan members who might need it more.

"Ma lady, if ye have the time, mayhap we could go over the ledgers," Angus offered quietly. She smiled up at the older man and nodded. While Bethea was hardly subtle with anyone, she and Angus had been thoughtful in how they approached Abigail, attempting to stave off loneliness and uncertainty. She appreciated their kindness.

"I have the time, Angus. Thank you." Angus led Abigail into Ronan's solar, where he laid out the ledgers on the massive wood table in the center of the chamber. Abigail forced herself not to keep glancing at Ronan's desk, wondering what he looked like when he sat there.

"Lass, he'll be home in two shakes of a lamb's tail. Then ye will find him underfoot and a nuisance just like ma Bethea finds me."

Abigail smiled wistfully at the desk before she looked at Angus. "Aye, and you and I both ken you do it on purpose and love every minute."

"Just like our laird will." Angus offered her a fatherly pat on the arm before they sat together to look over the accounts. One look at Angus's colossal build, and it was obvious he still spent hours in the lists. She'd caught sight of him sparring with Kieran. More specifically, she spied him knocking Kieran on his arse more than once. But the ledgers were in perfect order, all figures written in neat penmanship, and the tallies accurate.

"Angus, may I ask you something?"

"Of course, ma lady."

"What was the laird's mother like?"

"Och, Lady Glynnis was wonderful. Ye actually remind me quite a lot of her, except her hair was blonde, and her eyes were brown," Angus grinned. "She was kind and patient with everyone, especially our laird. He was a troublemaker as a child. He would give his parents fits. Clyde was just as bad. They often led one another astray, but they were adorable when they were wee lads, so it was hard to stay angry. She didna have an easy go of it when she arrived. People werenae vera welcoming, and the auld laird was a rake before he married."

When Angus went quiet, Abigail smiled encouragingly. "The laird told me aboot a conversation he had with his father aboot that."

"I suppose ye would have noticed," Angus mumbled, aware Abigail would have realized Ronan's inexperience. He cast an assessing glance at Abigail, and she wanted to shift in her seat.

"I cared no more than the laird cared aboot me and my past. But that must have been extremely hard for Lady Glynnis."

"It was at first. But like I said, she was kind and patient with everyone. It wasna long before people saw the good in her was genuine. She and the auld laird were a wonderful couple. Always respectful of one another, and it made them powerful leaders. It made the laird's father a better leader. Lady Glynnis was shy at first, but she loved to laugh. Ma Bethea took it harder than anyone but the laird when she passed. They were the best of friends, and Lady Glynnis never made Bethea feel like a servant."

"A housekeeper is a family member," Abigail whispered as she thought about Agatha at Stornoway. The woman practically raised Abigail and her siblings; she was the warmest and most maternal woman Abigail knew before Maude. She considered the years that she was ungrateful for Agatha's care. Abigail had worked hard over the last few years to make it up to Agatha. It had been the older woman who Abigail turned to when Adeline died. She looked up at Angus and smiled. "A housekeeper is often a second mother and grandmother to the laird's family. I didn't appreciate the woman I grew up with when I was younger, but I do now. Is the laird more like his mother or his father?"

"He's the best of both. He can be reserved and quiet like his mother was, but he's brave and commanding like his father was." Angus watched Abigail and knew the young woman took what he said to heart. He remembered when Lady Glynnis arrived, under much the same circumstances as Abigail had. Laird Gregor rode out a fortnight after Lady Glynnis arrived and was away for nearly a month fighting the MacQueens. Gregor hadn't been very discriminate in his choices of bedmates when he was a young man, and Lady Glynnis faced a chilly welcome. The differences between father and son relieved Angus. He knew Abigail wouldn't face the same challenge as Glynnis.

"I think that describes my husband perfectly, Angus. I wondered aboot how quiet he was when we met, but I realized he's very observant and never speaks without thinking."

"That is vera true, ma lady. I dinna ken what he told ye aboot all of us, but he couldnae stop smiling whenever he spoke of ye. If ye dinna mind me saying, he's vera smitten with ye."

"I don't mind at all, since I'm completely besotted." Abigail looked back at the ledgers, and the pair spent the rest of the afternoon going over the income and expenses the clan faced each month. But Abigail considered what she learned. It had seemed like so little, but when she considered all she heard about Ronan, it made sense. By the time the servants presented the evening meal, Abigail already felt like she was at home. There were suspicious looks from some, but overall, the clan was welcoming. She couldn't blame those who were skeptical, since their laird rode out to fight men she was distantly related to. But the only clan on Skye she felt a kinship with was the MacKinnons. She woke the next morning ready to face her first full day as Lady MacKinnon, chatelaine of Dun Ringill.

THIRTY-FIVE

Abigail straightened as her hand stopped kneading the bread on the kitchen table before her. Everyone in the kitchens froze. Bells pealed outside, but it wasn't the slow and steady rhythm announcing the laird's return. It was the urgent clanking of a warning. Abigail abandoned the dough, wiping her hands on her skirts as she dashed out of the kitchens and into the bailey. She pulled her arisaid over her head as she lifted her skirts to run to the steps leading up to the battlements. They were slick, forcing her to slow as she climbed.

"Who's coming?" Abigail called out as she reached the top. Her eyes scanned their surroundings until she squinted and spotted birlinns approaching. She turned to look back toward the mountains in the distance, the same direction Ronan traveled. "Mac-Leods? Not my brother?"

"Aye. Nae yer brother, ma lady."

"How can ye tell from here? They're barely specks."

A guardsman pointed to the anglers on the docks, hurrying to unload their catches. Then he pointed to the ones rowing furiously toward the shore. "Willy, Linus's grandson, came running to tell us."

Abigail watched as villagers scurried into the bailey, mothers dragging and carrying children. Men armed with axes and pitchforks followed. "Is this the only village nearby? Are there others that need warning?"

"Aye. There are three villages up the coast."

"Can a rider make it in the snow?"

"Mayhap, but I dinna think the people can make it here on foot."

"How long do you think we have until they make landfall?"

"With the midmorning tide, an hour, mayhap."

"Send the best rider to the furthest village first. Have him tell the people to head toward here. Send the best sailors up the coast to ferry people here. Have extra men posted at the postern gate to help those who take that path up. Do the storage buildings have false floors?"

"The granary is the only one. But there are storage rooms in the keep that have false floors."

"Thank you." Abigail turned away, then paused. "What's your name?"

"Timothy, ma lady."

"Thank you, Timothy." Abigail hurried down the steps as guards herded women and children into the keep. She ran back inside to discover Bethea issuing orders for the maids to find blankets and for Maisie to bring all the cheese, meats, and bread she had prepared. "Bethea, one of the guards, Timothy, told me about the false floors in the storerooms. Can all these people fit?"

"Only the ones here now."

"Then we need blankets, water, and buckets taken to the granary."

"Buckets?"

"Aye. What do weans do when they're scared?"

"Need to use the pot."

"Exactly. The women need somewhere for the weans to go, so none are tempted to leave their hiding place to keep the small space clean."

"Right, ma lady." Bethea turned to a passing servant and conveyed Abigail's orders. Abigail still knew few servants by name. "I'm going to the bailey, Bethea. The storage buildings first, then back up to the battlements. Then I'll come back to the kitchens."

"I'll ken where to look for ye." Bethea nodded her head in approval, impressed that Abigail thought to tell someone of her whereabouts. If the MacLeods breached the keep, she would be a primary target. Bethea would know where to send people to search for her. Abigail pulled the front of her skirts high enough to keep from tripping over them and tucked them into her belt. She made her way back out to the bailey as villagers continued to pour through the gates. She ordered guards to take the women and children to the granary, then pointed the servants with the supplies she requested in the right direction. She made a detour to the postern gate to tell the guard to expect villagers to arrive by boat and to urge them to use that gate since it was closer to the docks.

Abigail climbed another set of steps up to the battlements, shielding her eyes from the glare off the water. The boats were still small dots on the horizon, seeming not to have grown closer. She looked for the man assigned as captain of the guard while Clyde was away. She spotted him and called out. She slipped and slid her way to him. "Get the wall walk cleared of snow. Now. Do we have cauldrons and tar or oil?"

The man looked startled by Abigail's order and question. He nodded before he scowled at her, clearly deciding he didn't enjoy taking orders from her. She returned his glare in equal measure. When he opened his mouth to speak, she snapped, "Dinna even think to disagree with me. Ye ken both things need doing. The laird and his tánaiste arenae here. I am, and I'm chatelaine to this castle. I'm responsible for every person within these walls. That includes men who dinna need to break their necks while trying to defend our people. Clear the snow, even if it means ye're on yer hands and knees scooping it. Get the fires lit. I'll make sure yer men can get into the storerooms. Do it now."

The man looked at Abigail once more, then nodded. She watched him spin on his heels and start issuing commands to his men. She worked her way back to the kitchens, weaving through people running to find shelter. She scanned the wall walk, pleased to see more men on sentry. She yanked the door open and stepped inside. She locked eyes with Maisie, who looked terrified and resolute at the same time. Abigail suspected her expression matched the head cook's.

"If this is a long battle, the men will need food and ale. Have food set aside for them. More than for the villagers. There's naught for it. The men need it more. Where's the pitch stored?"

"In the storeroom closest to the fletchers."

"I'm going there now. Have men gather wood to bring in here, so once the fight begins, none of you have to leave. Get torches lit and in all the sconces where you and the women will hide."

"Where we will be? Where are ye going?"

"I don't ken yet. But have them as weapons. It'll keep men from coming within reach of you." Abigail looked at the keys hanging from her belt. "Do you ken which one opens the storeroom with the tar?"

Maisie rushed forward and examined the keys before she picked one. Impulsively, the cook pulled

Abigail into her embrace. The exchange took both off-guard, but Abigail hugged Maisie in return. "Dinna do aught foolish, ma lady. Remember the laird loves ye."

"I ken. And I love him. I'm going to do my best to make sure he has a home to come back to." Abigail spun away and made for the storeroom. She signaled men to come with her before she unlocked the door, issuing orders that they take all of it to the wall walk. She spied Bethea on the steps by the main door. She made her way to the housekeeper.

"Blankets, water, and buckets are with the women and weans. They ken nae to go down below until they must. I see ye have the pitch going up and wood too. I saw ye speaking to Norman. I'm guessing he didna take to ye suggesting what he should have started the moment the warning went up."

"Likely not, but I don't care. He can deal with me later. When we live through this. Where will you go when the fight starts?"

"To the kitchens with Maisie and the others. She told me aboot yer idea with the torches. I didna think of that."

"Where's Angus?"

"The armory or the blacksmith's."

"That's where I'm headed, then the fletchers. Go back inside and make certain there are no papers left out in Ronan's solar. If you can lock his desk, then do it. Lock his solar, too. Make sure the guards in the keep ken to block the chamber. I don't know what Ronan keeps in there, but it doesn't belong in another clan's hands."

"Aye, ma lady. Where will ye go?"

"I don't know, Bethea. Not because I don't know where to go," Abigail clarified as Bethea started to speak. "I don't ken where I'll need to be." Bethea nodded and went inside while Abigail went to the armory. She found Angus issuing orders to men as they gathered additional dirks and battleaxes. She stood out of the way until all the men were armed, and no weapons remained.

"Ma lady, Timothy told me what ye said to Norman. Ye were wise to have them clear the snow. They'll chip the ice away once they can see it. Can ye smell the tar warming? That'll be bubbling by the time the MacLeods arrive."

"Can we send anyone to Ronan or Clyde?" Abigail asked softly. She'd watched the heavy cloud cover for the past two days and knew Ronan was likely up to his knees in the white powder.

"I did. Ma son Willy." Angus smiled when he could tell Abigail was trying to remember where she knew the name from. "Ma son married Linus's daughter. Their son is wee Willy. Ma Willy is the best rider in the clan. Ronan kept him here in case he needed someone to fetch him."

"Angus, are we ready?"

"Aye, Lady MacKinnon. We're ready. We have five score warriors still here, along with the men from the village."

"Five score?" Abigail's eyes widened as she glanced at the barracks that adjoined the armory. She hadn't realized Ronan commanded nearly two hundred men.

"That's why the other clans raid at our borders or chase our fishermen. They dinna dare come close to the keep."

"But Cormag must assume Ronan rode out with a large contingent if he's willing to sail here."

"Aye."

"Angus, is Norman up to the task?" Abigail whispered.

"He is. He's a good leader, and the men trust him. He would have had the same ideas as ye. He just didna think of them as quickly. Are ye going to the kitchens?"

"Eventually. Where will ye be?"

"Inside the gate. I'll help keep them from breeching it, and I'll be there to fight if they do."

"Besides the portcullis, what do we have to protect the gate?" It would take a long time, but a battering ram would break through the wood posts of the mobile gate and the massive wood doors. At Angus's blank stare, Abigail grabbed his hand and pulled him outside. "How many wagons do we have?"

"Between what's here and what's in the village, aboot a score."

"Get them in here. When it's time to seal the gates, get them flipped on their sides and stacked three and four deep and just as high. Take the wheels off the remaining ones or flip them upside down and push them to lock into with the bottom ones." Abigail made a "t" with one palm and the fingertips of the other. "Stack bales of hay to the side if you can. Position archers on them to pick off any MacLeods who makes it through."

"Ma lady?"

"Aye?" Abigail asked, distracted now as she looked around the bailey, searching for anything that needed moving or reinforcing.

"Does the laird ken ye can lead an army?"

"What?" Abigail looked back at Angus's grinning face.

"Lady MacKinnon, I thank the blessed saints I'm on yer side. I dinna ken how many battles ye saw on Lewis, but ye ken all that needs doing and then some."

"It's been since before my father died that anyone tried to attack Stornoway, but I remember more than I realized. I remember what I heard my father and

Kieran ordering. I guess it came back to me. I haven't been thinking aboot how I came up with these ideas."

"Ye're a bright lass, ma lady." Angus grinned once more before he went to order the wagons into place. Abigail climbed the steps to the battlements once more, pleased to see the ice and snow gone from the brick walkways. She searched for the first guard she'd spoken to. When she spotted Timothy, she made her way to him.

"How much longer?"

"Mayhap a quarter hour, ma lady," Timothy said without taking his eyes off the approaching enemy. Abigail noticed the boats appeared larger and knew they were drawing closer. She turned to look in the opposite direction.

"The men are returning with the villagers." Abigail pointed when Timothy moved to see. "Are all the boats back? Fishermen and rescuers?"

"Aye."

"Thank you." Abigail swept her eyes along the battlements until she found Norman. She gritted her teeth but wound through the hurrying men until she reached him. She kept her tone even, wanting to give the man the benefit of the doubt. She had no reason not to trust Ronan's judgment if he'd made the man a commander. "Do you or the men need aught?"

"Nay, ma lady. Thank you for the food and water." Norman appeared sincerely appreciative.

"Can we seal the gates after the last of the villagers come through the postern?"

"Aye. That's the plan."

Abigail looked at the battlement walls for a moment as her brow furrowed with a thought. She pressed her lips together between her teeth as she considered her idea. "They'll likely use grappling hooks and ladders, won't they?"

"That's what we expect."

"I've been rushing around too much to notice, but now that I'm standing still, it's bluidy perishing out here. Water'll freeze within a few minutes of being out here. Can we pour water along the top and outsides of the wall? The ice'll make it impossible to keep the ladders from slipping, and the grappling hooks will have a hard time catching. We can use the tar to keep most of them from climbing."

"We can do the outsides, but I will nae do the tops. I dinna need any of our men sliding over the sides when they reach out to keep the MacLeods from breeching."

"Do your men have time to fill buckets, or should I have some women help?"

"Ma men will do it. Get yerself and the women locked away, Lady MacKinnon."

"Thank you, Norman."

"Ye're welcome, ma lady." Norman smiled, and Abigail feared his face would crack. But she returned it, hoping any animosity she'd created earlier would ease.

Abigail went to the granary and watched as mothers and children climbed down the ladder before pulling it away from the opening. Abigail closed the hatch before sticking her head outside and asking two men to move barrels and crates over the trap-door, hiding it from sight. She noticed the chain of men passing water buckets up to the wall walk and heard the splash of the liquid hitting the brick walls. She went into the kitchens, but the women were already gone.

Abigail moved into the Great Hall, finding only guards staring at her. She nodded to the men stationed near Ronan's solar before she checked the doors of each storeroom. She called out to the occupants of the ones with the false floors, reassuring the

315

occupants that she was just checking on them. She glanced at the stairs and considered retreating to her chamber, but the idea left her mind as quickly as it came. She wouldn't cower in the comfort of a bedchamber while others were on the ground floor and in places the invaders would look first. But she also realized she'd locked herself out of any secure hiding place. The storerooms didn't lock from the inside, and she would never trust her keys to anyone but Angus, Bethea, and Maisie. She'd already ordered guards to seal the granary. The only place she could think of was a storeroom in the undercroft.

THIRTY-SIX

R onan and his men trudged through the snow as they neared the Fairy Pools. He squinted as he tried to make out the shapes in the distance. It wasn't long before he recognized them as people. He signaled to his men, who drew their swords. They led their horses closer until the forms clearly became men. Ronan prepared to order his men to gather the horses and task a handful to remain with the steeds. The force they approached was on foot too, because of the snow. But he recognized a russet-colored mane.

"It's Clyde," Ronan called out. The men sheathed their swords as they plodded toward the other half of their army. Ronan called out when they were within earshot. The two groups met beside the first fairy pool. "How'd you ken to come here?"

"We found signs of them making camp, then changing direction to come here. We thought to trap them between us."

"The same for us. So where are they?" Ronan and the men gathered around him stared in every direction, but there was no hint that anyone passed by the icy pools. Some had steep drops from waterfalls that collected icicles, while others filled with

317

water from a babbling brook. There were no foot- or hoofprints in the area, but he was certain they'd followed the correct path. He'd found signs that someone traveled in the same direction as them, but now there was nothing.

"How did they just disappear?" Clyde wondered. Many of the men looked warily at the pools, and Ronan knew what crept into their minds.

"There are no more fae here than there are in the Black Cuillins or at Dun Ringill. It's more likely the falling snow has already covered their tracks. The fae didn't come from the water and ferry them away, nor did the fae suck them in. The only place left for them to go is Dun Ringill. We make haste and return to the keep. We can be there in four hours. With luck, we'll be in time for the midday meal." Ronan looked at the sky, then the mountains that spread out in the distance. "How was the crossing?"

"We barely made it. The snow's deeper in the hills, and the ice is thin at the loch."

They had two choices: head back in the direction from which he and his group came to skirt the mountains or attempt to traverse them in the foul weather. The continuing snowfall left him with only the former as a reasonable option, despite Clyde and his men taking the latter route the day before. With twice the men came at least twice the risk. Even if they circumvented most of the mountains by following the coast, they would still have to climb a small distance before making the dangerous crossing at the isthmus of Loch Coruisk. Ronan supposed that was the way the MacLeods went, but he didn't want to engage in battle while getting snowed into a mountain pass. Going back the route he came would only add a half an hour to their journey and was safer. He gave the command, and the four score of men turned northeast.

As the morning progressed, Ronan feared they would have to seek shelter once more. The snow was knee deep in many parts, and snow drifts came to the men's waists. But being unable to account for the Dunvegan men made everyone apprehensive. Ronan and Clyde weren't the only MacKinnons eager to return to their families. With heads down against the wind, they pressed on. Ronan was glad he'd ordered such an early start that morning. It had been one of the coldest he'd ever experienced before the sun rose overhead, but it gave them more time to wind their way across the width of MacKinnon territory.

Ronan was the first to spy the solitary figure approaching them on horseback. They'd been able to mount again when they drew closer to the shore of *Loch na Cairidh*. He recognized the MacKinnon plaid before he could distinguish the face. There was only one person with only one reason who would brave the elements.

"It's Willy," Ronan announced. The threat of imminent danger took hold of Ronan's heart. Something was terribly wrong at Dun Ringill if Angus sent his son out alone during a snowstorm. The man was trying to reach Ronan. He spurred his horse on, but he could go no faster than a trot. When he was certain Willy would hear him, he called out, "What's happened? Is it Lady MacKinnon?"

"MacLeods!"

A visit from Kieran wasn't a reason for Willy to search for him. It could only be his nemeses from Dunvegan. He looked back at Clyde; his dark look told him he suspected the same thing Ronan did. Whether Ronan, Abigail, and the other men escaped Dunvegan, there had always been a plan to attack by water. The men sent out on horseback were a diversion, or additional swords to attack by land. When Willy reined in, Ronan knew the attack would already be underway when he arrived home. It was clear from the urgency in Willy's expression.

"Most of their fleet was at the mouth of Loch Slapin when Da sent me. That was close to two hours past. They will have already made landfall by now." Willy said no more before all the men urged their horses on. Where the snow wasn't as deep and the road was easy to follow, the men pushed their mounts to move faster. The cacophony of battle reached them on the crisp air before the keep came into sight. When the village was within view, the men pushed their horses to a gallop, the land finally clear enough for their horses to run.

Abigail ducked into the armory as the first arrows rained down on the bailey. The volley didn't come from the shore. The MacKinnon lookout spotted the MacLeod riders only minutes before they launched their ground attack. MacKinnon archers returned fire, and Abigail heard the pained whinnies as they struck horses. She'd been too slow to enter the building before one of her husband's men pitched backwards over the wall walk and landed in the bailey with an arrow through his chest.

Abigail prayed the barracks and armory connected like they appeared to from the outside. She hadn't time to run to the undercroft after speaking with Norman. The cry went up, then the arrows appeared. Dun Ringill was a large keep with a wide and long bailey. A projectile was more likely to strike Abigail than she was to make it across. She didn't want to shelter in the armory, knowing that if the MacLeods stormed the castle, they would search for additional weapons. But she hoped they wouldn't bother with the barracks; it would be natural to assume that no man remained there while the fight was ongoing. She pushed open a door, welcoming the sight of additional doors leading to small chambers. She ran halfway down the corridor before trying the door to her right. When it wouldn't open, she tried the one to the left. Her racing heart eased as she slipped inside. She looked for anything that would block the door, but there was nothing. The chamber was dim, so she slid under the furthest cot, praying no one would see her.

More cries filled the air as arrows met their targets. She'd smelled the scalding tar that boiled in the cauldrons, and she prayed the men placed them strategically. The weather was still as frigid as it had been an hour earlier, so she knew the ice remained from the water poured along the walls. If the MacKinnon archers kept the MacLeod archers at bay, then they could also pick off the foot soldiers who tried to scale the walls. Those who avoided death by arrow faced the impossible feat of bracing their ladders or entrenching their hooks. Many would die either from burns or the tar immobilizing them. Abigail knew ten men easily fit on a birlinn, though it would be tight. She'd spied at least fifteen boats sailing toward their docks. The MacLeods likely brought their entire force minus the men who approached on horseback. They outnumbered the MacKinnons, and Abigail feared they would besiege the keep.

Abigail reached for the dirk sheathed in her boot as she laid on her belly beneath the low bed. She commanded herself to slow her breathing, so she made no noise and could think without her heart hammering in her ears. She needed a plan in case she couldn't remain in the barracks. If she was forced to flee the building, it was because MacLeods were nearby, and they were likely to find her. But she still didn't know where she could go, since the undercroft was too far. She refused to open any door into the keep, nor would she lead men to the granary. Even if she had time to unlock a storeroom, they didn't lock from the inside. She might have the strength to move some barrels or sacks, but that would hardly deter warriors from breaking in.

I'm stuck here. This might be where they find ma body, or it might be ma saving grace. I dinna ken, but it's the best I can do. I can only pray Ronan's figured out that Cormag's men got around him, and he's already on his way back. Mayhap even the weather will force him to turn back. Aught to get him home sooner. I dinna want to see him fighting, but St. Michael and all angels, we need him and his men.

Abigail shut her eyes, concentrating on her breathing until she no longer felt like her heart would beat out of her chest. When her body felt calmer—if not her mind—she channeled her focus into listening, trying to distinguish each sound or hint of movement. The minutes dragged on, but nothing hinted that the MacLeods stormed the bailey. There were still cries of pain and men's voices issuing orders. But there was no organized chaos that indicated that the MacLeods had broken through the gates. She heard pounding footsteps outside the door several times, but she suspected men were passing through the building to avoid the projectiles coming over the walls.

A corner of Abigail's mind whispered guilt. A sense of duty tempted her to leave her hiding place, feeling like her position dictated she do more. But there was nothing more for her to do. She couldn't wield a weapon, and those under her care were more safely hidden than she. The most reasonable action was to remain where she was, even if it felt cowardly and insufficient. She would remain in hiding until the noise ceased, or they forced her out.

"We won't get in," Ronan yelled over the pounding hooves. "We take a stand against those outside the main gate. We've chased them to our own door. They will not enter." He drew his sword as his knees squeezed his horse's flanks, bracing himself and spurring the beast on. Many of his men had bows and quivers with them, having brought them not only to hunt but for battle. The noise surrounding the keep kept most of the MacLeods from hearing them approach. Ronan and his clan fired upon their enemy, cutting down nearly half of their men before any MacKinnon was within sword's reach. His men fanned out, trapping their enemy between them and the walls.

Ronan leaned to his right before standing in his stirrups and lunging forward to drive his sword into a man's back. He yanked it free before swinging it again, severing an arm. The stump sprayed blood that splattered Ronan and his horse. Despite not being his preferred warhorse, his mount was experienced in battle. When two men came toward the steed's head, he reared back, his hooves his deadly weapons. Ronan was prepared, feeling the horse's bunching muscles signaling its intentions. The beast's hooves slammed into the men's heads, knocking them to the ground before crushing them.

Ronan whirled around, locking his sights on his next target. Many of the MacLeods had dismounted, and Ronan assumed they awaited a battering ram. But none was in sight, even though MacLeod birlinns were already at his dock. Arrows flew from the birlinns, but he watched just as many fly from his battlements. As he engaged with another mounted warrior, his horse's teeth clamped down on the other horse's nose. The MacLeod warrior's horse cried out in pain, distracting its rider. Ronan severed the man's head from his shoulders. He scanned the fight around him and noticed his men were prevailing. They'd cut down most of the MacLeods on foot, and there were only a handful of mounted warriors left. His forces greatly outnumbered those who'd crossed the island, and his combined army rivaled those who sailed to his home.

As he and his men claimed victory against the men outside his keep, waves of MacLeods poured off the boats. On foot, the men were easier targets for Ronan's mounted forces. One after another, Mac-Leods fell to the ground. Seeing Ronan leading the defense, Ronan heard Cormag order his sailors to approach from the opposite side. Ronan and his men raced to intercept the MacLeods, but their horses reared to a stop as the first cauldron of pitch streamed down the side. Ronan nor his men could approach, lest they become targets of the boiling, viscous ooze. He was certain that the gates were barred, so there was no way into the keep and little he could do to reach the rest of the enemy.

THIRTY-SEVEN

A bigail heard the bells ringing, no longer the constant jangle but the rhythmic one signaling Ronan's return. She knew he would remain outside the barmekin, since no one would open the main gate or the postern in the middle of a battle, but much of her fear eased. She wasn't so naïve that she believed the MacKinnons won the battle merely because Ronan returned with reinforcements, but she trusted her husband's leadership and warrior training implicitly. She recalled watching him in the lists at Stirling Castle, then again at Stornoway. She still marveled at how men followed his corrections without hesitation and how he bested each of his opponents, graciously helping them up. Confidence suffused Abigail as she continued to wait.

With the additional men fighting, the noise had grown louder, making it difficult for Abigail to distinguish what was happening. The tar's odor still permeated the air, but the smell of burning thatch soon joined it. Abigail sniffed as the second scent grew stronger than the first. There could only be a single cause, and it forced her out from beneath the cot. She darted across the chamber, but screamed and yanked her hand away when the circular ring handle burned her hand. Gathering her skirts and her arisaid, she used them to cover the metal as she pried the door open. The heat in the passageway already made the door swell within its frame. She tugged as hard as she could until it gave way. Smoke billowed in as heat scorched her face.

Abigail dropped to her hands and knees, thankful the flames blazed in the opposite direction from the armory. Her only known exit route headed in the armory's direction. On her feet once more, she burst into the armory, then out to the bailey.

"Lady MacKinnon!" Angus cried as he charged toward her. She used her sleeve to wipe ash from her face, then used the other to wipe her watering eyes. "Merciful saints, I had nay idea ye were inside."

Abigail and Angus turned toward the barracks as a creak, then a crack boomed from the barracks' roof before it caved in. If Abigail had waited any longer, flames would have engulfed her. Abigail scanned her surroundings, shocked to only spot a handful of dead bodies. There were numerous injured men lining the far wall, but she knew far more still fought on the battlements than were unable.

"Have any made it over the wall?"

"Nay. The laird defeated those who attacked near the gate. Cormag's ordered his men to approach from the postern side, but the tar is already stopping many. The ice is keeping the ladders from staying still. Our archers are exhausted, but currently they are our best defense. A few grappling hooks took, but most slipped as they tried to anchor against the wall. Norman had the men freeze the outside and the inside, but nay the top. It's doing the trick, ma lady."

"Do you think Cormag will retreat? Have you seen him?"

"I havenae been up to the battlements, but nay, I

dinna think he will. He's come to make a stand, to get revenge for his brothers' deaths."

"Is he fighting?"

"I dinna ken. If he is, I dinna doubt he and the laird will meet."

Abigail nodded as she huddled beside Angus, his body and targe shielding her from the fire's heat and the few stray arrows that soared over the wall. The diminished number of MacLeod archers among the land-based forces slowed the assault. She looked at the fire, her eyes narrowing. The flames continued to build despite men throwing buckets of water onto the blaze. Part of the building was already smoldering ash, but most of it was still alight. She watched as the men passed buckets to one another while another handful threw water onto the thatching of the buildings nearby, trying to prevent the fire from consuming anything else if it jumped from one structure to the next.

"How much tar do you think is left? Have they used most of it?"

"They've used all of it along the waterfront wall, but men are just dumping the first rounds above the postern gate."

Abigail looked at the armory again. It sat beneath the waterfront wall. She pictured the scene on the other side of the retaining wall and the distance to the docks.

"Who's your best archer, Angus?"

"Timothy, ma lady."

"The same mon I spoke to earlier?"

"Aye."

Abigail noticed the gleam in Angus's eyes as he answered. "He's one of your lads, too, isn't he?"

"That's right. Timothy is our auldest, then Willy, then Maisie. The rest are still youths, ma lady. They're with Bethea and Maisie."

"Can you take me to Timothy?"

"Nay! Ye canna go up on the battlements, ma lady. It's far too dangerous. The laird will have ma heid."

"Then give me a targe." Abigail put her hands on her hips, determined to show Angus she wouldn't back down.

"Nae even a sennight, and ye already sound like ma Bethea," Angus grumbled. "I'm still nae taking ye. I'd rather slip ye into a storeroom."

"Too late for that, Angus. I need to see what's happening. Do you think they intend to lay siege? Do they still have the men for that?"

"Only if they defeat the laird's men outside the wall. But even then, we have enough arrows to pick them off one by one if they try to trap us inside the walls."

"What if we trap them?"

"What do ye mean?"

"Take me to see Timothy, and I'll tell you."

Angus stood to his full height, and Abigail thought he was Goliath to her David. She prayed she could convince him without a stone between his eyes. If she hadn't known the man would never harm her, his size and the air of power surrounding him when he set his shoulders back would have terrified her. He studied her for a long moment before nodding.

"I dinna trust ye nae to find yer way up there. Like I said, ye're like Bethea." Angus raised the arm that carried the targe, the forearm through the two leather loops. With his sword arm raised behind Abigail, ready to ward off anyone who approached from behind, he angled his body to walk sideways up the steps, his shield blocking Abigail from sight as they rose higher.

Abigail peeked over the wall as they arrived at the top of the steps. She was unprepared for the carnage she found. Dozens of men lay dead, covered in layers of black sludge. Blood pooled around them and the snow beneath them. Mud tracks and churned grass showed through where patches of snow melted from the heat as the pitch rained down. She swallowed the bile that rose in her throat from the scent of burned hair and flesh. She didn't dare flinch or turn away after demanding Angus bring her up. He guided her until he spotted his son. Abigail noticed that most of the fires were out, and the tar no longer bubbled along that portion of the wall.

"Ma lady? Da, the laird will kill ye if he spots Lady MacKinnon up here!"

"Dinna tell me what I dinna already ken, lad."

"Timothy, can you hit the boats?"

"Hit them? Aye, at least several."

"How many men do they still have aboard them?"

"Only one or two each, ma lady. And that's only on a few."

"Timothy, do we have any more tar or oil left up here?"

"Oil. We havenae heated it because the pitch has worked so far."

"Can we get the oil to the laird and his men? Could they make it to the boats?"

"Mayhap." Timothy's eyes widened as he looked at Abigail and then his father. Abigail knew her idea registered with Angus when his expression matched his son's. "Aye. If the laird can make sure they douse the boats with oil, they'll go up faster. But even if he canna, I'm nay the only mon who can hit those targets. A volley of flaming arrows will sink many."

"Angus, can you find Laird MacKinnon?"

"Abby!" A roar rose from below, making Abigail cringe.

329

"I think the laird found ye instead," Timothy snickered.

"Dinna laugh, son. He's seen us both talking to Lady MacKinnon. Mayhap he'll give us neighboring cells."

Abigail ignored Angus and Timothy as she edged closer to the wall and looked down. She gasped when she took in Ronan's blood-drenched clothes, face, and hair. She couldn't tell if any of the blood was his. Sweat and dirt mingled with the blood he wore. With his blond hair peeking through the blood and grime under the sunlight, he looked like an avenging St. Michael.

"Can you get men to the docks?" Abigail called down.

"Abby!"

"Aye. Bellow at me later. Can you get men to the docks? Get them to pour oil on the birlinns?"

Ronan looked back over his shoulder. He'd sent half his men around to the postern wall from the opposite direction. He was running past the waterfront wall when he glanced up to see how his warriors fared above. He stumbled and nearly lost his footing when he recognized Abigail's dark hair. When she turned toward him and looked out at the battlefield, he hadn't thought twice before yelling up to her. He wanted her nowhere near the fighting. As he swept his gaze over the MacLeod fleet docked within his harbor, he wanted nothing more than to send them all up in smoke.

"Aye. Angus, get the vats lowered now. Timothy, get your men to dip their arrows before you light them. Don't wait. As soon as we get the oil on them, fire. We'll worry aboot getting ourselves back on land. For God's sake, Abigail, get down."

"Timothy, light the arrows from the barracks' flames licking up the inner wall from the armory,"

Abigail suggested as she turned back toward the steps. "Have they abandoned trying to force down the gates?"

"Aye. The laird defeated the men prepared to storm the gate, and Cormag ordered the next wave in the other direction. They didna bring up the battering ram."

"I'm going to the kitchens then. There are bandages and salves there that the men need." She moved forward, Angus once more protecting her. When they reached the ground, Abigail picked up her skirts and hastened to the kitchens while Angus went back onto the battlements to help lower the massive oil vats.

Ronan and his men tipped them on their sides and rolled them along the path until they reached the docks. Three men carried each cumbersome, awkward barrel once they pried the lids off and once more tipped them on their sides. His men made their way to the end of the MacLeod fleet, dousing them in the combustible liquid. When the last boat they could reach had the flammable oil poured onto its deck, Ronan waved his sword in the air. Abandoning the barrels, he and his men sprinted back up the dock as the lit arrows arced through the air before pummeling their targets. The boats erupted in flames, the wood and canvas catching immediately. Ronan raised his arms to shield his face from the heat as he and his warriors charged back toward the keep.

MacLeods turned toward the water as they watched the lit arrows land among their boats. They took in the horror playing out before their eyes. One boat after another caught on fire. The ones without oil poured on them ignited from those already on fire. Their only means of escape were sinking beneath the water's surface and crumbling into ash.

Ronan searched for Cormag, intent upon slaying his enemy. He'd left Cormag alive for the sake of politics. He knew King Robert wouldn't overlook the MacKinnons slaying all three MacLeod brothers, so he'd ignored his intuition that he should have killed Cormag back at Dunvegan. But his right to end Cormag's life was irrefutable the moment the MacLeods sailed into MacKinnon water and then set foot on MacKinnon land. With a renewed sense of purpose and deadly intent, Ronan set his sights on Cormag.

THIRTY-EIGHT

Abigail knew when Ronan succeeded with the fleet. The crackling of the enormous fire was deafening, and she could hear little more than the raging flames devouring the wood birlinns. She emerged from the kitchens with two baskets slung over each arm as she hurried to where the injured gathered. Two baskets contained linen strips and pots of salve, while the other two carried waterskins. She handed the skins out to the men while others gathered the bandages and began tending one another.

"Move to the Great Hall. There's water boiling in the kitchens. I found soap and whisky. I left them on the tables. I haven't met your healer yet," Abigail explained. "But I'll do what I can to stitch wounds." Abigail led the way through the kitchens, pointing to the supplies she'd left out. While many of her belongings sank along with the birlinn Ronan captained, the MacLeods left the other three untouched when they towed the MacKinnon birlinns to their docks. Since they were still moored there, the MacKinnons sailed their own boats back when they escaped. Abigail assumed that the MacLeods had planned to add the MacKinnon birlinns to their fleet, but she was grateful they'd ignored her belongings once she discovered that her childhood sewing kit—packed on a whim—survived the journey.

Abigail hurried up to her chamber to retrieve the sewing kit. By the time she returned to the Great Hall, the men were already helping the most severely injured onto tables. Bowls of steaming water appeared from the kitchens as the warriors scrubbed each other's wounds, both the wounded and the hale taking healthy swigs of whisky beforehand. Abigail triaged the men in her head before carrying a candle to the man who looked to be in the worst shape but still likely to live. She didn't want to turn her back on those who would likely succumb to their injuries, but she had to prioritize those she could save, lest the list of the dead grow longer.

She dipped her hands into a bowl of water before scrubbing them with soap. She hadn't realized how filthy they'd become from scrambling along the barracks floor as she escaped the fire. Once she had as much dirt out from under her nails as she could manage, she dried them, then rummaged through her sewing supplies until she found a needle and sturdy thread. She passed the needle and thread through the flame several times before asking the surrounding men to hold down her first patient.

There had been little need over the years for her to practice her suturing skills at Stornoway. Adeline had been a competent nurse and able to tend wounds that needed stitching, but since she adopted few of the skills of a chatelaine, she neglected to make sure her daughters learned those duties. Luckily, her clan's healer, Eara, insisted she and Madeline learn how to suture. As Abigail pressed the needle into the man's skin, she said a silent prayer of thanksgiving for Eara's persistent demands that she learned to stitch wounds.

Abigail moved from one injured warrior to the

next for hours, until her eyes burned and her back ached from bending over. She wondered how the battle progressed, but she didn't dare leave to find out. Her duty was to the keep—to the ailing and the dying. She swallowed her scream when the doors to the Great Hall burst open. Men in various conditions scrambled for their weapons until they recognized MacKinnon plaids flooding the gathering hall. Exhausted smiles greeted Abigail's eyes as she searched for Ronan.

Ronan's vision tunneled when he homed in on Cormag's location. The man was barking orders as his men continued to attempt scaling the Dun Ringill walls. The MacLeod swung his sword as MacKinnons moved in to surround him. As Ronan ran toward his target, he recited his clan's motto silently: *audentes fortuna juvat.* "Fortune favors the bold," he reminded himself. The words brought Abigail to mind, and he couldn't repress his grin. He was certain he looked like a madman charging through the fray while smiling. But his bonnie bride had been destined to be a MacKinnon because she was as bold as any man he'd ever met. She'd appeared demure at first, but she possessed the spirit of a lioness. He wouldn't overlook discovering her on the wall walk, but he was not truly surprised to find her there.

MacKinnon warriors cut Cormag off from the rest of his men, some fighting off MacLeods to prevent them from rescuing their laird, while other Mac-Kinnons kept Cormag in one place until Ronan reached them. The MacKinnons encircling Cormag shifted to allow Ronan to come face-to-face with his nemesis. With both hands wrapped around the hilt of his claymore, he raised it to shoulder height before launching himself forward, with the MacKinnon war cry *"Cuimhnich bàs Ailpein"* bursting from his mouth. His men echoed his battle oath, "Remember the death of Alpin."

"Where are your fae now, arselick?" Ronan sneered as he swung his sword toward Cormag. The latter blocked the blow, but it pushed him backwards. Ronan didn't relent, with a bone-jarring strike immediately following the first swing. He pounded Cormag over and over; the MacLeod laird was never able to launch his own strike. He struggled to defend himself against Ronan's prowess as a swordsman. Ronan battered Cormag again and again until he knew his enemy grew too fatigued to endure much more. "Lay down your sword, Cormag. Surrender with dignity. Your men will live if you do. You won't, but they will. Refuse, and we will butcher you all and hang your entrails out for the crows."

"You're awfully boastful for a mon who doesn't have his wife to protect him."

"I can put my faith in Abigail because she's real. I'm not the one whispering to imaginary creatures, praying they'll come save my arse. Where's your wee flag? Where are your wee fae? Nowhere to be found."

"You're no threat to Dunvegan," Cormag spat. "We don't need the fae to defeat you."

Ronan almost stopped fighting to laugh. The MacLeods were falling as fast as the snow had that morning. There were no boats left to carry them home. And their leader was only moments away from death.

"You need something because you aren't doing very well on your own. You ken all is lost. It's a question of whether you cause all your men to die or if some will have the chance to limp home."

"Limp home? In defeat? In disgrace? Never!"

Cormag roared the last word as he attempted to take control of the fight. He slashed his sword toward Ronan, but pride made him reckless. When he raised his arms to gain leverage, he left his chest unprotected. Ronan plunged his sword into his enemy's breast, just as he'd done when he discovered Gordon purloined his sword. Blood bubbled out of Cormag's mouth as he tried to speak, but his knees gave out. His legs buckled beneath him, sending him crashing to the ground. A cheer went up among the MacKinnons, and it spread to the men still fighting near the postern gate and on the battlements. The MacKinnons whooped and hollered, their victory uncontestable now that Cormag lay dead at Ronan's feet. The surviving MacLeods lowered their weapons in defeat as they looked at one another.

"Take them to cells. They shall be our guests until spring, when they can walk home," Ronan decreed. Without needing orders, the MacKinnons divided into groups that herded the prisoners through the postern gate, into the bailey, and down to the dungeon. Others moved among the injured and dead, searching for MacKinnon survivors and finishing off any MacLeods still breathing. Ronan searched the battlements, but he couldn't see Abigail. He sighed when Angus leaned over the wall and nodded. "Abby?"

"In the Great Hall sewing up the injured," Angus called down. Ronan breathed easier as he smiled up to his seneschal. The man had blood splattered across his face from the men he'd fought as the MacLeods tried to make their way over the wall. His hair stood out at all angles. He appeared the seasoned warrior he was, no hint of his bookishness apparent. Ronan noticed Timothy was near his father. He was the clan's best archer, but he was still young. As Ronan joined the search for MacKinnon survivors, he considered promoting Timothy. When he walked past Willy, he stopped.

"Does your da ken you're alive?"

"Aye, Laird. I heard him bellowing at Timothy to keep his wee brother alive unless he wanted Mama to take a rolling pin to him." Willy grinned, and Ronan chuckled. While not as large as their father, Timothy and Willy were among the tallest and strongest men in Ronan's guard. But all three of them would hide from Bethea if she had a weapon in hand. The men in Bethea's family had a healthy fear of the fiercely protective woman, but they were just as devoted to her as she was to them.

Ronan shook his head and carried on. Fatigue set in over the next two hours, as he helped men limp into the bailey or carried dead bodies to be laid on shrouds. Men helping with the wounded confirmed that Abigail was safe and busy within the Great Hall. But as much as he wanted to walk away from the death and destruction to find Abigail, he reminded himself that, as laird, he was the last man to find his family. He would see to his clansmen before he allowed himself to escape with his wife to their chamber.

When they recovered the last MacKinnon, and the MacLeods' bodies were burned on a hastily constructed pyre at a safe distance from the keep, he trudged up the keep's steps. His equally exhausted men followed, but another cheer went up as the doors swung open. The first cheer had celebrated their victory. This cheer celebrated their clan's ongoing survival and the warriors' return to their loved ones. Ronan stepped inside the Great Hall, his eyes a magnet to Abigail. She raised her head as she tied off her last stitch, spotting Ronan immediately. She glanced at the unconscious man on the table beside her before jumping to her feet. She hopped over the bench, lifting her skirts to her knees, before she flew toward Ronan. He rushed to meet her halfway, enveloping her into his embrace, neither caring about the blood and grime caked over Ronan's entire body. They only cared that they were holding one another once again.

THIRTY-NINE

"**A**bby," Ronan groaned as he lifted his wife off her feet. Like a bear climbing a tree, she wrapped her arms and legs around her husband, clinging to him. Steel bands encircled her, pinning her to his torso. Abigail shuddered as her mind absorbed her husband's presence, finally accepting that he was alive and safe. Neither husband nor wife needed anything more than to hold one another. They were oblivious to the world around them as women and children swarmed the keep from outside.

When Abigail finally lifted her head and looked around, she realized Angus must have opened the granary. She accepted she must release Ronan and go to the storerooms. The other women and children had a right to reunite with their men, just as she had with Ronan. But before she could release them, more women and children poured into the Great Hall. Abigail knew Angus had already done the task.

When Abigail caught sight of Angus's Herculean arms wrapped around Bethea, who clung to his neck, Abigail knew the warrior-turned-seneschal had been just as impatient to find his family as she'd been to see Ronan. Abigail and Ronan turned toward a cry as a blur of russet hair rushed past them, and a streak of blonde hair flew like a banner as Maisie and Clyde found one another. During most battles, Ronan and Clyde fought side by side, but they'd had to split once more to lead forces in different directions. Abigail lowered herself to her feet before Ronan clasped her hand. They walked to where Angus stood with his family. While the men appeared battered and bruised, none received serious wounds. As Abigail wrapped her arms around Ronan's waist, his arm pulled her against his side, keeping her close to him.

Witnessing his best friend and his most trusted advisor safely with his family created a powerful sense of security that nearly rivaled how he felt seeing Abigail when he entered the Great Hall. Abigail looked up at Ronan at the same moment he turned his gaze to her. The need to kiss drove them into a passionate embrace, the tenderness from only moments ago set aside. Their lips crushed together as Ronan's tongue swept the inside of Abigail's mouth. She sucked his tongue as he groaned, his cock hardening beneath his plaid. Were they alone, he would have rucked up her skirts and thrust into her until all their pent-up fear and need abated. The kiss drew on, no one caring as the Great Hall's other occupants were too distracted with their own families.

Breathless, Ronan and Abigail pulled apart. They looked around the gathering hall, taking in the warriors' conditions and the emotions displayed by their clan members. Abigail sighed as she looked at the many wounded who'd entered along with Ronan. She stepped away from her husband, a sad smile on her face. They both had duties to return to. She needed to tend to more wounds, and Ronan needed to check on his men.

"Abigail." Ronan entwined the fingers of both their hands. "I love ye, lass."

"Ronan, I love ye. I want to hold on to ye and never let go. Nae ever." Abigail's accent matched Ronan's, their voices laden with feelings that consumed them both. Duty would draw them apart for the next several hours, but their gazes promised time alone after they'd seen to others first. They drifted in different directions as Ronan moved around the Great Hall, checking on one family after another.

Abigail resumed her ministrations after meeting the clan's healer, Naida. The woman appeared with a basket full of medicinals after the women left the keep's storerooms. She tsked several times as she examined the men Abigail had already sewn, making Abigail narrow her eyes before the women turned a warm smile to her, praising her work. Abigail learned the woman quietly scolded the men for getting injured, not for the quality of Abigail's work. The patients who were conscious smiled at the older woman, clearly used to her clucking at them. Bethea joined Abigail and Naida as they saw to the injured. The uninjured, unmarried men, after reuniting with their parents, joined the three women's efforts by cleaning and bandaging wounds that didn't require serious examination.

The MacKinnons spent hours helping one another. The quiet sense of kinship filled the Great Hall as women served platters of food and children dashed back and forth to refill waterskins. The victorious euphoria waned as everyone set about their various tasks, but the peacefulness that came from surviving the attack also brought a sense of calm. The grieving huddled together as families gathered around them, offering solace. Abigail hadn't experienced an attack on her home since she was a child too young to understand the significance of the aftermath. Kieran and his men often rode out to prevent such events, engaging in skirmishes far from their home. Even when she'd helped tend the returning injured, she'd lacked empathy at the time. She'd barely mustered sympathy. But as she looked around the Great Hall, her heart broke for those who had no joyous reunion and for the men who would soon join the angels. It gave her purpose to work harder to heal the men stretched across the tables. She, Naida, and Bethea worked well into the night while Ronan met with the families who lost warriors and arranged funerals, investigated the damages to the keep, and inventoried the weapons.

Angus, Clyde, and Ronan examined the barracks' smoldering remains. He'd bent over and heaved when Angus let it slip that Abigail was in the building when it caught fire. The older man passed him a flask of whisky, which he gulped down as he forced his mind to rid itself of the idea of recovering Abigail's charred body from the ashes. They accounted for all his men, those who survived and those who didn't, so they knew no one else was in the building when the roof ignited. The carpenters and masons would set about rebuilding the bachelor warriors' quarters the next day. Until then, the men would bunk down in the Great Hall or with family.

The stars twinkled overhead in a cloudless sky by the time Ronan reentered the Great Hall. Abigail stood talking to Maisie, who was nodding at whatever instructions Abigail gave the head cook. Maisie smiled at Ronan before disappearing into the kitchens. Abigail turned to see who Maisie had been looking at. Ronan noticed the shadows under Abigail's eyes and how her shoulders drooped with fatigue, but her smile was radiant when she spied Ronan approaching.

"Abby, I could have lost ye today," Ronan whispered, his throat tightening. Abigail knew he'd learned that she'd been in the barracks. Her smile dimmed as she nodded. Their hands clasped as they came to stand before one another. "What happened? Angus could only tell me that ye ran into him as ye fled the smoke."

"I secured the women and weans into the storage rooms and the granary before I realized none locked from the inside. I dinna trust ma keys to anyone but Bethea, Angus, Maisie, and I suppose Clyde. I was going to hide in the undercroft, but the arrows started landing in the bailey. I'd spoken to Angus earlier, so I'd been into the armory. I suspected it connected to the barracks. I kenned the MacLeods would search the armory if they entered the bailey, but I figured they'd assume the barracks were empty and ignore it. I ran into one of the chambers and hid under the bed. I heard the bells tolling that ye'd returned. But it wasna long after that, that the building started to smell smoky."

"Angus said ye got out only moments before the roof caved in. Why didna ye hide when the other women did? Or why nae go to our chamber?"

"There was too much to do, and I couldnae bring maself to hide in the comfort of our chamber while the others huddled in freezing, dark holes in the ground. It didna seem right."

Ronan pulled Abigail into his embrace, still shaken from discovering how close she had come to death. He recalled seeing her on the battlements as he ran past. Without letting go, he asked, "What aboot when I saw ye on the wall walk?"

Abigail tightened her arms as the rumble of Ronan's voice against her chest felt steady and reassuring. "That was after I came out. The fire made me think aboot burning the boats. I insisted Angus take me up to Timothy. I'd asked aboot the oil and whether Timothy could hit the birlinns when ye went past. Timothy and Angus warned me ye'd be furious, but I stayed up there until I kenned ye could get the oil."

"I should be raging against yer recklessness, but I'm too damn relieved that ye're alive. Abby, I dinna ken if I could live without ye. Ye're everything to me."

"That's how I felt kenning it was practically a blizzard where ye trekked then kenning ye were fighting. I thought I would be ill when I saw ye caked in blood and dirt. Nae because of the filth, but because I kenned ye came to look like that because ye fought for yer life. I couldnae tell if any of the blood was yers."

"Some of it is." At Abigail's gasp and her attempt to pull away, Ronan cooed to her. "Just nicks and scratches. I'll have some almighty bruises by morn, but I wasna injured like some."

"Ma lady, ma laird," Bethea said quietly as she approached. "I've sent a bath up to yer chamber. Will ye eat down here, or would ye rather Maisie sends up a tray?"

"Down here," Abigail and Ronan answered together. Bethea offered a maternal smile of approval.

"Ma lady, I dinna ken if yer gown is repairable."

Abigail looked down at her clothing for the first time all day. Smeared ash covered her skirts from the knees down. Embracing Ronan covered her bodice and back with mud and sweat, and blood had splattered from the many wounds she tended. She had to agree with Bethea.

"I'll have the laundresses salvage what they can, then it can be cut down to rags." Abigail saw no point in wasting the fabric. She might not wear the gown again, but the fabric was still in serviceable condition. She realized that a younger version of herself would have dumped the gown in a corner for someone else to dispose of, and not thought twice about it. "When will Maisie serve the meal?"

"An hour and a half, ma lady."

"Thank ye, Bethea." Abigail and Ronan made their way to their chamber. When the door closed behind them, they fell into one another's arms again. The kiss contained a hunger they'd restrained in front of their clan members, but the privacy their chamber offered unleashed it. They tore at one another's clothes until they stood naked. Ronan lifted Abigail, and as when Ronan returned from the battle, she wrapped herself around him. He stepped to the door, pressing Abigail's back against it. He thrust into her, aggressive and determined.

Abigail moaned with pleasure as the sensation of being filled with Ronan's cock nearly triggered her release. They moved together, savage desire making their coupling rough. Abigail's heels dug into the small of Ronan's back as she held on. Ronan thrust into his wife over and over, unable to get enough, her moans urging him on. While the pleasure that came with release was always eagerly anticipated, this joining was about feeling the connection between their bodies, proving they were one, possessing as well as being possessed.

Abigail's back banged against the door as she encouraged Ronan to continue pounding into her as she rocked along his length. The feel of being pressed against the door, the virility that Ronan's desire held, and the possessiveness that came with his forceful movements spurred her on. He was claiming her, and she welcomed it. Their need wasn't just for the physical. It was for their very souls. Grinding their pelvises together pushed them over the precipice, making them shatter in one another's embrace. When Ronan eased Abigail to the floor, she covered her belly with her hands. Ronan's eyebrows shot up.

"Do ye think ye are..." He couldn't finish the thought.

"I hope so, but it's too soon to ken. But I could be. I want to be."

"Ye want a bairn?" Ronan whispered.

"Nae 'a.' Ours. Every time ye pour yer seed into me, I hope that it takes."

"Ye'll be a wonderful mother, Abby." Ronan pressed a gentle kiss to Abigail's lips. Abigail frowned for a moment, and Ronan's expression grew curious. She didn't know how to articulate her feelings. "What is it?"

"I dinna ken how to say what I'm thinking without sounding possessive—rather without admitting how possessive I am."

"Do ye like kenning that ye're the only woman who could ever bear ma child?"

"Aye. That when ye spill yer seed into me, I ken ye're entirely mine. It sounds horrible."

"Why? Do ye think I feel any differently? I'm the only mon whose bairn will grow inside ye. When I see yer belly grow round, I'll ken that I'm the mon who gave ye that bairn. I dinna ken if it's just some primal male instinct, but there is possessiveness and pride wrapped up in the love I feel thinking aboot that. Is it that different from how ye feel?"

"That's exactly how I feel. But it still doesnae sound good to say it aloud. I sound like a shrew."

"Nay, ye dinna. I think ye sound like a woman who loves her mon and was ready to set fire to an entire fleet herself just to make sure he came home." Ronan grinned as he pinched Abigail's backside. He led them to the bath and helped her to step in. He followed her before sinking into the water. "Mayhap ye shouldnae share this one, Abby. I'm disgusting. I dinna want ye covered in this too."

Abigail didn't want to admit to the same thoughts, especially not after she'd just claimed to want him so badly. She looked toward the fire and spied buckets of water before the hearth. There were empty buckets beside them. She pointed to them. "Bethea sent extra fresh water. She must have thought ye'd need at least two baths," Abigail grinned.

"Or she kenned ye shouldnae be in the same filthy water as me." Ronan helped Abigail to step out before slipping his head beneath the surface. He scrubbed his head, loosening the dried blood from it. When he surfaced, he accepted the soapy linen square Abigail offered him before she set to work cleaning his hair. She washed it twice, unsatisfied after the first round. When they were certain Ronan was clean, he stepped out and wrapped a drying linen around his waist.

They worked together to change the water before Ronan joined Abigail in the tub. The warm water lapping at Abigail's shoulders and Ronan's chest was both soothing and erotic. They soaked together while Abigail sat between Ronan's legs. They lay there for a long time, both with their eyes closed, but eventually the feeling of closeness turned to physical desire. Ronan massaged Abigail's breasts, rubbing her nipples as she clasped his thighs. She twisted to receive his kiss until the awkward position became frustrating. They adjusted so Abigail straddled Ronan's hips, and he slid inside her. Their movements were unhurried, the feel of the warm water heightening every sensation. Their kisses were languid and easy as their hips rocked together. Both intended to draw out this lovemaking, enjoying every moment of being together.

They stilled as heat and pleasure suffused them, holding one another, savoring the connection. Abigail rested against Ronan's chest as he ran the bar of soap over her arms and back. The sounds of people preparing for the evening meal forced them to hurry through Abigail's ablutions, and her hair was in a wet braid as they entered the Great Hall. Those recovering from serious wounds had been carried to their homes or given bedrolls around the gathering hall. The tables had been scrubbed clean, and Abigail noted the dirty rushes had been swept away. She would ensure the floors were cleaned and new rushes laid the next day. She and Ronan made their way to the dais, where Clyde and Angus already sat. It wasn't long before the servants presented the meal. It was a somber meal with simple fare, reminding them of what they'd just endured. With fewer dishes than normal making their way to the tables, Bethea and Maisie joined their husbands at the high table.

"Lady Abigail," Clyde spoke softly, keeping the informality to those seated around the laird and his lady. "Thank ye for making sure the women were safe. Maisie told me aboot yer suggestion to have the torches. Ma greatest fear when I ride out isnae that I willna come home. It's that I willna be there to protect Maisie. Kenning ye watched out for ma wife eases ma conscience, ma lady. Thank ye."

"Ye've all welcomed me into yer home and made it mine too. Mayhap ye can imagine what it's like to leave yer family and join a new one, kenning only yer husband. It's nae easy, but I'm proud to be a MacKinnon, and I'm proud to serve our clan. I appreciate the friendship Bethea and Maisie have offered since the moment I arrived. I'd do aught to keep ma family safe. That means all of ye."

"Ma lady," Angus spoke up. "I wasna jesting when I asked ye earlier if yer husband kenned ye could lead an army. Ye looked out for all of us, nae just the women and children. Ye thought to provide the men with food and water, ye helped our defenses, and ye risked yer own life to help our efforts to win. The laird has always been an intelligent lad, but he was almighty clever to find ye, Lady Abigail."

Abigail smiled at Ronan as they held hands resting on the table between them. Both knew there were long days ahead of them as the clan healed and moved forward, but neither could imagine a better partner with whom to share the joys and sorrows of leadership. Ronan kissed Abigail's temple as the conversation moved on to plans for the next day. The couple joined in, but both were subdued as they watched the people seated at the tables below them. The battle with the MacLeods was over, but the war was not. Abigail and Ronan knew it was only a matter of time before King Robert learned of the fight, and neither was eager to face the fallout.

FORTY

Abigail shielded her eyes as she handed the waterskin to Ronan. "I can't believe how much you've accomplished in a sennight. You would never ken an auld building stood here only days ago." Ronan and Abigail stood together as they surveyed the newly reconstructed barracks. The clan's laborers had worked from sunup to sundown to provide a new home for the bachelor warriors. Despite bruises that ached with each breath, Ronan had joined the men each day laying bricks. He'd carried bundles of thatch and cleared away snow. He'd smiled sheepishly at the end of each day as he trailed muck into the Great Hall. The sun shone each day that the men worked, quickly melting the snow and leaving mud behind.

Abigail aided the servants as they brought food and ale to the men throughout the day and flasks of whisky when the wind grew brisk. She'd caught herself distracted several times as her gaze lingered on her brawny husband. She watched his leine pull tight across his broad shoulders while the breeze lifted his blond hair from his shoulders. With the laces loose at his shirt collar, she watched the muscles in his chest bunch and ripple as he moved bricks and thatch.

Bethea found Abigail ogling Ronan more than once, generally when the older woman came out to watch her own husband. Abigail had never seen a man as strong as Angus. She marveled at what Ronan could carry, but watching Angus was mind boggling. He lifted twice as much as any other man and never looked nearly as winded as the others.

"He has the stamina of an ox," Bethea winked as she elbowed Abigail. "It's his fault we have seven children."

Abigail giggled as she glanced as her friend. She'd grown close to Bethea and Maisie in the brief time she'd been at Dun Ringill, and she was grateful for the companionship. Both women were patient when they explained tasks that Abigail was unfamiliar with or lacked the confidence to do on her own. They praised her for her efforts and her determination. Abigail discovered purpose to her life that had been missing in all her previous endeavors.

But her greatest happiness—when not making love with Ronan—was watching the ease with which Ronan interacted with his people. He hadn't exaggerated when he said that he wasn't hesitant or anxious around his clan. She saw a more easygoing man, who smiled most of the day and was often laughing the loudest. She discovered he had a wicked sense of humor when she overheard jests that made her face go red to the roots of her hair. She recognized that Ronan would never be as gregarious as Clyde turned out to be, but she preferred him the way he was. And his reserve made him well matched to Clyde's exuberance, and Abigail quickly understood why they'd been best friends since birth. Her admiration and respect for Ronan grew daily.

"What has my bonnie bride laughing?" Ronan asked as he wrapped an arm around Abigail and lifted her off her feet to make it easier to kiss her.

Abigail's cheeks went pink as she sucked her lips in. She glanced at Bethea, who shook her head and walked away. Abigail kept her voice low as she admitted, "Bethea claims Angus has the stamina of an ox, and that's why they had so many children. I didn't say this to her, but I was thinking we must be rabbits considering how often we couple."

Ronan nibbled at Abigail's neck before nipping her earlobe. "Wait here while I drop off these logs, then we shall see if we can make our own bunnies." Ronan put Abigail back on her feet, before scooping a bunch of logs and hurrying to deliver them. She watched as his plaid swished around his thighs. She pictured what she knew lay beneath it, and Ronan chuckled when he caught her staring. He bent at the waist and hefted Abigail onto his shoulder just as he'd been carrying the logs. The clan was already used to the newlyweds' antics and no longer bothered looking in their direction.

"Ronan, put me down. I can walk on my own."

"Your legs are too short."

"I'd say they're just the right length for what I need."

"Aye. Wrapping them around me and holding on," Ronan guffawed as he tapped her backside. He carried her to their chamber where he locked the door before they undressed. They were locked in a passionate kiss, stumbling toward their bed when a knock rang at the door. Ronan barked, "Go away!"

"I canna," came Clyde's voice from the passageway. "A missive from the Bruce just arrived."

Ronan wrapped his plaid around his waist while Abigail put her chemise back on and wrapped her plaid around her shoulders. Ronan opened the door and accepted the parchment from Clyde. Abigail wasn't certain if her husband's scowl was from their interlude being interrupted or having to deal with the king's message. She suspected it was both. They sat together to read the missive. When they were through, Abigail's scowl matched Ronan's.

"He expects me to account for my actions," Ronan growled. "He's going to say he'd demand the same from the MacLeods, but they're all dead now."

"Because of their own stupidity and greed."

"Aye. But Robert won't see it that way. He'll complain that I've created another headache for him now that the MacLeods will be in turmoil. He should thank me for doing away with Cormag and his ilk. His cousin is young, but the mon isn't nearly as brash. I saw him standing behind Cormag when Kieran and I stood together at the Dunvegan gates. But the mon wasn't with the riders we met, nor was he among the dead or the captured. He must have remained home to oversee the keep."

"How auld is he?"

"A couple years younger than me. Most likely close to your age."

Abigail turned her head sideways as she considered her time at Dunvegan. She looked back at Ronan, her brow furrowed. "Cecily is close to Madeline's age, so only a couple years aulder than me. I ken she has a lover because I heard her with someone. Do you think it might have been the new laird?"

Ronan's eyes widened as he looked at Abigail before he burst into laughter. "It wouldn't surprise me in the least. He's a strapping young mon who was a lovesick pup the last time I saw him around Cecily. She'd love a mon younger than her in her bed simply for her pride, never mind that the new laird of Clan MacLeod is handsome. He likely thought it was an accomplishment to be tupping his cousin's wife."

"Rather than the king harping at you, the new laird should send you a fattened calf as a gift. He'll get some of his men back in the spring, and you've opened the door to the laird's—and lady's—chamber for him."

"She won't marry him though."

"Won't she? It would allow her to keep her position as the clan's lady."

"It would, but she'll balk at the idea of marrying a replacement. At least that's how she'll see it. The woman is vain to the bone. She won't see the match as being good enough for her. She's more likely to return to court and demand a better arrangement."

"Demand?"

"Aye. Cecily is King Robert's third cousin or some such. They're related somehow. She'll use that to force Robert's hand."

"How do you know all this?"

"Because I listen more than I talk."

It was Abigail's turn to laugh. "You're plenty talkative with me. Especially when you're telling me just how you plan to ravish me."

Ronan let the parchment drift to the floor as he unwrapped his plaid. Abigail shed her chemise before they fell backwards on the bed together. His large palm rested on Abigail's backside as they gazed into one another's eyes. "Abby, I told you when we met that I may never be the most talkative mon. But I've never been as comfortable with anyone as I am with you. Not even my own family. I ken I can talk aboot everything with you. I think you've also seen that I didn't exaggerate when I said that I'm not as reserved at home as I am at court."

"I have noticed. It makes me so happy to see you among our people. But it also makes me feel so foolish for ever doubting you, Ronan. You're so much more than I imagined any mon could be, and so much more than I gave you credit for."

"We didn't know each other then, I thought I was

getting a quiet wife," Ronan chuckled as he rolled over Abigail, his fingers pressing into her sheath. She moaned as he sparked her arousal. "Not so quiet as I thought."

Abigail opened her legs to him, guiding his cock to her entrance. Ronan thrust into her and went still. "Not so shy after all."

They moved together as their hands caressed one another until their passion crested together, leaving them breathless. Ronan rolled to his side, and Abigail followed him. They exchanged light kisses before Abigail snuggled under Ronan's chin, listening to his steady heartbeat.

"You ken the Bruce will summon me at soon as spring is in the air."

"Aye. I've known that since I killed Donovan. Gordon and Cormag's deaths made it inevitable."

"Will you come with me?"

"If you'd like me to, of course."

"Abby, I want you to come because I don't want to be away from you, and because I enjoy your company. I don't want you to fear that I need you because I'm scared."

Abigail leaned back and scowled at her husband. "I never would have thought that, and I don't like that you did. I know you're not scared. I might have thought you were shy, maybe even too timid to lead, but I never once thought it scared you to present yourself before the king. I never thought you were a coward, Ronan. And it upsets me to think you ever believed I did."

"I know you don't think I'm a coward. That wasn't what I meant. I meant that I ken you know it makes me anxious to be around people I don't know well, and I take my duties seriously. I didn't want you to think that I was too nervous to see the king without you by my side."

"That is the same as worrying that I think you're a coward, Ronan." Abigail sat up, deeply upset that her husband thought she perceived him as such after their time together. Ronan sat up next to her and brushed hair from her shoulder before kissing it. "I made a mistake aboot judging you and could have missed my opportunity to meet the mon the Lord intended me to marry. But I realized how wrong I was, and I have never doubted you since then. I have unwavering faith in you, so it hurts me deeply to think you might doubt that." Abigail dashed away the tear that fell down her cheek. Ronan opened his arms, and she leaned against him. Her heart ached with guilt that she hadn't made her feelings clearer to her husband.

"Abby, I'm making a mess of this. I didn't mean that you're scared for me now. I know you don't think I'm a coward. How could I when you offer praise freely and often? I meant, I didn't want you to grow nervous aboot me attending court. I want you to know that I'm asking you to join me because I wish for your company, and I want to discuss clan matters with you as they come up. I trust your council, and I would have it while I'm there, rather than having to wait until I return here."

Abigail nodded, better understanding her husband's thoughts. She wrapped her arm across his belly as she pressed closer to him. He kissed her forehead as they both watched the fire snap in the hearth. Feeling more at peace, she shifted to kneel beside Ronan, so she could see him better. "I would like to come with you. I ken I won't always travel with you, and that's something I will have to learn to accept. But it means I won't spend sennights making myself sick with worry. Ronan, six moons ago, I couldn't imagine anyone ever saying they wish for my council. Kenning you and what a tremendous laird you are to our people, knowing you wish for and value my opinion means more than I can put into words."

"Abby, we're both better people for being together. We'll undoubtedly fight from time to time, but I think we bring out the best in one another."

"I dinna think it, I ken it," Abigail giggled as Ronan tickled her. She knew he preferred her without her refined speech, but she'd sounded like a Lowlander for much of her life since her Lowland mother disdained the Hebridean accent. She'd laughed when Kieran abandoned his Scots accent when he married Maude, who was a Highlander, but now Abigail understood why. It felt natural, even carefree. "Will we leave with the first thaw?"

"Nay. I dinna trust that to hold. It's nearly the end of January now. We willna go until nearly the beginning of April."

"There is nay way the king will wait two-and-a-half moons to see ye. He'll have men beating down our gates if ye keep him waiting that long."

"Bah. He kens the weather's unpredictable in the isles. That's as good an excuse as any. Things are still too unsettled with the MacLeods. I'd rather try to sort some of this kerfuffle out with Landry before the king gets involved."

"Landry?"

"Aye. His mother was French."

"I ken. I met a Landry MacLeod at court. I didna ken that he was the laird's cousin. I ken why Cecily fancies him. He's vera handsome but vera arrogant. At the time, he reminded me of Cormag. Now I ken why. If he doesnae gain some humility with his new role, he's going to be just as bad as his cousins."

"Aye. I ken him too. He has the potential to be far better than Cormag or his brothers. Hopefully, this defeat will give him that humility. Otherwise, it will only drive him toward revenge."

"That's true. But they dinna have the forces they did a moon ago. It'll be difficult for him to act on it without men to swing their swords. His clan will struggle until they can rebuild their fleet. I recognized many of the birlinns were used for fishing, too. Without them, they'll lose a substantial source of food and trade."

"That's what I'm counting on. I hope to broker a truce while they're downtrodden, but offer terms that will be acceptable even when they're strong again. The price of peace for them will be getting their men back. If Landry agrees to ma terms, then I'll release the men. If he doesnae…" Ronan didn't need to finish his thought. Abigail knew Landry held the power to decide his own men's fate.

"For his sake, I hope he kens the auld proverb, 'he who cuts off his nose takes poor revenge for a shame inflicted on him.' He'd do well to accept aught that ye offer. He isnae in a position to haggle."

"We shall see. When the weather clears, I'll send a messenger to let him ken I'd like to parlay. We'll see if he accepts. Ma terms will insist he comes to us, so be prepared to host our enemy in a fortnight or so."

FORTY-ONE

Ronan stroked Abigail's thigh, then patted it beneath the table as they sat listening to Landry MacLeod drone on. He'd accepted Ronan's invitation under duress, knowing he wouldn't rebuild his forces to their prior strength before spring. He understood that if Ronan chose to lead an attack on Dunvegan, the MacKinnons would decimate his clan. He couldn't ignore that the MacLeods of Lewis stood beside the MacKinnons and not their distant relatives. Unfortunately for his clan, he presented himself as brash and immature, though Ronan and Abigail understood he thought he appeared determined and in control.

"Landry, cease your prattle," Ronan interrupted. "You remind me of Cormag. And that's hardly a compliment, considering why you're here."

Landry spluttered as he looked at Ronan, then swept his gaze over those at the high table. He focused on Abigail, and Ronan felt her tense once more. He wanted to bash the younger man over the head for putting Abigail at unease, especially when he thought he'd just gotten her to relax. Landry MacLeod had swaggered into Dun Ringill's Great Hall, tossed Abigail a seductive smile, then spoke to

Ronan as though they'd been peers for decades. He'd set Abigail on edge when his comment about recognizing her at court was laced with innuendo. Ronan feared Abigail would stab the new laird before the end of the first course. He disliked Landry, but he was already familiar with his arrogance, while Abigail was not.

"You are new to the lairdship, but you are not entirely new to politics, Landry. You have some choices to make. You can accept your clan's defeat graciously, and we can broker an accord. You can pretend as though your losses weren't significant in an attempt to save face, but that will only make you look like a fool. You can feed your bitterness and let your anger fester until all you can think aboot is revenge. If you choose that course, you will be the demise of your clan. It will lead you to be impulsive and to put pride before the wellbeing of your people."

Ronan sat back as he looked at Landry, who was unprepared to discuss clan politics while they sat on the dais. When Ronan said no more, it turned everyone's attention to Landry, who struggled with what to say. Ronan felt sorry for the man. No one had trained him to be a laird; since he was third in line after Gordon and Donovan, no one imagined Landry would one day lead the clan.

"What would this accord involve?" Landry watched Ronan, realizing that Ronan had gained control of the conversation by being direct, without flowery language or braggadocio.

"We make clear the water each clan claims for fishing. We agree to open water channels around your cape. My wife and I will travel between Dun Ringill and Stornoway often. If you are foolish enough to make the same mistake as your relatives, you will find the MacKinnons and Lewis at your door. You will allow us safe passage without harassment."

Landry nodded. He knew whatever he brokered with Ronan would influence his relationship with the other branch of his clan. He was disinclined to allow the MacLeods of Lewis to grow stronger. He couldn't afford for that branch to expand and dominate both Lewis and Harris. It would set his own people at a serious disadvantage. It would also make him appear weak before the MacDonalds of Sleat. He'd received a warning that John of Islay, Lord of the Isles, intended to visit Dunvegan. The new laird wanted matters settled before his overlord turned up.

"Do you have my horse?" Ronan's question surprised Landry, who blinked several times.

"Your horse?"

"Aye. Do you have him?" Ronan crossed his arms, the muscles rippling in his forearms.

"I do," Landry confessed. "We rounded up all the MacKinnon horses that made it ashore."

"I expect them returned—as healthy as they were when you stole them."

Landry's expression turned thunderous, but he nodded.

"You will cease crossing onto my land unless you would like to lose every patrol you post. I will do more than lead a hot trot to recover my cattle. I will lay waste to your men along our border. This will open the gates to the MacDonalds, MacQueens, and MacNeacails. Once I have my cows and sheep," Ronan's lips turned down, "I don't care what happens."

"You do, because if any of those clans gain land from us, they will become more powerful than you."

"Land is not power, Landry. It's what you do with it that gives you power. The northern MacDonalds, the MacQueens, and the MacNeacails don't have the resources to expand their clans onto new land. They might hold it in name, but they won't benefit from it. I, however, will, if it means they weaken your clan. In addition to uncontested navigation through the Minch, our horses returned, and no more raiding our cattle, I expect two hundred pounds sterling."

"What?"

"Your clan sank one of my birlinns. On that birlinn were my wife's belongings. Be glad that I only expect you to compensate me for the boat, and not the costly courtly wardrobe Lady MacKinnon lost." When Landry glared at Abigail, she didn't flinch. She returned his stare with one of her own. Ronan draped his arm around Abigail's shoulders. The silent yet possessive gesture was the warning Ronan intended. Landry looked away but nodded.

"You will have those things. But in return, I expect to leave with my men."

Ronan snorted. "You will not. They will be returned once you meet my demands. Refusal will not only ensure I kill them, it guarantees that I will come for you too. I will reciprocate your cousin's hospitality by throwing you in the oubliette. Once you've languished there for a while, I will kill you as well." Ronan raised his chalice but didn't take a drink. He canted his head as he looked speculatively at Landry, knowing he made the younger man uncomfortable. "Perhaps I will throw you down there this eve and send a messenger back to Dunvegan with my demands. When they're met, then I'll consider releasing you."

"You would violate the pledge of your hospitality?"

"I never pledged to be hospitable, Landry. You did not come here seeking shelter. You came to negotiate a truce. Unfortunately, you are not the one with the upper hand. I am. If you don't accept my terms, then the negotiations are through, but you are still on my land." Ronan shrugged and took a long sip of his wine. He watched Landry over the rim of his chalice. He observed Landry mull over his options and knew when the man made his decision.

"All but the horses. Your wife murdered my cousin. Call their value a *weregild* for his life."

"You may claim your lineage is from the Norse, but I do not. I am descended from the first kings of Scotland and the kings of Ireland. I don't believe in a *weregild* any more than I do your Fairy Flag. Be glad you're not begging for that back."

"Be glad your wife still has her head," Landry snapped. Every MacKinnon man at the table rose and reached for their sword or a dirk. The MacLeods at the lower tables reached for their knives. Abigail sat forward and locked eyes with Landry.

"You are not speaking in your best interests, Landry, nor those of your clan. If you were smart, not only would you agree to each of my husband's terms—graciously, I might add—you would also seek his council on how to lead. You have no one left alive in your clan who has ever served as a laird. Your council is either weak or foolish, mayhap both, since they supported Cormag. Laird MacKinnon came to his position even younger than you. You sit at our table because he hasn't killed you, and he's considering allowing your men to live. A wise mon would spend more time listening and learning than speaking."

Ronan sat down when Abigail began talking. His men followed his lead, and the MacLeods went back to their meals. Without much thought, his hand rested where Abigail's neck met her shoulder, and his thumb grazed the skin of her nape. He was intrigued by what Abigail would say, and he thought her observation to be astute. He wondered if Landry would see the wisdom. When the young laird nodded, it pleased Ronan to see Abigail had gotten through to him.

"Laird MacKinnon, I will accept your terms. All of them, without condition. Lady MacKinnon is correct that there is no one with experience as Laird MacLeod left at Dunvegan. My cousins and I filled four out of nine seats on the clan council. Not only are three now vacant, but my cousins also forced the council to follow them, since we nearly outnumbered them. Mayhap we could speak in private after the meal."

Ronan nodded, curious about what Landry wished to discuss behind closed doors. He invited Abigail to join him and Clyde when they retired to his solar with Landry, but she declined. The man made her uneasy, and she wished to escape his company as soon as she could. Ronan watched from the bottom of the stairs as Abigail made her way to their chamber before he ushered Clyde and Landry into his solar. Two guards stood outside the door once the two lairds and the tánaiste were behind the closed door.

"MacKinnon, you and Lady MacKinnon made points I cannot ignore. I don't know what I'm doing, and I don't want to ruin my clan," Landry confessed. "I ken I made an arse of myself with my bravado, but I thought I needed to make a good show."

"I once told King Robert that the greatest lesson my mother taught me was that children should be seen and not heard, and that's a motto men can live by as well."

"Sounds similar to what your lady wife said."

"It is. She knows my nature. Come to the point of why you wished to speak in private. It's been a long day, and I prefer Lady MacKinnon's company to yours."

"The MacLeods and the MacKinnons will not thrive if we spend our resources feuding. We each have enough contention with the other clans on this isle without furthering our disagreements. I would rather be a leader like you than Cormag." Landry frowned but didn't look away when his gaze met Ronan's. "I don't ken how to be laird. I didn't even ken how to be a tánaiste. Now I must lead my clan. Not only do I agree to your terms, but I would also offer a pledge to cease all hostility toward your clan in exchange for you —for your—your tutelage." Landry blurted the last two words as if they left a sour taste on his tongue.

"You wish for me to teach you how to be a laird? You're a wee auld to foster, Landry."

"If you're going to be a smug bastard aboot it, then never mind."

"Take your pot off the boil," Ronan waved Landry toward a chair with a grin. "You don't have the luxury of remaining here while I teach you the duties of a laird. But I am willing to answer your questions this eve and in the future. If you're in doubt of how to handle a situation, send a missive, and I will do what I can to advise you. I suggest you consider every mon in your clan and decide who you trust and who would offer you sound advice. They should be your clan council, not just men who have held their position since before you were born. Your clan is aboot to make serious changes if you want to maintain a truce with me. Your council likely needs to change. Don't do this in haste, but neither should you dally."

"I assume King Robert's summoned you, like he has me."

"Aye. And I assume you're dreading appearing before him."

"That and managing my way around court. I

369

would rather I arrive kenning we are at peace than having King Robert intervene."

"I would prefer that too. That is why you sat at my table and are sipping my whisky now." Ronan stretched his legs out before the fire. He glanced at Clyde, who stood unobtrusively near the door. Neither man trusted Landry, but they would give him the benefit of the doubt until he proved as untrustworthy as his relatives.

"I—" Landry gazed into his whisky mug as he swirled the contents. Ronan waited even though he could guess what Landry wanted to say. When the MacLeod looked up at Ronan, he smiled tightly. "This is one of those times where you're being seen but not heard, isn't it?" Ronan nodded. "You'll wait for me to speak, rather than offer up more than you should."

Ronan nodded again. "You're learning already."

"When we're at court—" Landry's Adam's apple bobbed as he swallowed. "I don't want you to think that I'm weak and a pushover. You will severely underestimate me if you do."

"Settle. You needn't puff up like an indignant pigeon. When we're at court, you're hoping to observe how I interact with the men there," Ronan supplied.

"Aye."

"If you can remember to be seen and not heard, then I won't object. The moment you chime in and make my life difficult is the moment you find yourself out on your ear. If you do aught to jeopardize my clan or me, I will destroy you. So think twice if you intend to manipulate me. I will ken before you even start, and I will be merciless."

"That's fair. Thank you." Landry extended his arm to Ronan, who grasped his forearm. "I bid you goodnight, Laird."

"I bid you the same, Laird." Ronan and Clyde

watched the man leave before Clyde closed the door again.

"Do ye trust him?"

"Nae even by the wee hairs on his weak chin. But who kens? He might surprise us both, and for the better. That is yet to be seen. But I ken I dinna envy him the life he's just stepped into. I think it became far more real this eve when he faced Abby and me. I think she scares him more than I do."

"Och, I thought he was going to wet himself when we all stood. Then when Lady MacKinnon spoke, I expected to find a puddle under the pup." Clyde grinned, making Ronan chuckle. He'd shared the same thought.

"I'm for bed," Ronan announced. "He shall get his vera first lesson in the lists tomorrow when I knock him on his arse. We'll see if he has any humility there and if he can take instruction. If he canna do it in the lists, then he willna do it anywhere else. If that's the case, I wash ma hands of him now."

Much like they'd done countless times since Clyde and Maisie wed, Clyde left for his croft and Ronan turned toward his chamber. But unlike so many times before, he now had a wife to look forward to, just like his friend.

FORTY-TWO

"**R**onan, I canna appear before the queen with ma laces blowing in the breeze, but neither can I wear ma arisaid," Abigail huffed with impatience as Ronan tried to pull her gown closed. "When I agreed to travel with ye three moons ago, I didna ken ma waist would be thickening so fast. I didna ken it would be at all! I dinna have the right clothes."

Ronan turned Abigail to face him, her eyes welling with tears. He pressed her head against his chest before resting his arm against her back while he stroked her hair. His other hand rubbed the swell of her belly. When Abigail lost all interest in food not long after Landry's visit, Ronan feared she was unwell. When she cast up her accounts but insisted she was fine, he refused to listen and summoned Naida. The healer confirmed what Abigail suspected: she was with child. They'd considered Abigail remaining at Dun Ringill when Ronan finally planned his journey to Stirling, but neither was happy with that arrangement.

Unwilling to make Abigail ride on horseback for a fortnight—too frightened that the horse might throw her—he suggested a wagon. Abigail glared at him and said she would walk to Stirling instead of rattling her teeth loose in a wagon. They compromised and sailed. Even with the shorter trip, Abigail's middle expanded faster than she expected. She arrived at the royal court unable to lace her gowns closed without her chemise showing. While on the birlinn and even in the town of Stirling, wearing her arisaid was acceptable and hid her clothing difficulties. But she couldn't wear it when she was presented to the queen.

"I wish Laurel were still here. She doesnae ken, but I discovered she's an expert seamstress. I ken she made her own clothes."

"She made her clothes?" Ronan asked skeptically.

"Aye. I dinna ken all the details, but her father barely had a dowry for her and didna buy her what she needed. She started making her own clothes and even sold some gowns to earn pocket money. Anyway, if she were here, she could solve this."

"Are there any ladies here who ye could ask?"

"I dinna ken, Ronan. What am I going to do?" Abigail fought the urge to burst into tears. She struggled against her vacillating emotions, unprepared for how they frequently changed now that she was pregnant. Maisie had warned her, and Bethea had offered her a motherly pat on the arm. But she hadn't understood until the mood swings began. Now she felt like a watering pot.

"We'll go into town and purchase ye a new gown, or we'll find a seamstress who can adjust what ye have, Abby. We'll make it work. Dinna fash. I willna have ye showing up in front of the queen in yer shift."

Abigail offered him a watery smiled as she nodded. She leaned against him once more, stifling a yawn. She'd gotten little sleep while they traveled, often sleeping on the ground or on the deck. They'd stayed at inns when they could, but it wasn't every night. When Ronan suggested she climb into bed, she didn't disagree. She fell asleep to Ronan once again stroking her hair. When she awoke feeling refreshed, they ventured into town, where they visited two haberdashers. Abigail burst into happy tears when they returned to their chamber and laid out the four gowns they'd purchased. She smothered Ronan in kisses before they fell back into bed, but neither slept.

<hr />

"Lady MacKinnon," Queen Elizabeth greeted Abigail. "It appears marriage suits you." The older woman smiled as she glanced at Abigail's belly. Abigail wore a sapphire-colored kirtle with amethyst trim along the collar, cuffs, and hem. The gown fit her perfectly, disguising her growing belly while surprisingly comfortable. But it hadn't taken long before people detected her condition, and the women began gossiping. Abigail rubbed her hand over her belly and beamed.

"Marriage to Laird MacKinnon suits me very well."

"I can't say that I'm surprised. It was obvious from the start. You both appear very besotted with one another."

"I won't deny I love my husband, and he returns my sentiments."

"So much so that it appeared as though he didn't want you to return here." Queen Elizabeth looked around her solar.

"I haven't felt my best lately, Your Grace. Laird MacKinnon was concerned since I tire more easily."

"Abigail," Queen Elizabeth lowered her voice. "You deserve a doting husband, and I'm happy you've found one. We heard aboot what you endured at Dunvegan."

Abigail remained quiet. The woman hadn't asked a question, so Abigail offered no response. She wouldn't say anything unless she was pressed. She knew everything she told the queen would be repeated directly to King Robert. She didn't intend to say anything that might reveal more than Ronan wanted. They'd discussed their strategy while they traveled. Abigail would defer to him when she could, and demure to any questions she didn't want to answer. Queen Elizabeth narrowed her eyes before she nodded.

"You've matured, Lady MacKinnon. You seem more confident." Queen Elizabeth waited for Abigail to respond.

"Thank you, Your Grace." Abigail graciously accepted the compliment, but she had nothing more to say.

"You must be settled now at Dun Ringill. A battle just after your arrival must have been quite the ordeal." Queen Elizabeth's tone sounded sincere, but Abigail recognized the manipulation, which made the queen's voice seem patronizing. "It isn't easy when the mon you marry is at odds with your family."

"I'm blessed that Ronan and Kieran are like brothers."

"But that wasn't so with Cormag."

"Kieran and I never viewed Cormag as family. A very distant relative, but not family. The Sutherlands and Grants are family." Abigail referred to Maude's family and her sister Madeline's family-by-marriage.

"Right you are, Lady MacKinnon." Queen Elizabeth sat back in her ornately carved chair while Abigail continued to stand. Her back ached, and she wanted to rub it but didn't dare. "I see the Dunbar sisters are eager to visit with you. I'm certain there is time now before the evening meal."

Abigail dipped into a curtsy before turning toward Emelie and Blythe Dunbar. They made space for her and offered her the chair between them. Abigail chatted with them until the bell rang for the evening meal. She enjoyed conversing with her former fellow ladies-in-waiting. But she was eager to learn what happened while Ronan and Landry met with the king. She also wanted to let Ronan know that the queen was fishing for information.

"Your Majesty, while I cannot excuse my relatives' actions or their choices, I strive to improve relations between my clan and the MacKinnons. I do not subscribe to my cousin's beliefs," Landry said with a confident tone despite glancing at Ronan. He and Landry stood before King Robert in the sovereign's Privy Council chamber. Ronan stood silently while the king addressed Landry. A tinge of sympathy pulled at his heart as he watched Landry and remembered the first time the king summoned him to stand before him and account for his clan's decisions.

"And what do you subscribe to, Laird MacLeod?" King Robert wore a speculative expression as he watched the young man.

"Peaceful coexistence, Your Majesty. It is what's best for my clan as we recover from our losses."

"And once you are recovered, you intend to revert to your previous contentious relationship."

Landry shot Ronan a nervous glance, but Ronan kept his focus on the Bruce. Ronan clasped his hands behind his back as he stood tall, his shoulders back, his expansive chest an imposing sight. He would only answer the king's questions, volunteering enough information to represent his clan's expectations and role in the events. Before Landry departed Dun Ringill, Ronan's first lesson to Landry was not to be too eager to speak before King Robert. As Ronan listened, he knew Landry had already forgotten what he'd learned. He'd been too eager to answer the Bruce's questions, volunteering too much information too early on, and now the king was backing him into a corner.

"Those are not my intentions, Your Majesty," Landry backpedaled. "I intend to keep the peace."

"The path to hell is paved with good intentions, Laird MacLeod. What will you do when your council and clansmen are braying at the moon for blood?"

"Laird MacKinnon and I have brokered a truce that should keep either clan from wanting any bloodletting."

"And just like that, a conversation between a novice laird and an experienced laird has brokered a truce between clans at war for generations. To both clans' satisfaction."

"I—we—I can live with the terms," Landry stammered.

"For how long?"

Ronan watched beads of sweat form along Landry's temples before they trickled past his ears to his chin, where they dangled for a moment before slipping onto his neck. The young man's discomfort both amused him and pricked at his conscience. Once Landry disabused himself of his bravado, he'd proven to be surprisingly levelheaded and cooperative. In the fortnight before he and Abigail embarked upon their journey to Stirling, the horses and two hundred pounds sterling arrived without argument. Ronan continued to house the MacLeods in his dungeon, unwilling to release them until Landry proved himself trustworthy for a prolonged amount of time.

"Until circumstances decide otherwise," Landry responded.

"So you expect Laird MacKinnon to be the aggressor, to be the dishonorable one."

"N-n-nay, Your Majesty." Landry looked to Ronan. "That's not what I meant at all. I—I…" Landry trailed off, finally realizing that silence was a better tack than trying to justify himself. King Robert waited, but Landry said no more.

"MacKinnon, what say you?"

"I believe everything has already been said."

"Taciturn as always."

"No need to repeat what we just heard," Ronan hedged with a shrug. "The MacLeod and I have come to an agreement between us with terms I accept."

"Terms you likely set," King Robert grumbled.

"We've agreed," Ronan reiterated.

"But you still have MacLeods languishing in your dungeon."

"Those were part of the terms."

"And you accepted them, MacLeod?"

"I understand Laird MacKinnon's rationale."

"But that doesn't mean you accept them. Will you strike back to rescue your men?"

Landry looked to Ronan once more, wanting to squirm since he was well beyond his depths in this conversation. He'd hoped to be presented before the king, admit to his clan's culpability, state that he agreed with Ronan's demands, then retire to a pub and a willing woman. King Robert kept them waiting for most of the morning, and he'd been grilling Landry for nearly an hour. He wanted to throw up his hands and beg for mercy.

"It is unfortunate that any MacLeod was captured, and I regret that these men are the price of peace. But Laird MacKinnon assures me they are not being abused, and he has given me no reason to doubt his word. I even suspect they are properly fed and given blankets. I cannot, in good conscience, stage another attack to rescue them. It would not bode well for my clan's survival."

"You are notably different from your cousins, Landry." The king sounded bemused.

"I wish to grow auld."

The simple statement made King Robert guffaw, and Ronan fought to suppress his grin. It was the wish of the young and inexperienced. Ronan intended to do just that with Abigail beside him, but he understood that many lairds didn't see that wish fulfilled. He would fight to his last breath to live a long life with Abigail, but he accepted there were no guarantees.

"Don't we all. Don't we all," King Robert mused. He turned his focus back to Ronan. "I won't ask you whether you feel the same, since we both ken wishes are wasted on the young. What I would like to ken is why you've resolved this matter so easily when you and Cormag could barely be in the same chamber without drawing blood."

"I don't recall ever being the instigator or the aggressor," Ronan stated.

"You don't recall. Fine way to say it was Cormag's fault." The Bruce crossed his brawny arms, the muscles belying his age and his time spent away from the battlefield. "Young MacLeod looks to you often, as though you might offer him advice. What would you say?"

Haud yer wheest. "We must all be quick to listen, slow to speak, and slow to anger."

"Another pearl of wisdom from your mother, I suppose. She did well to teach you your scripture."

"That one came from my father," Ronan corrected.

"They were a fitting match. Is that a proverb you intend to drill into your mentee?" King Robert watched Ronan and Landry. Only Landry reacted with surprise. As the Bruce had come to expect, Ronan's expression shared none of his thoughts. The man never spoke without thinking first, and he was always predicting a conversation's course to have his response at the ready.

"He who has ears, let him hear," Ronan quoted. The king scowled but nodded his head.

"The way of a fool is right in his own eyes, but a wise mon listens to advice," King Robert said to Landry, who nodded, his eyes darting between the king and Ronan. "It seems I am not needed for this truce to move forward. But should it dissolve, the survivor will come to bear testimony before me."

Neither Landry nor Ronan missed King Robert looking at Ronan. Landry once again wanted to squirm, uneasy that the Bruce already assumed Ronan would defeat him. He knew it was the most likely outcome, but he wished his sovereign had faith in him. He supposed only time would tell, but he had no wish to fail. He'd accepted the MacKinnons' victory and knew he'd do well to watch and learn because, inevitably, the truce would fail at some point. It would prepare him to face the MacKinnons. Ronan narrowed his eyes as he looked at Landry, and the young laird suspected Ronan could read his thoughts.

"MacKinnon, you've grown impatient. I assume you're eager to find your wife." King Robert sighed when Ronan gave no reply. "Lady MacKinnon should be readying for the evening meal. Go to her before you begin pacing and wear a hole in the bricks. MacLeod, we are finished." The king sighed again when Ronan bowed, but Landry did not. "That means you are dismissed, lad."

The two lairds left the Privy Council chamber in silence, but once they were in the passageway, Ronan stepped in front of Landry and turned to him. "I am not your tutor, but I will advise you as you request. I said as much at Dun Ringill. I ken you think to listen and learn to prepare for when you must strike out against me. I will never teach you all that I ken. There will always be something more. Underestimate me as your cousins did, and you will lie beside them. Cross me, and I will grind your clan under my boot and claim Dunvegan as mine." Ronan spun on his heel, not waiting for Landry to reply. As he turned the corner, he glanced back at Landry, who stood watching him. His expression gave none of his thoughts away. Ronan couldn't decide if Landry was learning, or if the man was a far better politician than Ronan assumed. He would remain wary of the MacLeods of Skye.

"How do you fare, Abby?" Ronan whispered as Abigail walked beside him to the evening meal.

"Tired, but I'm well." Abigail paused outside the doors. They were the same ones she'd entered the night Ronan told her he wanted to court her. They were the same ones that she'd believed he would pass through moments after her. They were the same ones she'd watched throughout the first course, only to be disappointed.

"I'm walking through them with you," Ronan stated, his heart filling as Abigail beamed up at him. He moved them to the side, allowing others to pass. "I'm a different mon from the last time I was here. I would have avoided the noise and small talk at all costs. But now I don't notice them. I'm still not inclined to talk needlessly, but I can tolerate them with you by my side."

"I'm not partial to it either, but sitting beside you is far better company than any of the ladies. You put me at ease, Ronan. I feel comfortable and confident when I'm with you."

"You do the same for me, Abby. I can face aught in this world when I ken you're there. You're surely an angel sent down to save me from myself."

"Would that we could skip this meal altogether and return to our chamber. I would prefer feasting on you," Abigail said before licking her lips then tugging her lower lip between her teeth.

"Do that again, and I'm carrying you back to our chamber over my shoulder," Ronan said, his voice husky. It sent a shiver along Abigail's spine.

"Do you promise?"

Ronan growled as he led Abigail into an alcove. Hands yanked to move clothing aside before Ronan sank into Abigail, their sighs blending. "Abby," Ronan groaned.

"I ken." They moved together until release swept through them, leaving them depleted and clinging to one another. They kissed as they straightened their clothes.

"I think I've been an apt student," Ronan chuckled.

"The very best," Abigail responded breathlessly. "We've come a long way in such a short amount of time. I can't believe what we've been through in the last couple of moons."

"Hopefully, life will be quieter until the wee one is here."

"Then it will hardly be quiet again." Abigail leaned against Ronan's chest; his heat permeated her skin. "Are things truly resolved with Landry?"

"As best we can hope for. We'll have safe passage to Stornoway any time you wish."

Abigail squeezed Ronan's chest as she burrowed closer to him. The shy man she thought she'd met never existed. Instead, Abigail discovered a wise and observant leader whose people trusted and respected him. She found love she never imagined she'd claim as her own. She had a partner in all things, and she knew she was becoming a woman she could be proud of. Despite the tribulations they'd endured during their brief marriage, she'd never been happier.

"Thank you, Ronan. For everything. For forgiving me my shortcomings, for trusting me, for loving me, for making a life together with me. I love you."

"Abigail, I've loved you from the very start. You've helped me free myself of guilt that I carried for years. You put me at ease in situations that irritate me, and you make me smile whenever I think of you. I wasn't a patient child or young mon, but I have never been more appreciative of aught than waiting until I met you. I wouldn't share what we have with anyone else."

Abigail swallowed before she stepped away from Ronan. "Does it bother you that I can't say the same? You've said it doesn't, but it would bother me."

"You didn't have what we do. Besides, someone had to know what we were doing." Ronan grinned as he pressed Abigail back against the alcove wall. "I may be an apt student, but never was there a more desirable teacher. I think there is much for me still to learn."

"I'm learning along the way, just like you. Mayhap you can teach me how to make you groan like you did last eve."

"Gladly, wife. The only place we're dancing together this eve is our bed. We eat and then we slip away."

"I would follow you anywhere, husband."

Ronan and Abigail entered the great hall with Ronan's arm around Abigail's waist. They sat with their guards, enjoying lively conversation, but when the first strains of music began, they made their escape. They moved to the music their bodies created as they came together in synchronicity.

"**A**unty Abby!" Tawny braids flew behind the little
girl as she launched herself into Abigail's arms,
likely knocking her over if Ronan weren't behind her
as they came to the door at Stornoway. "Uncle Ronan! Where're Glynnis and Catriona? Where's
Gregor?"

"I'm—" Three youthful voices chirping beside
her interrupted Abigail.

"Here we are, Amy!"

Five-year-old Glynnis and three-year-old
Catriona grabbed hands with their eight-year-old
cousin, barely sparing Amy's twin Graham a passing
wave. Abigail supposed the girls were headed abovestairs to Amy's chamber. Their two-year-old son Bram
kicked and waved his arms as Maude, Kieran, Madeline, and Fingal approached. Madeline carried her
youngest, a baby girl named Finley. Abigail noticed
Madeline and Fingal's older three children, Magnus,
Adeline, and Sarah, played with Graham near the
hearth.

"I see ye're still vastly outnumbered," Ronan
grinned at Fingal. "Three daughters and a wife to
one wee lad and—ye."

"I dinna see ye doing much better. Two lasses

and a wife keeping ye and yer brawny lad alive."
Fingal clapped Ronan on the back as they came to
stand together. Maude and Abigail peered at Finley,
as the babe blew bubbles in her sleep. "Would ye
have it any other way?"

"Nae even for a minute."

"Where's Mairi?" Abigail asked Maude.

"Likely driving Eara into an early grave, pes-
tering her with questions aboot how to heal every animal the lass sees," Maude grinned. Eara had been
elderly even when Abigail, Madeline, and Kieran
were children. They used to whisper secretly that the
ancient healer would live forever. They seemed to
have been correct. As if summoned by thought, Eara
and Mairi entered the Great Hall from the kitchens.
Mairi released Eara's hand and dashed to her cousins
before the fire.

"I think yer lad is auld enough for his first wee
nip of whisky—for his gums, of course," Kieran pretended to gasp when Abigail's elbow landed against
the hard planes of his belly. Kieran led his brothers-
by-marriage to his solar, Bram reaching forward and
tugging on the tawny locks Kieran had passed onto
his children.

"Maude, the Great Hall looks magnificent," Abigail said as she looked around her former home.
"Ye've outdone yerself this year."

Garland, holly, and lavender were draped over
the mantles and around the banisters. Clusters of
holly sat on the high table, while the rushes smelled
of fresh rosemary. Sweet smelling candles burned in
all the sconces, and the gathering hall held a cheery
glow. While Abigail attempted to make the Great
Hall at Dun Ringill festive when the MacKinnons
hosted their extended family for Christmas, she never
achieved what Maude did. The atmosphere strengthened their sense of kinship as they came together to

celebrate Christmas, Hogmanay, and Epiphany. The trappings of being lairds and ladies, heirs and tánaistes fell away, with refined accents and pretensions cast aside as they gathered as one large and extended family.

"We have much to celebrate, and it's nae nearly often enough that we're all able to gather. I would make it special," Maude explained.

"It's as beautiful as ye made ma wedding day." Abigail recalled walking down the stairs from the chamber she and Ronan would share that night. Only the births of her children matched the excitement she'd felt that day. As she looked at her older sister, the wistfulness on Madeline's face struck her. "Madeline?"

"I wish we could have been at each other's weddings. Things were different back then, I ken that. But it's one of the few regrets I hold on to," Madeline answered.

"We've made up for it by being together for the holidays and attending the births of our nieces and nephews," Maude reminded them.

"Blessings from our Lord," Madeline whispered. Despite her years away from the convent, some old trappings of her life among the nuns remained.

"When will the others arrive?" Abigail asked.

"If the weather holds, Mama, Da, Lachlan, and Arabella will be here with the weans in a couple hours. Hardi and Blair should be here with their weans before nightfall."

"The keep will be bursting at the seams," Madeline grinned. "I ken ye wouldnae have it any other way, would ye, Maude?"

Maude wrapped her arm around her sister-by-marriage, a woman who had once tormented her mercilessly. With years and the court at Stirling behind them, Maude and Madeline were almost as close as Maude and Blair, and Madeline and Abigail. The four women laughed and teased as kindred spirits.

"This is exactly perfect," Maude sighed wistfully. "Christmas has been ma favorite time of year since I was a bairn. Mama says I used to clap when the cold air blew across ma face. I like it now because of the beauty that comes with the snow and ice, but more than aught, I like it because I ken we will all be together. I couldnae ask for more."

Abigail's cheeks sucked in as she tried to stifle her giggle, but she failed. It came out more like a snort. When Maude and Madeline turned toward her, she waved her hands as she tried to compose herself enough to speak. "That's such a lovely sentiment. I shall only ruin it if I say what I was thinking."

"Now I must ken," Maude grinned.

"I'd say ye've been asking ma brother for quite a lot more." Abigail placed her hand over Maude's swollen belly, making her sisters laugh along with her.

"Ye're one to talk. Dinna wake the bairns this year, Abigail," Madeline teased as she laid her hand on Abigail's rounded belly.

❧

"How was the journey?" Kieran asked Ronan as he poured whisky for his brothers-by-marriage.

"Just as I like it. Uneventful."

"Landry still keeping to himself?" Fingal asked.

"At least for the holidays. Cecily would never forgive him the impropriety of ruining her holiday celebration by attacking us, or worse, causing us to disturb her festivities."

"I still canna believe she married him," Kieran mused.

"I canna believe she bellowed at the king, refusing an earl because she loves Landry," Fingal chuckled.

"The pair are suited to one another," Ronan noted. "Besotted while still bringing out the worst in one another. Landry will be back to trouble the day Epiphany ends, but likely nae looking our direction. He kens after the last time that I didna exaggerate all those years ago. I didna teach him everything, and I will always ken more. It's Cecily who urges him on, leading him by the cods. Hopefully, their sons have more sense than him."

"He's sniffing around here, hoping a couple will foster here in a few years. I canna stand him any more than I could Cormag and his brothers, but it serves our purposes for me to train his sons to suit us."

"I feel the same, since he's hinting I should eventually take the other two."

"I would," Fingal chimed in. "All the MacLeods and the MacKinnons allied? John of Islay willna ken what to do."

"Visit Sleat more often, then ride over to eat me out of house and home," Ronan grumbled. "Hardi can help pay for it, since it'll keep that MacDonald away from Lochaber and the Camerons."

"To the isles," Kieran toasted before snickering at Fingal. "Och, and I suppose to the Highlands."

"Dinna let Hamish hear ye," Fingal and Ronan said together. Built like a bear, Laird Hamish Sutherland was every child's favorite person, but he still terrified all the men. Kieran, Fingal, and Ronan chuckled, waking the sleeping Bram, who gurgled and grinned.

By the time the evening meal laid before them, the Great Hall was filled with laughter and children's voices. The dais overflowed with people, children sitting on their parents' laps, while husbands and wives were wrapped in one another's arms. The MacLeods of Lewis, the MacKinnons, the Sutherlands, the Grants, and the Camerons filled Stornoway with love that only comes from a family who cherishes one another.

"Are ye happy, Abby?" Ronan murmured against Abigail's ears.

"Blissfully. I love ye, Ronan."

"Just as I love you, Abigail."

THANK YOU FOR READING

Celeste Barclay, a nom de plume, lives near the Southern California coast with her husband and sons. Growing up in the Midwest, Celeste enjoyed spending as much time in and on the water as she could. Now she lives near the beach. She's an avid swimmer, a hopeful future surfer, and a former rower. When she's not writing, she's working or being a mom.

Subscribe to Celeste's bimonthly newsletter to receive exclusive insider perks.
Subscribe Now

Have you chatted with Celeste's hunky heroes? Are you new to Celeste's books or want insider exclusives before anyone else? Subscribe for free to chat with the men of Celeste's *The Highland Ladies* series.
Chat Now

THE HIGHLAND LADIES

THE CLAN SINCLAIR

His Highland Lass **BOOK 1 SNEAK PEEK**

She entered the great hall like a strong spring storm in the northern most Highlands. Tristan Mackay felt like he had been blown hither and yon. As the storm settled, she left him with the sweet scents of heather and lavender wafting towards him as she approached. She was not a classic beauty, tall and willowy like the women at court. Her face and form were not what legends were made of. But she held a unique appeal unlike any he had seen before. He could not take his eyes off of her long chestnut hair that had strands of fire and burnt copper running through them. Unlike the waves or curls he was used to, her hair was unusually straight and fine. It looked like a waterfall cascading down her back. While she was not tall, neither was she short. She had a figure that was meant for a man to grasp and hold onto, whether from the front or from behind. She had an aura of confidence and charm, but not arrogance or conceit like many good looking women he had met. She did not seem to know her own appeal. He could tell that she was many things, but one thing she was not was his.

His Bonnie Highland Temptation **BOOK 2**
His Highland Prize **BOOK 3**
His Highland Pledge **BOOK 4**
His Highland Surprise **BOOK 5**
Their Highland Beginning **BOOK 6**

PIRATES OF THE ISLES

The Blond Devil of the Sea **BOOK 1 SNEAK PEEK**

Caragh lifted her torch into the air as she made her way down the precarious Cornish cliffside. She made out the hulking shape of a ship, but the dead of night made it impossible to see who was there. She and the fishermen of Bedruthan Steps weren't expecting any shipments that night. But her younger brother Eddie, who stood watch at the entrance to their hiding place, had spotted the ship and signaled up to the village watchman, who alerted Caragh.

As her boot slid along the dirt and sand, she cursed having to carry the torch and wished she could have sunlight to guide her. She knew these cliffs well, and it was for that reason it was better that she moved slowly than stop moving once and for all. Caragh feared the light from her torch would carry out to the boat. Despite her efforts to keep the flame small, the solitary light would be a beacon.

When Caragh came to the final twist in the path before the sand, she snuffed out her torch and started to run to the cave where the main source of the village's income lay in hiding. She heard movement along the trail above her head and knew the local fishermen would soon join her on the beach. These men, both young and old, were strong from days spent pulling in the full trawling nets and hoisting the larger catches onto their boats. However, these men weren't well-trained swordsmen, and the fear of pirate raids was ever-present. Caragh feared that was who the villagers would face that night.

The Dark Heart of the Sea **BOOK 2**
The Red Drifter of the Sea **BOOK3**
The Scarlet Blade of the Sea **BOOK 4 Coming March 2021**

Leif **BOOK 1 SNEAK PEEK**

Leif looked around his chambers within his father's longhouse and breathed a sigh of relief. He noticed the large fur rugs spread throughout the chamber. His two favorites placed strategically before the fire and the bedside he preferred. He looked at his shield that hung on the wall near the door in a symbolic position but waiting at the ready. The chests that held his clothes and some of his finer acquisitions from voyages near and far sat beside his bed and along the far wall. And in the center was his most favorite possession. His oversized bed was one of the few that could accommodate his long and broad frame. He shook his head at his longing to climb under the pile of furs and on the stuffed mattress that beckoned him. He took in the chair placed before the fire where he longed to sit now with a cup of warm mead. It had been two months since he slept in his own bed, and he looked forward to nothing more than pulling the furs over his head and sleeping until he could no longer ignore his hunger. Alas, he would not be crawling into his bed again for several more hours. A feast awaited him to celebrate his and his crew's return from their latest expedition to explore the isle of Britannia. He bathed and wore fresh clothes, so he had no excuse for lingering other than a bone weariness that set in during the last storm at sea. He was eager to spend time at home no matter how much he loved sailing. Their last expedition had been profitable with several raids of monasteries that yielded jewels and both silver and gold, but he was ready for respite.

Leif left his chambers and knocked on the door next to his. He heard movement on the other side, but it was only moments before his sister, Freya, opened her door.

"That armband suits you well. It compliments your

muscles," Leif smirked and dodged a strike from one of those muscular arms.

"At least one of us inherited our father's prowess. Such a shame it wasn't you."